Praise for Debra Webb

Deeper Than the Dead

"Expertly plotted and whip smart, *Deeper Than the Dead* is an exceedingly clever crime thriller filled with secrets, betrayals, and complex characters. Webb manages to hit that sweet spot between family drama and police procedural. This one is sure to be a hit in the crime-thriller genre. A wild and massively entertaining ride."

—Christina McDonald, *USA Today* bestselling author

The Last Lie Told

"A complex case fraught with angst and danger ends with surprising revelations."

—*Kirkus Reviews*

"Debra Webb writes the kind of thrillers I love to read. Sure, there is a murder or more. Yes, there's a twisted mystery to be solved. Once again, in *The Last Lie Told*, her characters are fully rendered and reveal themselves authentically as her novel unfolds and careens to its stunning conclusion. *The Last Lie Told* is her best yet. Webb is the queen of smart suspense."

—Gregg Olsen, #1 *New York Times* bestselling author

Can't Go Back

"A complex, exciting mystery."

—*Kirkus Reviews*

"Police procedural fans will be sorry to see the last of Kerri and Luke."
—*Publishers Weekly*

"Threats, violence, and a dramatic climax . . . good for procedural readers."
—*Library Journal*

Gone Too Far

"An intriguing, fast-paced combination of police procedural and thriller."
—*Kirkus Reviews*

"Those who like a lot of family drama in their police procedurals will be satisfied."
—*Publishers Weekly*

Trust No One

"*Trust No One* is Debra Webb at her finest. Political intrigue and dark family secrets will keep readers feverishly turning pages to uncover all the twists in this stunning thriller."
—Melinda Leigh, #1 *Wall Street Journal* bestselling author of *Cross Her Heart*

"A wild, twisting crime thriller filled with secrets, betrayals, and complex characters that will keep you up until you reach the last darkly satisfying page. A five-star beginning to Debra Webb's explosive series!"
—Allison Brennan, *New York Times* bestselling author

"Debra Webb once again delivers with *Trust No One*, a twisty and gritty page-turning procedural with a cast of complex characters and a compelling cop heroine in Detective Kerri Devlin. I look forward to seeing more of Detectives Devlin and Falco."

—Loreth Anne White, *Washington Post* bestselling author of *In the Deep*

"*Trust No One* is a gritty and exciting ride. Webb skillfully weaves together a mystery filled with twists and turns. I was riveted as each layer of the past peeled away, revealing dark secrets. An intriguing cast of complicated characters, led by the compelling Detective Kerri Devlin, had me holding my breath until the last page."

—Brianna Labuskes, *Washington Post* bestselling author of *Girls of Glass*

"Debra Webb's name says it all."

—Karen Rose, *New York Times* bestselling author

CLOSER THAN YOU KNOW

OTHER TITLES BY DEBRA WEBB

Vera Boyett

Deeper Than the Dead

Finley O'Sullivan

The Last Lie Told
The Nature of Secrets
All the Little Truths

Devlin & Falco

Trust No One
Gone Too Far
Can't Go Back

CLOSER THAN YOU KNOW

DEBRA WEBB

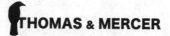

This is a work of fiction. Names, characters, organizations, places, events, and incidents are either products of the author's imagination or are used fictitiously. Otherwise, any resemblance to actual persons, living or dead, is purely coincidental.

Text copyright © 2025 by Debra Webb
All rights reserved.

No part of this book may be reproduced, or stored in a retrieval system, or transmitted in any form or by any means, electronic, mechanical, photocopying, recording, or otherwise, without express written permission of the publisher.

Published by Thomas & Mercer, Seattle

www.apub.com

Amazon, the Amazon logo, and Thomas & Mercer are trademarks of Amazon.com, Inc., or its affiliates.

ISBN-13: 9781662516191 (paperback)
ISBN-13: 9781662516207 (digital)

Cover design by Shasti O'Leary Soudant
Cover image: © DEEPOL Bengt Hedb / plainpicture

Printed in the United States of America

Dedication

The release of CLOSER THAN YOU KNOW marks twenty-seven years since I received "the call" and sold my very first book. What an amazing journey through nearly three decades! I am so very grateful to all the folks involved in the process, but most of all, I am thankful for the millions of readers who have spent their time and money on my stories. Thank you, thank you, you are the reason this journey continues!

It's the unexpected—the niggling worry haunting the edge of your thoughts—that is almost always closer than you know.
—Me

1

Tuesday, March 4
Old Lincoln County Hospital
Maple Street, Fayetteville, Tennessee, 11:30 p.m.

He didn't want to do this.

But he had no choice. His future depended on it.

Well, that might be an exaggeration. But how could he expect a career breakout if he didn't do something extraordinary? Something no one could ignore . . . something big? Really big?

"You sure this is the right place, man?"

Nolan Baker turned to the friend he'd asked to help with this peculiar meeting. They had known each other all their lives. Played football together in high school—well, Joel played. Nolan spent most of his time on the bench. Even then he knew he wasn't sports material. But his father wanted him to play, just as he had played.

The only thing Nolan had ever wanted to do was to report the news. So far he hadn't made it beyond the local newspaper. This might be just the story he needed. To that end, he was here—the last place he'd ever expect to find his big break.

"The message said to meet him at the old hospital." Nolan glanced around at the dilapidated building.

More than a century old, the former college turned regional medical facility had been abandoned for better than two decades. The building had fallen into disrepair, and vandals had broken windows, added graffiti, and basically trashed the place. Anything left inside had long since been stolen or damaged beyond repair.

The only thing that remained were the ghosts.

Riding out the shudder that quaked through him, Nolan suffered a sudden urge to get back into the car and drive away. He'd grown up hearing the tales about the "little girl" ghost and the many other apparitions sighted by those who lived nearby or who dared to venture into the place at night. The hospital had been the focus of a number of nationally syndicated television specials. Frankly, he wasn't surprised the person supposedly behind the series of recent abductions wanted to meet here.

In his opinion, the setting screamed "faker." This whole business was just a little too overdone. But, hey, he would take that big break any way he could get it.

"Well," Joel said, obviously losing patience as he scanned the dark parking lot, "doesn't look to me like he's coming." He set his attention on Nolan. "You want to keep waiting?"

"We're here. Might as well."

Joel was taller than Nolan, heavier as well. He'd always been a big guy. His job at the local John Deere dealership seemed to satisfy him. Married his high school sweetheart and had a kid, as well as another on the way.

The idea that Nolan hadn't managed a steady relationship ever and had no house of his own, just an apartment over his parents' garage, nudged him.

Nolan reminded himself he wasn't jealous of his friend or anyone else. He much preferred the potential excitement and adventure his five-year plan offered. He would, however, be grateful when the excitement finally kicked in.

Time and the right opportunity were all he needed. And patience, of course.

The three unexplained disappearances around the county in the past four weeks had garnered statewide attention. Just this week, a bigtime reporter from Nashville did an exposé that was set to go national. This really could be the opportunity that would launch his own career to the next level.

Nolan hadn't shared the message he'd received with anyone. Not even Joel knew exactly what this meeting was about—only that someone claiming to have information about the abductions had asked to meet. This anonymous source wanted to provide information that might help the authorities find the truth. Joel was all too happy to help Nolan out. Maybe Nolan's lifelong friend needed a little excitement that didn't include changing diapers and keeping his wife happy.

In truth, this could turn into real danger. Because tonight he might actually meet the so-called Time Thief—if the message sender was telling the truth.

The sender had claimed he wanted to tell his side of the story. Nolan experienced another shiver, this one from the actual excitement that tonight might be his big moment—the launching point for the next level of his career.

A flash of light in an upper window made Nolan jump.

"Did you see that?" Joel asked. "That third-floor window." He pointed to the one in question. "That's the one where people sometimes see a strange light. I know a bunch who claim to have witnessed it." He let out a long, low whistle. "Shit, man, I never believed it. But I definitely saw a light of some kind just now."

Light flashed again.

Nolan's heart thumped faster. "We should go up there. It could be him." He glanced around the parking lot. "Makes sense he wouldn't want to meet out in the open like this."

Joel released a big breath. "If that's what you want to do, I'm with you, buddy."

It didn't sound as if that was what his friend wanted to do. Nolan glanced away and smirked. Maybe Joel wasn't such a brave, tough guy after all. The little flare of glee he felt at the notion was undeniable.

Nolan pushed all else aside and gave a single, succinct nod. "Let's go."

He'd barely gotten the words out when snowflakes started to fall. He hesitated a moment and peered up at the sky. There had been snow in the forecast, but it rarely actually happened, particularly this close to spring.

"I'll be damned," Joel said as he pulled the hood of his sweatshirt up over his head. "My kid is going to love this. If it keeps up, maybe I'll help him build a snowman in the morning."

Nolan, on the other hand, would be shoveling his parents' sidewalk. One of these days he had to get his own place.

As they entered the double doors that had once served as the emergency room entrance, Nolan activated his phone's flashlight app. Why he hadn't thought to bring an actual flashlight was beyond him. Too late to wonder now. The place was an even worse wreck than the last time he'd done a walk-through. The new owner had wanted the newspaper to cover his attempt to find a use for the massive property that would benefit the community.

The graffiti and mildew on the walls were nothing new. The dank smell of the place he remembered from the visit last year. He had turned the visit into an exposé—past, present, and potential future. It hadn't gone beyond the local paper, but he'd received a good many favorable comments about the piece.

Silence was thick in the musty air. He'd have to remember that for the story. It was important to capture in words the intensity and drama of the moment. He hunched his shoulders, drawing the collar of his jacket up around his ears. It was cold for early March, but somehow it felt even colder in here. *As cold as death,* he mused, committing the line to memory.

Joel opened the stairwell door, and they entered the narrow space that led down to the basement as well as upward to the second and third floors. To his surprise, the stairwell was even chillier than the main building. What did they say about temperature drops? Ghosts were in the vicinity. Maybe. Though he wasn't much of a believer when it came to the paranormal.

Not at all, really. Except when it was part of a story. Accepting the idea as possible was an important part of the work during these occasions. Readers needed to believe that he believed.

Using his own phone's flashlight to guide them, Joel started up the stairs first. Nolan would never say as much, but he was glad. If the guy who'd requested the meeting was some crazed psycho, he didn't want to be the first to encounter him. It would be much better to witness all that happened from somewhat of a distance—for the story, of course.

Though the so-called Time Thief hadn't really harmed anyone so far, if he was some sort of psychopath, the situation could escalate at any moment. To date, his modus operandi—MO—was to sneak up on his victims, drug them, and then hold them for forty-eight hours before releasing them in some random place where he and his vehicle wouldn't be seen. The victims remembered nothing from the ordeal. Blood work revealed they had likely been drugged for the entire time. None were harmed, unless you counted the Sharpie illustrations on their bodies. Some were like maps of the solar system. Others were odd drawings of strange beings and animals. There was always at least one note written on each victim's back, related to something about them. *Too unreliable* or *too obnoxious*. Some characteristic or the other that appeared to be the reason they weren't kept for further observation by the abductor.

The police hadn't found a single clue. No prints, no nothing. Of the three abductions so far, all had happened in the surrounding county, just outside the city limits—keeping the case in the jurisdiction of the sheriff's department. Nolan guessed that if another victim was taken, the Tennessee Bureau of Investigation would be called in. Particularly since after a month and three victims, there was still nothing known about the person responsible or the potential motive for the abductions.

Maybe it was just someone having fun. A local who wanted to shake things up. Seriously ridiculous in Nolan's opinion. This requested meeting could be the perpetrator's way of coming clean. Perhaps a confession before disappearing. If it helped Nolan's career, he could turn it into something not so ridiculous. Make it seem important. Wasn't it a reporter's job to make stories interesting? To build the hype? The whole truth was rarely as titillating as something with a little added drama or speculation.

They emerged from the stairwell onto the third floor.

"Maybe we should turn off the lights," Joel whispered. "No need to give him a heads-up that we're coming."

Nolan agreed. He took one last long look at the corridor before them, then turned his app off and tucked the phone into his back pocket. As they moved forward, he held his breath in hopes of hearing even the slightest sound.

Slowly, as quietly as possible, they walked toward the room at the end of the corridor—the one from which they'd seen the light in the window. Some amount of moonlight filtered through the windows of the rooms they passed, sending faint rectangles of light over the floor. The meager glow wasn't much, but as their eyes adjusted, it was better than nothing. Kept them from tripping over the trash and random items scattered about.

Their destination, the room at the end of the corridor, was darker than the rest. Had the mysterious person closed the blinds after flashing the light they'd seen from the parking lot? Most of the coverings on the windows in the other rooms were damaged and dangling uselessly. It was possible the stories about the little girl who haunted this particular room had kept the vandals away from it.

Always intent on being the hero, Joel held up a hand as they approached the open door. He glanced at Nolan, then entered the room first.

Nolan waited a beat, then followed, scanning left to right. He'd been correct—the blinds were closed. Not even a single bent louver allowed a sliver of light into the space. There was a murky kind of darkness in here. He should pull out his cell and use the—

A thud and then an *oomph* made Nolan jump. A crash against the floor had him reaching into the near-total darkness for his friend.

"Joel?" Then he grabbed for his cell to get some light in the room.

Something pricked his neck.

Nolan twisted, stumbled away from the threat.

Something or someone moved in the darkness.

"Joel?"

The room started to spin, and Nolan swayed. His head began to swim. *Needle. Drug. Damn. Time Thief.*

He collapsed to the floor.

Just as his eyes closed, he felt something on his face . . . warm breath. He wanted to scramble away, but his body wouldn't move.

"Good boy."

The words followed him into nothingness.

2

Wednesday, March 5
Boyett Farm
Good Hollow Road, Fayetteville, 6:00 a.m.

Vera Boyett shoved a pod into the coffee maker and pressed the Start button.

It was cold. Too damned cold for March in southern Middle Tennessee. Thirty degrees, for God's sake. As if that wasn't bad enough, when she peered out the window over the sink, she saw there were at least six inches of snow on the ground.

"What in the world."

Vera shook her head. It wasn't like it didn't happen. There was the occasional snowstorm in March—even in April sometimes. When forecasting this event, her favorite meteorologist had provided data about just how many times it had happened in the past hundred years. She doubted the statistics would do a single thing to make folks feel better. All the schools would be closed, as well as a good many businesses.

She exhaled a big sigh, leaned a hip against the counter. Chances were, it wouldn't last long. By tomorrow the white stuff would be nothing more than an annoying memory for those who had to drive to work in it. Didn't really matter to Vera since she had no particular place to be this morning. A little smile toyed with her lips. That was the best part of being self-employed.

The money was enough to get her through when her services weren't needed. She worked from home, ensuring there was no overhead for the business: the family farm was paid for, so there was no mortgage or rent. She'd also paid off her SUV when she'd cashed out her 401(k), rather than rolling all of it over. She was in a good place financially. She'd barely noticed the loss of income after resigning from her position at the Memphis Police Department.

Life was good. No stress. No unattainable expectations. No more jaded outlook.

She bit her lip. That was the part that worried her. When things were going this well . . . trouble was bound to be right around the corner.

"Don't even go there, Vee." She had never been very good at accepting how things were at face value. She was always looking for the hidden agenda or bracing for the other shoe to drop.

She supposed that was what happened when you spent fifteen years as a cop in a city like Memphis. You never assumed anything . . . not if you were smart. The one time she had, her career had crashed and burned.

She forced the memory away. Not going there for sure.

The coffee maker sputtered and stopped humming, a sign her hot liquid caffeine was ready. Putting aside the notion that life was a little too good right now, she grabbed her cup and walked to the table, then slid onto one of the stools.

This was her routine every morning. She got up, brushed her hair, and—mostly to boost her self-esteem—added a touch of makeup. Sure wasn't to impress anyone. She dressed comfortably, in jeans and sweaters or tees—sweatshirts if it was really cold. As winter had started to show, back in December, she'd even picked up a pair of boots. But mostly she wore her sneakers. Casual attire was the norm in Fayetteville. No one expected her to show up at a crime scene or even a conference room wearing a suit or a dress with heels. Thank God. She did not miss any aspect of those days.

There was something truly relaxing about the idea of spending the rest of her life in jeans. Gone were the days of dressing for the ruthless climb up the career ladder. She had learned the hard way that the higher she climbed, the farther she had to fall.

Okay, so she hadn't quite killed off that jaded side just yet.

Truth was, she'd fallen all the way down from the high place she had achieved in her fifteen-year career. But, in true determined-female fashion, she had picked herself up and started over. Finding a new beginning could have happened anywhere, but she'd ended up back home in small-town Fayetteville. She surveyed the big country-style kitchen of the house where she'd grown up. She'd been here for seven months now. But her career debacle wasn't the only reason she'd landed back where she started.

The thought of all those remains found in that cave—the cave she and her sister Eve had played in as children right here on the family farm—still shook her.

"Not going there," Vera announced. Walks down memory lane were overrated.

Keeping the past behind her was, admittedly, a work in progress. And though she might never say it out loud, being here again had been good for her soul. She'd spent more than two decades after high school graduation immersed in the insanity of big-city living, first at university and then in an intense career. She'd never once considered that she could ever be happy living in a small town again—especially *this* small town. After high school she'd wanted only one thing: to get as far away from home as possible.

She laughed softly. Now, less than a week from turning forty, she was back here, living in her childhood home.

Forty.

Something like defeat sagged her shoulders.

"Forty." It sounded old. Not to mention she had spotted a gray hair this morning. Since she had blond hair, it was harder to see, but it was there. Despite the old saying that plucking out one would cause six more to show up for its funeral, she had ripped that sucker out with a vengeance. Although she loved dressing comfortably and forgoing all those old makeup routines, she was not ever going to be happy with gray hair.

Down deep, where she hid the things she didn't want to look at, the idea of forty prompted some of those old feelings of failure and unfulfillment. But a quick reminder that she did not need anyone or anything else to be happy with herself usually did the trick.

As if to challenge her assertion, the image of Gray Benton flashed in her mind.

She rolled her eyes at the dirty trick her mind liked to play. Bent was the sheriff. Yet another of the unexpected discoveries when she came home seven months ago. Bent had been Vera's first love and one more of the many reasons she had fled this place.

So much for not taking that walk down memory lane. Frustrated with herself, Vera stood and wandered to the back door, then stared out through the panes of glass that made up the top half. So weird to see snow at all, but especially this much. The backyard was white. The trees and shrubs . . . her mother's potting shed—they were all topped in a thick blanket of white.

Depressions or dips in that solid mass snagged her attention. She frowned and pressed closer to the glass to stare at the inconsistency. Tracks, she decided. Something or someone had walked through the snow. The tracks were too large to be from a deer or a dog. She grabbed her coat from the rack next to the door and stuffed her feet into her boots.

Outside, the wind was stronger than she'd expected. She grimaced and eased carefully down the steps in deference to the slippery conditions. The tracks in the snow were definitely human shoe prints. Big—probably male. They didn't come up the steps to the back door. Instead, they went to the pair of side-by-side windows that looked into the kitchen. The trampled snow in the area suggested the trespasser had lingered at the windows for a bit.

What the hell now? She'd had way more than her share of snooping reporters and other lookie-loos over the past few months already. Enough was enough.

Irritation flaring, Vera stepped back inside and grabbed her father's shotgun from behind the door. Then she followed the tracks. The cold seeped through her coat and into her bones far more quickly than she had expected as she trudged along. The temperature wasn't as low as it could be, but the wind gave the cold a sharp bite.

The tracks passed the potting shed and well house without veering off and led straight toward the barn. She was out of breath by the time she opened the double doors of the big old structure. Though she had restarted her workouts a few months ago, trudging through the snow and cold was a little tougher than a typical run on the treadmill.

No tire tracks that she could see. Evidently, the trespasser had parked at the road and snaked his way through the woods and into the barn on foot, then walked to the house. Unless he had arrived before the snow, then waited. If that were the case, maybe the tracks were a message. She'd been sent a few since her return. You didn't help bring down bad guys without making an enemy or two along the way.

Vera flipped the switch for the lights inside the barn. With the fixtures hung so close to the cavernous ceiling, the combined glow still left far too many shadows. Not to mention that the array of farm equipment and other junk provided way too many spots for hiding. She braced the butt of the shotgun against her shoulder, held the barrel at the ready, and performed a walk-through. She didn't really expect whoever had been here to still be in the barn, but the question was, had he taken anything?

Or left something?

She would prefer the former to the latter. Better a thief than someone setting a trap.

She looked through each stall, the tack room, and the larger side of the space, which had once housed cows and horses but now served as storage. Her search revealed nothing out of place. She stared upward for a moment before walking to the ladder that ascended to the loft. She climbed it slowly, considering the shotgun she carried. Once her head was higher than the floor, she scanned the space. A few bales of old hay but nothing else.

She climbed down. Settled one foot back on the ground, then the other.

A crash made her jump around to face the front.

It took a moment for her heart to calm and her brain to assimilate the realization that the wind had blown hard enough to send one of the doors slamming shut.

Damn. "You need more coffee, Vee."

She shut off the lights, closed the remaining door, and headed back to the house. She stalled long enough to take a few pics of the tracks with her cell phone, zooming in to get the tread imprints.

On the back steps, she stamped her feet to rid her boots of the excess snow, then went inside. She locked the door and set the shotgun aside. She'd just gotten her coat hung up when the doorbell rang. Given the hour—not quite seven in the morning—and the snow, she was surprised to have a visitor.

Taking her time, she made her way to the front of the house and peered out a window to see who was on her porch.

Bent.

The usual trickle of heat rushed through her. It annoyed her immensely that even after all these months, she hadn't gotten past that initial reaction each time she encountered him. It wasn't like he was naked, or all dressed up. For God's sake, he wore jeans—always. This morning he'd added a denim jacket with a sherpa lining over his usual Lincoln County Sheriff's Department shirt. But she knew, damn it. She knew it was the cowboy hat and those well-loved boots that gave him that little extra *something*. Something she refused to define.

Maybe if she wasn't so deep in denial about her physical needs . . .

"Stow it, Vee," she grumbled as she unlocked the door. She plastered on a big smile and opened it. "Morning, Sheriff. You're out early."

A smile stretched across his lips—slow, easy, as if he had all day. He removed his hat, like the gentleman he was, and gave her a nod. "Morning to you, Vee. You mind if I come in?"

"Sure." She backed up, opened the door wider. Once he was inside, she closed out the cold air. "You up for some coffee?"

"Actually"—he held his hat in his hand and pinned her with the blue eyes that had always made her weak—"I need your help."

So this was work. Okay. Good. "Let me get my coat."

On the way to the kitchen, she grabbed her cell phone, tucked it into her back pocket, then pulled on her less-than-sexy boots and retrieved her coat. Like the boots, the down-filled lightweight jacket was a purchase she'd made after moving here. Also like her boots, it was black. She might not be fashionable, but at least she matched.

"What happened?" she asked, pulling on her coat as she walked back toward Bent.

"You been keeping up with the Time Thief case?"

"I have. Sort of. We talked about it that once." There had been three disappearances so far.

"We have another one."

She frowned, reached for the buttons of her coat. "You're not calling in help from TBI?" He'd mentioned something to that effect before.

He nodded. "I did, but as you know, it might be another day or two before they get here. Right now, we have nearly every deputy in the department, as well as borrowed personnel from Moore and Franklin counties—not to mention community volunteers—all working to find our latest victim." He shrugged. "We're doing all we can, but the victim's mother asked me to see if you would get involved."

Her recognition as a crime analyst—one who often consulted with local law enforcement—had heightened her profile around town. Not that her assistance had offset the other less-than-flattering stories about the notorious Boyett sisters. Some folks would never change their minds about the past. Didn't matter really. When those same folks called on Vera for help, she simply reminded herself that even the most devout churchgoers would call on the devil himself if necessary when tragedy struck.

"Who's the victim?"

"Nolan Baker."

Her eyebrows rose in surprise. Baker was the local reporter who'd harassed her younger sister Luna to no end during the investigation into the cave remains. Vera knew him, all right. Knew his parents, too—in particular, his mother.

"His mother asked for me?" Considering that Elizabeth Baker—Bogus before she married—had made Vera's life miserable back in high school, she couldn't help feeling surprised.

"She did," Bent confirmed. "She's really worried, as you can imagine."

Vera did another of those slow nods. "Anything different this time?"

If the perp followed his usual MO, Nolan was in no serious danger. But that could change in a heartbeat.

"Apparently, the perp or someone who knows the perp set up a meet this time. Claimed to have information for Nolan. There was a friend with Nolan—Joel Keeton. He was left unconscious at the scene. He has a concussion, but he's fine otherwise. Unfortunately, it was dark, so he didn't see anything."

The information gave Vera pause. If the perp had changed his MO, there was a distinct possibility that he was escalating. Never a good thing.

"Take me to the scene. Then we'll talk to the friend."

If this Time Thief had decided to change his game, Nolan Baker might be in far more trouble than anyone realized.

3

Old Lincoln County Hospital
Maple Street, Fayetteville, 7:00 a.m.

The last time Vera had stood in this hospital, her mother was in the emergency room being officially pronounced dead.

The image of her father standing quietly next to the gurney that had been used to wheel his wife into a room, with poor Eve—Vera's younger sister—flung across their mother's cold, dead body was one Vera would never be able to exile from her brain. She had hovered at the foot of the gurney in a sort of shock that wouldn't allow the tears to flow until later, when she was alone in her room.

Grief was that way. It either poured from one at the moment of trauma or buried itself for a later eruption.

That day had been the worst of her and Eve's lives.

"The room where Joel Keeton was found is on the third floor," Bent said, drawing her attention back to the present.

They'd entered the building through the old emergency room entrance. The same way she and her family had come in all those years ago.

"Lead the way." Vera gestured for the sheriff to precede her.

He gave her one of those nods—every woman knew the sort. The kind only a man like Gray Benton could pull off. The vague gesture had many meanings. *Yes. Okay. Whatever.* The impact was in the execution. And no one ever questioned it.

Vera narrowed her focus to the reason she was here. A young man—arrogant though he might be—had gotten himself into what would likely prove to be deep shit. But like most reporters, Nolan Baker wanted the story and was willing to do most anything to get it. She wondered if he felt that way now . . . assuming he was still alive. Then again, there was no reason to believe he wasn't, based on the perp's MO so far.

Broken glass and other debris littered the floor of the long corridor they entered next. The seemingly endless walls had once been white. Now they were mostly gray, speckled and streaked with something darker from the mildew and mold. Amid the collage of gray hues were a few not readily identifiable stains. On the way here Bent had explained that the chief of police had someone checking on the place each night to ensure there were no vagrants hanging out. Still, without a guard 24–7, it was difficult to keep out those who had mischief in mind. The curious could be a problem as well. Not to mention the desperate, who just needed shelter. Particularly in weather like this.

For the life of her, Vera would never understand why cities didn't make repairs to old buildings like this and house those with no place to stay, especially during cold weather. Realistically she understood the financial and legal ramifications might very well be overwhelming. But there was just something intrinsically wrong with the idea of people sleeping on the streets when buildings like this one stood empty.

In the end, she supposed it all boiled down to whether or not the city owned the property. In this case they did not. Long ago life had changed from the simple terms of right and wrong to the far more complicated concepts of why and whose opinion reigned.

"You're probably aware of the stories about the little girl who haunts the place," Bent said as they entered the stairwell and began the climb upward.

"Eve has mentioned the stories over the years." She recalled her sister saying there had been television-docuseries-type shows about the old hospital. Vera had never watched any of them. Maybe she would when she got home. The perp had chosen this place for a reason. Learning as much as possible about it could prove useful.

Another flight of steps disappeared behind them with nothing more than the sound of Bent's cowboy boots, as well as her own nondescript ones. Bent wasn't a big talker. He spoke when he had something to say. Small talk wasn't a part of his top-cop toolbox. Never had been a part of who he was. As much time as they had spent together during their brief love affair twenty-odd years ago, very little talking had taken place.

She shivered at the memory . . . or maybe because it was so damned cold in here.

When Bent moved to open the stairwell door, curiosity got the better of her, and Vera braced a hand against it to stop him. "Do you believe the rumors—about the little girl, I mean?"

Bent studied her for a moment. She clenched her jaw and refused to blink—not an easy task. Of all the men she had met in her life, Bent was the only one who could look so deep inside her. Back in the day, he'd been what folks around here referred to as a "lady's man." The women adored him and gladly forgot all about their boyfriends and husbands for a moment of no-holds-barred pleasure with Bent. At seventeen, Vera had thought he was the most amazing man on the planet. At least until he disappeared, leaving her heartbroken.

He gave her a vague shrug. "I believe there are people who believe they've seen her."

Exactly the answer she'd expected. Vera dropped her hand. Bent was a good man and a good sheriff. Maybe one of the best cops with whom she'd worked.

They stepped into the center corridor on the top floor. The gathering at the other end told her the two forensic cops in the department were on site already. The forensic duo was relatively new for the county. Bent had been working on building a team since becoming sheriff.

Finally, early last year he'd brought two new deputies, both educated and trained in forensic science, on board. Another deputy appeared to be standing guard. No TBI agents so far.

And she didn't see Nolan Baker's mama. That was the real surprise.

"I imagine Elizabeth has attempted to visit the scene already," she said as they neared the ongoing activity. A face-to-face with her was not something Vera looked forward to, even if the woman had asked for her.

"Chief Teller talked to the family personally. He assured both the mother and father that he'd give them a walk-through when the forensic work was done."

Of course he would. No one ever said no to Elizabeth. Vera wasn't surprised it was the chief who'd done the talking. The incident occurred inside the city limits, making it Police Chief Ray Teller's jurisdiction. But the ongoing investigation was the county's, and that made it Bent's problem. Teller likely had no issue with leaving the bizarre case with the sheriff's department. If Vera recalled correctly, Teller had a daughter who had been friends with Elizabeth back in high school. He would no doubt have taken the initiative of informing the parents either way.

"Teller passed along Elizabeth's request about me?"

"He did." Bent turned to meet her gaze. "You still don't like her?"

Vera almost laughed. "Ah, unless you can tell me she's not the snobbish bully she was in high school, yeah, I suppose I don't."

A smile played with one corner of his mouth. "You're right. You don't."

Vera shook her head. Some things never changed.

Before entering the room, they donned gloves and shoe covers. Vera was fairly confident Bent kept a special size on hand for his boots. The boots and the hat were details that made the ladies like him more. The tight-fitting tee he wore under that sheriff's department shirt only added to his appeal.

Don't be an idiot, Vee. Focus on why you're here.

As with the rest of the former hospital, the room they entered had been vandalized. Blinds were open. Graffiti and those other unpleasant discolorations marred the once-white walls. The commercial-grade vinyl tile covering the floor was dirty with random debris lying around. Beer bottles, some broken, along with beer cans and miscellaneous trash. No small number of cigarette butts.

Deputy Will Conover, the lead forensic investigator, nodded to Bent. "We're just finishing up. Be out of your way in about fifteen seconds."

"Take your time." Bent scanned the floor. "Did you find any fresher cigarette butts?"

It went without saying that he hoped for genetic evidence.

"I did," Conover said. "But none smelled very recent, so I wouldn't get my hopes up. We dusted for prints in the most obvious places, but"—he surveyed the room—"it's like looking for a needle in a haystack. There's been a lot of people through here."

In Vera's opinion, there was little in the space that would provide anything in the way of usable evidence—unless they got really, really lucky. The sheer notoriety of the place ensured far too many visitors.

Considering no evidence had been found at any of the places where the previous victims were taken or left suggested this perp planned carefully. He was organized and smart. Too smart to leave something as elementary as a fingerprint. Either that or he'd been damned lucky so far.

The other deputy—Vera didn't recall her name—grabbed the last of their gear and headed out.

"If you find anything," Bent said to Conover, "call me."

"Will do."

With that, the two deputies were gone, leaving only the one assigned to guard duty in the corridor.

"Keeton said it was dark when they entered the room. The blinds were closed. Perp probably closed them for that reason. Keeton hit the floor here," Bent said as he moved toward the right and closer to the window. "When he regained consciousness, Baker and the perp were gone. Keeton was tied up with nylon rope. It took him a while to free himself. His cell was taken, along with the fob to Baker's car—which was likely in his pocket. Once Keeton was outside, he banged on doors in the neighborhood until someone answered and let him use a phone."

Vera moved toward the spot where Keeton had fallen, then turned all the way around. "So the perp was waiting in the room for them. He must have known Nolan wasn't coming alone."

Bent walked the few steps to the window. "Baker's car was parked in the lot in clear view of this window. The perp probably watched them enter the building, then closed the blinds to block any moonlight."

The blinds were open fully now. Bent or one of his deputies likely opened them once the initial crime scene photos and video had been taken. Vera peered out the window. She thought of the tracks she'd found behind her house this morning. "No tracks in the snow down there?"

A multitude of vehicle and person tracks littered the melting slush now. Reporters had started to line up outside the perimeter the deputies had put in place.

Bent shook his head. "Keeton said it had just started to snow when they came in last night, so I'm assuming our perp got Baker out before the snow piled up."

"No other vehicle in the lot when the two arrived?"

"No. If there was a vehicle on the property, it was well hidden. And," he went on, "we've canvassed the area, and no one who lives nearby saw or heard anything."

Well, that answered her next question.

"With the other victims, he waited for them where they lived or worked or some other place they frequented," she mentioned, her brain running through scenarios.

"The first was taken from home around ten p.m.," Bent explained. "Number two was taken from the gym after closing time. The parking lot was empty. There was no one else inside except the employee closing up, who didn't see or hear anything." He surveyed the room. "The last victim was putting flowers on her mother's grave in the middle of the afternoon."

At Blanche Cemetery over near Taft. Not at Rose Hill, where Vera's parents were buried. The ache of having buried their father just two months ago was still fresh.

"This one is a sizable step out of his usual MO," Vera said, pointing out the obvious and moving on from thoughts of her father.

"That's what worries me," Bent agreed.

"Maybe he's ready to tell his story," Vera suggested. "Nolan Baker is a reporter. He has extensive local connections, which makes him high profile. Maybe Nolan is the big finale—the point he hopes to make in all this."

Bent shot her a look that said he hoped to hell not. Okay, that wasn't what she'd been going for.

"I mean," she clarified, "to achieve whatever glory he's hoping for. Perps like this one aren't in it for the violence; this is all about proving something. Showing off. That sort of thing." At least, that appeared to be the case so far. There certainly was nothing in his MO that suggested otherwise—at least until now.

"We can hope it doesn't involve murder."

Murder. Vera had helped bring many murderers to justice, and she'd kept at least two murders hidden. Basically, she'd been a part of the deed from both sides—going way back. Better to keep that to herself too.

Funny, she'd never seen her sister Eve or their daddy as killers. But they were . . . weren't they? No matter that the act in both instances had been self-defense. Still, people were dead.

There were times when she wondered if she was one of the good guys or not. *Not tap-dancing around in that minefield.*

She squared her shoulders and suggested, "We should walk through the other rooms on this floor. Look for any sort of staging area."

"We walked through earlier." Bent waited for her to take the lead now. "Didn't find anything, but a fresh set of eyes is always a good idea."

As soon as they were out of the room where the attack had occurred, they removed their shoe covers. Vera left her gloves on just in case. The other rooms were not unlike the one where Joel Keeton had found himself unconscious on the floor. By the time they reached the fourth room, Vera had noted the one undeniable consistency that did not extend to the scene of the attack.

"All the windows"—she gestured to the one in the room where they currently stood—"are basically bare. The curtains and blinds are either gone completely or hanging by a thread. But the window in the room where the abduction took place has a workable set of blinds."

Bent's gaze narrowed as he considered her point. "Let's take another look."

They walked back to the room and, not bothering with the shoe covers this time, took a closer look at the intact blinds on the window.

"Looks the same as the damaged ones on the windows in the other rooms," Bent noted, "but this one is in working order."

"Maybe the perp picked this room because it was the only one with an intact set." Made sense, Vera supposed.

"Otherwise," Bent said, "he picked the best of the window coverings, since the windows are all about the same size, and moved it here. This is the room where sightings of that mysterious light and the little girl most often occur. If cashing in on the notoriety was his point, this room was the one to choose."

"He would unquestionably do that. He's careful, organized," Vera said. "We know this from the other abductions. His victims have all been locals, all around the same age. And all taken with no witnesses and no evidence left behind. Sticking to a precise routine has prevented any missteps so far."

"If we find the window where this blind came from," Bent considered out loud, "assuming that's what happened, we might find prints. Removing a set of blinds is a pain in the ass if you're wearing gloves."

"Are we checking every window?" Vera did a quick mental tally of all the windows she'd seen.

Bent shook his head. "That last show some ghost-hunter group made is still on YouTube. They went from room to room. We should be able to see which one had what we're looking for."

"Excellent idea." Vera grinned. "Your office or mine?"

"I have the investigation details laid out at my home office."

"But does it come with the offer of breakfast?" Vera was suddenly starving.

He smiled. "I can make that happen."

"Best offer I've had all morning."

Back on the first floor, more uniforms guarded the entrances. News had spread, and a few lookie-loos were in the parking lot along with the reporters.

Vera groaned at the number of news vans lining the perimeter. "Oh yippee."

"All we have to do," Bent said, leaning closer to her, "is make sure they don't follow us."

Before she could respond, two women and a cameraman breached the yellow tape and stormed toward them.

"Oh hell," Bent murmured.

He headed toward the three to cut them off while Vera climbed into his truck. She appreciated the move. He knew how she hated this sort of thing. She had nothing against reporters in general, but she'd suffered through more than her share in her career. Now that she was a private contractor, she didn't have to talk to reporters if she didn't want to. No chain of command to keep happy. No public to appease.

"Vera Mae!"

She would have recognized that voice anywhere. Another groan welled inside her. Elizabeth "Boggie" Bogus Baker. Vera would lay odds that the woman had chosen a man with a last name that began with a *B* just so she didn't have to change any of her monogrammed self-indulgences.

"Mrs. Baker . . . ," Bent was saying.

"Vera Mae, please, I need to speak with you." Elizabeth's face was red and puffy, but it was the pain there that did the trick.

Vera took a breath and climbed out of the truck. Putting off the inevitable was a waste of time anyway.

Bent glanced at Vera as Elizabeth rushed past him.

"I'm so sorry to hear about what's happened, Elizabeth," Vera said with complete earnestness. Having a child in danger—even an adult child—was a parent's worst nightmare. "We can talk at Bent's office—have more privacy."

"I know." Elizabeth grabbed Vera by the shoulders. "But I just couldn't wait. Please, just please promise me you won't let anything happen to my son. I know if anyone in this world can find him before he's hurt, it's you. Please promise me."

Vera could feel the various camera lenses zooming in on her. The other woman who'd made it as far as Bent would allow was obviously a reporter. She appeared to be directing the guy with the television camera on his shoulder. She produced a smile when she noticed Vera watching her.

Vera shifted her attention back to Nolan's mother. "I can promise you, Elizabeth, that Bent and I will do everything we can."

Tears flowed down the woman's face. Funny, she had not a single wrinkle under all that puffy redness. She looked perfect. Vera, on the other hand, had plenty of lines. Truth be told, Elizabeth had always been perfect, from the top of her flawlessly styled black hair to her elegant designer boots.

"Thank you, Vera Mae." She yanked Vera against her, hugging her tightly. "Thank you. I just want my son back safe and sound."

Vera glanced at the reporter. Now the whole town—possibly the country—would know that Vera Mae Boyett had promised to find the victim, in a case where the victims were typically released basically unharmed anyway. She wasn't sure which one of them would come off looking more foolish, she or Elizabeth. Then again, it wasn't Vera's son missing.

She just hoped like hell this was not the moment this bizarre perpetrator decided to escalate into the kind of violence that did more than inconvenience and temporarily disable his victims.

At least not before Vera could find that little shit, Nolan Baker.

4

Benton Ranch
Old Molino Road, Fayetteville, 8:00 a.m.

Bent had gone into the house to prepare the promised breakfast. Vera had opted to remain in the home office he'd created out of an existing potting shed behind the cottage he called home. The first time she'd come here, she'd been surprised.

The main house, a wood-and-stone cottage, sat a good half mile off the road, on a rise overlooking a meadow where horses grazed. Just passing by on the main road, one would never know there was a house deep within the woods. It was one of the most beautiful properties Vera had seen, and she'd seen a few. The idea that this naturally pristine and tranquil property belonged to the womanizing boozer who'd stolen her heart and introduced her to sex twenty-odd years ago stunned her. No, not stunned—shocked her.

More startling had been his reason for buying the place. When he was a child, his mother had worked as a cleaning lady for the then owner. She'd mentioned how much she would love to have a home like this—it was her dream home. Even decades after her death, Bent hadn't forgotten the way his mother had spoken about the place. When he returned to Fayetteville and learned it was for sale, he bought it.

Truth was, Bent hadn't been a bad person back when he and Vera collided, just a wild twenty-one-year-old who had nothing and wanted nothing except to feel something besides neglect and abuse. He used his looks and sex, as well as plenty of alcohol, to assuage that emptiness. Loss and need brought the two of them together.

But Bent knew he wasn't what Vera needed, so he ran off and joined the army. She was devastated. They hadn't seen each other or spoken in better than two decades until seven months ago, when those remains were found and Vera had to come back home to protect her sisters and to handle the situation.

She stared at the two whiteboards on the far side of the room. The first time Bent had brought her here, to his home workspace, the remains and other evidence found in the cave on the Boyett farm had lined both. All those bones . . .

The only ones Vera had known about were the remains of her and Eve's stepmother. She had helped Eve put the vicious bitch's body in that cave. She shuddered at the memory. Twenty-odd years later—when the bones were discovered—she and Eve faced no charges for what they had done as kids. Their father and Sheree, the wicked stepmother, had argued, gotten physical when she'd tried to drown Luna—Vera and Eve's baby half sister, only nine months old at the time. The fall and subsequent head injury that had caused Sheree's death were ruled an accident. The trouble was, Sheree's remains weren't the only ones in that damned cave.

Enough of that.

She blinked away the memory and eased down onto a stool next to the vintage planks and posts Bent had put together to create a large table, which served as his desk. Seven months. They'd been working together on some level the whole time, and so far he'd been careful not to cross the line she had drawn in the sand. They would be friends and nothing more. It wasn't always easy—for her anyway—but it was the best course of action.

She looked around the room, which reminded her of him in so many ways . . . it smelled of his subtle aftershave—an oldie but goody. Something earthy and lightly scented. She'd always loved it. Once, maybe twice she'd run into a man wearing that same aftershave. Except no one had worn it the way Bent did. Somehow his natural scent or maybe the small amount he used, perhaps both, mingled and made the most amazingly subtle fragrance.

She cleared her throat and stood, walked up to the first of the two case boards, where the victims of the Time Thief were displayed. Beneath each photo were the details of the victim and the event. All three in their twenties. All White. Two males, one female. The details of the abductions varied very little. The time and day of the week changed. Location too. But the events that occurred were exactly the same each time. The victim was drugged and kept that way until he or she was released around forty-eight hours later.

Photos of the drawings on the bodies showed those were fairly consistent as well. Very little variation. That was the part of the case that confused Vera. The drawings—images of odd beings and animals, as well as crude renderings of the solar system—were simple, adolescent almost. For someone so carefully organized and seemingly clever, the diagrams didn't fit. She wondered if this was just a game to the perp. Bent had made notes about a few social media sites where he'd found similar drawings, but none linked with criminal activity. Most were associated with finds in caves or other remote locations around the world. These same sorts of drawings were regularly affiliated with people and groups with strong opinions about UFOs and aliens. For some the belief was like a religion. But not a single one of those drawings was connected to this town or this case—at least not that they had found so far. Was their Time Thief using what he found on the net to give himself authenticity of some sort?

The door opened, luring her gaze in that direction. Bent walked in, carrying one of those post office trays made for holding sorted mail. No envelopes in this one. There was a carafe with two cups and two wrapped sandwiches.

He kicked the door shut behind him and carried the tray to the table. "I hope BLTs work for you."

Vera inhaled the aroma of bacon and coffee. "Oh God, it smells fantastic."

He passed her a sandwich swaddled in a paper towel. "Whoever invented microwave bacon was a genius." He pointed in her direction. "By the way, I added mustard to yours."

She was surprised he remembered. "Thanks."

He poured the coffee, and for a minute they only ate. The lettuce and tomato were really fresh. Vera swallowed. "I can't believe you had lettuce and tomato on hand. If I have any in the fridge, they're probably dead. I buy them and then forget about them."

Bent set his coffee aside. "I wouldn't have had any, but I stole it from the leftover salad Renae brought last night."

Time slowed for a second as Vera analyzed his statement.

"Renae?" She blinked to hide her surprise. They rarely talked about that part of their lives. She didn't actually have *that part* anymore—the personal part. She had, it seemed, been unaware that he apparently did have one. Her last personal or intimate relationship had been back in Memphis with a guy she still considered a friend. But dating wasn't even on her radar.

Bent tore off another bite and then nodded as he chewed. After swallowing, he explained, "She's divorced, moved here about three years ago. Just after I came back."

Vera forced another bite, the lettuce and tomato suddenly tasting bitter. "I see," she mumbled around chewing.

He studied her a moment. "She's just a friend."

The idea that he saw right through, right to the sting of jealousy that had burned her, annoyed Vera inordinately. "We all need friends."

She forced her focus onto the coffee and the sandwich. Took another bite and worked on it until she could swallow, then licked her lips. "Tastes surprisingly good for store-bought veggies this time of year."

"She has a greenhouse. Grows her own."

Of course she did. She probably milked goats and made cheese as well. Vera set the remainder of her sandwich aside. Her appetite had vanished. "Wow. I'm impressed. She sounds nice."

Bent shrugged, the move barely visible. "She is. Nice, I mean."

Good to know. Not.

"If the Time Thief follows his usual MO," she said, moving on, "he'll drop Nolan off somewhere tomorrow night."

Bent finished off his sandwich and sipped his coffee before commenting. "If we're lucky and nothing changes, he will."

But things had changed. Unease slid through Vera as she twisted on the stool and reviewed the case board's detailed timeline. Having been a cop and crime analyst for so long, she couldn't help forming conclusions based on the information available to her. It was the nature of the beast.

"His work has been confined to Lincoln County," she offered, "suggesting someone local or who used to be local. Perps typically prefer to hunt where they feel most comfortable. His choice of victims as well as the time and place of each abduction indicates a preference for low-level risk—which significantly lessens the thrill." She shrugged. "Given he has consistently worked outside any city's jurisdictional lines—until now—he obviously prefers keeping a low profile."

"I agree." He braced his forearms on the table and stared at the timeline he'd created. "We've interviewed all the high-profile extraterrestrial believers in a tricounty area. We found more than one club with members who believe they've been abducted and released by aliens. One in Tullahoma in particular seems very active."

Vera frowned. "You didn't mention that part when we talked before." They had discussed what was happening with the case over the past few weeks. And it wasn't like she could escape the details anyway—the Time Thief was all anyone was talking about. Besides, what else did two investigator types do when they got together for a meal or ran into each other at the supermarket? The options she had relegated to the farthest recesses of her brain instantly pushed front and center, but she banished them.

Not going there for sure.

"Since you're officially working on the case with me now, I figured you should know."

True enough. In deference to his need for a more open mind, she threw out another feasible scenario. "Perhaps someone a bit more fanatical is responsible for the abductions, in an effort to spur belief or interest. Some folks need to escape what's happening around them, and going overboard on something like this could be the chosen remedy."

"Definitely a possibility," he agreed.

She studied the photos of the victims after being released. "I've seen those rudimentary-type diagrams before from people who claimed to be abducted. Not in person," she clarified. "Online. I also watched a program about victims who believe they've had that experience. What I found when comparing their stories is that the images seldom vary but the steps in the abductions are rarely so carefully executed as what we're seeing here. There are generally all sorts of variances."

"Maybe this alien enthusiast is more detail obsessed," Bent suggested.

She laughed. "Maybe so." She took some time to consider any other potential scenarios. This was what she did, after all, and she was very good at it. "Another possibility I'm seeing—and this is a stretch at best," she proposed, "is that maybe the perp is someone who has a grudge against the department or you and wants to make you look bad." She shrugged. "I mean, what better way than to set up a case you can't solve. If it's a former deputy, then he knows how to avoid all the pitfalls that get perps caught."

It really was a stretch for sure, but when Bent had taken over, there had been cleanup to do. The former sheriff had recognized the trouble, but with his age and health conditions, the issues were too big for him to handle. He'd left that to Bent, and he'd done the job, all right. Replaced nearly half of the department.

"I've considered the possibility." He looked from the board to her. "I have Myra looking into the whereabouts and activities of those who were fired."

Vera gave him a nod. Myra Jordan, his assistant, was the perfect choice. She had been with the former sheriff for twenty years. She knew the department inside and out and everyone who lived in the area. Vera could see her quickly ferreting out anyone targeting the department.

"Another scenario," she went on, "is that we have a perp who's looking for his fifteen minutes of fame—even if only in the local paper." She pondered the idea a moment. "The idea that the perp is either trying to draw attention to the existence of otherworldly beings, or maybe to himself, feels more feasible, don't you think?"

"Those are the most logical, yes." He considered her a moment before asking, "What are your thoughts on the way our perp contacted his victim this time—leaving a message tucked under his windshield wiper while he was shopping at Gerald's? That was a big step away from his usual MO of no advance warning."

The small-town supermarket had no video surveillance of the parking lot, which the perp no doubt knew—maintaining that low risk level. "It's possible this was nothing more than his not being able to catch Nolan in the right situation without going a new route. Then again, at least two aspects of his MO this time are different. If this move is about taking his work to the next level or making a big, splashy finale, abducting a reporter would certainly do the job. Especially since Nolan is the son of one of the most prominent families in town."

They sat in silence a moment, both staring at the case board.

"But we can't be sure this is his final victim," Bent countered. "He's a repeat offender. At this point we don't know where he's going. He could be a fledgling serial abductor. Testing his wings before he flies. Baker could end up his first kill."

"True . . . except," Vera argued, "this perp, so far, has no message. Nothing. Other than vague observations written on the bodies of the victims he releases. He's told us nothing. What is he accomplishing?

He's taken nothing but time from the victims. He's used up time and resources from your department. But otherwise, what does he get from his actions? What need is he fulfilling? What does his work say?"

Even as she said the words, the "fifteen minutes of fame" scenario was gaining ground as the more likely of the two options. And it was one she felt confident no one—including Bent—was going to like.

"Not much," Bent admitted. His gaze narrowed. "Where does that leave us in terms of most likely scenarios?"

She braced herself and went for broke. "What if this latest victim—the reporter—either created the whole damned thing or is taking advantage of the Time Thief's MO to create a stir of his own for a little notoriety." No one—not even Bent—could deny the scenario was feasible. "After all, Nolan is Elizabeth's child. Being an attention hog at all costs runs in the family."

Bent mulled over her scenario for a bit. "You really think Baker would set this up for the headlines?"

"Think about it. No one is harmed—not really. The vics are released fairly quickly. And we both know that Nolan is an ambitious guy who would do most anything to get what he wants."

"True enough," he allowed, but his expression told her he wasn't convinced.

Vera turned her hands up then. "There is obviously the possibility that I'm suggesting this, in part, because he was so mean to Luna during the cave investigation and his mother was so awful to me in high school."

She imagined the idea had crossed Bent's mind without her having to say as much. It was no secret she was not a fan of Elizabeth or her offspring. No matter the training and experience under her belt, Vera was only human.

"Bottom line," she went on before he could respond, "what we have are three seemingly uneventful abductions that resulted in nothing more than worry for the families, the community, and the sheriff's department. Then suddenly we have a deviation. A reporter is abducted. There's a note sent to him to set up a meeting—a note you have not seen. None of the others received notes. There's a witness to the abduction—a witness who actually heard and saw nothing. There were no witnesses of any sort to the other abductions."

He nodded. "I'm with you so far."

"Whether," she said in conclusion, "this is some guy out to make you look bad, or an extraterrestrial enthusiast hoping to gain support—*or* a desperate reporter out to gain a spot in the limelight, my gut tells me this is not just an escalation but a setup to some sort of finale." She pointed a finger at Bent. "And just in time to avoid involvement from an outside agency. If this one resolves in the usual forty-eight hours like the others, the TBI will scarcely have arrived, and the whole thing will be over."

"I can see merit in what you're saying," Bent said slowly. "With that in mind, I say we take a close look at each scenario. See where each one takes us."

Vera laughed—a dry, surprised sound. "You know that a scenario where Nolan is involved in any way with illegal activities will not sit well with the Bakers."

Elizabeth's husband, Carl, owned the biggest bank in the county. The man had inherited well via his marriage and invested even better. He would not appreciate any negative light cast on his only son.

"I guess we'll have to be careful, then, and make sure they don't find out until we have concrete evidence one way or the other." He stood, grabbed their breakfast remains, and tossed them back into the postal tray.

"I could talk to some of his colleagues at the *Elk Valley Times*," Vera suggested.

Bent pushed the tray aside. "Carl has given me permission for a more detailed search of his son's home."

"That tops colleague interviews anytime." Vera slid off the stool. "What're we waiting for?" Having a look into the intimate space of a victim could provide important details as to why that person may have been victimized.

Or why he was victimizing others.

"The TBI will be picking up Baker's laptop and going through it."

"You heard from them, then." Vera reached for her coat.

"Got a call while I was preparing breakfast. Oh, and I also scanned that episode of *Ghost Adventures*. There was only one window with a blind intact at the time the show was filmed. Not in the room where Joel and Nolan encountered the bad guy though. So our perp probably did relocate the one working blind. Good catch."

"It was a joint effort." They worked well together. Maybe that was what they were destined to do.

He considered her a moment. "You sure you want to go to Baker's place? He lives over the garage at his parents' house. Elizabeth could be there."

Vera grimaced. "Can one of your deputies call her into the office to look at mug shots or something? This will go a lot more quickly and smoothly without her asking questions."

Bent raised his eyebrows in question.

"It's a logical step. Nolan could have a new friend. Maybe Elizabeth has seen someone new hanging out at his place?"

Bent crooked an eyebrow. "I guess we can make that work." He retrieved his phone from his back pocket and called the office. "Myra, I need a favor."

While Bent explained how he wanted Deputy Boyd Fowler to bring in Elizabeth Baker to review mug shots, Vera wandered back to the case board. She studied the diagrams again, noting once more the primitiveness as well as the similarities to other ones she had reviewed on the internet.

Was the Time Thief nothing more than a copycat out for notoriety?

There was the possibility the whole thing was a bizarre hoax of some sort. The abduction of Nolan Baker in a way added to that idea.

Granted, going straight to the hoax theory without further consideration of other possibilities would be a bad move.

Still, Vera couldn't get past the idea that Nolan was a reporter looking for his fifteen minutes of fame. What better way than becoming the next victim?

He was just as likely to be involved as not, in her opinion. But she would keep an open mind—however hard that proved. It was too early to assume anything. Whatever the case, she really needed to find him unharmed. Living in the same zip code as Elizabeth Baker was bad enough. Failing to save her only son from himself or some other nutcase out for a little of the limelight would be unbearable.

5

Baker Residence
Mulberry Avenue, Fayetteville, 10:00 a.m.

Carl, Elizabeth's husband, came home to let them into Nolan's apartment before going to the sheriff's department to review mug shots with his wife.

Vera should have felt guilty, but she didn't. This was the best way to proceed. Elizabeth would only get in the way and cloud the investigation if she were home during their search.

And get on Vera's last nerve.

A set of stairs inside the quadruple garage led up to the apartment. Elizabeth certainly wouldn't have wanted her son to use exterior stairs. He might get wet in the rain or cold in the winter. This way he could drive right into the garage and have the entrance to his home nearly right in front of him.

No wonder the guy still lived at home.

The snow had melted from the streets and sidewalks already. About all that remained was the white stuff around the bases of trees and against the foundations of homes. Anyplace there was a shady spot. The temperature was already heading toward forty, so none of it would last much longer.

At the top of the garage stairs, there was a small landing and the door to the apartment. Bent went in first to check the place.

Vera rolled her eyes. As if she couldn't protect herself if someone was hiding inside. Oh well, let him play the hero. She'd spent enough time struggling with perps during her time at the Memphis Police Department. She had nothing to prove.

Except maybe the idea that she usually didn't miss the little things that led to disaster.

No looking back, Vee.

It was basically impossible to look back on her career without seeing the bad.

"It's clear," Bent said, snapping her back to attention.

She nodded and walked into the apartment.

Based on the size of the garage, it was no surprise there was a relatively large main living area as well as two bedrooms and two bathrooms in the apartment. From the sleek hardwood floors to the cozy furnishings and modern light fixtures, the place was like walking onto the pages of an interior design magazine. No expense had been spared to create this warm and inviting space.

Nothing was too good for Mama's little boy.

"Does he have an office here?" she asked.

"Carl said the second bedroom doubles as an office."

"I'll take that room." She headed toward the hall.

"Course you will."

She glanced over her shoulder and grinned. He held her gaze a moment before shooting her one of his own trademark grins and then moving on to prowl around the main living space.

Bent knew her too well.

She often wondered if allowing him closer would only lead to disaster, considering the secret she kept for her sister.

The odds of him never finding out weren't that good either way. Still, when it came to her sister, Vera had decided that Eve's secrets were best explored on an as-needed basis. No need to go looking for trouble.

That worry was for another time. Vera dismissed the troublesome subject and surveyed the room Nolan Baker used as a home office.

There was no file cabinet or credenza, just a desk and a bookcase. Vera sat down at the desk and reached for the middle drawer. It was filled with pens, pencils, sticky notes. The usual . . . she paused in her search, surveyed the surface of the desk. Typical desk blotter—no notes written on the white expanse—but there was a *phone*. Nolan had a landline. Who had landlines anymore? She visually traced the line to the wall, where it connected to an old-fashioned jack. A real landline, not the kind that came with internet or cable service.

Not surprising, really. The house his parents lived in was one of the town's most treasured historic homes. On the same highly sought-after street as former Judge Preston Higdon's in fact. Vera rolled her eyes. Another pompous ass. Anyway, these houses would have been hardwired for phones decades before cell phones and Wi-Fi phones were invented.

When she closed the middle drawer, she paused a second time. There was a voicemail on the answering machine. Not a new one but one he'd listened to and hadn't deleted. Might be from the person who'd invited him to last night's meeting. Maybe not deleting that message was Nolan's way of leaving a breadcrumb just in case.

Vera pressed Play. *Tuesday, 6:45 p.m.* Only a few hours before Nolan disappeared.

"Mr. Baker."

Female voice. Vera frowned. Sounded vaguely familiar. The volume was set so low that she had to lean forward to hear better.

"This is Teresa Russ returning your call. Yes, I can be available to meet with you tomorrow if you'd like to make an appointment." There was a pause. "I can't promise I'll share what I've learned so far, but if you want to talk about the Norton Gates case, I'm willing to listen. You have my number."

The thud in Vera's chest stole her breath for three, four, five seconds.

Russ was a private investigator that Vera had encountered before. Apparently she, and maybe Nolan, too, were investigating Norton Gates—the college professor whose remains had been tucked into a crevice in that damned cave. The man Vera's sister Eve had killed. Well, that sounded worse than it was . . . Eve hadn't just randomly killed him. The man had tried to rape Suri—he'd sexually abused her when she was his student—and Eve had stopped him the only way she could at the time. With a cast-iron skillet to the back of the head.

"Son of a . . ." Vera gritted her teeth. And then she did the unthinkable. She turned the volume all the way down and deleted the voicemail.

Regret bloomed in her chest the instant she had done it. She shouldn't have . . .

But it was necessary. Norton Gates—the scumbag—had been a serial rapist and an overall piece of shit. No one even missed him. Thankfully, the investigation into the man's death had gone nowhere because no one had a damned clue what had happened to him. But Vera understood with utter certainty that if and when the facts ever came to light, Bent would not forgive her for failing to share the details about Eve's involvement.

"Find anything?"

She jumped.

"Sorry." Bent stood in the doorway. "I haven't found anything so far other than the man's fetish for peanut butter M&Ms and gummy bears."

"Still looking." Vera grabbed for the next drawer. *Don't look at him. He will see the lie in your eyes.*

While she pilfered through the crisp, clean notepads, Bent walked to the bookcase and picked through the paperbacks and hardcovers stored there. Nolan Baker appeared to be an avid reader.

"Am I keeping you?"

Her gaze shifted to Bent. "What?"

"I thought I heard you talking to someone. If you need to leave, just let me know."

Her throat went dry. "No. No. It's just . . . I'm having lunch with Eve. I told her I'd be there when I could. No worries about that. I'll catch her later."

"If you're free after lunch, we can visit some of Baker's coworkers."

She nodded, swallowed, even with her dry throat. "Sounds good."

Bent wandered out of the room, and Vera continued the search of Nolan's home office. Didn't take that long. She imagined anything important was on his laptop or his cell phone. Basically, the effort proved a waste of time. Nolan had no notes whatsoever on the Time Thief—at least not in his home office. Maybe if he had an office or cubicle at the newspaper, there would be something there.

Otherwise, the idea that he hadn't made notes suggested he didn't need to. He already had the details and answers others might be looking for.

She would have a look at his official workspace when they spoke to his colleagues.

Somehow her brain couldn't seem to focus on Nolan Baker or the Time Thief.

The only thing on her mind right now was Norton Fucking Gates.

Vera thought of the tracks in the freshly fallen snow behind her house this morning. Those tracks had come from the barn, which wasn't all that far from the cave. Someone had been there and obviously hadn't cared that she knew about the visit. Evidently wanted her to know . . . to worry. To wonder.

Bottom line: no matter that Gates's remains had eventually been moved to a cemetery in Madison, Alabama, his ghost was still here in Fayetteville. Rattling around the edges of Vera's and Eve's lives.

Why the hell hadn't Eve buried him in a place no one would ever look?

6

Barrett's Funeral Home
Washington Street, Fayetteville, 11:30 a.m.

Vera's sister Eve was four years younger than her. She had been ecstatic when her parents brought her home. For Vera, having a little sister had been like having a real-life baby doll all her own. They had the same blond hair. Vera still wore hers long, while Eve preferred a short, spiky style. Same blue eyes. But the coloring was pretty much where the resemblances ended. Vera was taller, thinner. Bossier, Eve would say.

By the time Eve was around six years old, it had become very clear there were other differences. Eve was fascinated with the dead. Whether it was insects, animals, or humans, the child was drawn to anything no longer living. Not really in a bad way—at least not at first. Whenever they had come upon something dead—any sort of bug or bird or whatever—Eve insisted there be a proper burial, including a prayer.

Visits to funeral homes were not so different. Eve would spend more time at the deceased's coffin than anyone else in attendance. More than once she was caught talking to the corpse. On one occasion she ended up asleep under a row of chairs in the viewing room, and a miscommunication between their parents and grandparents resulted in Eve being left at the funeral home. An attendant found her hours later, still asleep, except she was no longer on the floor under the chairs. Eve was in the coffin with the deceased.

It was no wonder, after years of failing at various jobs and a number of false starts in college, she ended up in mortuary school and then working at a funeral home.

Also not surprising that her best friend and girlfriend had the same occupation at a competing funeral home across town. Eve's whole life, so to speak, revolved around the dead.

Vera took a breath and knocked on the door to the mortuary room. She hadn't bothered asking in the office where her sister was. Eve spent her breaks, more often than not, right in this room where the dead were prepared.

The door opened, and Eve made a face behind the plastic shield protecting her from various types of body fluid splatter. "What're you doing here?"

Judging by her expression and the obvious reluctance to have company, one would think something nefarious was going on in that room.

Eve sported the usual heavy-duty rubberlike apron over her scrubs, as well as plastic shoe covers over her sneakers. In addition, there were elbow-length gloves. Based on the attire Eve wore regularly, always scrubs and sneakers, black in color, she looked as if she worked at a hospital or a doctor's office. But that was not the case at all. Eve had no desire to work with the living. Ever. She barely associated with those still breathing, including her sisters. Eve was the quintessential loner. The only breathing human she gravitated to was Suri.

Vera suppressed an eye roll. "We need to talk. Privately." Which meant a mere phone call was out of the question. Cell phone records and transcripts were too easy to subpoena.

Eve did roll her eyes. "You need to suit up."

Rather than argue, Vera stepped into the room and did as she was told while Eve walked back to the stainless steel table where her latest *visitor* waited. She didn't like referring to the dead as *corpses* or using any other term generally associated with bodies. Instead, she called them *visitors*. She took great pride in preparing her visitors for their final soiree—the viewing and/or funeral.

Last, Vera slipped on shoe covers. While she adjusted her mask into place, she headed across the room. The female on the table was young. Painfully so. No one Vera recognized.

"What happened?" she asked as she took a position on the opposite side of the table from her sister.

"Car accident." Eve carefully made an incision in the carotid artery and then another in the jugular vein. Once the incisions were made, an embalming fluid pump tube was placed in the artery and then a drain pump tube was placed in the jugular. While one drained the fluid from the vessels, the other pumped the disinfectant and preservative in. The whole preparation took only a short time.

"She looks"—Vera shrugged—"strangely good for an accident victim." Beyond the bruising in the chest and abdomen area, anyway. No visible lacerations or mutilations. No twisted limbs.

"Internal injuries," Eve said, confirming Vera's assessment.

Once the machine was turned on and working as expected, they stepped away from the table. The distinct hum and occasional gurgling confirmed the ongoing process. Vera worked extra hard at not thinking about how those very fluids being replaced had until recently flowed freely inside this young woman, keeping her alive. A shudder quaked through her.

"What's up?" Eve asked, her impatience showing.

Vera hesitated; her attention suddenly fixed on a tiny pinkish speck on her sister's face mask.

Eve glared at her. "What?"

"You . . ." Vera pointed to the speck. "You have something on your mask."

"Why are you here?" Eve demanded, ignoring the speck.

"Okay." Vera squared her shoulders and focused on her sister's eyes, a mirror of her own. "Did you hear that Nolan Baker is the latest victim of the Time Thief?"

A line appeared between Eve's brows. "No. I've been here since really early this morning." She nodded toward the table. "She and her husband *and* her younger brother were all killed in the accident. The families want to have the funerals together."

"Damn." Vera grimaced. What a horrible tragedy for the families. "Anyway," she explained, shaking off the thought, "Nolan was taken late last night."

Eve barked a half laugh. "I'll bet Boggie is all over you and Bent. You better find that guy alive and undamaged or—"

"I know," Vera cut her off. "I'm not as worried about Nolan as I am about what I found in his apartment."

Eve glanced at the progress across the room. "Okay, so what did you find?"

"Nolan had a voicemail on his landline from Teresa Russ."

That line between her sister's brows deepened. "The private investigator in Huntsville?"

"That's the one. Evidently Nolan asked her about Norton Gates. The message gave me the impression that the two of them have been looking into his case."

"Fuck me," Eve muttered.

"Yeah," Vera agreed. "Fuck us both."

For years as a deputy chief in Memphis, Vera had carefully monitored her language even around her colleagues. Not that cops didn't swear plenty, but her job had involved far too much politics. It was important to set the right example and to present the proper image. And although politicians were some of the biggest liars on the planet, they preferred more refined language during meetings. Since coming home, Vera had regressed to saying the first thing that popped into her head when she was with her sister . . . or alone, for that matter.

So much for the new Vera she'd worked so hard to build after escaping this place.

Eve blew out a breath of frustration. "Maybe we'll get lucky, and Nolan will—"

"Eve," Vera cut her off again, "you don't mean whatever you were about to say. Anyway, it was difficult to determine what either of them knows, based on that one-sided message. I'm guessing Nolan is trying to dig up some big break to boost his career. Which, in my opinion, might actually be why he's missing right now."

Her sister's gaze narrowed. "You think this is a fake abduction for the attention."

"Maybe. We can't be certain of anything at this point, but if that's the case and it comes out, anything he does in the future would be less than credible. That said, having him poking around in the Gates case could create a snowball effect by generating interest." Vera scrubbed at her forehead. "Frankly, the part that worries me more is the idea that Teresa Russ is involved. We both know she isn't one to give up."

"Good point." Eve searched Vera's eyes. "What do we do?"

"*We*," Vera said with emphasis, "do nothing. Let me sort this out. And don't tell Suri."

"But what if Russ calls her or comes to see her? She'll find Suri's name on those class-registration rolls the same way you did."

Eve was right. "Okay." Vera set her hands on her hips. "Tell her she shouldn't talk about what happened between her and Gates to anyone. He was her professor for a couple of classes. End of story."

This was the same story Suri had given Bent when he reviewed the class rosters for the final semesters Gates had taught before disappearing. There were some things Bent didn't need to know. If Vera had her way, he never would.

Eve nodded. "Who knew that cave would turn into such a nightmare all these years later."

"No kidding."

Eve's mouth dropped open. "I just remembered something you need to know."

Vera's stomach knotted. "I swear to God, if you tell me there's another body hidden somewhere . . ."

"No," Eve griped. "I don't kill people. Not on purpose, anyway."

Vera drew in a big breath. She sure hoped Eve was telling her the truth. Just because she had no social skills and spent most of her time with the dead—preparing them and talking to them—didn't mean she was a psychopath. Maybe. Probably.

"What do I need to know, then?"

"Rumor is"—Eve glanced around, her gaze resting a moment on the corpse a few feet away before returning to Vera—"that Nolan is gay."

Vera made an exaggerated face. "So? This is not twenty years ago, Eve. Being gay is just being who you are."

Eve executed another eye roll. "Seriously? Like I don't know that. I'm gay. But this is Boggie's only child we're talking about. His mama was captain of the cheerleading team. Prom queen three years in a row. Having high school football star Carl Baker for a daddy doesn't help either. Nolan cannot be gay and live in this town—not because of the town but because of his parents."

There was that. "Okay, so how did you hear about this?"

"Suri and I saw them in a club in Nashville. They didn't see us, so Nolan has no idea I know."

"Maybe he was just playing the field," Vera argued. "Stretching and exploring his boundaries."

Eve shook her head, a goofy grin on her face. "No . . . this was way more than that. Trust me, I know the difference."

She supposed her sister would. It had been so long since Vera felt anything like that for another person, she might not recognize it when she saw it. Except maybe all those little feelings Bent elicited. She chased away the thought. Apparently having forty bearing down on her was really messing with her head.

"Who was this other person?"

"A big deal attorney from Huntsville, Liam Remington. His family's firm is like one of the biggest in the Southeast."

Remington. Vera had heard about the firm. They had huge signs all over the place. No one wrangled bigger settlements than the Remington firm, or so the billboards boasted.

"Liam is the younger of two sons," Eve went on. "His father is some highly decorated retired military guy. His grandfather is a war hero too. They're all part of the firm. Seriously hard-core conservative types. Nolan isn't the only one keeping secrets about his sexuality."

Vera couldn't say she blamed either one. Sometimes family could be . . . *difficult*.

"He might know what Nolan was up to," Vera considered out loud.

Eve walked back to the table and checked on her work. "Couldn't hurt to talk to him."

Vera wandered in that direction. "Nolan hasn't talked to you or Suri about Gates or the cave, has he? Recently or back during the investigation?"

"No way." She shot Vera a look. "I would have told you."

Probably true. But with Eve it was difficult to ever be completely certain.

"I guess I'm heading to Huntsville, then."

If Bent managed to set up a meeting with Nolan's colleagues, he would just have to go without her. She could follow up if he learned anything worth the trouble.

"If Bent calls," she said to her sister, "tell him I was here with you at lunchtime."

Eve nodded. "Be careful," she warned. "I don't trust lawyers."

Vera laughed and gave her a little wave goodbye. No one trusted lawyers. Not if they were smart.

7

Remington & Sons Law
Jefferson Street, Huntsville, Alabama, 1:30 p.m.

Just her luck that the office was on the square in downtown Huntsville. Parking was insane. She found one spot, which only required a two-block walk. Good thing she wasn't wearing high heels.

She'd taken the time to run home and change for this. The dampness in the cool air had her thankful she'd chosen her long trench coat. She'd had it forever, but the black color and classic style ensured she never had to worry about it going out of fashion. Strapped across her coat was her favorite new accessory: a cross-body-style bag to make hanging onto a purse easier. The hands-free ease of the bag made her happy. Relaxed her. *Avoid stress* was her motto now. She couldn't think why she'd never bought one before.

Speaking of stress, so far she'd ignored two calls from Bent. He'd left a voicemail the last time, but she hadn't listened. It was difficult enough to ignore him; she damned sure didn't want to punish herself by listening to his voice. If it was really important, he'd send an SOS text.

Pushing the thought aside, she opened the door to the law firm.

The lobby was quiet, elegant. Lots of glossy magazines and potted plants placed strategically around the room. The reception desk had a sleek wood grain with brass trim. Not really a desk—a counter. Three employees were stationed in the generous space behind it. Two on the telephone and another, who glanced up at Vera, offered a gleaming smile, and said, "Good afternoon. How may I help you?"

"My name is Vera Boyett. I'm here to see Liam," she said with the sort of familiarity that suggested they were friends.

The woman with the neat brown bob and matching chocolate-colored turtleneck sweater made a pouty face. "I'm so sorry, Ms. Boyett, but unless you have an appointment . . ."

Vera smiled. "I do not have an appointment, but if you'll let him know this is his friend from Fayetteville, I'm sure he'll make time for me."

One carefully manicured eyebrow lifted slightly higher than the other. "Give me one moment, please."

The receptionist picked up the phone and tapped a button on the base. "I apologize for interrupting you, Mr. Remington, but there's a Vera Boyett here to see you." She listened a moment, then said, "She mentioned being a friend from Fayetteville."

Surprise flashed on the receptionist's face. "Of course. I'll show her to your office."

Vera kept the smugness that wanted to claim her own expression at bay. Not an easy task.

"This way." The receptionist rounded the end of the counter and gestured toward a corridor that exited the lobby to the right.

There was also one to the left. The space was far larger than Vera had expected. A sort of maze likely designed for creating privacy. She glanced toward the other corridor as they left the lobby. There appeared to be a large conference room in that direction. Maybe more offices beyond.

The receptionist paused at a door on the right. "You may go on in."

"Thank you." Vera waited until the woman had started back to the lobby before opening the door.

Inside, the office was very much like the lobby, lavishly appointed. Lots of deep, rich colors and heavy wood tones. The man standing behind the desk looked to be in his early thirties and was extraordinarily handsome. Obviously very smart. So this was Liam Remington. No wonder Nolan liked him.

"Ms. Boyett," he announced with a dazzling smile, "welcome."

Vera walked straight up to the desk and extended her hand. He shook it. "I'm here about Nolan."

He nodded slowly, as if uncertain of whom she spoke.

For the first time since she left Fayetteville, Vera hoped like hell her sister knew what she was talking about.

"Nolan . . . ?" he prompted.

"Nolan Baker. A reporter in Fayetteville. Tennessee," she tacked on, though he hopefully was aware.

No response. Closed reaction.

"He disappeared last night. We have reason to believe he was taken by a serial kidnapper."

Liam Remington's face went deathly pale, and he sank into the elegant leather chair behind his desk. Okay, good. Eve was right.

"Oh my God. Are you certain? What are the police doing?" He put a hand to his chest. "I'm certain his parents are—"

"Beside themselves," Vera finished for him. "The police are doing all possible. I'm a consultant working with the Lincoln County Sheriff's Department. I have a few questions, if you're amenable."

"Of course. Anything." He touched his forehead. "Sorry. Please have a seat."

Vera sank into one of the two plush chairs in front of his desk. The worry on his face, the fear in his eyes further confirmed that Eve had judged the relationship accurately. This man cared deeply for Nolan.

She kicked off the conversation with "Are you aware of anything in particular that Nolan was working on recently?"

"This Time Thief series of abductions," Liam said, as Vera had expected. "He was keen to learn what the police had not. But he didn't discuss specifics with me."

Typical reporter. They always thought they could do a better job of investigating any given case than the police.

"Did you hear from him at all yesterday?"

Liam hesitated. "Is there some reason why you were sent to speak with me, rather than someone from the sheriff's department?"

"No one in the department knows about you, Liam. I have other sources; that's how I was able to find you."

Recognition flared in his expression. "I know who you are. You're the cop from Memphis—the one who had bodies hidden on her family farm."

Great. "That's me. I'm sure Nolan had plenty to say about me."

They stared at each other for a moment. Vera wondered if pushing harder would be necessary, or if the man was just recalling whatever Nolan had told him about the Boyett sisters.

"Our relationship," he said quietly, "mine and Nolan's—"

"I understand," Vera assured him. "I'm not here about your relationship. I'm here to learn anything I can that might help us find Nolan. So, did you speak to him yesterday?"

"Yes."

"Did he mention a late-night meeting with a contact related to his investigation of the Time Thief case?"

"No. He only said that he had plans with his family and that he would call me this morning, but he hasn't." The worry reappeared. "I've tried him twice. No answer."

"You're certain he's said nothing to you about any case—old or new—that he's looking into besides that one?"

"Nothing. We . . . don't typically talk about work." Some realization had him hesitating. "But he mentioned recently that he still had thoughts on the case that involved that cave on your farm. Is that why you're here, Vera?"

Smart man. "No. As I said, I'm working with the sheriff's department to help solve this case and Nolan's abduction. Anything you can tell us about Nolan's frame of mind recently could be useful." She paused a moment. "Frankly, I'm worried that he may have been digging into the case and stumbled upon something that got him into trouble. The sooner we find him, the less likely he is to . . . well, you know."

A new surge of fear tightened his features. "His frame of mind has been normal—no change at all that I've noticed." Liam looked away a moment. "That said, he really wants to break out. I feel confident he would take any and all risks to make that happen. But I am unaware of any steps he has taken or contacts he's made in this thing that's going on right now."

"Thank you." Vera stood. Reached into her bag and removed a business card. "Please, call me if you hear from Nolan or think of anything that might help us find him." She placed the card on his desk.

He pushed himself to his feet. "You may rest assured that I will." He looked away for a moment, then said, "Was his cell phone found?"

Text messages and/or photos. She got it. They were the riskiest elements that should never be part of a secret.

"No. It was not."

The hope in his brown eyes vanished. The man had nice eyes. Not to mention he was tall with dark hair. Nolan had good taste.

"As I said, I work with the sheriff's department. Closely. The sheriff and I are old friends. If the cell phone shows up . . ."

His gaze lit once more. "There . . . might be photos. We're careful, but . . ."

"Don't worry," Vera said. "I'm sure there won't be any photos of concern discovered."

He nodded. "That would be very good. And I will be in your debt."

He surely would. "Thank you. I'll let you know when we find him."

"Please do . . . he . . ."

Vera nodded.

She understood.

Now she had even more reason to find Nolan Baker.

She needed the leverage just in case his investigative skills were sharper than Vera thought.

8

Baker Residence
Mulberry Avenue, Fayetteville, 3:30 p.m.

Bent was in a meeting.

To her credit, Vera had attempted to return his calls—not once but twice. Both times, the call went to voicemail. As she had arrived back in Fayetteville from her interesting and potentially useful trip to Huntsville, she'd called Bent's assistant, Myra. At the moment he was on a conference call with TBI and the local brass. Apparently, a meeting between Bent, Fayetteville's chief of police, and the mayor had been set for 3:00 p.m. According to Myra, Bent had tried to reach her so she could attend the meeting with him.

At least now she knew what his calls had been about. Nothing new on the case, unless of course something came out of the meeting. He would fill her in later. She wouldn't mention the fact that she was exceedingly happy she'd been unavailable for the meeting. Those sorts of torturous events were just one more thing she did not miss about her former career. The politics of police work was something she could live the rest of her life without.

She stared at the mansion that stood at the end of the long driveway. Vera would wager that Elizabeth had watched this house for years in hopes it would become available. The instant the previous owner had passed away or decided to move for whatever reason, she probably rushed to any remaining family and made a ridiculously generous offer to ensure the home was hers. Nothing wrong with going after what she wanted. Elizabeth had gotten the guy she wanted too. She was an only child whose father had owned the bank her husband now owned and operated. The ambitious woman left nothing to chance.

Made sense she would do the same for her only child. He'd graduated from the University of Tennessee just as his parents had. But since returning home one year ago, the job offers from larger outlets hadn't materialized. His work at the *Elk Valley Times* was a good way to gain experience for his résumé, but that would never be suitable enough for Elizabeth. She would want more for him.

Vera suspected Nolan had inherited that sense of determination from his mother. He'd shown his true colors during the investigation into the remains found on the farm. In Vera's opinion it was absolutely plausible that he would attempt to use the Time Thief case to his benefit. What better way than to become a victim himself? What was the real perp going to do? File a complaint? Cry foul? Unless, of course, Nolan was the Time Thief. She actually had considerable difficulty seeing him in that role. It was a potential scenario, of course.

And if Nolan had taken the liberty of putting himself in the position of victim, the actual perp might very well react in a manner not consistent with his MO. Unfortunately, that was the prospect Nolan may have failed to consider. He could very well cause the real perp to commit a more egregious act to wrestle back the lost attention and regain control of the narrative.

Vera emerged from her SUV and closed the door. She shivered as the chilly air cut through her. Though the snow was gone, the wind remained sharp. Spring couldn't come soon enough for her. Walking quickly, she headed to the front entrance of the Baker home. By the time she climbed the steps, the door had opened and Elizabeth stood in the doorway. Though to Vera's knowledge she didn't have an actual job, Elizabeth dressed as if she was expected at a very important meeting. Black fitted trousers and a cream-colored sweater, topped by a matching scarf that swirled around her neck like a puffy noose. Her hair and makeup were impeccable—even her red lipstick looked fresh.

"Is there news?" Her voice quivered ever so slightly.

The mixture of fear and hope on her face had Vera doubting her theory for a second or two. But then, this woman had always been a very good actress. Besides, there was a chance Elizabeth was unaware of what her son was up to—assuming he was up to anything other than being abducted. Vera would bet money she had no clue about his love life.

"Not that I'm aware of," Vera admitted, standing in front of the other woman now.

Elizabeth's shoulders sagged. "Please. Come in out of the cold."

Vera followed her inside. "You holding up okay?" Dumb question, but it was the expected one.

Elizabeth turned her hands up, as if she wasn't sure what to do with them. "I suppose. I keep reminding myself that none of the victims have been harmed—not really, I mean—so there's every reason to believe Nolan will be unharmed." Her lips trembled. "But I just keep thinking about what could happen."

Tears burst from her eyes and flowed down her cheeks.

Vera stiffened, glanced along the entry hall beyond her former classmate. "Is Carl home?"

A shake of her perfectly coiffed head was the answer.

Vera surrendered to the necessary and gave the woman a perfunctory hug. "Don't cry. We will find him, and he'll be okay."

"I keep telling myself that." Elizabeth's voice rose with the building emotion, but, thankfully, she drew back. She dabbed at her cheeks with her fingertips so as not to smear her makeup. "I just don't know what to do with myself. I had no luck with those mug shots. Once we were back home, Carl had to rush off to the bank and a meeting he couldn't ignore. I guess, sitting here alone, I just sort of fell to pieces."

"It's difficult to just stay home and wait." Vera suffered a tiny pang of guilt about the mug shots.

Elizabeth pressed a hand over her mouth, as if holding back a sob, and nodded.

Silence lapsed, and for a moment Vera allowed it to linger, in hopes Elizabeth would pull herself together.

"Do you have a few minutes to answer a question or two?" She decided what the woman needed was a distraction. "I want to do all I can to help—if this isn't an imposition."

Elizabeth stared at her in confusion or something on that order, then blinked it away. "Of course. I . . . I can't seem to maintain any level of focus." She waved toward the other end of the hall. "I need tea. Would you join me?"

Vera smiled. "That sounds lovely."

The entry hall cut through the center of the house, with the usual rooms on either side. French doors stood open, revealing the expected soaring ceilings and shiny original hardwoods in the extravagantly appointed parlor, library, and dining room. Lots of antiques and exquisite pieces adorned the rooms. The space at the rear of the house on the first floor had been opened up to create a generous kitchen and lounge area. Perfect for entertaining. Exactly what Vera would have expected of a home belonging to Elizabeth Baker.

She slid onto a stool at the large island while Elizabeth lit the flame under the kettle. The woman of the house settled two delicate cups and matching saucers on the marble counter and returned to another cupboard for a canister.

"My favorite," she said, opening the container with trembling fingers.

The scent of peppermint reached Vera's nose.

"I have peppermint tea," Elizabeth explained, with a wobbly smile, "every afternoon. I so love it." She placed a bag in each cup. "I loved the candy as a child, but"—she smoothed a hand over her black-clad hip—"unnecessary sugar is a no-no, especially after you reach a certain age."

Vera doubted the woman, who was only two years older than her, had consumed a grain of sugar since she was ten years old. Back then she'd been a little plump. The talk in the school cafeteria was that her mother put her on a diet. Vera really couldn't say if the rumor was true, but the girl had lost all that weight, and her whole personality had changed. Not surprising. If Vera gave up sugar, she would turn unpleasant too.

"I wish I had your willpower."

The kettle started to sing, and Elizabeth turned off the flame. She poured the steaming water into the cups. "Look at all you've accomplished." She flashed a brighter smile at Vera. "You survived losing your mother and a perfectly terrible stepmother. You were at the top of your class in everything you set out to do." She set the kettle aside. "Why, look at what you achieved in Memphis. Amazing, just amazing. All of it. You should be very proud of yourself."

Except for the last part, Vera didn't say. The cutting-edge team of investigators she'd helped build had been disbanded after one killed another and then herself. So much for being amazing. The media frenzy afterward had destroyed all credibility related to the specialized team.

"I know what you're thinking," Elizabeth said. "You're thinking that what happened before you moved back here negates all that you accomplished. Well, Carl and I have discussed it at length, and we are certain none of it was your fault. You just took the fall. It happens all the time. There always has to be a scapegoat." Tears gathered in her red-rimmed eyes once more. "Nolan said the same thing."

Except they were all wrong. It had been Vera's job to spot potential issues. She should have noticed the trouble before it became a tragedy.

"Tell me more about Nolan," she said, moving on. She hadn't come here to talk about herself and definitely not about her past.

Elizabeth removed the tea bag from her cup with one of the delicate spoons that Vera hadn't noticed she had placed next to each cup. "He's brilliant. Really." She met Vera's gaze, paused a moment to gather herself. "I know I sound like a bragging mama, but it's true. In time, he'll find his place and make a name for himself. His father and I will support him every step of the way."

"He never wanted to go into banking, like his grandfather and father?"

She sipped her tea. "Oh no. Never. Nolan has a wonderful relationship with his father, but he has always had his sights on the media. In fact, when he was a child, all he talked about was becoming an actor." She let go a beleaguered breath. "His father and I did all possible to dissuade him from that idea. Finally, when he was about ten years old, he watched an exposé on a serial killer by . . ." She frowned, as if attempting to call the name to mind. "Ah, yes. Patricia Patton presented it. I think it launched her career to the next level."

The name and the time frame bored into Vera's skull like a bullet. "The Messenger." The hiss of air was barely audible . . . the words not really words at all, more a desperate expulsion of sound.

"Yes," Elizabeth enthused. "That big case you solved. What? Twelve . . . no, thirteen years ago!"

Vera snapped from the haze of disbelief that had swaddled her. It was the same every time. Whenever the subject of the Messenger came up . . . it seemed to knock her into that place of shock and disbelief. With good reason. She closed out the sounds and images that attempted to fill her mind. It was her first big case as a detective . . . a serial-killer case. Not just any serial killer, either. One who had evaded the police and the FBI for a decade.

She forced a smile. "Wow. How interesting that he zeroed in on one of my cases."

"Well." Elizabeth took another sip of her tea, reminding Vera that she hadn't touched her own. "It was likely because Carl and I were absolutely enthralled by the investigation. I think everyone in town who knew you or your family was captivated. You were one of us, and suddenly you were this big hero." Though her eyes remained red and puffy, the tears had dried, and she even managed a decent smile.

"Well, thank you." Vera focused on removing the tea bag from her cup and properly tucking it on the saucer as Elizabeth had. She downed a gulp of the hot liquid, let the burn recenter her, then cleared her throat. "It was a . . . strange time."

She almost winced. *Strange time?* Was that the best she could come up with?

Christ.

"Anyway," her hostess went on, "your media success was Nolan's inspiration. I think he's followed you ever since. I know Carl and I have."

More tea slid down Vera's throat. The taste wasn't so bad, but primarily Vera needed to do anything to make the dryness go away.

"Anyway." Elizabeth waved a hand in the air, as if erasing the most recent part of the conversation. "I'm sure you're aware what a celebrity you are around here. Your incredible ability is the reason I knew we needed you to find him." That shine was back in her eyes, and she seemed to need a moment before she could go on.

Vera cleared her throat, but the thickening sensation and the dryness lingered. "I imagine Nolan has been captivated by the Time Thief as well."

Elizabeth stared into her cup. "Sadly, yes. He's been utterly focused on the case. You may or may not read the paper, but he's written pieces on every abduction. Interviewed the victims at length." She squeezed her eyes shut, as if hoping to hold back the tide.

Vera had known about Nolan's articles. Though she didn't spend a lot of time watching or reading the news—not since the tragedy in Memphis—Bent had brought her up to speed. He'd mentioned Nolan's close following of the ongoing investigation once or twice over the past few weeks.

For several seconds Elizabeth said nothing. Vera wondered if she was waiting for her to respond to that last comment. In her experience it was better to delay and see what the other person said next. No one liked the spans of silence during a conversation . . . especially if that person was leaving out pertinent details related to the conversation. In this case, the pause might very well be emotionally driven.

"I've been asking myself all morning," Elizabeth went on, as Vera had known she would, "if he somehow veered too close." Her gaze lifted to Vera's. "Nolan firmly believes the person behind these abductions is someone local."

No question. "Did he ever mention any names? Maybe someone he spoke with more than once?"

"Just one." Elizabeth shivered visibly.

Vera's instincts sharpened. Her fingers tightened on the delicate handle of the teacup. She forced her hand to relax rather than risk breaking it.

"You may or may not remember him, but he was in my class." Elizabeth flattened her palms on the cool marble. "Fisher Owens. He was one of those guys who spent all his time totally zoned out on one drug or the other. Most recently I heard he was into crystal meth."

Vera did remember him . . . vaguely. Bent hadn't mentioned him, and the guy's name and face hadn't been on the case board. "What made Nolan suspect Owens was involved?"

"The few people who associate with Fisher know he has this bizarre fixation on extraterrestrials. He talked about it even back in high school. Evidently he still does—ad nauseam. Nolan felt he fit the profile for the person behind these incidents."

Ah, yes. Another armchair detective. The endless parade of crime shows over the years had far too many people believing they could profile perps as well as the cops could. This affliction was particularly prominent in reporters—ones exactly like Patricia Patton, who believed she knew more than the police or anyone else.

Vera kicked the woman out of her head. Patton was just another of her bad memories from Memphis. Like a buzzard, she showed up circling wherever she smelled potential trouble.

"Did he give you any other specifics on why he believed Owens was the one?" Vera felt confident there was nothing to the scenario, but she never allowed her personal feelings to get in the way of an investigation. Well, most of the time, anyway. There had been a failure or two in her time. Then again, considering her hostess, this could be one of them.

"He said Fisher had newspaper clippings and notes about the victims all over his wall in that shack where he lives. He told Bent." She shook her head, looked heavenward. "Bent is a good sheriff, but sometimes he can be . . ." She sighed. "Well, you know."

Vera knew exactly what she meant. Sometimes Bent didn't do a good job of covering how little tolerance he had for people like Elizabeth and, no doubt, her son. Still, once Vera pushed past defending him, she did wonder why he hadn't mentioned Owens. And why the guy's photo hadn't been on his board.

"You have Fisher's address?"

Elizabeth spouted it off as if she frequented the place.

"Since I'm working with Bent on this one, I will follow up on it." Vera stood, forced a smile into place. "Thank you for the tea."

Elizabeth reached across the island and clutched Vera's hand. "Find my son, Vera Mae. Please. This was not supposed to happen. He—" Her eyes rounded with something like surprise or shock. She blinked. "He . . . he has this bright future, and I can't bear the thought of losing him."

Vera promised she would do all in her power, then made her exit. All the way to her SUV, she kept wondering what Elizabeth had almost let slip.

Once she was on the street headed away from the Baker home, she pulled over in the parking lot of the Whiskey Creek Grille. She put the address into her GPS to confirm the directions. She hadn't lived in Fayetteville in a very long time until a few months ago. She was still finding her way around, to some degree. A check of her cell showed Bent had returned her call. If she told him her plan, he would demand to go with her.

If Fisher Owens was a tweaker, chances were he wouldn't be very forthcoming with the sheriff around. Vera would unquestionably have better luck alone.

Only one way to prove her theory.

9

Owens Residence
McDeal Road, Fayetteville, 4:45 p.m.

The small house, or "shack," as Elizabeth had called it, was over half a mile off McDeal Road, down a "more dirt than gravel" road. If it had a name, there was no sign. She had assumed it was a driveway, and it turned out it was. It came to a dead end in front of a sagging shack of a structure.

Vera climbed out of her SUV and closed the door.

It was damned quiet out here. The woods prevented anyone who might drive by on the paved road from seeing the tiny house, much less whatever was going on in or around it. Not a whole lot to observe, actually, except for a couple of junky vehicles. One, a car that was likely about her age, had no wheels and sat on concrete blocks. Dead for the winter, waist-high grass surrounded it. The other vehicle was a pickup. The lack of tall grass in the area where it sat suggested it had been driven recently. Lots of other junk decorated the yard. An old washing machine, a refrigerator with no doors, and a couple of lawn mowers in various stages of deconstruction.

The house itself had once been white but was now chippy and a more grayish color. The metal roof was rusty. And the porch sloped to one side.

Before the grass had died for winter, it had been at least knee high around the house. A narrow path appeared to have been trampled between the truck and the porch, confirming Vera's initial conclusion about the vehicle.

She clutched her cell phone—luckily she still had service—and made her way to the porch. The lack of sound coming from inside the house sent alarms blaring in her head. Anytime things were this quiet, it could only mean one of two things—either no one was home or there was something bad waiting inside. Knowing her luck, it would be the latter.

There was electricity. The line ran to the meter at the end of the porch. She noted the disk on the old meter turning ever so slightly. Most houses in the area had digital meters now. Apparently this one had been missed, or maybe this address was outside the Fayetteville Public Utilities coverage area.

She pulled at the wooden screen door, which opened with a screech. The screen was torn in two places and sagged in another. The wooden door behind it was molting an old coat of pale-blue paint. She pounded a couple of times on the door. More loose paint chips drifted to the porch floor. Still no sound inside. The phone in her hand buzzed, and she jumped.

Bent.

Shit. She had to hurry, or he'd send out a search party for her. She wouldn't put it past Elizabeth to have called and informed him of Vera's visit just to prove she was aware of something he wasn't.

Maybe not, though, considering her emotional state. Her son was missing, and she was terrified of losing him. Or so she seemed. Vera hadn't completely let go of her skepticism.

She banged the side of her fist against the door again.

Still nothing. Not a single sound.

"To hell with it." She was no longer a cop and was not bound by their rules, unless Bent was with her.

She reached for the knob and turned it. The door opened with a rusty squall. Inside, the place was dark. Smelled bad. Not "decomposing corpse" bad but "rotting food and trash" bad.

Vera felt along the wall for a switch but didn't find one. She turned on her phone's flashlight app and scanned the room she'd entered.

Worn, lumpy sofa. A side table loaded with beer cans and dirty plates. Two gold dots flashed. *Eyes.* Vera jumped back and slammed into the door, flattening it against the wall. A hiss echoed, and a black cat jumped from a chair, rushed past her and out through one of the holes in the screen door.

Vera pressed a hand to her chest. "Damned cat." She turned back to the task of surveying the room. "Mr. Owens! It's Vera Boyett. Are you home?"

Still all quiet.

The front room was one long area. The living room on the left, and on her right was a small kitchen, as well as a table and two chairs. The once–mint green cabinets were dingy and sported sagging doors. The sink was loaded with more dirty dishes. Open, presumably empty food cans cluttered the short span of countertop. Some were overturned, probably by the cat. A pan with a serving spoon stuck in the center of something not readily identifiable sat on the narrow stove. Not the usual size of stove for a house—more like for a travel trailer. There was a small fridge with a dented door. Next to the fridge was an open door, with a toilet visible beyond it. No way was she going in there.

All in all, the place was downright filthy, with no sign of the inhabitant. She finally spotted a string hanging from the ceiling in the center of the room. A quick yank, and a dim overhead light came on. The few windows were covered with stained yellow blinds.

The single bare bulb wasn't much help in the way of illumination, but it was better than nothing. She could open the rickety-looking blinds, but she'd just as soon not touch anything unnecessarily. She should have grabbed a pair of disposable gloves from the console in her car.

She stretched her neck, one way, then the other. Another door lay behind the sofa. Vera steeled herself and started in that direction.

"Mr. Owens, are you here? I'm concerned for your welfare. Are you all right?"

She paused at the door, steadied herself, then grasped the knob. If the man was in this room, he could be in a manic state or having a delusional episode. The lack of noise suggested that probably wasn't the case. Braced for battle in any event, she opened the door and met with the same darkness as when she entered the house. She clicked on her phone's flashlight.

The wall directly in front of her was covered with newspaper clippings about the Time Thief. Photos of the victims cut from newspapers were there as well. This was what Nolan had told his mother about. Poster-board-size squares of white were here and there, all filled with the same sorts of images and diagrams as found on the victims.

With effort, Vera forced her gaze away from the wall and checked the rest of the room. A derelict dresser. Drawers partially open, one drawer front missing entirely. Parts of socks or other clothing were hanging out here and there.

Then she settled her attention on the bed. Unmade. Several quilts and comforters piled in a mound in the center of the mattress. Smelled like a boys' locker room near the end of the school year, with a couple of dead rats thrown in the mix.

She snapped her gaze back to the mound of covers and started toward the bed. There was something . . . a *toe*. Big toe. It peeked just beyond the pile of soiled fabric.

Vera reached out slowly. "Mr. Owens, are you all right?" She dragged back layer after layer until there was only the man and the dingy sheet beneath him. Wrinkled T-shirt and jeans were twisted around, as if he'd tossed and turned in his sleep; long, stringy hair was matted to his head.

She stared at his chest . . . her own rising and falling too rapidly.

Is he dead?

Reaching out, she touched the fingers of her right hand to his carotid artery.

The faint but distinct pulse there sent air rushing into her lungs. *Good. Still alive.*

A scream pierced the air.

Not hers.

The man's eyes flew open wide, and another scream escaped him.

Vera jumped back. Stumbled over a lump and hit the floor hard on her butt. Pain radiated up her spine. Her phone flew from her hand.

She scrambled after it, grabbed it, and shot to her feet. Air sawed in and out of her lungs as she stood stone still. No movement from the bed. She roved the light over the man lying motionless there, his eyes closed once more. Then she searched the floor for what had made her stumble.

A bag of apples. A few decaying cores were scattered around it. Damn. Evidently the man liked apples.

For a long moment Vera didn't move. She listened intently for the slightest sound. The occasional shallow breath whispered in the air.

Still breathing. Good. Okay. Her attention shifted back to the wall. This could be nothing but the delusions and paranoia of a drug addict. But there was no way to be certain what fed his dive into the subject of the Time Thief. Whatever the case, she should call Bent.

Easing a few steps farther from the bed, she made the call.

Then she waited. She'd run into her share of tweakers in the past. The one thing she understood with reasonable certainty about a person with a methamphetamine addiction was that they could be unpredictable.

And dangerous.

10

Owens Residence
McDeal Road, Fayetteville, 6:00 p.m.

Bent wouldn't have been surprised when Vee called him even if she'd told him she had landed on the moon. He'd learned to expect the unexpected when it came to the Boyett sisters, especially this one. He glanced at her, and she pretended not to notice.

They waited while the paramedics struggled to strap Owens to a stretcher. The man hadn't moved or said a word when he was picked up and loaded onto the gurney, but as soon as the first strap was pulled over his chest, he came to life.

A half minute was required for the sedative to take effect. As suddenly as he'd started, he stopped fighting.

"We're gone," Paul Graves, the lead paramedic, said to Bent.

Bent gave him a nod and watched as they navigated out of the shack. After they'd loaded him into the ambulance and headed to the hospital, Bent turned to Vee. "Start from the beginning."

Somehow Vera Mae Boyett just didn't get the concept of teamwork. When they worked together, he kept her informed, and she was supposed to do the same.

Except she never did—not fully.

She stared at him. "Do you mean from when I arrived here?"

She knew damned well what he meant, but that was another thing about Vee: she never made this sort of thing easy.

"From the moment I last saw you today, shortly after eleven."

"Oh." She glanced around. "We need more light in this place."

She moved about the room, opening blinds—the ones that worked anyway. Not that it did that much good, considering the sun was setting. The evasive tactic warned that she was attempting to decide what she intended to share and what she planned to keep to herself. If he'd learned anything from his adventures with the Boyett sisters, it was that they worked very hard to keep their secrets. As well as he believed he knew Vee, he recognized there were things she didn't tell him. He was okay with that—unless it involved *his* investigation.

She dusted off her hands. "I went to see Eve."

"You had lunch together," he reminded her, since she appeared to have forgotten the story she'd told him.

"But we couldn't really. Have lunch, I mean." Seeming to gather herself, she squared her shoulders and lifted her chin. "There was a car crash, and three family members were killed. She was working on preparing them for a family-style funeral. She couldn't take a break."

He nodded slowly. "I heard about that. The accident happened in Hazel Green, but the family is from Park City." Bad, bad situation.

Vee shrugged. "I didn't ask about the specifics. But anyway, she couldn't leave for lunch, so we talked there."

"I tried calling you." He watched her closely. "I spoke with Nolan's friends at work."

"Sorry, I got caught up on a lead of my own." Her expression closed completely then.

"Was this lead about Baker or the Time Thief?"

"It wasn't about this investigation, no. Sorry. The call came and I had to check it out."

The fact that she held his gaze steady without flinching made him smile. No matter that he was certain what she'd just said was not the whole truth, he couldn't help himself.

Her face became lined in confusion. "Why are you smiling?"

"Because I know you're evading the question."

She exhaled a put-upon breath. "Fine. Eve told me about a friend Nolan had—a possible boyfriend. I went to see him. He said Nolan was focused on the Time Thief, but he had no idea about last night's meeting or anything else about the case. My impression was that they don't spend a lot of time talking when they're together."

Bent nodded. "You're confident he knows nothing we need to hear."

"I am."

"All right." He glanced around the room. "If he didn't tell you about Owens, how did you end up here? *Alone?*" He would think she'd learned her lesson about taking chances like this, but then again, this was Vee he was talking about. *Chance* was her middle name.

She laughed. "You mean Boggie didn't call you and blab about my visit to her?"

"She did not." Now there was a shocker. Elizabeth Baker generally liked to share anything she knew—particularly if the person with whom she intended to share with didn't already know the details. Then again, she wasn't herself, under the circumstances.

Vee glanced around the shabby room. "Which means she had an ulterior motive for sending me here."

Maybe. Like Vee, Bent wasn't completely convinced this Time Thief business was what the perp wanted the world to believe. Did he suspect Nolan Baker? He did. Vee's analysis of the situation was brilliant—as always. Still, until he had more, it was only one of a couple of possibilities.

"The forensic team is on the way," Bent said. If this was a setup, he wanted to know ASAP. Why the hell couldn't people just tell the truth?

Like you always do?

He dismissed the voice that haunted him all too often. He did what he had to do to get the job done. At least that's what he told himself.

Vera walked back into the bedroom. Bent followed. She opened the blinds there and then stood a few feet from the wall Owens had decorated with information about the Time Thief and his victims. Mostly newspaper articles and crude drawings. Nothing they didn't already have—other than his drawings, assuming they were his.

"Do we know anyone Owens hangs with?" she asked. "Who his supplier might be?"

"Owens is a loner. I have ideas on who supplies his needs. I talked to both of those guys as well. The consensus was that Owens is a head case." Bent purposely left out the names. He was not about to have Vee trying to question those two deadbeats. Though he couldn't prove anything related to their activities, both were dangerous.

"Apparently you've looked into Owens." She pointed an accusing look at him then. "Why didn't you tell me about him? Why wasn't he on your case board?"

Good of Elizabeth to pass along her son's concerns. Bent wouldn't have expected less. "Because there was nothing here. No reason to consider him a person of interest and certainly no reason to have you showing up here alone." Which was why he'd taken Owens off his case board before he invited Vera to consult on the case. He had known she would do something exactly like this.

"I suppose I had that one coming," she tossed back.

"Our missing reporter," he went on, grateful for the reprieve, "came to me last week. He'd been here, and I guess Owens made a comment that led Baker to believe he was hiding something. He wasn't real clear on the details. Anyway, I came that same day and talked to Owens. Most of this," he gestured to the wall, "was not here then. There were a couple of articles from the local paper. Nothing else. Anyway, he talked the same stuff most of the folks who believe in alien abductions spout. The stuff he sees on television or reads." He nodded to a pile of books and magazines on the floor at the head of the stack of mattresses that served as a bed.

"What now?" Vee turned to him.

"I get forensics to do their magic, and we see from there."

"They'll find my prints," she said. "I had a look around after I called you." She shrugged. "He appeared to be down for the count, and I wanted to see if there was anything hidden that might be useful to the investigation."

"We usually get a warrant for that sort of thing," he reminded her.

"Yeah, well, I felt there were exigent circumstances. For all I knew, he'd OD'd on something. In that situation it's always helpful if the medical staff knows what they're dealing with when they get the call."

"Works for me." Bent eyed her cautiously. "Did you find anything?"

"No cell phone." She shook her head. "No drugs. No nothing. Not even a business card from Baker, which I totally expected to find."

Bent figured if she was keeping anything from him, she would tell him eventually. "While we wait for Conover to arrive, we could have a look around the yard before it gets too dark?"

"Good idea."

Outside, he grabbed flashlights from his truck, handed his extra one to Vee. They started with the vehicles parked out front. He'd had a look in those when he came last week, but a follow-up wouldn't hurt. The trunk on the car was held closed with a bungee cord. Same as last week—nothing but trash inside. A plastic gas can and a couple of bags of trash were piled in the bed of the truck.

"I'll have Conover's people go through all the trash," Bent mentioned. If he was going to waste resources, he might as well do it right.

"Someone's going to love that detail." She looked toward Bent. "I've been assigned to it plenty of times myself."

"You don't know dirty details," he warned, "until you go through the army's basic training."

"You win," she agreed.

Vee was the only reason he'd survived those weeks and then the years that followed. Knowing that he'd done the right thing by Evelyn Boyett's daughter had gotten him through. He'd owed Vee's mother that. The woman had been far too good to Bent for him to risk ruining her daughter's life.

Vera Boyett had done well for herself. He was grateful to have her in his life again.

Bent forced his mind back onto the task at hand as they picked through the discarded appliances. They found nothing, so they moved on to the backyard. There was an old shed. Bent had looked inside it as well when he was here before. Owens had been completely agreeable to a thorough walk-through of his property. But the shed had been empty. No trash in there, which, looking back, Bent felt might have been a little suspicious, given the condition of the rest of the place. Could have been for no other reason than Owens being too lazy to walk that far to dump anything.

The last of the daylight was fading into the treetops as they reached the shed. It was one of the less expensive metal ones. Maybe eight by ten, with a few decades of rust showing. He slid the doors apart with an annoying screech and roamed the beam of his flashlight over the interior.

Not empty this time.

There was a sleeping bag, a couple of empty water bottles, and the wrappers from snack crackers and chip bags.

Vee crouched down at the door for a closer inspection of the ground. There was no floor in the old shed. It sat directly on the dirt.

"Well, well," Bent noted, "looks like Owens has had some company. Maybe one of his junkie friends or a supply source who stepped on the wrong toes."

Since the shed didn't have a lock, they could assume whoever had been here wasn't being held against his or her will.

"This wasn't here last week?" she asked.

"It was not." Bent put his flashlight under his arm and tugged on gloves before stepping inside. He picked up the sleeping bag by one corner and gave it a shake. An object tumbled out and hit the ground.

Vee's flashlight highlighted the item before Bent's. Black. Cell phone.

He picked it up, and the screen lit with a series of notifications, which included several calls and text messages from *Mom* and someone designated as *LR*. He showed the screen to Vee.

"That has to be Nolan's phone," she said without even touching it, her gaze colliding with Bent's. "LR is probably the boyfriend."

Bent pulled out his own cell and called the hospital. He identified himself and then said, "I need whoever's in charge in the ER." Half a minute later he had the doctor in charge on the line. "I need an update on a patient just brought in, Fisher Owens." A few seconds were required for the doctor to get the information. Bent then thanked him and ended the call.

"Owens is conscious but in psychosis. They had to sedate him. We can't talk to him until he's on the other side."

Vee bit her lip. "Which could take a few hours or a few days. Maybe weeks."

"Meanwhile, we'll search the entire property and the surrounding area."

"Just one thing." She cleared her throat. "There may be photos on the phone."

Bent's eyebrows went up. "I'm guessing so. Most folks have photos on their cell phones."

"No." Vee shook her head. "I mean photos with LR. Photos that could damage his career, as well as Nolan's."

Bent got it now. He looked at the phone. "We need a passcode. His mother may know it."

"Is it all right if I check with the boyfriend first?"

Bent was stunned. Was she asking for his permission? Wow. This was a first. "Why not?"

Vee stared at him kind of funny. "Okay. I'll give him a call." She stepped away from the shed.

While she spoke quietly to the boyfriend, Bent spotted headlights bobbing through the trees. That would be Conover.

"It's zero-zero-zero-zero," Vee said, drawing Bent's attention back to her.

He entered the passcode, and sure enough, that was it. He passed the phone to Vee. "You know what you're looking for." When she pulled on a glove and reached for the phone, he held on to it for a moment. "Just make sure you don't delete anything we need."

"Never," she promised.

By the time she'd done a quick perusal, the forensic crew had parked and were climbing out of the vehicle.

"Nolan is smart," she said, passing the phone back to Bent. "He has very few photos on there, and the ones he does have are related to stories he's working on. FYI, he has a photo of the wall in that bedroom—exactly the way it is now." She pointed to the shack Owens called home.

Which meant Nolan had been here since Bent's visit.

Maybe the ambitious reporter was only following up on a lead. But then, Bent had already let both Nolan and Elizabeth know there was nothing to be concerned about with Owens. Evidently, someone wanted him to believe he was wrong.

Bent wasn't particularly worried about that right now. Keeton had said in his statement that Baker had his phone with him last night when they'd arrived at the old hospital. Which would mean the device ended up at this location *after* his abduction.

There was only one conclusion to be reached from there: someone was lying.

11

Boyett Farm
Good Hollow Road, Fayetteville, 10:30 p.m.

Vera sat in her SUV. She'd been sitting here for a while now. The cold had overtaken the warmth and had her on the verge of shaking. She should go inside. She should eat. Her stomach rumbled, reminding her she hadn't eaten since . . . she frowned. She had no idea. Maybe breakfast. Had she eaten breakfast? Yes, at Bent's.

Evidently her memory was failing now that she was so very near forty. The new treadmill she'd ordered for Christmas was turning into more of a clothes rack than a workout feature for her room. She was getting soft. Complacent.

And desperate.

It had been a really long time since she'd been physically intimate. Back in Memphis she'd had Eric Jones. He was a colleague in the department and a good friend, had been for years, before she moved back to Fayetteville. The couple thing hadn't worked out, but being friends had suited them. They had been friends first, long before the other development. Until she moved to Fayetteville, she could rely on Eric at times like this—when she really needed a thorough, *physical* workout.

Bent's image filled her head, and she closed her eyes. Going down that road with him would not be smart at all. There was too much history between them. They were better, sort of, at the friends thing.

No matter that Bent was an incredibly good-looking man and had the sexiest voice she'd ever heard. God, and those blue eyes.

Vera closed her own and fought the wave of need.

The memories of their many secret rendezvous all those years ago rolled through her mind like a favorite old movie.

Maybe it was the whole idea of turning forty and never having been married, no kids, no traditional anything. The last time she'd been in love was when she was seventeen and was head over heels for Bent. The fact that her life had spiraled in reverse, landing her back in Tennessee, with no career and no love life and in the middle of a murder investigation involving her family had been plenty with which to deal.

Now she was about to be forty, her parents were gone, and both her *younger* sisters were in relationships. Life was calm . . . simple, for the most part.

That was the problem. There was nothing to distract her from the other.

The cold penetrated her coat, and she shivered again. Going into that big old empty house was maybe the issue tonight. It was late. She was tired and hungry, and the house was dark and empty. Eve had moved in with Suri, and Luna—the youngest Boyett sister—had gotten married.

That was enough to make a girl feel out of sorts.

She thought of how they'd found Nolan's cell phone in that shed. How the hell had Owens gotten the phone? Had he found it somewhere? Or had Nolan been hiding in that shed while he pretended to be abducted? Certainly, someone had been using the sleeping bag in that shed, and there had been food remains lying around.

But if Owens found the phone somewhere . . . why not turn it in when the news broke of Nolan's abduction, assuming he heard about it? Were the man's delusions driving him? There was no improvement in the last update from the hospital. Who knew when the guy would be able to answer any questions—if ever, for that matter. Long-term meth use could cause brain damage, among other terrible things.

The trouble was, if Owens wasn't the Time Thief and Nolan wasn't . . . that meant they still had no true evidence in this case. How could four people go missing and no evidence be left behind? Either they had one hell of a good perp, or it was a hoax that had been planned very carefully. No evidence of that either.

Basically, they had nothing.

The only good thing to happen today was that she'd been able to call Liam Remington again. He'd sounded relieved that there were no intimate photos to be worried about. But the reality that there was still no sign of Nolan hadn't been news he'd wanted to hear.

Still, Vera had been able to deliver on her promise to the man. He now owed her one. The thought of Teresa Russ and that voicemail she'd deleted had her nerves twitching again.

Finally, she reached for the door handle and got out of the car. The wind cut through her like a knife. She didn't remember March being this cold when she was a kid. Hundreds of daffodils had formed yellow puddles all around the front yard. Tulips had already pushed their way through the soil but hadn't started blooming just yet. Her mother had been a consummate gardener. The evidence bloomed all around the house from early spring until the dead of winter.

Vera had never fully appreciated all those blooms until the past few months. Considering all that had happened with the discovery of those remains in the cave, her mother's sea of blooms had been a comfort all last summer, through one trauma after another.

She slid the key into the lock and gave it a twist. Inside, the sound of the alarm had her going straight to the keypad to disarm it before closing and locking the door once more.

She tossed her keys and her bag aside, shrugged off her coat, and hung it on the nearest hook. Then she headed to the kitchen. She needed something hot to drink. Maybe with a shot of whiskey. With her favorite oversize mug under the drip basket, she set the coffee to brew and went for the Jack under the sink. Her stomach rumbled, reminding her that she needed food too. The memory of having BLTs with Bent popped into her head. Along with Renae's homegrown tomatoes.

Vera rolled her eyes. She'd have to go on social media and find this tomato-growing, salad-making *friend* of Bent's. Not that she was jealous or anything. Why would she be? She and Bent were only friends. Sure, she was attracted to him. What woman—or man, for that matter—still breathing wouldn't be? The man was . . .

"Stop it, Vee," she grumbled.

She poured a shot of Jack into the mug with the steaming coffee. Beyond ready for some sort of relief, she lifted the mug to her mouth and savored the heat and the taste of the promise Jack made with every damned drop—bottled right up the road in Lynchburg.

A sting of cold washed over her body. Was the heat off? It felt unusually cold in this big old kitchen. That was the thing with old houses. The heat or air-conditioning was never exactly right. Too many cracks and odd spaces—not to mention the lack of insulation—to keep the climate properly controlled.

Mug in hand, she trudged to the thermostat near the stairs. Seventy-two. It was warmer here by the stairs, but it certainly wasn't seventy-two degrees in the rear of the house. She walked back into the kitchen. Why was it so cold near the sink? This was more than just drafty.

She checked the back door. Locked. She went still. As she stood by the door, a stouter breeze swept past her. She turned to her right and recognized the cold was coming from the laundry room/mudroom. She walked through the cased opening, flipped on the light.

The window over the washer and dryer was up—not just a little, either. It was up all the way.

"What the hell?"

She set her mug aside, grabbed the stepladder from the corner. Had Eve or Luna been over here today? But why would they open a window? She should call and ask before she overreacted.

Climbing onto the top of the washing machine, she lowered the window and tried to lock it. Didn't work. Lots of these old windows no longer locked. Damn it. The windows were the original ones and were slathered with more than a century's worth of paint.

Once her feet were on the floor again, she put the stepladder away and picked up her mug once more.

The memory of this morning's tracks in the snow just outside her kitchen nudged her. It was entirely possible the window had been opened by an intruder. A new wave of cold washed over her, but it had nothing to do with the temperature. They'd had alarms put on the doors, but they'd opted not to include the windows since there were so many of them and it was crazy expensive.

A lump thickened in her throat.

Had someone been in the house?

She dragged her cell from her back pocket and called Eve. She downed the rest of her coffee and Jack before her sister answered. It felt wrong to be drinking alcohol while talking to Eve, who was a recovering alcoholic.

Plus she needed her free hand for her daddy's shotgun, which she hefted under her arm as she started a walk-through of the house.

"Do you know what time it is?" Eve demanded rather than saying hello.

It wasn't that late, but Eve sometimes had very early-morning starts at the funeral home.

"Did you come to the house today?" Vera asked, ignoring her question.

"What? No. I didn't leave the funeral home until an hour ago. I had to eat both lunch and dinner in the mortuary room."

Vera suppressed a gag. How her sister could eat while preparing a body was beyond all reason. "Someone was here."

"Maybe Luna came over. Did you ask her?" She yawned, as if the conversation couldn't be over quickly enough.

"I will, but I called you first." The living room and library were clear. The bathroom under the stairs too. That left the second floor. She started up the stairs.

"Why do you think someone was in the house?"

"The window in the laundry room was open, like someone used it for climbing in."

At the top of the stairs, Vera used her cheek and shoulder to hold the phone so she could position the shotgun properly in the event she had to shoot at an intruder.

"You really think someone's been in the house?" Eve's voice was suddenly at full attention.

"I hope not," Vera said, "but I can't think of another explanation."

"Call Bent," Eve practically shouted. "Do you have Daddy's shotgun?"

"I do." Her room looked clear, but just in case she checked the closet and under the bed. Not an easy task while holding the shotgun and keeping her phone in place.

"I'm hanging up and calling Bent."

"No," Vera growled. "Just stay on the line until I've checked all the bedrooms."

Eve's room was next. All clear there too. Hall bathroom was as well. The same in Luna's room.

"Going in Mama and Daddy's room now," she said, her heart beating faster.

The sound of her sister breathing on the other end of the line kept Vera steady. That and the shotgun in her hands.

Under the bed . . . in the closet. All clear.

"Okay." Vera let out a breath. "No one's in the house."

"I swear to God, if you go poking around outside without calling Bent . . ."

"There were tracks in the snow this morning." Vera sat down on the end of her parents' bed. The Jack had kicked in and given her a light buzz, considering she'd had no food in more than twelve hours. "They came from the area of the barn all the way to the back door and that window next to it. Looked as if whoever was out there stood around for a while, packing down the snow under that window. Just looking inside, I guess."

"Are you kidding me? I am calling Bent."

"Eve, I checked it out." Vera considered again that she hadn't seen tire tracks by the barn. So whoever was here had come from the woods beyond the barn. A long walk in all that snow.

And, as she had pondered this morning, maybe he parked on the road, walked to the barn and waited for the snow . . . but then how had he gotten back to the road or anywhere else without her seeing his return tracks? If he'd walked in the same tracks, it would have been obvious . . . unless he'd been very, very good at walking backward.

It could be only one of two ways—he either sprouted wings and flew or he'd gone through the house. The thought settled deep in her gut and started to swell. Why would anyone go to all that trouble? While she was asleep inside? He would have had to remove his boots to prevent leaving a telltale mess, climb into her house, make it to the front, and go out . . . a window. Opening the door would have set off the alarm.

The idea made her throat tighten.

"You can call him, or I'm calling him," Eve threatened.

"Fine. I'll call him."

"Okay. I'm hanging up now, but if I find out you didn't call him, I will be so pissed—you don't even know."

"I will call him. Night, Eve." Vera ended the call before her sister could say more.

She would call Bent. But not tonight. She was too exhausted . . . too out of sorts.

Instead, she went downstairs and started checking windows. The very first one next to the front door was unlocked and not quite pushed all the way down. Fury roared through her. She closed and locked it. It was one of the few that actually locked. Why the hell hadn't he at least partially closed that back window too?

He had, she suddenly realized. She would have noticed when she made coffee this morning if he hadn't. Which meant he'd been back again after she'd left for the day.

Son of a bitch.

She stormed back to the kitchen and poured another shot of Jack. Forget the coffee. She sipped it as she put her father's shotgun away and walked through the downstairs again. More slowly this time. She hadn't looked to see if anything was missing the first time. Not that the Boyett family had anything of any real value. Just a lot of stuff that prompted memories.

There was no one in the house, and there was nothing missing, as best she could tell.

It was possible the news had gotten around that she was helping with this Time Thief investigation. Some low-life reporter or, worse, someone involved with the kidnapper could have come in to see if she had anything relevant to the case in the house.

She shook off the endless possibilities. "Food." She downed the rest of the shot. She needed food.

After a scan of the fridge, she went for a peanut butter sandwich—well, half of one. There was only one slice of bread. Since she needed something to wash it down, she poured another shot of Jack and snagged a bottle of water. She downed the shot and left the mug in the sink. The one-sided sandwich and the bottle of water she took to her room and placed on the dresser.

A shower would have to wait until morning. She was way, way too tired for that. She clawed at her sweatshirt and finally managed to get it over her head. Then she peeled off her jeans. The bra hit the floor, and then she grabbed her favorite sleep shirt: a Bon Jovi tee Bent had gone to great lengths to get for her more than twenty years ago.

"Means nothing," she grumbled as she grabbed her sandwich and took a bite.

Her head swam from the booze. She took her sandwich, water, and phone to the window and settled there. As a teenager she'd ensconced herself by this window, all the time dreaming of when she'd grow up and escape her small town. Later, after her mama had died, she would sit here and watch for Bent.

She stuffed another bite of sandwich into her mouth and closed her eyes. The memory of twenty-one-year-old Bent and that damned cowboy hat he always wore had her smiling. She'd loved taking it off his head, running her fingers through his long, thick hair.

Her cell vibrated in her lap. She jumped, almost dropped her half-eaten half sandwich.

She tore off another bite and stared at her phone. *Bent.*

"Damn it, Eve."

She swallowed, took a drink of water, then accepted the call. "Hey." She swiped at her mouth.

"You okay?"

She was going to get her sister back for this. "I'm good. Really. Everything here is fine. Really. Fine."

The fact that she sounded inebriated was not lost on her.

"Good."

She wanted to demand to know if Eve had called him, but on the off chance that she hadn't and this call was about work, she didn't.

"What's up?" She downed a swallow of water, then ate the last of her sandwich. Licked her fingers.

"I was on my way home, and, well, I thought I'd check in on you. You look comfy."

She stopped licking and stared out the window. Right there, beyond the trees, was his truck . . . parked exactly where he'd parked all those nights when she'd sneak out to meet him.

The water bottle slid out of her hand. "Shit." She jumped up, grabbed it before it completely emptied on the floor. "Sorry." She grabbed her sweatshirt and tossed it onto the puddle. "I dropped . . ." She stared out the window, her throat so dry she could hardly speak, much less swallow. "I dropped my bottle of water."

"I like the T-shirt."

It hit her then that with the lights on in her room and him sitting in the dark out there, he could see her clearly. Oh God. He'd probably seen her underwear when she bent over to pick up the water.

"An oldie but goody," she said, trying to sound nonplussed as she settled on the window's deep ledge once more.

Silence filled the air for a long moment. The lack of talking had never bothered her, or him. They'd spent long minutes just listening to each other breathe.

"You'd tell me if something was wrong."

She moistened her lips. "Sure."

"I could come in, you know. Sleep on the couch."

He'd done that more than once back in July when all hell broke loose with that damned cave.

The words . . . words she knew better than to say . . . crowded into her throat. How many times since July had she wanted so damned badly to ask him to stay the night . . . not on the sofa downstairs but right here in her bed? How many hours had she spent daydreaming about how Bent the man might make love? The memory of how the twenty-one-year-old made love was seared on her brain. No imagination was necessary to envision his body now. Twenty years in the military had given him the patience and endurance of a warrior. He had a great body. She'd seen him without a shirt more than once.

She ran her fingers through her hair just to have something to do with them. She didn't know why she did this to herself. She was a grown woman. If she wanted to have sex with the man, she should just do it.

Except the one thing she knew with absolute certainty was that if she did, there would be no turning back. She recognized with complete certainty that it would change everything.

"I'm fine," she said, the breathless quality in her voice immensely frustrating. "Good night, Bent."

"Night, Vee."

The call ended, but she didn't move. She sat there and watched him drive away, the urge to call him back and invite him to come inside a pulsing, throbbing need.

When he was gone, she got up, walked to the bed, and collapsed onto it.

The thought of how much she wanted something more than the emptiness she felt at that moment followed her into the darkness of sleep.

12

Nolan couldn't stay awake.

He tried. He tried so hard.

This wasn't supposed to happen.

His mouth was so dry he could barely swallow. His arms and legs hurt. He'd been secured this way for too long. He needed to move.

He needed to talk to the person who had brought him here.

Good God, was Joel okay? Had he hurt Joel?

His father would say he had been asking for something bad to happen. After all, what intelligent, rational person responded to a letter tucked under the wiper on his windshield?

He'd wanted this story so bad.

His tongue slid over his dry lips once more. That's all. The story. His big break. No one else had a clue what was happening with the Time Thief. This had been his big chance to move up.

Except now he wasn't so sure.

The man, woman, whatever hadn't said a single word to him. He'd felt the prick of a needle more than once. The drug kept him so far out of it that he could hardly open his eyes.

This was the Time Thief's MO. And if this was the Time Thief, like the message had said, then he should let Nolan go in the next twenty-four hours. His parents were probably worried sick. Liam . . . God, Liam would be tormented.

His mother would completely understand his need to take this risk. Liam too. But his father . . . his father would be very disappointed in his carelessness.

Nolan drew in a deep breath. At least he was alive. Thank God for that.

But would his luck last?

The first time he'd woken up enough to have a coherent thought, he'd wondered if he was actually alive and if he would stay that way. Just because the Time Thief hadn't killed anyone so far didn't mean he wouldn't start.

Nolan didn't want to die. He just wanted to do bigger stories. To move to a larger market and report the sort of stories that made a difference.

The prick of a needle made him jerk.

"Wait! Talk to me." The words sounded sluggish. Drunken. "Let me tell your story," he managed, before the creep of darkness overtook his ability to get the words out.

Laughter echoed in the space around him, but Nolan couldn't respond . . . he barely hung on to a shard of consciousness.

"Not to worry, Mr. Baker."

The words jolted him, but Nolan still couldn't open his eyes or make his mouth work.

"*You* are the story."

13

Thursday, March 6
Boyett Farm
Good Hollow Road, Fayetteville, 6:30 a.m.

Vera stood in the shower until the water started to cool.

Dragging herself from the bed this morning had required enormous effort. Although she was confident the whiskey had helped her go to sleep and stay that way, she wasn't sure the resulting hangover was worth it.

Her head felt stuffed with cotton, and that distant ache suggested it was only going to get worse.

She shut off the water and climbed out. Moving slowly to avoid contributing to the nausea threatening, she used the towel to squeeze and rub her hair partially dry, then swab the dampness from her body before hanging the towel over the side of the tub.

The steamy air in the room made breathing even more difficult. Never again would she drink like that on an empty stomach.

She walked to the sink and reached for her hairbrush. Her gaze snagged on the fogged mirror. Words were written on the steamy glass.

I've missed you, Detective

Vera stared at the mirror, squeezed her eyes shut, and then looked again just to make sure she hadn't imagined the words staring back at her. She squeezed her eyes shut once more. *Not possible.* If she was lucky, it was a hangover hallucination.

But it wasn't . . . the words were still there. Her heart thumped harder and harder.

Her first instinct was to reach out and smear them away, but the deeply rooted cop training wouldn't allow the move.

This was the Messenger's MO. His wording . . . but that was impossible.

Where the hell was her cell phone?

Her mind replayed her movements after dragging out of bed . . . the window. Closing the door behind her to hold in the heat and steam, she rushed back to her room and grabbed the phone from the window ledge where she'd left it last night.

"Don't be dead," she muttered.

Five percent. Thank God.

She hurried back to the bathroom and snapped a photo of the mirror. Luckily, the foggy glass around the words kept her reflection from the photo. Having Bent or anyone else see her bare breasts was . . .

"Stop." She grabbed her towel and hurried back to her room. She stuck the charging cord into her phone, left it on the bedside table and went in search of clothes. Her usual fare. Jeans. Tee and sweatshirt. She tossed the items onto the unmade bed and dug for underthings. As quickly as possible she dried her body and dressed.

She sat down on the bed, and while she dragged on her socks, she called Bent.

"Morning, Vee."

"I need Conover at my house." With her socks on, she picked up the phone, took it off speaker. "Someone was in my house while I was gone yesterday."

"You okay?"

Big breath. "Yes."

"Is it possible there's someone still in the house?"

The idea only then settled like an elephant on her chest. "No." She relaxed as the details of last night cleared in her mind. "I don't think so. I set the alarm when I came in and checked the house. A window was open, so I think someone had been in here but left before I came home."

No need to mention the other unlocked window. It was possible it had been unlocked for weeks or months. But that cop instinct of hers said she'd been right last night about why it was open. Which meant, she kept to herself, that someone could have come in again last night. Damn it.

"Where are you?" Movement rustled in the background on his end.

"In my room."

"Lock the door. Pull something—anything in front of it. I'm sending the nearest unit to you, and I'm on my way. I'll call Conover en route."

Vera ended the call. She wasn't sure if she'd thanked him or even said goodbye. Her gaze settled on her bedroom door. She blinked. Considered her options. No way was she hiding in here.

She grabbed her phone and slid it into her back pocket and walked out. Moving quickly, soundlessly, she checked the other bedrooms. Clear. On her way toward the stairs, she paused at the bathroom door, stared at the words now melting on the mirror. Couldn't be what it looked like. No. Way.

Not possible.

She swallowed the lump lodged in her throat and moved on. To the count of ten, she stood at the top of the stairs and listened. Nothing save the ticking of that old grandfather clock in the entry hall that she forgot to wind up more often than not. Her gaze surveying left to right, she started down the stairs. Room by room she searched. Living room was clear. Library and bathroom too. She eased into the kitchen . . . clear.

Thank God. She so needed coffee right now.

Then again, she supposed someone could have been hiding somewhere she'd failed to look last night. Set up the message and hung around to see her reaction.

"Not his style." The serial killer known as the Messenger would have gotten in, left the words for his victim, and gotten out. No deviation. No hanging about with a vic in the house. He did not take those sorts of risks. But leaving notes on mirrors like this was his favorite method of delivery.

Stop. Where the hell had that thought come from anyway? The Messenger was in prison. Had been for a dozen years. Vera shook herself. Last night's overindulgence had obviously rattled her brain.

She dismissed any further thoughts about that part of her past. *Not going there.*

Someone—maybe someone related to the Time Thief case—was messing with her head. Couldn't be anything else. Finding information about her biggest cases during her tenure with the Memphis Police Department was easy enough to do on the internet.

Satisfied with her assessment, she prepared a pot of coffee versus a single cup. Conover and Bent might want coffee as well. Besides, she doubted one cup would get her through this hellacious morning.

8:30 a.m.

Vera watched as Conover reached for his bag of tricks in the middle of her bathroom floor. "So, what's the verdict?" she asked.

He looked from Vera to Bent and back. "Without giving you the exact type or brand, I'd say laundry detergent. Maybe from your own laundry room, since that's where the window was opened. But, as you know, I can't be sure of anything until I've run all the necessary tests. I'm basing my preliminary assumption on the scent and the oily feel of the residue that was on your mirror."

Whatever hope Vera had held out that it would be some other substance, like plain old alcohol, deflated. The answer Conover had given fit the MO she didn't want to think about. But the Messenger was an old case that could not possibly be back in her life. No way. Even the idea was implausible. The memory of Elizabeth bringing it up echoed in her head. Had to be a coincidence.

The whole concept was ridiculous. Could. Not. Be. Him.

She nodded at Conover. "I understand."

Conover looked to Bent. "You want me to lift prints from the window?"

"And this door." Bent nodded toward the bathroom door.

"Will do."

Vera headed for the stairs. The frustration building inside her was not something she wanted Bent or Conover to witness. So maybe not only frustration. More like shock, worry, *fear*. Damn it, she hated feeling this way. No matter what she told herself, some flaw in her reasoning wouldn't let go of the remote possibility that yet another part of her past was back to screw with her.

Bent was right behind her as she took the final step and turned toward the kitchen.

"You want to explain to me what's going on?"

More coffee wouldn't help, so she stalled a few feet from the kitchen doorway. Food damned sure wouldn't provide any relief, either, so no need to go to the kitchen. She wasn't a stress cook like Luna. She'd always thought she wasn't a stress drinker like Eve, but then last night had seemed to disprove that conclusion.

Vera opted to go to her mother's library rather than stand in the entry hall and have this unavoidable conversation. "I'd made detective," she began. "Thirteen years ago. The chief really wanted me on the admin side, but I was determined to be an investigator. Reluctantly, he caved, and I was assigned to the homicide division. Being at the bottom of the food chain seniority-wise, I always got the shit tasks and cases. The ones no one else wanted to deal with—meaning the routine stuff. The easy-to-solve, 'anyone can figure it out' sort. But then a few months later, I arrived at a routine scene that changed everything."

Why the hell was she even talking about this? The person—whoever left that message—could NOT be him.

"The Messenger." Bent's jaw worked for a moment. "That's how you got involved with the case."

Just hearing him say the name made her gut clench.

"I made an impression pretty quickly." Vera nodded. "The first message I received from him was left on the mirror in my bathroom—like this one. My apartment was a low-end one, so breaking in wasn't difficult. He used laundry detergent to write the words on the mirror so that when I took a shower, the steam covered the glass save for where the detergent was—revealing his message to me." She blinked, took a breath. *"I see you, Detective."*

Biggest mistake of his fucking life. Vera was the one who figured out who he was and nailed his ass.

This is not him. Nope. Can't be.

"I was stationed in Europe during that time," Bent said, "but I followed both you and Eve on social media. The bastard's in prison, right?"

"He is." Vera reminded herself to keep her cool. She did not want Bent to see her lose it. "This morning, while I waited for you to arrive, I called a friend in Memphis, who confirmed it for me."

Riverbend Maximum Security Institution was in Nashville. Not nearly far enough away to suit Vera. When she'd been in Memphis, at the time of his sentencing, she'd been glad he would be hundreds of miles away from her.

But now that she was back in Fayetteville . . . he wasn't nearly far enough away.

Why was she still thinking about him? She ordered herself to stop.

"Tell me about him."

But Bent kept wanting to hear more . . .

Vera took a breath. "If it's okay with you, I'd like to hold off going there until there's reason to. Anyone could have read about him and decided to do this. I haven't exactly been a local favorite. And if someone who's holding a grudge knows I'm helping on this case, it may have stirred up those feelings."

"For now," Bent allowed, his expression stony. "But if anything like this happens again, we are going there."

"Thanks." With effort, Vera pushed the worries about the writing on her mirror aside. "Did Conover have any news on Owens's shack or Nolan's apartment?" Bent had already told her there was no news on Nolan Baker, but he hadn't been specific as to the case overall.

"There were no prints at all on the newspaper clippings in the bedroom," Bent told her. "But the poster-board drawings were covered with Owens's prints. There's still a lot to go through from the shed out back and in the shack itself. As for Nolan's apartment, nothing so far that we didn't expect. His prints. His parents'. No word back yet about his laptop. Nothing unexpected on his cell phone."

There hadn't been any calls to or from Teresa Russ on his cell phone. Vera had checked. No voicemails either. Thank God.

"There were prints on that window at the old hospital where the blind was removed and then on the one where it was installed."

Vera perked up. "Seriously?"

"Seriously. No match yet. Conover and I were at the old hospital when you called."

"Sorry." She folded her arms over her chest. "I could have waited... I just got spooked."

"Never wait, Vee. Always trust your instincts." Bent put a hand to her back and ushered her toward the entry hall. "You should eat and have more coffee."

He knew her too well. "That would mean I'd have to cook."

"I'll cook. An omelet sound okay? Assuming you have the fixings."

She scoffed. "Why don't I go grab a few things from my greenhouse garden?"

A grin tried to make an appearance, but he kept it at bay. "Let me have a look in your fridge."

While Bent figured out if there was anything to prepare, Vera wandered to the laundry room, where Conover was now focused on the window over her washer and dryer.

He glanced at her. "You should have better locks on these windows."

Yeah, she had an idea for that. "You're right. I'll take care of that today."

She had a lot to do today. Dropping by the hardware store for a new power drill and some long screws for securing the windows was first on her agenda. Next, she intended to get in touch with Teresa Russ. Then she would follow up on leads related to Nolan Baker—not that she had any, but she planned to find at least one today. If the Time Thief's MO played out per usual, Nolan would be released tonight.

But Vera had a bad feeling about that. Maybe the message she'd found on her mirror this morning was the reason that nagging sense of doom wouldn't fully dissipate. Her instincts were humming.

Some would say it was a sure sign she needed to brace herself because something bad was coming.

Vera didn't think so. She was pretty sure it was already here.

14

Boyett Farm
Good Hollow Road, Fayetteville, 1:00 p.m.

Bent had made breakfast as they'd waited for the lengthy forensics process to finish. Now, a trip to the hardware store and two hours of work later, Vera had bored the second screw into the final window. She wasn't sure what Luna would think of her securing the windows shut, but she was reasonably confident Eve wouldn't care. Come summer, Vera would likely be dragging out this handy new power tool and removing the screws so she could raise the windows.

Probably would have been simpler to just have the security company come back out and add sensors to the windows. But there was something infinitely satisfying about knowing she had personally thwarted the efforts of any would-be intruders.

She climbed off the stepladder and set the power drill aside. "Try getting in now, you bastard."

A check of her cell showed there was still no response from Russ. Vera had left her a voicemail. Hopefully she would call soon. The waiting was driving her nuts. She had no more windows to work on. She'd cleaned up the kitchen already. Bent was a good cook, but he'd made a hell of a mess, and she had refused to allow him to stay and clean up. She'd had things to do. It was bad enough that the deputy who'd showed up first thing that morning had hung around, followed her to the hardware store and back.

Having someone watching her made her antsy. She could take care of herself—at least that was the line she gave Bent and anyone else who suggested otherwise.

What now? Put away her tools and then maybe check in with Bent to see if he had any news. Waiting was another of those things that made her edgy.

She grabbed the power drill. The best place for her new tool, she decided, was under the sink. Since she might need it again sooner than she thought. A few strides and a quick squat, and that was done. The stepladder went back into the laundry room. She called it a room, but it was really just a nook her father had carved out of kitchen space to create an organized place for the laundry stuff. Vera remembered how happy her mother had been with the change. How Vera wished life was so simple now.

Her cell vibrated with an incoming call, and she jumped. Held her breath in hopes it was Russ. *Bent.* Her hopes sagged. No offense to him—she had questions for him—but she really, really needed to have a conversation with Russ. Maybe she would just show up at the PI's office.

"Hey." Vera's attempt at an upbeat tone didn't really hit the mark.

"Hey," he said back. "I managed to make appointments with all three of the Time Thief's released vics. You busy, or do you want to come along for new interviews?"

"Sure, I want to come along." She was supposed to be helping with the case, after all. "You coming now?"

"I'm outside your house."

She should have known. "Headed that way."

She ended the call and did a quick survey of the kitchen to ensure she'd locked the door and all was turned off—coffee maker, stove. On the way to the front door, she checked her hair. The ponytail she'd tied it into was looking a little wispy, but it would just have to do. Since she'd had to forgo blow-drying her hair this morning, taming it with a hair tie had been her only option that didn't take too much time. At the door she grabbed her jacket, dragged it on, then her shoulder bag and looped it over her neck.

She set the security system, and then, once outside, she closed and locked the door. Checked it just to be sure. Obviously, paranoia was creeping in.

Keeping busy had been the key to her not thinking about the Messenger as the morning had dragged on. As creepy as the message on the mirror had been—not to mention it had put her instincts on edge—she had no actual reason to believe it was from him.

Couldn't be. Couldn't be.

The idea really was ridiculous. He was in prison. If he'd had a partner during his killing years, there had been no evidence, and there had been nothing from that person since the Messenger's arrest, which pretty much negated the possibility—killers rarely just stopped killing. This, Vera suspected, was likely someone trying to rattle her. Maybe some other creep she'd ensured went to prison and who had recently been released. With the media circus generated around the Messenger case, anyone who hadn't lived under a rock would know that was the case to use if they wanted to get to her. And there was always the possibility that someone the Messenger had befriended in prison was out now and was doing him a favor by harassing Vera. Both were possibilities she would look into if the need arose.

The case had been the subject of numerous special reports and documentaries. Finding a few details online would be easy enough. As for her recent activities, the investigation into the remains in that damned cave had been far more high profile than this Time Thief thing. If that very personal investigation hadn't stirred the Messenger's interest and prompted some sort of action, she couldn't see how this case would.

"Who are we going to see first?" she asked as she climbed into Bent's truck. The deputy in the cruiser was no longer parked at her house. She supposed Bent had sent him on his way.

"Kayleigh Marshall."

"That's the one I don't know," Vera mentioned. The other two, the males, were sons of people she had known growing up in Fayetteville. Oliver Randall was the son of Scott Randall, the guy with the fruit orchards and pumpkin farm. His family had made quite the name for itself in Lincoln and numerous surrounding counties with that farm. Vance Honeycutt's father owned the most popular restaurant on the square—the one his grandfather had started many decades ago.

Kayleigh was the only one who hadn't grown up in Lincoln County.

"Her family moved to Fayetteville when she was already at UT," Bent explained. "She actually lives in Nashville, but her mother died last year, so she spends a lot of time in Fayetteville with her dad."

"The three have nothing in common," Vera said, recalling the details, "based on your reports. Does Baker's abduction change that?"

Bent glanced at her as he made a turn onto Molino Road. "It does. Randall and Baker were on the high school football team together."

Vera shrugged. "It's a small town. It was bound to happen."

Bent nodded slowly. "Except Randall's uncle was the football coach, and there was some rumbling about favoritism. I don't know the details, but I did hear he retired in the middle of a season."

Vera scoffed. "Let me guess, Elizabeth and her husband were the ones rumbling."

"It was all kept very hush-hush, so I can't say for sure." Bent slowed for a turn.

"If Nolan was involved, you know it was," Vera argued. "It's the most logical scenario."

Bent glanced at her. "You only say that because you don't like her."

"As my mama always said, you made your bed, now lie in it. I truly hope Nolan is released, like the others, and that he's okay. But nothing in this world is going to make me like Boggie." And that was assuming the little bugger wasn't the Time Thief himself. Frankly, the idea of Nolan kidnapping three other people, holding and drugging them before releasing them, and then pretending to kidnap himself was a little over the top. Even if the notion did keep nagging at her.

Bent said no more, but Vera recognized how hard he was working to keep a smile from making an appearance. Most folks only tolerated Elizabeth. She was, as Vera's mama would say, a mess.

Vera set her gaze straight ahead. There were parts of her past that weren't worth the effort of analyzing, and her dislike of Elizabeth Baker was one of them.

A final turn into the neighborhood called the Avenues, and a few moments later Bent parked. The Marshall home was a newer one. Brick. Modern. Certainly not the typical style of the neighborhood. Probably had windows that worked and locked the way they were supposed to and weren't bloated with layers of paint.

"Kayleigh hasn't gone back to Nashville?" she asked, spotting a car with Davidson County plates.

Bent shut off the engine. "Her father had a health scare while she was missing. She doesn't want to leave him until he's back on his feet."

"Health scare?" Vera nudged.

"He started drinking again and took a tumble down the stairs." Bent reached for his door. "He's a recovering alcoholic."

Damn. She thought of Eve and the idea of how alcoholism was a forever battle. "I'm glad she can be here for him."

Bent nodded. "He's a lucky guy."

Kayleigh Marshall was waiting on the front porch when they reached it. "My father is napping; do you mind if we go around to the screened porch? I've started a fire in the outdoor fireplace."

"Sure," Bent agreed. "We'll follow you."

Kayleigh led the way around the corner of the house to the patio. Not only was there a huge fireplace but there was also an outdoor kitchen and a lovely sitting area. Very nice.

Once they were seated around the roaring fire, Kayleigh made a face. "I'm sorry. I didn't think about refreshments. Would you like coffee?"

"No," Vera hastened to say. She'd had far too much caffeine today. "Thank you."

"None for me," Bent said.

Kayleigh seemed to relax then. "All right. You said you wanted to talk about what happened."

"Kayleigh," Vera spoke up, "we really appreciate your time and don't want to keep you any longer than necessary. I've read the reports including your statements, so really I just have two questions."

She waited expectantly.

"Have you remembered anything new that perhaps you feel is relevant or significant in some way?"

The young woman thought for a moment, then shook her head. "No. I've already told the sheriff everything I can remember. I've had a few nightmares, and sometimes I find myself dwelling on it, but it's always the same."

Vera gave her a wide smile. "I'm sorry to hear about the nightmares. I'm sure they'll pass once we have the person who did this in custody."

Kayleigh nodded. "Hope so."

"Did you know any of the other victims before the events occurred?"

The younger woman shrugged. "I don't think so. I mean, I can't say for sure—I've maybe seen them at a community event or just walking around the square, but I didn't *know* them. We've talked since—Vance, Oliver, and I." She looked to Bent. "You mentioned that it might be useful if we talked informally to see if it sparked any new memories."

Great idea. Vera never ceased to be surprised by what a good investigator Bent was.

"I'm glad you decided to do that." Bent gave her a nod of approval.

"What about Nolan Baker?" Vera ventured. "Were you acquainted with him before?" An idea had the wheels turning in her mind. This could be something.

Kayleigh made a face, not sad or angry . . . maybe annoyed. "I don't really know him. But three years ago when we were both still at UT, he asked me to Christmas dinner with his family. It was sort of strange because we had only one class together, and we really weren't friends or anything. I don't know. It was like out of the blue. But since my family was in Fayetteville, too, I figured why not. It was a free ride, and he seemed nice. But . . ." She drew in a big breath. "The whole time we were at his family's home, he was . . ." She shrugged. "I don't know, behaving as if we were a couple. No, not just a couple. A serious couple."

Maybe not as strange as Kayleigh thought. "Was that the only time the two of you interacted?"

She nodded. "Other than the one class we had together that semester, we really didn't see each other. It was like he didn't know I existed before or after that one dinner. I didn't care, but it was just odd. You know when something or someone gives you that creepy feeling? That's how I felt afterward."

"Thank you, Kayleigh." Vera turned to Bent to see if he had anything to add.

He settled his hat in place. "We appreciate your time."

Vera kept quiet until they reached the truck, but her instincts were vibrating. "You have to know this is far too big a coincidence to ignore."

"Agreed. But I'll restrain myself from jumping to conclusions."

Vera gave him a look. "Who's jumping to conclusions? The whole 'come to dinner' thing was likely just to make his parents think he was dating a girl. When she never came again, he probably told his mother she dumped him. Elizabeth would not have been happy about that."

Bent laughed. "I admit that you could be onto something, but let's see what the other two have to say before we go closing in on a single scenario."

No problem. Vera smiled to herself. She was right, and he knew it.

15

Randall Residence
Washington Street, Fayetteville, 2:45 p.m.

The interview with Vance Honeycutt had been much like Kayleigh Marshall's, quick and to the point. He and Nolan had classes together in school. They had known each other their whole lives. But they were never friends. In fact, they hadn't liked each other back in high school and still did not. The trouble had started when he and Nolan both ran for class president. Nolan started the rumors that caused so many of his classmates not to vote for Vance. Nolan swore it wasn't him, but then when Vance took over the restaurant from his father, Nolan ensured the story was buried. If Vance had felt any doubts all those years, that move relieved him of every single one. Vance considered Nolan to be arrogant and far too "me focused."

Vera couldn't deny that Nolan Baker, bless his heart, was both of those things.

It was on to Oliver Randall then.

"Mr. Randall," Vera began.

"That's my dad," Oliver said. "Just call me Ollie. My friends do."

Vera nodded. "Ollie. The sheriff and I were discussing whether you were acquainted with the other victims before the abduction."

"I went to school with Van and Nolan. Van is a good guy. Hard worker, let me tell you. We're not close, but not for any particular reason. We go to different churches, and truth is, we're both busy with our respective family businesses. Like I said before, I don't know Kayleigh much at all. She's come into our restaurant since . . . what happened, but if she came before, I never noticed."

"You and Nolan Baker," Bent said, "played football together as well."

Ollie paused, as if he wasn't sure how to respond to the comment.

"Team members are usually pretty tight," Vera pointed out.

"I played football," Ollie said, his tone growing noticeably hard. "Nolan played being on the team. He got the spot because his daddy is Carl Baker. Otherwise, a jersey would never have been wasted on him."

And there it was . . . the thread that tied them all together.

"But your uncle was the coach," Vera argued. "Some may have thought you had your spot on the team because of his position."

He laughed. "No offense, ma'am, but I still hold the all-time record for the most catches and the most touchdowns for any player in the history of Lincoln County High School. I was on that team because I was good, and I worked hard. Nolan Baker couldn't catch a house if it landed on him, much less a football. And he sure as hell couldn't carry it to a win."

Vera could hardly hold back the "I told you so" she wanted to say to Bent.

"Tell us," Bent prodded, "why your uncle resigned in the middle of the season. Why not finish out the year?"

Ollie's face showed all the disdain he had for the answer to that question. "The Bakers insisted he wasn't being fair to their son. Nolan was spending all his time on the bench, and that was unacceptable. My uncle chose to sacrifice his position so that I could still play without all the drama. The next coach made the same decisions as my uncle. The Bakers still put up a fuss, but they let it go after a bit. Anyway, we're not friends—Nolan and I. I hope he's released soon. Unharmed, as we were, but otherwise I got no sympathy for him."

"If you remember anything else relevant to your abduction," Vera said, "please let us know." She had heard all she needed to hear.

When they were back in Bent's truck and on the road, she spoke up. Rather than *I told you so*, she said, "This is beginning to smell rotten, Bent."

"You were right." He glanced at her. "Doesn't help that I received a text from Conover while we were talking to Randall. He's found some trace evidence from all four victims in that shed behind Owens's shack." He braked for a traffic light at Lincoln Avenue and College Street. "I think we both know Owens is not capable of pulling this off. And that shed looked far too ready to collapse to serve as a place to hold a hostage. Unfortunately, we still can't question the guy because he hasn't recovered from his psychotic episode. But this is clearly a setup."

Vera lifted an eyebrow. "That just leaves two suspects, in my opinion—Nolan or his mother—and I'm leaning toward the mother. Maybe dear old Boggie wanted some sort of big event to boost her son's fledgling media career. Mothers have done far worse to get what they wanted for their child. Even one all grown up."

"Could be the husband," Bent countered. "Or some crazed fan of Nolan's."

Vera wasn't even going there. "If the perp was after Nolan, why bother with the others? All three of the previous vics are people who don't like Nolan. Who could be seen as having wronged him somehow. This"—she turned to Bent—"is about that and boosting his name. Nothing else."

"You're right," he repeated, and ducked his head in acknowledgment.

"Well then, why're we beating around the bush?" Vera demanded. "It's time to confront Boggie."

"We will do that," he promised. "Soon. But we need to take a minute and talk about what happened at your house first."

She got it now. He was holding the confrontation with the Bakers hostage until she agreed. Damn it.

Vera's heart had bumped into a faster rhythm. "Did Conover find a match with any of the prints?"

Bent parked at a popular Mexican restaurant on the square. "He did not. But I want to hear more about your interactions with the Messenger. All of it. I know you don't want to talk about it, but I need to be prepared just in case."

"I think the discussion is premature. It can't be him," she argued. Couldn't be. The scumbag was in prison.

"Premature or not," he said as he reached for his door, "we're having it."

Vera stared at the restaurant. Funny how Bent somehow always managed to make sure she had her next meal. Although the topic of conversation he'd chosen was hardly appetizing. Before she could climb out of the truck, Bent was at her door. They entered the restaurant together and followed a server to a booth.

When they'd given their orders, he looked to her. "Talk."

"As I told you already," she said, weary of the subject before she'd even started, "it was a mistake that I ended up on the case. No one already working the investigation wanted me there. But once I was digging around and the Messenger acknowledged me, there was no turning back. The FBI agent leading the investigation was thrilled, and so was I. This was my big chance. I wanted to make the most of it."

The server brought their drinks. When she'd moved on, Bent said, "Tell me what you learned about him."

She poked a straw into her sweet ice tea. "Dr. Palmer Solomon turned out to be the Messenger." She made a sound meant to be a laugh, but it fell short. "He's the epitome of a cliché. A psychiatrist who knows how people think and who used it to get his thrills. A regular old Hannibal Lecter. He would select his prey—a long and careful process. Always someone who would be classified as lonely. No social life. Busy with work. No family, or nearly none. Few friends. The easy targets."

Vera felt a little sick at the idea that she had fit the profile of his preferred victim. She imagined the federal agent in charge had noticed as much and that detail had gone into the decision process for adding her to his team. The cops—no matter the rank or the agency—who truly wanted/needed to solve their cases at all costs would do most anything to make that happen. Including using a new, inexperienced detective who just happened to fit a serial killer's profile.

Special Agent Xavier Alcott had wanted desperately to catch the one who had been evading him for a decade.

Their food arrived, and though it smelled wonderful, she wasn't sure she would be able to eat a bite.

"The FBI determined that Solomon had been actively killing for ten years . . . which," Vera said, thinking back, "I found a bit unusual since he was sixty at the time. Most serial killers begin well before that, as Alcott no doubt knew. Hell, the whole team did. But there was no evidence to support the theory in his past beyond that ten-year mark. He was careful. One victim per year, unless he used a different MO or we just didn't find them. Considering how he loved to show off, I don't believe that's possible."

"He would have had eleven if not for you," Bent said before taking a bite of spicy rice and cheese.

Vera forced herself to lift her fork and taste her own rice. A bed of it was covered with cheese. There was chicken in there somewhere, too, but she wasn't sure she could manage to eat any meat just now.

When she'd swallowed, she continued with the story. "He'd been watching Gloria Anderson for months. When he was ready to make his move, he gave her the usual caution. A message warning that he was coming. For Gloria, he had put it in her email. He'd used a computer at a library and a Gmail account listed to M. Messenger to send her an email. He'd gone into her office and opened her email so that when she started work that morning, it would be the first thing she saw when she touched her keypad."

He'd proven to be such a smooth, highly intelligent operator. He'd known how to get in and out and how to stay just under the radar. Some killers were that way . . . cunning, clever . . . elusive.

When her lapse into silence persisted, Bent said, "The messages were all very similar."

"Yes. *I'm coming for you. You're next.* That sort of thing. But only one. Always, only one message before he struck." She picked at the rice with her fork. "Until I came into the picture. He sent me three. First was *I see you*, then *I'm intrigued by you*, but the last was something different." Her gut tied itself into a dozen knots.

"*I'm going to enjoy killing you*," Bent said.

Vera resisted the feeling that went with that memory. "The first was on the mirror in my bathroom. Since it was February and cold as hell, the second one was on the windshield of my car."

"But not the last one," Bent said, his face reflecting the worry twisting inside him. "It was carved into the woman you found before he could finish his game with her."

She nodded, forced a forkful of rice into her mouth. The fact that he took the poor woman that second time just to send Vera a message still tortured her dreams.

"His victims were always women," Bent said. "He appeared to love torture."

"The worst kind of monster," Vera confirmed. "A torture-murderer." Inside, where Bent couldn't see, she shuddered. The things the Messenger did to his victims were merciless. He carved them up, inducing incredible pain, but never deeply enough to cause a quick death. His process ensured death was slow and intentional. She forced the memories away. "And, yes, his intended victims were always women. Anyone else was just someone who got in the way."

"How did you find him?" Bent abandoned his fork, half his rice and cheese and chicken gone.

Vera had barely taken two bites. "I'll be completely honest with you, Bent. I think he let me find him. Maybe it was some subconscious way to stop himself. I don't know, but he left me several clues. He never left evidence. Ever. Maybe he just wanted to see if I would follow them without involving the rest of the task force."

"And you did," Bent said pointedly. "You risked your life."

"But I saved Gloria Anderson's life." Vera exiled the thought. Going back to that place was not something she wanted to do just now. Not with Bent. At least not until she had no other choice.

"I need you to promise me, Vee," Bent said, leaning toward her, "that you will not do that if this happens again—with any perp."

She smiled, shook her head slowly. "I can't make a promise like that, Bent. You know it as well as I do. Sometimes you just have to do what you have to do."

He drew back, anger tightening his features. "Then maybe you shouldn't be involved with police work anymore."

"Maybe not." If he'd meant to hit her where it hurt, he'd done so. But his wasn't the only law enforcement department around who called on her for assistance. She was a civilian consultant. Over the past several months she had worked for a number of different southern Tennessee law enforcement groups. As long as there was crime, she would always have work.

He held up his hands, his expression repentant. "I'm sorry. That was out of line."

"I can promise you this," she said, in hopes of smoothing things over.

"I'm listening."

"Unlike twelve years ago, I will never put myself in a position that I know up front I cannot handle. I will be careful and smart, Bent. I'm not that naive newbie with something to prove anymore." This was exactly why there were things Bent never needed to know about the Messenger case—about all that happened at the end . . . with her and Eric. Eric had gotten in the way and ended up being the bastard's first known male victim, and that was her fault.

"Fair enough." He glanced at her plate. "Now eat. We have work to do."

On some level Vera hoped Elizabeth Baker and maybe her husband and her son had set up this whole Time Thief thing. That would mean there was no crazed alien-obsessed wacko running around out there abducting people. That would also mean that Nolan was most likely safe and would be released soon.

Tonight, if the usual MO played out.

That said, if it was Elizabeth or her husband, the two were really, really award-winning actors. They had already done two television interviews begging for the release of their son. The fear and anguish had looked real. Certainly there were those who relished putting on a good show. As much as Vera didn't like Elizabeth, the woman truly loved her son. Would she really be able to fake that level of concern if she was responsible for his abduction?

If the person who'd taken Marshall, Randall, and Honeycutt was not the same person who'd taken Nolan Baker, then he was in trouble. Serious trouble. Because the sheriff's department was looking for the same perpetrator . . . not someone different.

As much as she did not want to entertain the idea even for a second, it was there, waiting on the edge of her thoughts. And it tore at her insides.

If, by some bizarre twist of fate, the Messenger was involved in Nolan's abduction . . . if he had for some reason chosen this time to come after Vera through some other means—a surrogate, maybe someone he'd met in prison—he might capitalize on an ongoing situation. It was the perfect path to worm his way into her life. With the Messenger, nothing was outside the realm of possibility.

And if that was the case, Baker would last two or three more days at most, depending on his ability to keep the bastard entertained, and then his throat would be cut. He would bleed out on the ground or wherever he was left to die—some place that had meaning for him.

If the Messenger was in any way involved, it would turn everything—not just this case—upside down. No one, least of all Vera, wanted to learn that Solomon had found a protégé interested in creating heinous crimes similar to those of his past.

Because if there was a new partner, the bigger question was, What the hell had that deviant been doing all this time? Watching his idol . . . waiting for his turn . . . training for the big production? Whatever the case, he, too, might very well have left in his wake a trail of mayhem that hadn't been found yet.

Or was Nolan Baker to be his first?

16

Baker Residence
Mulberry Avenue, Fayetteville, 4:50 p.m.

Bent wasn't looking forward to how this would likely turn out. Elizabeth and Carl Baker were high-profile citizens, and if by some chance he and Vee were wrong . . . this could be a real pain in the ass for a very long time to come. People like Elizabeth Baker didn't forgive and forget.

But he and Vee weren't wrong . . . he was damned certain of that conclusion now.

He glanced at Vee as he knocked on the door. She tucked a stray blond hair, which had loosened from her ponytail, behind her ear. He should know better than to worry in the first place. She wouldn't be wrong. The woman was very, very good at figuring out the real story behind all the layers. She had been extensively trained in collecting crime statistics and predicting patterns in criminal behavior, as well as coming up with deterrents. She was good . . . damned good.

Vee looked at him suddenly, as if sensing his attention on her.

She scowled. "What?"

When she snapped at him that way—which was fairly often—a little line formed between her eyebrows. But it was the way her lips pursed that really got to him. Didn't matter how often or why she got mad at him . . . he loved every minute of it.

Maybe his low-down daddy had been right—he wasn't too bright.

Bent banished thoughts of his father and lifted one shoulder in a purposely vague shrug. "Nothing." He knocked on the door again.

"You think I'm wrong." She crossed her arms over her chest and eyed him with a narrowed gaze. "I hope I am. It would be far better for Nolan and his family if that's the case."

"The thought never crossed my mind," he insisted, his attention fixed on the door, which he hoped would open now. Maybe he had resisted the idea at first, but deep down he had known she was onto something.

She made a disagreeable sound.

Lucky for Bent the door flew open just then. Elizabeth stood there, her eyes red and swollen from hours—no, days—of crying. Man, this was really going to suck.

Fear stole over her face. "Have you found him?" she asked, her voice trembling.

Bent figured she used the pronoun *him* instead of her son's name because it hurt less. Oh hell. Unless Nolan Baker was suddenly released in the next few hours with obscure drawings all over his body, this would not end well for anyone involved.

"No, ma'am. We have not, but we feel another look in his apartment is in order. If you're good with that."

She seemed to shake herself, as if she'd expected different news and wasn't quite sure how to process Bent's words. "Oh. Well . . . sure. Sure. I'll get the key."

Elizabeth disappeared into the house.

"Are you going to ask her, or am I?" Vee demanded quietly.

He glanced at her. "I'm thinking we should wait until we've had that look. It'll make things easier."

She made another of those ornery grunts. "Chickenshit."

His lips twitched with the need to smile despite present circumstances. The last time she'd called him that, she'd been seventeen years old and had dared him to kiss her. He hadn't wanted to—well, no, he had wanted to. But out of respect for her mama—no matter that she'd been dead for months by that time—he hadn't wanted to cross that line. Even at twenty-one he had known there would be no turning back. But Vee had lugged him right across it with her fearlessness. She had been the prettiest girl he'd ever seen. And the most intriguing.

"Some things require a little more patience and compassion," he suggested, dragging his head out of the past.

"Whatever."

What Vee wanted was to sound totally unaffected. This was an archenemy from her high school days. For her, watching Elizabeth Baker squirm would be undeniably cathartic to some degree. He got that. Vee was only human. Except he knew Vera Mae Boyett better than that. She might pretend to be as cold as ice at times like this, but she wasn't. It was the shield she held up to prevent anyone from ever thinking for one second that she was weak or soft.

This was the way she had learned to protect herself after one too many tragedies in her life. Everyone had their technique for healing . . . and sometimes just for hiding.

Elizabeth reappeared at the door with the key. "I'll wait here if that's all right."

Bent nodded. "Course. We'll come back to you when we're done."

"Thank you, Bent." More tears slid down Elizabeth's face.

Vee turned away first, and Bent followed. The sound of the door closing was a sharp reminder that no matter how this ended, the trouble was far from over. Either the Bakers would be clawing their way out of deep shit or something worse was right here waiting to be discovered. Maybe both.

They entered the garage through the side door. The second key on the ring Elizabeth had provided unlocked it.

"Has anything been found in his car?" Vee asked as they climbed the stairs to the second-floor apartment.

"Nothing relevant to the case." Bent pushed the key into the lock. "The man keeps his vehicle immaculate."

"Maybe Conover should check the windshield and mirrors for any sort of oily residue that may have been a message."

"Good idea." Bent sent the necessary text. This time of year, folks often started their cars well before leaving for work, and windows would sometimes fog up. Baker could very well have gotten a message in that way. But he'd told his friend he'd found it under his windshield wiper.

Vee walked into the apartment. "He keeps his apartment in perfect order as well. I imagine he never got dirty as a child. Never left toys on the floor. Boggie would have flipped out."

"Sounds about right," Bent agreed, closing the door. "Where would you like to begin?"

"The mirrors," Vee said. She walked to the bathroom, where there was the expected mirror over the sink as well as a full-length one on the opposite wall. She flipped on the light, then turned on the hot water in the shower and in the sink. "We can have another look around while we wait for the steam to fill the room."

Bent asked, "Any place in particular you want to look?"

"He might have a message in his email," she said as she closed the bathroom door, "but Conover has his laptop. He find anything?"

"Nothing."

"It's possible," she went on, "that it was someplace Nolan didn't notice, but that wouldn't fit the Messenger's MO. He wants his messages to be easily discovered. He always went to great lengths to ensure that happened."

"In that case," Bent allowed, "we can safely say Baker received nothing by email—assuming he didn't delete it and then empty his trash."

"Determining if he did that would take a much deeper dive." She surveyed the main room. "If we don't get anywhere with the mother, we could have Conover call someone with that particular skill set."

Bent grunted his agreement. "How did the Messenger begin once he'd made his selection?"

"He made it a point to know a person's routine." Vera wandered through Baker's main living area. "It was part of the excitement for him.

Learning everything about them. Then doing little things to make the victim wonder. Make her sweat." She glanced at Bent. "Check the refrigerator. If Nolan added creamer to his coffee each morning or had milk or whatever each night, we might find a message there. He may have noticed something and tucked it away to analyze later, then forgot it."

"So we need to look at anything he would have done daily."

"Basically."

The search was on, this time for a written message that may have been overlooked before because no one was looking for a short note written in some manner in an unexpected place.

Long minutes later, Bent was confident there was nothing to be found unless it was on the mirror in that bathroom. Conover had confirmed there was no oily or soapy residue on the windshield of Baker's car or on any of the car mirrors.

Vee opened the bathroom door and stepped inside. Bent did the same, closing the door behind him.

And there it was.

The message on the mirror above the sink was short and to the point.

See you soon.

Bent's gut tightened. He gave himself a moment by stepping over to the shower and turning off the water there and then at the sink. Vee stood as still as stone, staring at the words.

"We need to know," she said without taking her eyes off the mirror, "if anyone has been in this apartment—besides law enforcement—since Nolan went missing."

Bent braced for the answer he didn't want to hear. "You believe this message wasn't meant for Nolan."

"I can't be certain."

The brittleness in her tone told him otherwise.

"The primary problem is," she said in that same rigid tone, "the Messenger never took a male victim. Only females."

Bent nodded slowly. "You said something earlier about him doing little things to make the victim wonder."

She pulled her cell phone from her jeans pocket and snapped a photo. He should have done that already. Then she turned to him. "Like moving something a victim used every day to make her think she'd forgotten or that she was losing it. Changing the temperature setting on the thermostat while she slept. Taking a piece of mail out of the mailbox and putting it back on the table when it was meant to go out that day. Little things to make her wonder." She turned away from him so he could no longer see her eyes. "Like leaving footprints in the snow leading right up to your window. Or leaving a window up."

Son of a . . . "I'll check the windows just in case someone entered that way."

Vee nodded, still staring at the message as the letters started to run.

Bent checked the windows. None were unlocked or appeared to have been tampered with. There were two doors—the one accessed from the stairs in the garage and one in the bedroom that led out to a balcony overlooking the backyard. The locks showed no indication of having been tampered with. Conover had gone through the place thoroughly the morning after Nolan's disappearance. It was unlikely they had missed anything as blatant as an insecure or compromised lock on a window or door.

But the bastard got in somehow.

"Anything?" Vee asked as he joined her in the living room.

"All secure." Another thought nudged him. "Is it possible," he began, "since a month has passed and nothing really big has come of this Time Thief business . . ." The idea might seem a little far fetched, but at this point, he was just about ready to believe anything. "Maybe Baker did some digging into the Messenger case and decided to evolve this thing into . . . something bigger."

Vee considered the idea for long enough to have him second-guessing having even put it out there. Then she said, "It's possible, sure. But that would mean he did some serious digging and took some major risks. Peeking in my windows only hours after allegedly being abducted. Coming inside and leaving a message on my bathroom mirror." She shook her head. "That's a lot for a missing guy to get done alone—in the snow."

"When you lay it all out like that," Bent confessed, "it doesn't really work."

"You want it to work," she said, understanding him better than he understood himself. "I want it to work. Having Nolan Baker do something stupid like this is a lot easier to deal with than the alternative."

"No question." No more beating around the bush. "We should get this next part over with."

"The sooner the better," Vera agreed.

When they reached the door of the Baker home, Elizabeth was waiting. "Did you find anything?"

"We need to ask you a few questions," Bent said, bypassing her question.

"Come in." She moved away from the door and led the way to the living room. She settled on one end of the large sectional sofa and clasped her hands in her lap. "Sit wherever you like."

Bent waited until Vee sat down, and then he did the same.

"Maybe," Bent offered, "you should call Carl to join us."

Her face crumpled, and the howls of agony that emanated from the woman were gut wrenching. "No. No. No. He has to be all right. Please, please." She looked to Bent then, her face twisted in pain. "Please tell me you've found him and he's okay. Please, please, Bent . . . I can't bear it."

Bent shared a look with Vee.

"Elizabeth, we haven't found Nolan," Vee assured her. "We're not here to tell you anything like that."

A shudder rocked through Elizabeth, her whole form quaking with it. "You're not here to tell me he's . . . dead?"

"No, ma'am," Bent said. "We have questions for you . . . related to the Time Thief case. There are some inconsistencies we believe you can help us with."

She blinked. Once.

"Why don't I call Carl?" Vee suggested gently. "He should be here for you."

For a long moment Elizabeth stared, first at Vee, then at Bent, as if a new realization had dawned on her. Her jaw sagged, but no words came out. The tears had slowed, drying on her skin, leaving messy paths in her makeup.

"No," she finally said, her voice so low it was nearly inaudible. "I don't want him here for this."

Well hell. As nice as it was to be right about a conclusion, this wasn't the sort of situation that gave anyone pleasure. "All right then. But I need to advise you of your rights—"

"No." She shook her head adamantly, lifted a hand to stop him. "I waive my rights. An attorney can't help me, and he sure as hell can't help my son."

"Elizabeth," Vee urged, "you need to think about that for a moment, because anything you tell us can be used against you. You're emotional right now, you may not be thinking straight. We don't want you to regret this decision tomorrow or next week."

"It's too late for regrets," Elizabeth said, her lips quivering. She swiped at her cheeks with her fingers. "It was me. Carl had nothing to do with it. I watched the three I selected very carefully. I . . . I was extremely cautious about everything. The dosage of the drug. All of it." She turned her hands up. "I didn't want anyone hurt." She shook her head, drew in a ragged breath. "But I suppose I did choose the ones I did for a little payback. Is that what tipped you off?"

Rather than answer her question, Bent asked, "Was Nolan to be the fourth victim?"

She nodded. "I left him the message on his windshield. I was going to meet him that night at that old shack where Owens lives. I'd already set everything up. I would do exactly as I did the others so he wouldn't know it was me . . . but he never showed up." Her face pinched with agony. "I was certain Nolan had figured it out. Then, when he didn't come home, I thought he was angry at me. I was up walking the floors all night . . . until Chief Teller called." Her voice quavered. "I never intended to hurt anyone. I just wanted . . ."

"You wanted," Vee offered, "to give Nolan that big story he's been waiting for."

Elizabeth jerked her head up and down, her lips clamped together. "I had no idea I might be inviting some evil person to get involved."

"First," Bent said, "as far as what you've done goes, the good news is you didn't harm anyone—not really. But you need to understand that this is kidnapping, Elizabeth. This is a very serious situation. At least a second-degree felony. Then there's the false imprisonment."

"I don't care about that," she argued, her voice frantic. "All that matters is finding Nolan." Tears streamed down her face once more. "Someone had to be watching me . . . switched out my message. They took my son." Her cries again turned to agonized howls.

Bent looked again to Vee, who made a face at him. She should know how to handle this part better than him. Three seconds passed before she finally spoke up. "Elizabeth, we're doing all possible to find him. But we need your help if we're going to be successful. Can you pull yourself together and do that?"

Elizabeth swiped at her eyes, this time with her forearms—mascara and foundation smearing on the silk sleeves. "Yes. Yes. Of course. Whatever I can do. After what I've done, this is probably God's punishment." She fell apart again. "It's my fault. Oh God. It's my fault."

Bent grabbed the box of tissues from the coffee table and took it to her. "What we believe happened," he said gently, "likely was not because of anything you did."

"And you can rest assured that God," Vee tossed in, "had nothing to do with this." She waited until Bent was seated once more. "Unless you left another message besides the one on Nolan's windshield, we have reason to believe this has something to do with someone from my past."

Elizabeth stared at her, the tissue clamped between her fingers and tears still streaming down her cheeks. "What?" She shook her head as if to clear it. "I don't understand. What other message?"

"We don't know anything for certain just yet," Bent countered, hoping to head off what he suspected would be a meltdown.

"I'm not following." Elizabeth scrubbed at her cheeks with the deteriorating tissue. "You have some idea who took him?"

"We have another potential suspect," Bent explained carefully. "What we need from you is to know if anyone has gone into the apartment since we were here on Tuesday."

She slumped. "I . . . I'm . . . let me think . . ." She looked to Bent. "You and your people were here first. Wait, no. Chief Teller came first after that call from Joel. So he was first, but then he called you. So, I guess you and your people went into Nolan's . . ." Her lips trembled. "Nolan's apartment next." She moistened her lips and took a breath. "Then you and Vera. I don't think there was anyone else."

Bent nodded. It was possible the person who left the message on the mirror had picked the lock, but he had left no marks whatsoever. It took someone very skilled to manage that feat.

"Wait, no." Elizabeth's forehead wrinkled in thought. "There was someone here this morning. Carl mentioned it on his way out the door. He said someone from the sheriff's department had needed to get back in." She stared at the floor. "I slept in. Couldn't seem to drag myself out of bed. I hadn't slept at all the night before . . . the night he was taken." She shook her head. "Anyway, Carl gave the key to whoever it was—that's why I didn't remember."

"Why don't I call Carl?" Bent suggested. "We'll meet him at my office, and he can tell us about this other person."

Elizabeth pushed to her feet. "I'd like to call him. Prepare him for . . . the rest."

Bent stood, as did Vee. "All right. We'll wait at the front door. You let us know when you're ready to go."

Elizabeth left the room. Vee jerked her head in the direction Elizabeth had disappeared. "Should I keep an eye on her?"

The sound of her voice as she called her husband drifted toward them.

"As long as we can hear her, I think we're good."

Vee made a sour face. "You're really taking her in?"

"Do I have a choice?"

As badass as Vera Boyett wanted to pretend to be, she was not as merciless as she would have anyone believe. She felt sympathy for her old enemy.

"You should talk to the DA and see if she can be released on her own recognizance. At least until Nolan is found."

Bent bit back a smile. "You think that's a good idea?"

Vee threw up her hands. "It's not like she's going to leave all this."

He let the smile go then. "I think we can arrange something along those lines."

Elizabeth returned to the living room. She cleared her throat. "Carl is on his way here. He'd like to drive me, if that's all right." She looked from Bent to Vee and back. "Since this is a first for me, what happens next?"

"While you're giving your statement, Carl will work with Vera to try and nail down a description of this morning's visitor. We may be able to get a sketch artist, but that could take some time."

"When . . ." Elizabeth cleared her throat again. "When will I be arrested?"

"We'll work all that out at the office," Bent assured her.

For now, he needed to get the details of whoever had left that message. Because it sure as hell hadn't been for Nolan Baker.

That message was for Vee.

17

Boyett Farm
Good Hollow Road, Fayetteville, 8:30 p.m.

Vera paced the distance between the kitchen and the front door for about the hundredth time. As exhausted as she was, she had to keep moving. The DA had gone along with Bent's suggestion that Elizabeth Baker should be released on her own recognizance. Vera imagined there would be a favorable deal worked out eventually. No doubt one that included a big settlement for the victims to persuade them not to file charges. Vera wouldn't put it past her to talk the three into saying they had begged to be a part of the plot—like some sort of independent film production. An equally large donation to the sheriff's department to compensate for their wasted resources would likely keep the city officials happy as well.

A win-win situation.

Except they still didn't know where Nolan was. She supposed that alone was punishment enough.

Vera was too exhausted to work up any real irritation at the woman. A tiger never changed her stripes. To expect Elizabeth to stop doing all in her power to be the one on the pedestal for all to see and honor was like expecting the sun not to rise in the east. Still, Vera felt an enormous amount of sympathy for Nolan. The fact that his mother was a narcissist wasn't his fault, and yet he was the one paying the price. Then again, he wasn't exactly Mr. Nice Guy himself.

"Whatever." Life wasn't fair sometimes. Family was often the biggest pain in one's ass.

Except, *if*, as Vera feared, the Messenger was somehow involved in Nolan's disappearance, then this was on her, not the Bakers.

Sadly, it was growing difficult to ignore the possibility that the Messenger had someone here orchestrating his plan. Either a colleague who had worked with him on some level all those years ago, or someone he'd prompted recently to do his bidding. The question was, Why now? What had tripped his trigger? Set him on the path of a new evil scheme?

This was the part that prevented Vera from jumping fully to that conclusion. Why would the Messenger—Dr. Palmer Solomon—suddenly start meddling in her life now? Better than twelve years—nearly thirteen actually—was a very long time to wait for revenge. His circumstances had not changed. It wasn't like he was suddenly a free man and could do what he'd longed to do all this time. So why not do this last year, or ten years ago?

As much as she didn't want to pursue that line of thought unnecessarily, she also didn't want to ignore the possibility glaring right at her either.

Just as likely was the possibility that this was a copycat. Someone who had dug up enough details to lend authenticity to his work. No question that there were plenty of scumbags who held a grudge against her for ending their criminal careers.

Well, whoever it was, he had her full attention.

The memory of waking up to find those tracks in the snow and then, later, finding the open window and the message on her mirror nagged at her. Whoever was behind this had been in her house, and he'd wanted her to know it.

She thought of Nolan and the message on his mirror that was left just today.

That message was meant for Vera. She knew it. No point pretending.

If not the Messenger, who?

The endless list of creeps that knocked around in her head was mind boggling.

At this point, regardless of the perp's true identity, she had to prepare for the worst. Which meant her sisters weren't safe.

"Damn it." She pulled out her cell and called Luna. Jerome Andrews, her new husband, answered. The two had decided to get married back in January rather than wait until June. "Hey, Jerome, is Luna around?"

"Sure thing. Hold on."

Vera wasn't entirely convinced that Jerome liked her. His family didn't like any of the Boyett sisters, not even their new daughter-in-law. Vera didn't really care, other than she wanted her baby sister to be happy.

"Hey, Vee," Luna said, sounding breathless, "everything okay?"

Vera winced. Had she interrupted the newlyweds? "I'm not sure," she managed. "Is this a bad time?"

"No," Luna said, "we were just working out. You know Jerome is really focused on physical fitness."

For God's sake. The man was twentysomething. Tall, lean, and handsome. How much more fit did he need to be? "Sorry. I can call back later."

"Don't be silly. What's up?"

If she were talking to Eve, explaining her feelings and concerns would be easy. But this was Luna. Nothing was ever easy with Luna. Then again, Vera supposed she should just be thankful that Luna had forgiven her and Eve for burying her mother in that cave and then allowing her to believe for the next twenty-odd years that her mother had abandoned her. At the time, the only thing that mattered was that Sheree, Luna's mother, was dead—no fixing that, so why tear apart the rest of the family? Vera and Eve had thought their decision to hide her body would keep the situation from turning into something far worse. Luna had been nine months old—she wasn't going to remember her mother anyway.

Except they hadn't considered the future ramifications. They were kids. Luna had felt the sense of loss far more profoundly as she grew older, and that was squarely on Vera and Eve.

Their relationship with Luna had been tense for a while. Though it hadn't been easy, Vera and Eve had given her the time and space she needed. What else could they do? In fact, Vera was relatively certain the nightmare they'd kept secret from Luna was the reason she and Jerome had moved up the wedding date. Thankfully their baby sister had come around eventually.

"Look." Vera cleared her throat, forced away the painful memories. "Remember I told you about that window I found open and the tracks in the snow?" No need to mention the other unlocked window. Or the message left on the bathroom mirror.

"I do," Luna said slowly. "Is everything okay?"

"Well, unfortunately there's a possibility the intruder was a bad guy related to my time at MPD. He may also be responsible for Nolan Baker's abduction. We don't have any real evidence right now, so I'm not getting too worked up about it, but I want you to be careful. Keep your eyes open for any stranger who gets too close. Let me know if you receive any sort of odd message."

The next five or so seconds of silence told Vera that her sister was reaching for patience. Maybe even wondering what the hell else was being kept from her.

"Thank you for letting me know, Vee. I'll tell Jerome. Don't worry, we'll be vigilant."

"Good." Immensely relieved, Vera took a breath. "I'm sorry about this . . . thing. Occupational hazard."

"You stay safe, too, Vee. Love you. Good night."

"Love you too. Night."

Things still didn't feel exactly right with Luna. Not that Vera could blame her. She and Eve had brought this on themselves.

Next she called Eve.

"If this is about *him*, I can't talk right now."

"Hello to you too," Vera snapped. Eve and Luna were totally opposite. Really nothing alike at all, personality-wise. "And no, it's not about *him*." Norton Gates was just another issue hanging over their heads.

"What's going on?"

"Remember that serial killer, the Messenger?"

"Ye . . . ah." Her sister said the word as if it were two.

"There's a chance someone he's using or maybe someone who wants to be like him is the one who broke into the house. He may also be the one who took Nolan Baker."

"Are you fucking serious? I remember reading about that creep. I think he had a thing for you."

Vera closed out the voices that echoed Eve's words. There were those, including her former boss, who were convinced the Messenger had some sort of obsession with Vera. She later learned the FBI had believed so as well and had used the idea to their benefit.

"Anyway," Vera said, moving on. "You and Suri keep an eye out for strangers. Stay aware—the threat to anyone close to me may be real. Also, look for strange messages via email or left at your house or in your car. Basically anywhere."

"Got it." Eve hesitated. "Anything from Russ yet?"

"Not yet," Vera admitted. "If I don't hear back from her tomorrow, I'll go to her office. For now, don't worry about that problem. Just keep your eyes open." She'd meant to follow up with Russ today. Damn it.

"Okay. Did you talk to Luna?"

"Yeah. She promised to be careful."

"She sound okay to you?"

"Pretty much." Sort of.

"I'm not sure she's ever going to completely forgive us, Vee."

Vera laughed a humorless sound. "Do you blame her? I mean, we let her believe her mother had abandoned her for most of her life. We suck at being big sisters."

"It was Sheree's fault," Eve argued. "She did this to all of us."

Vera closed her eyes. "No, Eve. Daddy did this to us. Sheree just egged it on."

The woman had been young, only a few years older than Vera at the time. She'd glommed on to their father—made him forget all about his dead wife. She'd tricked him into marriage by getting pregnant, and then she'd taken everything she could get her hands on and continuously cheated. She'd ignored her baby, and on her last day of life, tried to drown the child in the bathtub. Still, no matter her horrific deeds, their father—God rest his soul—was the one who brought her into their lives.

"I guess you're right," Eve admitted. "Thanks for letting us know about this Messenger guy."

"Sure thing. I love you, Eve." Vera stamped her foot in frustration as emotions she didn't want to feel rose inside her.

"Love you. G'night."

The call ended, and Vera was left with those old feelings of loss and regret. They'd had the perfect life—the perfect family—then their mother had died, and everything had gone to hell. The only good thing to come out of that time was Luna, and somehow she and Eve had screwed that up.

Vera blinked the memories away. She had things to do here and now. There was no time for dwelling in the past and on things she could not change.

First, she was not going to hang around here waiting for something else to happen. She intended to start at the beginning and look for anything she may have missed now that she knew what she knew.

She tucked her cell phone into her pocket and grabbed a flashlight, then walked out the front door. She went straight up to the deputy that Bent had insisted keep watch over her tonight. The deputy powered the window down as she approached his cruiser. His name tag read *Olson*.

"Deputy Olson," she said, "FYI, I'm going down to the barn to have a look around."

"I'll follow you, ma'am."

"Suit yourself."

She headed through the yard and around the house. She wanted to take the same route the person who'd left those tracks in the snow had taken. The tracks, she suspected, had been left on purpose. He wanted her to know he'd been here. If she didn't know better, she'd swear he had ordered that damned rare snowstorm.

But even the worst of the worst were only human.

Behind her the deputy's footfalls echoed in the darkness. He'd pulled out a flashlight of his own and was lighting his path. Smart man. Vera's mother had lots of flower beds and bird fountains and other yard ornaments around. If a person didn't know the path, he could easily end up tripping in the dark.

The trail to the barn took a few minutes and went right past the potting shed and well house. Vera decided to check both before continuing to the barn. She wished she'd worn her coat. It was colder than she'd realized. Probably because she'd been far too pissed off when she came home to really notice the temperature. The idea that Elizabeth had manufactured this Time Thief business to boost her son's career was just over the top. But it would all work out just fine in the end. Nothing ever kept a Baker down.

Then again, Vera supposed she couldn't say much, considering she was keeping her sister's secret about Norton Gates. At least Elizabeth hadn't murdered anyone. *Probably,* Vera amended.

The well house was empty, save for the usual stuff—rakes, hoes, et cetera. Most of those yard implements had been in there for decades. No one had really done any gardening around here after her mother died. Maybe she would give it a try this spring.

Entering her mother's potting shed was like walking into a tomb. No one besides her or Eve ever came in here. Every single thing inside was far too precious . . . held too many painful memories.

Vera cast the flashlight's beam around, as she had in the well house, until she was satisfied that nothing had been disturbed.

Then on to the barn. She shivered. Damn. She wished again that she had worn her coat. Her cell vibrated, and she dug for it. Probably Bent, or maybe Eve or Luna.

Eric.

Surprise shot through her, putting Vera on alert. "Eric, hello."

"Vera." He made a sound, something like a sigh. "You were going to call me back."

Damn, she'd promised to call him back with any updates when they'd talked this morning. She'd forgotten. "We found a second message." Her shoulders sagged. "It's the same MO as the Messenger, but like you said . . . he's in prison."

All those other thoughts and possibilities she'd been going over and over would have to wait. She was not up to all that tonight.

A moment of silence. Well damn. Now he was disappointed in her.

"We both know," he said finally, "prisoners reach out from behind bars all the time. The questions are, Does he intend to do more than attempt to rattle you, and Why now?"

His words set her off. Had fury rising inside her like smoke billowing from a raging fire. She hadn't wanted to talk about this, but now she had no choice. "If this is his doing, the only thing he did was piss me off."

Dr. Palmer Solomon was an arrogant bastard, rightly enough. She wouldn't be surprised at anything he did. In her opinion, the timing was the big mystery here.

"I'll talk to the warden. Get some sense of who visits him—if anyone. And I'll look into the possibility of him getting messages out."

"I appreciate that, Eric." She forced herself to calm down as she paused at the front of the barn, roved the beam of light over it. "I should go. It's been a long day."

"Understood. Just wanted to make sure you were okay."

"Thanks. You're a good friend."

"Always."

The call ended, and Vera shook off the old feelings of regret that always came when she interacted with Eric. Before she had the phone back in her pocket, it vibrated again.

"What now?" She shouldn't have asked . . . *Remington*. "Hello, Mr. Remington." Vera glanced back at the deputy waiting a few yards away, squinted at the beam from his flashlight.

"Ms. Boyett, please tell me you have news about Nolan. I'm barely holding on to my sanity here."

Vera tucked the flashlight under her arm and reached for the barn doors. "Well, we don't have anything new on his whereabouts, but we're hoping to have more soon."

No way was she talking to him about the person they suspected had taken Nolan. She'd leave that up to Bent's discretion. At some point there would have to be a press conference. As for what Elizabeth had done, Nolan could tell his boyfriend about that—assuming he lived through this nightmare. Then again, if the story leaked to the media, he would hear about it.

Not dealing with that tonight.

Vera walked through the doors, grabbed the light from under her arm, and shined the beam around the space.

"Just please call me as soon as you know anything at all," Remington pleaded.

"I will. You have . . ." Vera's light hit something pale. She moved the beam over that space again.

Flesh . . . human. Naked backside of a body. Dark hair.

Adrenaline charged through her. "Mr. Remington, I'll have to call you back." She ended the call, shoved the phone into her back pocket. "Deputy!"

Olson moved up next to her. "Holy shit," he muttered.

"We need an ambulance, right now."

Vera turned on the interior lights and rushed to the body on the ground.

Nolan Baker.

Fuck. Please don't let him be dead . . .

She touched his shoulder. He groaned. *Thank God.*

Hope fired through her. She didn't dare move him until she had a firmer handle on his condition. She crawled around to the other side to see his face and the front of his body. His chest shuddered with an intake of breath.

"There you go. Keep breathing, Nolan," she murmured.

There was a lot of blood. She grimaced. What she needed was to get a better look at the injuries and see if she could stop the bleeding.

God only knew how long he'd been out here. Could have been hours.

His eyes suddenly flew open, and he screamed.

Vera toppled onto her butt.

Nolan flopped onto his back and screamed bloody murder.

Vera scrambled closer once more. "Nolan, it's Vera Boyett. We have an ambulance on the way. You're going to be all right."

His hands went up in a defensive move as he squirmed and thrashed in pain.

"You'll be okay," Vera urged.

Then he flipped onto his belly. His continued writhing had his skin parting . . . blood and dirt from the barn floor moving on his skin. A gasp echoed in the air . . . *her* gasp. She watched, her heart pounding, as his movements parted the bloody, dirty lines where his naked flesh had been carved. Words formed . . .

I'm coming for you.

The bastard had left a message in Nolan's skin. Just like with Gloria Anderson . . . just like with all the others.

Vera gritted her teeth and pushed aside the feelings that tried to swarm her brain. *Focus on the victim.* This moment . . . this part couldn't be about analyzing the words. She did what she had to do. As much as she didn't want to spoil any evidence, she was well versed in this bastard's MO. The Messenger never left evidence. His minion or a copycat would likely attempt the same. She stroked Nolan's head gently and took his hand with her free one and held it to her chest as tightly as she dared.

"You're safe now, Nolan. We'll get you to a hospital. Your parents will be there."

His wailing stopped, and he started to sob.

The anger that welled inside her had her struggling for breath.

She would get this son of a bitch. One way or another.

18

Lincoln Medical Center
Medical Center Boulevard, Fayetteville, 10:50 p.m.

The throng of reporters outside the ER had not diminished. Lincoln County deputies, with the help of Fayetteville's finest, were keeping them out of the hospital.

Vera could see the parking lot from the small conference room where she and the Bakers had been sequestered. Bent had gone back with Nolan more than an hour ago. What the hell was taking so long? Surely he had been stabilized and questioned by now.

Deep breath, Vee. These things take time.

Nolan's parents were seated at the long table, and another deputy was stationed right outside the door. The glare Elizabeth kept on Vera prevented her from being able to sit. Instead, she paced, occasionally pausing at the window to peek through the slats of the blinds.

This was her fault. She got that. But it wasn't like she had asked for any of this. It would be nice to have a normal life, but that was apparently not in the cards.

Then again, what was normal?

Besides, Elizabeth Baker had no right to judge anyone. Damn it. She had organized no fewer than three kidnappings. Held people hostage—drugged them. Set up all sorts of evidence to suggest poor drug-addicted Fisher Owens was the perpetrator. She'd even admitted to finding Nolan's phone on her own front porch the night he disappeared—obviously left there by the person who'd actually abducted Nolan to make sure she understood someone else was in charge of her little game now. Elizabeth had hidden it along with the other evidence in that metal shed at Owens's place just to make it look as if the victims had all been held there. What worried mother took the time to hide her son's phone that way when he was missing? The woman was a psychopath if Vera had ever seen one.

She tightened her arms around her chest and turned in the other direction to pace some more. Dropping her arms to her sides was not an option with Nolan's blood staining the front of her sweatshirt. Better to keep it covered as best she could.

She had sent a text to Liam Remington to let him know Nolan had been found and was undergoing a medical evaluation of his condition, which she believed was relatively good, under the circumstances. Liam had headed this way immediately. Then she'd called Eric and updated him about Baker and the new message left to her on the poor guy's back. Eric was going to brief all the folks in Memphis who needed to hear the news before the media blitz that was no doubt coming. She'd warned Bent that MPD would likely be contacting him.

"Vera."

Startled, she turned to the man who'd spoken.

Carl Baker, one arm around his wife, peered up at her. "You should sit down. You must be exhausted."

Elizabeth pointed a glare at her that said she did not feel the same way as her husband. Maybe that was the reason Vera decided to take him up on the offer and collapse in the nearest chair already pulled away from the table. Getting off her feet had her body aching with relief. She was exhausted. Disgusted too.

"We," Carl said, sitting a little straighter in his chair, "appreciate all you did to help Nolan. Todd Wiley, one of the paramedics, told us how you were comforting him when they arrived." He looked away a moment as his emotions visibly got the better of him. "It means a lot."

Elizabeth pulled away from his hold, her glare still intent on Vera. "But she's the reason this happened," she snarled. "That monster came here and took our son because of her."

"Liz," Carl murmured, "don't do this. Our son is alive. We need to be thankful."

"Alive?" She aimed her fierce glare on him now. "Yes, but look at what was done to him. He may never recover mentally. My God, PTSD can devastate your life." Her head moved side to side. "His career may be over. He will be heartbroken."

"I'm just glad he's alive." Carl looked away from her.

Vera decided it would be in her best interest to keep her mouth shut. You couldn't win in a situation like this one. People saw what they wanted to see. Changing their minds was rarely possible. And when it involved a child—even a grown one—things could get ugly fast.

"You have nothing to say?" Elizabeth demanded.

Then again, sometimes the choice was taken from you.

Vera met her furious gaze. "You want an apology?" The emotions she'd ignored for the past two hours shook her hard. "Yes, I am very sorry this happened to Nolan. I would never have wished this nightmare on my worst enemy." She pressed her lips together to prevent a tremor from showing. "Happy now?"

"No." Elizabeth's face pinched with mounting rage. "You've brought nothing but pain to this community since you came back. Your family is rotten to the core. Look at those people who were buried on your farm! What kind of person helps hide a body when they're barely seventeen years old? You and your sister are just evil."

Sister. She'd left Luna out, which was only fair. Vera lifted her chin but kept her lips pressed tightly together. What could she say? The woman had her there.

Elizabeth stood, leaned over the table, and braced her palms against its smooth surface. "They should run you and Eve out of this town."

Carl attempted to usher her back into her chair. "Liz, please."

She jerked away from him. "Look at what the two of you did to poor Luna."

Vera flinched. She was well aware of what they had done to Luna, and no one regretted it more than her. But to argue with this woman would be a waste of time.

Elizabeth straightened to her full height, pointed a finger at Vera. "This is your fault. You're the reason my son was almost killed."

"That's enough."

Vera's head snapped toward the door. *Bent.*

Thank God.

He closed the door behind him, his presence suddenly flattening the escalating tension in the room. "Nolan is doing well. The doctors say he'll make a full recovery. The damage was almost entirely superficial." This he directed at Carl and Vera. Then he turned to Elizabeth. "I understand this is difficult, but you need to be careful how you proceed from here."

Elizabeth shot him a dismissive look. "I'm aware of your relationship with Vera. I'm not surprised you would take her side."

Vera almost laughed out loud. Where was the terrified mother who had begged Vera to find her son? Oh well, once a bitch, always a bitch.

"Under the circumstances," Bent said, his tone about as far from friendly or understanding as it could go, "I would advise you to bear in mind that any public displays similar to this one would not be in your best interest."

Elizabeth laughed long and loud.

Carl winced. "Liz."

"You expect," Elizabeth went on, "me to keep quiet about this? Absolutely not. I intend to see that everyone in the whole town knows." She sent a poisonous look at Vera. "I want them to run her out on a rail."

"It's a free country." Bent placed his hat on the table and pulled out a chair. "But bear in mind that if the DA opts to proceed with charges against you—and that is the most likely path—the people in this town are your jury pool. I'd be on my best behavior if I were you. The grateful, humble mother persona is a far more sympathetic one. No one likes a haughty defendant."

Elizabeth turned away then. "I need coffee."

Carl rocketed to his feet. "I could use a shot of caffeine myself." He ushered her from the room.

Vera sagged with relief. She turned to Bent. "Can I talk to Nolan now?"

He searched her gaze, sympathy in his. "Sorry about leaving you in here with her for so long." His expression shifted to doubt. "Talking to Nolan is not a good idea, Vee."

She figured he would say that. "For the record, I don't need your sympathy; I need the facts. At least give me a replay of all he said."

"It's not a lot," he warned. "The only message he received was the one tucked under his windshield wiper—the one that replaced his mother's."

According to Elizabeth, her note had instructed Nolan to meet her at the shack where Fisher Owens lived, but he'd never showed. She'd had no idea—even after finding his phone—until the next morning that somehow her latest move in the Time Thief game had gone awry. She'd assumed that Nolan had figured out what she was doing and wanted her to worry.

"He was drugged the entire time," Bent was saying. "He heard a voice now and again, but he doesn't remember much about it except that it sounded male. He has no idea where he was kept or how he got there, much less how he arrived at your barn."

Wait just a minute. Vera sat up straight, mentally reviewing all that Bent had just said. "The Messenger relished interaction with his victims. The fear he induced. Their cries. The agony. He wouldn't get any pleasure from keeping one drugged and compliant." She shook her head. "This is wrong." But the messages—the one on her mirror and on Nolan's mirror and body—were right. "Are you sure he was telling you the truth? Maybe he was told not to talk about his experience and he's afraid to do otherwise. He could still be suffering some level of shock."

"That's possible." Bent studied her a moment, probably noting the fear she did not want him to see. "But I didn't get the impression he was hiding anything. I'll talk to him again in the morning. Possibly when he's rested and full of pain meds, he'll be more forthcoming—assuming he's holding back."

"Thank you." She tried to feel satisfied with his plan. What was another eight or so hours?

It was a lifetime. Her tension started to build again. This was wrong. Completely wrong. "Did you see any other indications of torture?"

Bent shook his head. "The only injuries were the words carved onto his back. The doctor confirmed what we talked about at the scene—the knife work was almost all shallow. Deep enough to ensure plenty of bleeding and that the message was visible, but not enough so to cause serious injury."

"This is way, way off, Bent. Whatever this person is up to, he knows about the messages, but this is *not* the person who killed all those people in Memphis." Someone had started a game—one quite possibly being manipulated from prison by Palmer Solomon. Copycats often interacted with their idols. Son of a bitch!

As obvious as the concept was . . . she couldn't be certain of anything. Jesus Christ, she did not need this sudden uncertainty. Not right now, damn it. *Think! Focus!*

"The messages were talked about in depth in the media." She said this as much for herself as for Bent. "But not the one carved on Gloria Anderson's back. We never released anything about it, and Gloria refused to talk about what happened to her with the media." Vera shrugged. "I suppose she could have confided in someone who eventually told someone else. Or maybe someone on the hospital staff or one of the cops assigned to the investigation—there were plenty who knew the details who might have spilled. But I never heard about it. There was nothing about it in any story that's been done, and there have been several."

And there was Eric... those details had not been released either.

"So we don't know with any measure of certainty what we're dealing with here," Bent said, voicing her primary concern. Worry deepened the lines around his eyes.

"That would be my conclusion." And yet it made no sense. "The only thing, based on what we know so far, that makes any measure of sense is the idea that Solomon set this all up from his prison cell. He's suddenly decided he wants to torment me."

"There's no chance he was working with a partner before you stopped him?"

Vera couldn't deny having wondered about the possibility during the original investigation. "There was never any evidence. I considered the idea at one point, but then he was caught, so I let it go." She shook her head. "Now, all these years later I think it's safe to assume he didn't. Most of the time serial killers don't just stop killing, unless they've been stopped the way Solomon was or they're dead."

Bent nodded his understanding. "All right then. Let me take you home. I've arranged for my truck to be brought around to the back. We can get out of here without all the fanfare."

"The sooner the better." She needed a long hot shower and sleep.

Vera had a terrible feeling that this nightmare had just begun.

As they walked away from the conference room, she spotted Liam Remington. "That's Nolan's boyfriend," she explained to Bent.

He gave her a nod and went to the younger man. They spoke briefly, then Bent rejoined Vera. "Let's go."

"What did you tell him?" She watched Remington head to the bank of elevators.

"I gave him Baker's room number. He's to tell the deputy to call me for confirmation that he's allowed to see his friend for a few minutes."

"Thank you." Vera breathed a sigh of relief. Even Nolan Baker deserved to have the people he cared about close at a time like this.

Boyett Farm
Good Hollow Road, Fayetteville, 11:55 p.m.

There was a white van parked at the road when they reached Vera's house. A reporter who'd figured out the best way to get to her was to wait for her at home.

God, she hated reporters sometimes.

"Stay put. I'll take care of this," Bent said, getting out.

Vera was only too happy to let him play the part of hero right now. She twisted in the seat and watched as he approached the driver's side of the van. He stood there for a half minute, then turned and walked away. The lights on the van came to life, and the vehicle rolled away.

"Good." Vera reached for the door and got out. She was on the porch before she realized she didn't have her bag. She'd left it in the house when she'd gone to the barn. "Damn it." Then she stalled, stared at her door. She hadn't locked the house . . . she'd been too frustrated and too angry.

"Don't worry," Bent said, coming up beside her. "I had Olson come back and keep an eye on the place." He knocked, and a few seconds later the door opened.

Deputy Olson looked from Vera to the sheriff. "All clear in here."

"Good. You can go home now," Bent told him. "I've got Price coming to take over for the night."

"Yes, sir." Olson nodded to Vera. "Night, ma'am."

When the door had closed, she said, "I didn't see his cruiser."

"I had him park it down by the barn so the house would look empty. I figured if our perp wanted in your house, he might give it a shot while we were at the hospital."

"That was a good idea. Interesting that he didn't bother. I guess he had nothing else to say to me at the moment."

"Guess so," Bent agreed.

"Who was in the white van?" Vera was almost too exhausted to care.

"An old friend of yours."

Vera felt her brow furrow. "Who?"

"Patricia Patton."

She should have expected her to show up. Just another too-familiar element of this new nightmare.

"Thanks again for putting Boggie in her place." Vera was fading fast. She really needed to get in the shower before she lost the ability to stay vertical.

"I'll check in with you in the morning. See what we know then."

"Thanks, Bent."

He hesitated. "I can stay, you know. If you'd be more comfortable."

She smiled. "I appreciate the offer, but I need sleep." What she really needed was time to think.

"Night then."

"Night."

He left. Vera closed the door and locked it. Then she dragged herself upstairs. One of these days she was going to shock the man by saying yes.

But just look how that turned out last time.

19

Friday, March 7
Lincoln Medical Center
Medical Center Boulevard, Fayetteville, 6:30 a.m.

Vera parked around back of the hospital, in view of the maintenance entrance. When she spotted an opportunity, she entered with a member of the maintenance crew. She didn't know him, but he recognized her from stories in the *Elk Valley Times*. He thought the work she did with various police departments around the area was very cool. Sometimes the media and a reporter could be your friend—unlike the one she had come here to visit.

As she reached Nolan Baker's room, the deputy on duty smiled. "Morning, Ms. Boyett."

She tried her best to always be nice and friendly to the deputies. Those in uniform were an important resource. Particularly to someone who relied on assumptions as much as she did. Like the maintenance man, this deputy had seen her around the department enough to believe she was one of them. He obviously realized she was consulting on this case.

"Good morning, Deputy Houser." She smiled brightly. "How's our patient this morning?"

"Last time I checked, he was still sleeping like a baby."

"Has the doctor been in yet?" Not likely, but it was the right question to ask.

"No, ma'am. A nurse checked his vitals at about five, and no one's been in since."

"Thanks." Vera eased the door open and stepped into the room without hesitation—just like it was her job this morning. Deputy Houser wouldn't think twice about it. She closed the door behind her and stood for a moment watching Nolan sleep.

Bent had warned all deputies with this particular assignment that no one outside the department—not even Nolan's parents—was to be in the room with him alone. Whatever was done and said, Bent wanted to know it.

Vera had never appreciated the man's prudence more. It would be just like Elizabeth Baker to try telling Nolan what to say and do going forward. The woman made helicopter mothers look like negligent free rangers.

She walked the short distance across the room, the only sound the monitors tracking Nolan's vitals. His face was pale, his dark hair tousled. He lay on his side, probably in deference to the injuries on his back. The IV running to his left arm likely provided the fluids, antibiotics, and pain meds he needed.

No matter that Nolan could be a real shit, she felt bad for him. No one should be subjected to this sort of nightmare. But he was alive, which was far more than could be said for all but one of the Messenger's other victims. Vera still tried on some level to rationalize the idea that this couldn't be the serial killer's work, but deep inside she understood that he had likely orchestrated it step by step, which ultimately made it his work and unquestionably made Nolan's survival a near miracle. He was enough like his mother that he would probably turn the whole affair into an award-winning story.

When she drew closer to his bed, his eyes fluttered open. He visibly tensed. "Why are *you* here?"

Strike her previous assessment. He was exactly like his mother.

"You're aware I work with the sheriff's department and Fayetteville PD. I'm here to follow up on your interview with Sheriff Benton."

His gaze narrowed. "I already told him everything."

Last night Vera had spent a lot of time thinking about Nolan's answers to Bent's questions. He was lying. Had to be. It was the only possibility, given the events leading up to his discovery in her barn. Who else would want to leave her that particular message carved on the man's damned back? It had to be the Messenger's minion, and if that was so, then Nolan was not telling the whole story.

She figured she had his number.

"You think holding back is going to build the momentum for your big story." Vera smiled. "All you're going to do if you persist with this version of events is piss him off. He left you alive so you could tell me something." Vera braced her forearms on the bed rail. "So do it."

"He left you a message on my back." Pain and fear or something on that order flashed in his eyes. He blinked it away. "I don't know what else you're talking about." He closed his eyes. "Now leave me alone. I'm tired."

"The Messenger gets off on watching his victims' pain, so either this was not the Messenger's commissioned work or you're lying." No response. "Torture is his thing. There's no way you were unconscious all that time with him."

Nolan said nothing. Time to stoop to his level. "Fine. I can go outside this hospital right now and tell all those reporters what I believe happened and steal your glory, or you can tell me, and I'll keep it to myself. The choice is yours."

His eyes opened, and his jaw clenched. He glared at her for a few seconds. "All he talked about was you." He drew in an uneven breath. "The last few hours he said plenty. He said you took something from him, and he was going to make sure you paid for it."

Vera's pulse rate fired into high speed. "Did you see his face at any time?"

He squeezed his eyes shut once more. "No. He wore, like, this . . ." He touched his face. "A mask. Like one of those characters in a horror movie. A hockey mask, I think."

The Messenger had worn a mask. Made sense his surrogate would do the same. Vera committed the detail to memory and moved on.

"Did he wear gloves? Long sleeves? Did you see any exposed part of his body?" Vera took a breath. She needed to slow down. Otherwise, she'd spook Baker. She was damned well spooked herself. But she needed the whole story.

"He wore gloves. Long sleeves . . ." Nolan frowned. "Like a sweatshirt. I didn't see anything other than the mask and the sweatshirt."

Vera moistened her lips, struggled to calm her frantic heart. "What did his voice sound like?"

"Deep. Smooth." Nolan's gaze locked with hers. "He sounded intelligent. Well educated. He didn't use any contractions or slang terms—very proper grammar. His tone was condescending." He shuddered. "Like I was completely irrelevant beyond his plan for me."

Gloria Anderson had talked about the way he made her feel worthless. Irrelevant. It was his way . . . Vera knew firsthand.

"Thank you, Nolan. Noticing those sorts of details is really important to an investigation." Vera gave him a moment to relish the compliment. "Did he tell you anything else? Anything at all."

He searched her eyes, his own showing a building agitation. "You swear you won't tell anyone else."

"I swear I won't tell anyone else unless what you're about to say will protect another potential victim." That was as close as she could come to giving him what he wanted.

"He said all he wanted was you. He wouldn't hurt anyone else. Just you. He said delivering this message to you was the only reason I was going to live."

Tension tightened in her throat. Just like Gloria Anderson. He'd given her basically the same message to pass along. "Why didn't he want you to tell Sheriff Benton or anyone else?"

"He said they would put you in protective custody and then he couldn't get to you."

Made sense. "So you did as he said and didn't tell the sheriff those details."

Nolan nodded. "Exactly like he said."

Wow. Nice to know her life was so low on this guy's priority scale. "What would you get in return for keeping his secret?"

"An exclusive," Nolan whispered. "Once he had you, he would do an interview without the mask."

And this chump believed him. Jesus Christ. This was why Nolan Baker hadn't been tortured the way the others had been and was still alive. Not because the Messenger's minion—whoever the guy was—had any intention of going easy on him, but because he intended to lure him back in for the kill. That had to be providing a whole new level of excitement and anticipation. The torture and eventual kill could wait for the big finale—double the pleasure.

"Okay." Vera produced a smile, no matter that she wanted to bop Nolan upside the head. "I'll be ready for him."

Concern stole across the little shit's face.

"Don't worry," she assured him, "not to prevent you from getting your story. I'll make sure you get that. I just want to survive to tell it."

He blinked. "Sure. Of course."

Bent would be pissed she'd kept this from him, but it was the only way to avoid having a dozen deputies swarming her at all times. She needed the opportunity to draw out this bastard.

Nolan moistened his lips, glanced at the table next to his bed. "Do you mind giving me a drink of water?"

Vera forced a smile. "Yes, I do mind."

She walked out of the room, nodded to the deputy, and then headed out the same way she'd come in.

No sooner had she settled into her SUV than another vehicle rounded the corner of the building. The hearse from Barrett's Funeral Home. Curious, Vera watched until the long black Cadillac funeral coach was parked. The driver wouldn't have seen her SUV, since the maintenance truck sat next to her. The driver's side door of the hearse opened, and a figure emerged. Black scrubs. Short, spiky blond hair.

Eve.

Damn it. Vera got out of her SUV and headed in her sister's direction. As soon as she was close enough, she hissed, "Eve!"

Eve whirled to face her. "Hey." She glanced around. "What are you doing here, Vee?"

Vera waited until she was toe to toe with her. "I suspect I'm here for the same thing you are."

Eve shrugged. "Doubtful. I'm here for a pickup."

Vera's gaze narrowed. "Since when did you start doing pickups again? I thought they hired someone for that."

Eyes rolling, Eve heaved a disgusted breath. "Fine. I hoped while I was here, I could talk to Nolan. Do you blame me?"

Not really, but Vera was not going there. "That would be a huge mistake. We have no idea what he knows about Gates. If you question him, that's only going to confirm whatever he suspects. You cannot do that."

Eve's eyes narrowed. "Did you talk to him?"

"About his abduction, yes," Vera growled under her breath. "But he never mentioned Gates, and neither did I. He needs to believe we have nothing to fear about that investigation. That we know nothing, got it?"

"Fine." Her sister's shoulders slumped. "Have you heard from Russ yet?"

"No, but I will today, or I'll be paying her a visit. I already told you this." Then again, that was yesterday.

"Keep me posted, will you? This is driving me nuts."

Obviously.

"I will," Vera assured her. "I just need you not to do anything until we know more."

Eve nodded. "I'll see you later, then." She turned back to the hearse.

Vera frowned. "I thought you had a pickup."

"That was just my cover story in case I ran into Bent."

Vera shook her head as her sister walked away. "Hey," she called after Eve.

She turned, her expression expectant.

"Remember to watch out for trouble. I don't want anything happening to you."

"Yeah, yeah." Eve waved her off and got back into the vehicle.

Vera watched her drive away. She wasn't sure who was worse, her or Eve. The two of them had learned early on that sometimes lies and subterfuge were necessary to survival. But lying to each other was downright dangerous.

Elizabeth Baker's hateful words echoed in her head. Maybe she and Eve were a little bit evil. Vera headed back to her SUV. She preferred to view it as cautious. The Boyett sisters, at least the two older ones, had learned the hard way that the truth did not always make things better.

Vera had just settled behind the steering wheel when her phone vibrated. She glanced at the screen. *Bent.*

Oh hell. She hoped he hadn't spoken to Houser already and learned about her visit. If she was really lucky, the deputy wouldn't mention it and Bent wouldn't ask.

"Good morning," she announced in the most chipper tone she could summon.

"I didn't wake you, did I?"

Good, he didn't know she'd left the house yet, which meant that he hadn't checked in with the deputy he had watching her house or the one watching Nolan Baker. A pang of guilt stabbed at her chest for allowing Bent to believe she wouldn't go behind his back like this. Then she remembered that he had just up and left her after stealing her heart all those years ago, and the guilt vanished.

"No. No. I'm up." Truth was, no matter what happened in the past, she hated lying to Bent. Technically, she hadn't lied yet. Just hadn't mentioned where she was or what she was doing.

"Can you be at my office at eight? I know it's short notice, but I just got word that Memphis PD wants a conference call, and they'd like you to be here for it. They're not wasting any time."

Cold sliced through her. Vera had warned Eric last night about this new development. She had expected MPD to contact Bent, just not so quickly. Interacting with the folks likely to be on the call wasn't exactly a treat for her. But there was no avoiding it.

She shook off the dread. "Sure, I can be there. And don't be surprised at their tactics. Big-city cops—especially the higher-ups—cut their teeth on legalistic-style policing, and jurisdiction is everything."

"Thanks, Vee. I'll see you then."

The call ended.

She glanced at the time on her phone. She had just over half an hour before the call. If she was going to be talking to anyone who'd been on the task force thirteen years ago, she would need real fortification.

Vera left the hospital and drove straight to the Dunkin'.

20

Lincoln County Sheriff's Department
Thornton Taylor Parkway, Fayetteville, 7:50 a.m.

Balancing her large coffee and the box of goodies she'd picked up on the way, Vera paused long enough to leave an individually wrapped donut on Myra's desk. Then she walked into Bent's office and offered him one of the three remaining in the little box.

"I made a stop on the way." She'd inhaled two donuts in the car, but she wasn't about to admit as much.

He accepted one of the two glazed confections in the box. Good. Chocolate covered was her favorite, and there was only one left. She snagged it and placed the container on his small conference table. She intended to float through the coming conference on a solid wave of high-octane sugar and caffeine.

She settled into a chair. "Who called to make this appointment?"

"Chief William Talbert."

Will. Her former boss. Thirteen years ago he had been lead from the Memphis PD on the Messenger task force. "He knows the Messenger better than anyone."

After Dr. Palmer Solomon had been brought in, Will sat in on all the interrogations. The monster's confession had prevented his one surviving victim from having to testify in court. Gloria Anderson had been incredibly relieved. It was the one good thing the bastard had done.

Vera polished off her third donut, then licked chocolate from her fingers. Even now, all these years later, she wondered what had prompted the Messenger to leave Anderson alive. It was almost like he'd wanted to be caught that last time. The concept wasn't impossible. Killers sometimes wished to be freed from their need to keep killing. But it was rare. Or maybe the idea was just another way Vera unconsciously justified her finding him. Certainly, it hadn't been her experience or skill at tracking down serial killers. She'd been a newbie. The one thing she would never, ever tell anyone is that she felt a sort of connection to the man.

Dr. Palmer Solomon had liked her, Will had insisted. He'd been drawn to her youth and inexperience. Vera had no idea. All that mattered was that he appeared to have invited or lured her to the place where he'd been keeping Anderson. He practically surrendered to her after he finished playing with her and torturing Eric. She forced the memory away. At the time she'd been so wired up . . . so charged with adrenaline, that capturing him—whatever the reason—was all that mattered . . . and Eric had paid the price. This was the part Bent still didn't know. If he fully understood just how close she had come to Solomon, he would have her in lockdown right now. That shared nightmare was part of the bond she and Eric had forged. Part of what had kept them friends long after the romance was over.

Still, when it was done, Solomon had confessed. It was as if he'd wanted one last playtime—with two cops no less. His statement had been brief and to the point. He had killed ten people. Names, dates, and locations were provided, along with enough pertinent details to convince all involved. And it was over.

Not a single event had been attributed to the Messenger since his incarceration.

Until now . . .

Bent had set his half-eaten donut aside and now focused on his coffee and watching her lick her fingers. Vera cleared her throat and grabbed a napkin. Thank God he had no idea she'd had two donuts besides the one he'd just watched her scarf down. She felt like a real hog.

"Deputy Houser said you stopped by to talk to Nolan this morning." Well hell.

"I couldn't help myself," she admitted. "I hoped after a night's sleep he might remember something useful—like you said."

Those blue eyes that Vera knew all too well studied her. "Did he?"

"Same story as last night." Liar, liar, pants on fire. "Have you talked to him?" she asked, turning the tables on him.

"I did. Like you said, his story hadn't changed." His gaze narrowed. "But I did get this feeling—"

Myra appeared at the door. "Sheriff, that call you've been expecting is on line one."

Saved by the bell, Vera mused.

"Thanks, Myra. Close the door, please."

Bent waited until the door shut before he tapped the necessary button to take the call, then set it on speaker. The phone was just an extension of the one on his desk. No fancy conference system.

"Sheriff Benton here. I have Vera Boyett in the office with me." He glanced at her.

Maybe it was her guilty conscience, but she could swear she saw disappointment in his eyes. Damn it. The things she did might not always be the right things, but they were nearly always necessary. He should know that by now.

"Good morning, Sheriff Benton. *Vera.*"

Will's voice echoed in the room, setting her on edge. She and her former boss had been close. They'd shared an almost father-daughter relationship. She'd trusted him, respected him. But things were different now. This thing happening in Fayetteville had nothing to do with Memphis PD or her former boss. This, she had every reason to believe, was about her. The more outside interference, the more complicated the situation would become.

In her opinion, ultimately this was likely about revenge of some sort. Getting even. Though she had no idea why as to the timing, she understood with utter certainty that her conclusion was correct on some level and whatever the Messenger's plan, it was going down. Now. Here, in Fayetteville.

Still, there was that other little detail that prevented his actions from making any sort of sense—that niggling idea that he had wanted her to catch him all those years ago. So why the encore now? If he'd wanted to be caught, why seek revenge? Maybe this was just a copycat who had a connection with Solomon, and the bastard's old urges had him happy to advise a protégé on how to have the most fun.

"Morning, Will. Thank you for finding time to touch base with us. I know how busy your schedule is," Vera said. Always be the diplomat. It was the first rule of negotiations, and this would no doubt be a negotiation. MPD wanted something. Quite possibly to ensure their reputation was not further tarnished by Vera Boyett.

"I have Special Agent in Charge Xavier Alcott with me."

The agent from the Bureau who served as lead on the Messenger task force. No surprise, she supposed.

"Morning, Sheriff Benton, Vera," he said. "I wish we were catching up under better circumstances. Resurrecting an old case is never an ideal situation."

"Certainly not," Vera agreed. She looked to Bent, who watched her intently. "Sheriff Benton will bring the two of you up to speed on what's been happening here."

His eyes still steady on her, he began with "I'm not sure we're resurrecting anything. It's possible your case was never quite dead."

Vera bit back a smile. She felt confident the two top dogs in Memphis weren't exactly overjoyed by the comment. Although there had never been any evidence the Messenger worked with a partner, it was certainly remotely possible. Just because the murders had stopped after Solomon's arrest didn't completely rule out the possibility. It did, however, make the idea far less likely—as she'd told Bent. But she understood. He wanted to put it out there. Even if the idea of a surrogate was by far the most likely scenario, no need to overlook a single other option just to avoid ruffling feathers.

Besides, this was Bent's jurisdiction . . . his case—the top cops in Memphis needed to understand he was no easygoing good old boy.

From there Bent walked the two through the details of the past twenty-four or so hours. Vera found herself enthralled with the sound of his voice . . . the stillness of him, but most importantly by the weight of his gaze on her. It was more like he was talking only to her; the words were for the others while the context was solely for her.

He would do whatever was necessary to protect the citizens of his county and the apparent target of this perpetrator. He wanted her to trust him . . . to let him take care of her. Vera managed to pull herself away from the trance he wove around her. Stared beyond the window, anywhere but at him. She hadn't allowed anyone that level of power over her since she was seventeen. It had only ever been him.

"Based on what you've told us," Will said when Bent had finished speaking, drawing Vera back to the conversation, "I'm confident what you have is a copycat. Wouldn't you agree, given what we all know about the Messenger case, that conclusion is far more likely?"

"No." Bent glanced toward the window beyond his desk, maybe to look for whatever Vera had stared at for so long. "I've done my homework, Chief, and I'm confident"—his gaze shifted back to her—"that based on what we've seen so far, the Messenger is either orchestrating this or he's here. We can't ignore the possibility—however remote it might be—that you got only half of a team twelve years ago."

Vera's heart stumbled. It felt as if Bent had reached deep inside her and pulled out her deepest, darkest fear. She'd never dared to allow the idea to form fully in her mind. Not when all the evidence had seemed to suggest otherwise.

He waited then . . . they all did . . . to hear her reaction.

Rather than leave Bent hanging, she said, "Although there was no evidence of an accomplice or partner of any sort involved, it is a possibility that, in light of current circumstances, we need to consider. The lack of activity on the part of an accomplice would certainly suggest that one did not exist. There is also the idea that without Solomon to lead him, he went dormant. But maybe something has awakened those urges and brought him out of hibernation. We simply can't risk ignoring the possibility."

Five seconds of silence warned them that the two men on the other end of the call weren't completely surprised by her and Bent's conclusions.

"Otherwise," she went on, "we need to find out why and how Solomon has reached out to prompt a surrogate to do his bidding. Frankly, it's the timing that raises the most questions for the sheriff and me."

Another extended moment of silence.

"I have spoken with the warden at the prison," Agent Alcott said finally, "and I've interviewed Solomon, without discussing our suspicions about what's happening in Fayetteville. He has had no new visitors—no visitors at all, really. His son stopped coming to see him recently. Solomon has received no letters other than the usual from the kind of fans these types get. Frankly, we have no reason to believe he's orchestrating anything from his prison cell. As for having an accomplice when he was active, it doesn't fit the profile. As you know, all involved firmly concluded that was not a possibility."

Vera got the message loud and clear. They were not prepared to go there. "You're confident this is nothing more than a copycat."

Sure made life a lot easier for MPD.

"Yes," Will hastened to confirm. "What we've heard so far has all the earmarks of a copycat."

Bent said nothing; instead, he waited for Vera to say what was on her mind.

"Sheriff Benton"—she paused to see if he wanted to speak instead; when he made no effort to stop her, she went on—"and I will proceed under the assumption that we're dealing with the Messenger's accomplice or surrogate, and we would appreciate any assistance the two of you can provide from there."

"Is that your plan, Sheriff?" Will countered.

Vera silently steamed at the question. The man was her former boss. They had worked together for thirteen years. That he would question her analysis this way was infuriating.

"Vera is the expert in this case," Bent said, his eyes still steady on her. "Whatever she says goes."

"Very well," Will agreed, though he didn't sound agreeable. "We will send a liaison to keep the communication open between our office and yours."

"If you feel that's necessary," Bent said with loads of "don't bother" indifference. "But I think we've got it under control in terms of manpower."

God, she really appreciated him backing her up. Almost made her feel guilty for not being completely honest with him this morning about Nolan. *Almost.*

"Eric Jones will be there by the end of the day."

Her former boss's announcement sent a shock wave through Vera.

"We appreciate your keeping us informed, Sheriff Benton," Will went on, "and we believe you'll find Eric a true asset."

This would not work!

"Will," Vera argued, purposely using her former boss's nickname, "it's not necessary to send Eric here. He and I can coordinate on the phone. I'm aware just how busy he is. No need to interrupt his work."

"We," her former boss challenged, "do feel it's necessary."

Bent held up a hand for her benefit. "Send him. As long as he doesn't step on any toes, we're good."

Vera pretty much zoned out for the rest of the call. She considered Eric a good friend, and he would unquestionably be an asset. But . . . to have him here with Bent. It just felt wrong.

"Vee."

She snapped from her distracting thoughts. She hadn't realized the call had ended. "I'm sorry, I was thinking about . . . the case."

"Who is Eric Jones?"

This felt really, really wrong.

"He's an analyst." To call him a mere analyst seemed offensive. "He started out in forensics, but his ability to find information no one else could garnered him the attention of the top brass, and they moved him into more of an intelligence position. He has a knack for finding things. It's uncanny. Anyway, we worked together closely at times. There's no denying he could be useful to our investigation." She might as well get past the awkward feeling. "In fact, I would say we can fully trust his allegiance to our investigation. Eric does not play politics."

There, she'd gotten it all out . . . except the part about the two of them having a thing.

Bent nodded slowly. "Sounds as if you know him well."

She smiled, ordered the strange arrhythmia in her chest to settle. "I know him well, yes."

A flash of something darkened Bent's eyes, but it was gone too quickly for Vera to analyze it.

"You trust him."

"I do."

"Good."

Vera's cell vibrated, making her jump. She'd left it tucked in her back pocket. She dragged it out, checked the screen. *Teresa Russ.* "I have to take this."

Saved by the bell twice already this morning. How lucky was she?

Then again, depending on what Russ had to say, she might not be lucky at all.

She tapped Accept Call and said "One moment" to her caller. Vera grabbed her coat and bag. "Talk to you later," she said to Bent.

"Noon," he said as she backed toward the door. "Here." He pointed to his desk. "We need to review all we have so far before your friend arrives."

"I'll be here," she promised.

Vera rushed out the door and through Myra's office before pressing the phone back to her ear. "Sorry about that. I was in a meeting."

"I understand. No problem." A sigh whispered over the line. "Honestly, Vera, I feel like we should do this in person."

Vera agreed, no matter that the other woman's statement put her further on edge. "You're right. We should. Are you available now?"

With Bent's demand that she be back in his office at noon, she didn't have a lot of wiggle room. Unless, of course, she put the meeting with Russ off until later this afternoon, and she did not want to wait any longer than necessary. This was one thing she needed to get done ASAP.

"I can be available in about an hour. Does that work for you?"

"Sure. Your office?" That meant a drive to Huntsville. So not what she wanted to do this morning. Not with all that was going on here.

"How about I meet you in Hazel Green at ten? That's a lot closer for you, and I'm in a meeting close by, so it works for me."

Much better. "Name the place."

"There's a coffee shop, Jackie's, right on the highway just past the Taco Bell. They always have the best donuts."

Vera grimaced. The idea of another donut made her stomach roil. "See you there."

She hurried to her SUV and climbed in. Guilt had her waiting until she was out of the parking lot—thus not staring at Bent's office—before calling Eve.

"Make it fast," her sister griped, "I'm working."

Vera imagined her hunkered over a corpse—*excuse me, a visitor.* "Russ called. I'm meeting her at ten."

"How did she sound?" Eve lowered her voice, as if she feared the corpse was listening.

Vera shook her head. "She sounded like she always sounds."

"So you couldn't tell if she knows or suspects something."

She shouldn't do this, but Eve was getting on her last nerve. "She did say that she felt we should talk in person."

The silence that followed warned that Vera had made a mistake.

"This is good," she hurried to add. "If we talk in person, there's no record. We can come to an agreement."

"'Kay. Let me know what she says as soon as you're done talking."

"I will." Her sister was really worried. Damn it. "Don't worry, Eve. We've got this."

"I know. Talk to you later."

Vera tossed her phone onto the passenger seat. What was one more lie this morning? On top of that, Eric was coming. *Today.*

Why did it all have to happen at once?

21

Jackie's Coffee Shack
US Route 231/431, Hazel Green, 10:00 a.m.

Teresa Russ waited at a table as far away from the entrance of the little coffee shop as could be gotten. Russ was an attractive woman, sixty, blond, and trim. Vera waved to her before going to the counter for a bottle of water.

Between the sugar and caffeine she'd already consumed, she was literally vibrating. She figured the additional adrenaline charge still rushing through her veins from Russ's call wasn't helping either.

Vera thanked the barista, grabbed her bottle, and headed for the table.

"I appreciate," Vera said as she settled into a chair, "you meeting me."

"No problem." Teresa took a breath. The vibrant blue sweater she wore highlighted the lighter blue of her eyes. "I suppose we should get straight to the point."

Vera twisted the top from her water bottle. "Never helps anyone to beat around the bush," she agreed. *Especially if the bush is on fire.*

"Norton Gates." Russ stared at the latte in her stoneware mug. "How he wound up in that cave just kept haunting me."

The bastard had haunted far too many people even before he was murdered.

"Meaning," Vera prompted, her stomach twisted into one big, writhing knot.

"I couldn't get right with the idea that someone might be wondering what had happened to Gates. Obviously he was someone's son, perhaps a brother or father or husband."

Vera wanted to feel sympathy, but she just couldn't work it up, so she said nothing, waited for Russ to continue.

"I started digging."

Those three words unsettled Vera inordinately.

"Of course, he had been all those things—except for the father part," Russ went on. "His parents had passed away, and his wife had divorced him years before he disappeared. The ex-wife basically made it clear that she hated him and was glad he was dead." Russ shook her head. "He had no real friends that I could find. No colleagues who appeared to care one way or the other."

A new kind of anticipation started to build inside Vera. Still, she kept her mouth shut and let the other woman talk.

"What I did find," the savvy PI said then, "was more than a dozen women who had been abused by Norton Gates."

Vera's heart bumped hard against her sternum. "Really?"

Anyone who actually looked would have found the same thing. The trouble was, for all those years that the bastard took advantage of his position as a professor at a respected college, no one wanted to talk about it. Either the victims refused to go to the authorities, or those who threatened to do so were scared off with a warning of dire consequences. Typical bullshit assholes like Gates had gotten away with it all through history.

"He used his position," Russ went on, "to prod sexual favors from his students. If the college had known, he would have been fired immediately. But no one ever dared to tell. Not even the two colleagues I believe, based on my interviews with them, suspected his predilection."

Happened all the time. It was disgusting and despicable. "That's terrible," Vera commented. "Just terrible."

Russ waited, as if she expected Vera to say more, but she knew better. *Never say more than necessary* was her motto. It was sure to come back and bite you in the ass.

"But one student fought back."

Vera went completely still inside. Her thought processes, even the need to breathe, seemed to pause.

"I think you know her," Russ said with a pointed look at Vera. "Suri Khatri. She lives in Fayetteville. She's a mortician, like your sister Eve. In fact, they're friends."

Vera said nothing. Russ already knew. No point confirming.

"Like the others," Russ said, her fingers turning the half-empty mug, "Suri had let the incidents with Gates go. She had gotten through the two required classes he taught for her certification and moved on." Her head angled toward her shoulder as her gaze connected fully with Vera's. "But then he found her again. You see, the last few years of his life, he'd come face to face with the MeToo movement. Women were no longer allowing him to pressure them into sex. I suppose that's why he jumped at the opportunity to go after Suri again. He had her pegged as an easy mark."

Vera forced down a sip of water. "Sounds like your story has a happy ending."

"I spoke to Suri this morning. That was the meeting I mentioned."

Apprehension wound its way through Vera. Obviously Eve did not know about this.

"I had tried to talk to her several times, but she avoided me. This time she didn't. We met at the funeral home where she works, and she told me everything."

The silence went on for five or so seconds.

"Which was?" Vera prompted. She certainly wasn't going to offer any scenarios, least of all the one she knew to be the truth.

"Suri told me that she killed Gates when he showed up at her house and tried to rape her."

Holy shit. Vera blinked . . . kept her lips pressed tightly together.

"She also told me about how Eve, your sister, kindly offered to help her hide his body in that cave."

The urge to scrub at her forehead, where her brain was vibrating... or to lick her dry lips . . . or shift around in her chair was a building, pulsating need. But Vera held perfectly still. She stared directly at the other woman and manufactured a surprised expression. "Wow, that's some story."

"Don't worry," Russ said, bracing her forearms on the table and leaning closer. "I'm not telling you this because I'm planning to go to the police or somehow use this information to my advantage or the advantage of my business."

Intrigued now, Vera imitated her move, leaning closer, her arms braced on the table. "Then why are you telling me this story?"

"Because I want you to understand that I get it. Norton Gates was a piece of shit who got exactly what he deserved. Sadly"—she shook her head—"not as soon as he should have. In my opinion, Suri is a hero who did what needed to be done."

Okay. Vera was on the same page so far.

"The problem is," Russ said, "Nolan Baker."

Of course it was Nolan Fucking Baker. Vera inwardly cringed. "You talked to him?"

"No." Russ shot a look heavenward. "And I will not. As soon as I did some digging around, I realized he was likely not going after this story for the women Norton Gates victimized but for himself. The problem you and I have is, sadly, he's not going to stop."

Tell me something I don't know.

"Yeah, that's Nolan." Vera suspected he already knew way too much about the Boyett sisters.

"I'm sure you realize," Russ went on, "the best way to see that this ends the right way is to get ahead of it and direct the narrative."

Vera stilled again. She knew exactly where this was going, and as right as Russ was, this was bad for Eve. "You're suggesting a confession."

Russ nodded, her face somber. "Suri is a victim. What she did was self-defense. If she goes to the police, I'm guessing—since I know the DAs in both Madison County, Alabama, and in Lincoln County, Tennessee—that she will likely not be charged with anything. No one wants to try a case like this and risk losing support in the court of public opinion. This," she reiterated, "will protect Suri and anyone else involved from the likes of Nolan Baker."

Except Suri didn't kill Gates.

"It's a risk for her," Vera argued.

"There's always risk in a situation like this," Russ agreed. "But it's the best scenario if she wants to be able to move on with her life without that cloud hanging over her head."

"Maybe." Vera wasn't saying anything that could be used to prompt Suri to do one thing or the other.

"It's out of our hands anyway." Russ leaned back in her chair. "Suri made a decision to confess today."

Son of a . . .

"She told you this," Vera demanded.

Russ nodded. "Just before you arrived, she sent me a text and said she was at the sheriff's office. If I were you, I would leave right now and be there for her."

A knowing look passed between them.

"Thank you for the update." Vera stood. "Nice seeing you again."

Vera forced herself to walk out the door and climb into her SUV. She waited until she was driving away from the coffee shop before calling Eve. The call went straight to voicemail.

"Damn it."

At the next traffic light, Vera googled the number for Barrett's and put through the call. She had to talk to her sister before she did something based on emotion.

As soon as the call was answered, Vera plowed right over the greeting. "I need to speak with Eve Boyett. It's an emergency."

A beat of silence, then, "Vera?"

"Yes, this is her sister. Please, can you get the phone to her? I know she doesn't like to be disturbed, but this is an emergency."

"Well, I would, but she's not here. About fifteen minutes ago she rushed out of here like the place was on fire."

Oh hell.

"Thanks anyway. I guess she already heard." Vera ended the call and put through another to her sister's cell.

No answer.

She stamped down harder on the accelerator. She had to get to Bent's office.

Why was it that trouble always came in pairs?

For once she would love to be able to handle one problem at a time.

"Christ." She felt sick.

On top of that, Eric was coming.

"What else?" she groaned. Then she snapped her mouth shut.

As her mother would say, it was never smart to tempt fate.

22

Lincoln County Sheriff's Department
Thornton Taylor Parkway, Fayetteville, 10:45 a.m.

Bent probably should have been recording this conversation. He also really should have had Myra in here as a witness.

But he'd done neither of those things, and now there was no going back.

"Suri." He laid down the pen he'd been using to take notes and settled his gaze on the agitated woman seated in front of his desk. "Let's take a minute, okay?"

She nodded. Her long red hair was tied back in a ponytail. Her face looked pale. Suri had always been a little thing. Petite. Bent had known her brother. He'd worked at the supermarket on the corner of Lincoln Avenue and College Street all through high school. Nice kid, never in trouble. He'd grown up and moved to Huntsville and started his own chain of convenience stores. Suri had stayed in the little house she'd inherited from their grandmother and gone to work at the funeral home.

He couldn't see her doing what she'd just confessed to in damned vivid detail.

"Sheriff," she said, her voice firm despite the way her lips trembled, "I'm telling the truth. I'm sorry it has taken me so long to come forward, and I'm even sorrier I didn't tell you the truth when you found his remains." She exhaled a big breath. "I was afraid I'd lose everything." She shrugged. "I don't want to go to jail. It isn't fair. I was only protecting myself."

This was one part of the job he didn't care for. Suri Khatri was a victim, not a killer. To have her go through what this confession could very well entail twisted his gut. To make matters worse, she had ignored his every warning about her rights. She'd refused to call for an attorney. She'd just forged ahead with her story, whether he wanted to hear it or not. She was determined—he'd give her that.

"How about we take a break, and then we'll go through your story once more, make sure we didn't miss anything." He needed to talk this over with the DA before he made any assurances.

Shouting outside his office door drew his attention. "Give me a minute." He stood and walked to the door. As soon as he opened it, he saw the trouble. Myra was attempting to prevent Eve from coming into his office.

"Bent," Eve shouted, "I have a right to be in there."

"Sheriff," Myra said, clearly flustered, "I tried to tell her she needed to wait."

"It's all right." He gave Myra a nod. Keeping Eve out would be like trying to prevent a bull from charging once the matador waved his cape. He stepped to the side. "Come on in, Eve."

Eve rushed to Suri, who was now standing. They hugged fiercely. Bent closed the door and rounded his desk. He said nothing, just sat down and waited for the two to decide what they wanted to do next. The tears had started, and that knot in his gut tightened a little more.

All he needed now was Vee, and the party could really get started.

What the hell were the Boyett sisters thinking? They had to have known about this. No matter that Suri had insisted she'd taken Gates to that cave and put him there all by herself—that was impossible. Gates had been a grown-ass man, and Suri likely didn't weigh a hundred pounds soaking wet. It was possible, he supposed, that her brother had helped her, but Bent's money was on Eve. Vee had been in Memphis, so she hadn't likely been involved. But he knew as sure as he was sitting here that she had been brought up to speed about it once those remains were discovered.

"Don't do this," Suri warned.

Eve pulled away from her and looked to Bent. "Suri didn't kill Gates. I did."

Holy hell. "How about the two of you sit down, and you," he said to Eve, "start from the beginning?" Might as well hear both sides of the story—not that he expected either one to be the whole truth.

The two sat, Suri sulking and Eve leaning forward, looking determined.

"You have the right . . . ," Bent said.

Eve waved both hands in the air. "I know my rights, and I waive whatever I have to waive. I do not want an attorney."

"Vee won't like it," he warned.

"Do you want my confession or not?" Eve snapped.

Bent held up his hands. "By all means, proceed."

Suri dropped her face into her hands and started to sob in earnest.

Bent got up and went to the door. "Myra, can you take Ms. Khatri to the lounge for . . . a few minutes?"

"Sure thing, Sheriff."

Myra hustled into the room and ushered Suri up and out in no time flat. Myra knew how to deal with emotional visitors. Bent was immensely grateful she had stayed when the former sheriff retired.

He closed the door yet again. "All right then, where were we?"

"I don't know all that Suri told you," Eve began as Bent settled behind his desk once more, "but if she told the whole story, then you know I was there when Gates showed up and attacked her."

"She told me about Gates and the things that happened when she was his student. She explained that she didn't report it out of fear of being failed in his class—which was required for her certification."

Eve nodded adamantly. "The man was a piece of shit."

"Tell me about when he came back into her life."

"We were out shopping one day and ran into him, and, I don't know"—Eve shrugged—"it like tripped some forgotten obsession, so he started showing up around here. Watching her. It felt like he was following her. Then he came to her house and tried . . ."

"I got that part," Bent assured her, when she couldn't seem to find the right words. "What did *you* do when this happened?"

"It was Saturday, and I'd spent the night. He didn't know I was in the house, so when I heard what was going on, I ran in there. I grabbed the first thing I saw—a cast-iron skillet—and I hit him with it. Then I—"

"Let me stop you right there, Eve." Bent held up both hands once more to shut her up. According to Suri, she had wrenched free of him and grabbed the cast-iron skillet and done the deed as he tried to grab her again. At least the two women agreed on the murder weapon.

Eve blinked twice. "But why? I'm trying to tell you the truth."

"Because"—he lowered his hands and took a breath—"Suri is the victim. The DA will look at this from an entirely different perspective if Suri is the one who killed him. It won't be quite the same for you." At her look of frustration, he urged, "I'm not trying to tell you what to say or what to do about this. What I am suggesting is that the two of you find your story and stick with it. I appreciate that you want to protect each other, but be aware of the consequences either way you go. Because once the statements are official, it's damned hard to go back."

Just when he had thought his day couldn't go any farther downhill, this situation walked into his office. He would be more than happy to get the Gates case off his plate, but this was not exactly how he'd expected it to play out. He'd learned not long after the remains were identified that Suri had been a student of Gates's, and he'd suspected that one or both of the older Boyett sisters knew the whole story of how he'd ended up in that cave. But he'd figured, when he had no choice but to get around to it, he would have to dig that truth out bit by bit from one or the other. He sure as hell hadn't expected a confession from not one but two sources.

One thing he could count on in this job: there was no end to the unexpected.

The door opened, and Suri was back. She'd pulled herself together—for the moment anyway. She sat down next to Eve.

"Why don't I give the two of you a minute to figure out how we're going to proceed?" He got up and walked out, closed the door.

Myra raised her eyebrows at him. "I know," he said.

This was more than a little unorthodox.

Bent checked his cell. Reviewed the latest text messages he'd received. Nothing new. In just a few hours this *Eric* guy would arrive. He wondered again about the relationship between him and Vee. Jealousy spiked inside him, and he kicked it aside. He had no right to be jealous of her in any shape, form, or fashion.

"Sheriff?"

He turned to find Suri waiting in the door of his office. She looked like a little girl who'd been sent to the principal's office.

"We're ready to talk calmly now."

"All right." He sent another look at Myra.

"You've got this, Sheriff," his assistant whispered.

He chuckled. "Maybe." He went back into his office and closed the door. When he'd resumed his seat, he gestured for whichever one wanted to start to do so.

"It was me," Suri said. "I couldn't go through that again. He'd tormented me for too long already. I'm ready to make an official statement."

"I want to give a witness statement," Eve echoed.

"I'll have Myra come in to assist with any questions you have. You'll each handwrite your statements, and Myra will witness the documents, and I'll enter them into the case file and contact the DA to see how we're going to move forward."

Both nodded their understanding. Bent exited the room once more and explained the situation to his assistant, though he figured she'd already heard most of the details. The conversations hadn't exactly been quiet, and the walls in this place were thin.

"I'll take care of it." Myra gathered what she needed and disappeared into his office.

Bent collapsed into one of the chairs facing Myra's desk. This had been one hell of a long day, and it wasn't even half over yet.

The door from the corridor swung open, and Vee burst in.

He'd wondered when she would show up. "Hey, Vee."

"Where are they?" she demanded, anger or fear—maybe a little of both—in her voice.

"They're writing their statements."

She dropped into the chair next to him. "Well damn."

He turned to her. "I assume you knew about this?"

She blinked. "Knew about what?"

"Give it a rest, Vee." He chuckled, rubbed at his eyes. "Both Eve and Suri have confessed to killing Gates." The look of horror on her face had him wishing he'd couched the news a little better. "I've advised them on the consequences either way they go. With that in mind, they've decided Suri is the one who will confess, and Eve will back up her statement as a witness since she was there."

Relief slumped Vee's shoulders.

He almost hated to ask the question burning in his brain, but he'd never be able to survive the day without at least inquiring. "Seriously, did you know about this?"

She considered the question at length. Damn, how long did it take to say yes or no?

"I think I would be wise to take the Fifth on that one."

He laughed, a dry sound. "I think I'd probably do the same."

Vee sank deeper into the chair. "She's a victim, Bent. She shouldn't have to go through a trial."

"I'm with you," he confirmed. "I really don't think that will happen. It's a clear-cut case of self-defense. According to Suri, that PI—Teresa Russ—has a whole list of other women he abused. Going through all that would be a major waste of resources. It doesn't hurt that our new DA is a woman. I think Suri and Eve will be okay."

"Good." Vee relaxed visibly. "This has been a hell of a day," she said, echoing his earlier thought.

"And it's far from over," he noted. "Heard from your friend who's headed this way?"

Vee didn't look at him, just held up her phone to display a text message. "Eric says he'll be here by four."

Eric. Bent hated that the man's name got under his skin, but he couldn't restrain the reaction.

"Great." If this *Eric* helped find and neutralize this new threat to Vee and the citizens of Lincoln County, Bent could overlook the idea that Vee had obviously been involved at some point with the guy. Sure. Yeah. He could do that.

"Anything new with Nolan?" she asked. "I'm assuming forensics has come up empty handed. The Messenger never left evidence—ever."

"Conover checked in an hour ago. He got zilch. I visited Baker again, and he's sticking with his story that he remembers nothing new. His mama was there. Maybe he didn't want to talk in front of her."

"Are you still having the guard stay close whenever his parents visit?"

"I think we're past that now. We have his statement. Any change he tries to make would seem suspicious." He turned his head to stare directly at her. "What about you? Anything new you need to share?"

"No." She shook her head. "I've told you everything."

"Good." He let it go at that, no matter that he doubted she was being completely honest with him.

Not that he could blame her. He was just one of the many bad things that had happened to Vee before she left Fayetteville. He had made a mistake, but she had paid the bigger price.

When they were kids, he'd selfishly allowed her to fall for him. There were things she needed, like to go to college, and he certainly couldn't help make that happen. Hell, he couldn't have given her anything. He'd had nothing to offer except himself, and at the time, that wasn't so much. But more recently, he had no excuse, and he'd still made a mistake. She had been back in Fayetteville for seven months, and he hadn't made the first move. He wanted a relationship with her beyond work. Beyond just being friends. Because she wasn't the only one who'd fallen all those years ago.

Obviously he was a coward. That was his only excuse. The grown-up Vee was way out of his league. But if he was going to try . . .

She was about to turn forty, and he was forty-four. What the hell was he waiting for?

"If it's okay," she said, "I'll hang around to talk to Eve and Suri. Then I'll get out of your way."

"You are never in my way, Vee."

She smiled. "I'm sure that is not true."

"After you've spoken to Eve and Suri, why don't we go to lunch? We could both use the break, and I'd really like to keep you close until this business with the Messenger or his minion is behind us."

She studied him for a moment. The request had sounded reasonable. The Messenger or whoever was behind these threats was targeting Vee. Made sense to keep a close eye on her. This was a viable threat directly against her.

"Sounds good." She relaxed into her seat once more. "I'm sure I'll be busy with Eric after he gets here."

He'd walked right into that one.

As long as Vee stayed safe, he could deal with a few days of having her ex around.

Protecting her from the Messenger was all that mattered right now.

23

Lincoln County Sheriff's Office
Thornton Taylor Parkway, Fayetteville, 4:10 p.m.

Vera had intended to be on time for the meeting, but that hadn't happened—at least that's what she told herself. Instead, she'd spent two hours with Deputy Conover going over the scene at the old hospital where Nolan had been taken and then at his apartment. It was ridiculous actually. She had known there was nothing to find, but the effort helped distract her. She'd been doing a lot of that lately. There was no easily or readily identifiable reason why . . . just a need.

In the end, she and Conover had arrived at the same conclusion—the one she had known they would reach. The perp at the hospital, as well as the one who had entered both Nolan Baker's apartment and Vera's home, hadn't left fingerprints or any damned thing else. The ones Conover found on the old hospital's windows—the ones where the blinds had been removed and then reinstalled—had belonged to a local who'd spent the night in the place on a dare months ago.

Conover wasn't happy about not finding anything at any of the three scenes, but Vera had reminded him that no one, not Memphis PD or the FBI, had found a single shred of evidence at ten crime scenes during the Messenger's decade of activity. The bastard had been far too careful. Some said there were no perfect crimes, only imperfect investigations. Others insisted that in cases like the Messenger's, given time, a perp—no matter how smart or how careful—was bound to make a mistake.

But not the Messenger. Not until Gloria Anderson. And Vera was convinced that misstep had not been a mistake.

Maybe that was the part that had always bothered her. She'd been a brand-new detective with only a few cases under her belt, and certainly none as complex as the Messenger case. She had followed the case closely from a distance. The whole city had. Even after ten years, the police were no closer to finding the serial killer than when they had started.

Victim eleven, Gloria Anderson, disappeared, and that long-standing record changed. Suddenly there was a variation in his MO. Or maybe Vera's unexpected involvement had caused the mistake . . . the misstep.

Or maybe there had been another perp—an associate or protégé—and he got ahead of himself and caused the misstep. Without evidence, it was an unprovable scenario. It also wasn't nearly as likely as the idea that Solomon was orchestrating this current situation from his prison cell.

She entered the long corridor that would take her to Bent's office. Eight, no, ten minutes past four o'clock.

Bent would not appreciate her lack of punctuality.

Outside the door with **Lincoln County Sheriff** displayed across the front, Vera paused to draw in a deep breath. She squared her shoulders and walked inside.

Myra looked up over her reading glasses. "They're waiting for you."

Vera flashed her a fake smile. "Thanks."

She opened the door and entered the office. Both men stood. Bent from behind his desk and Eric from one of the chairs on this side.

"Vera." Eric stepped toward her and gave her a hug.

"Eric." She drew back, smiled. "Good to see you."

The sparkle in his eyes reminded her of all the times she'd returned from training in some other city and Eric would be waiting. He looked great, as always. Navy designer suit, matching shirt and tie. He could be a model from the cover of a popular magazine or the hottest new media influencer. With Eric everything was always perfect. Flawless mahogany skin and the darkest chocolate eyes. An enviable wardrobe by anyone's standards, draped on a very handsome man. More important than all the rest, a kind heart and a fiercely intelligent brain.

Vera felt utterly underdressed and wholly ill prepared. Eric likely wondered how she'd gone downhill so far in only seven months.

"Why don't we sit," Bent suggested, "and get started?" His gaze held Vera's a moment before shifting back to Eric.

"I apologize for being late." Vera settled into a chair. "I've been running behind all day. I hope the two of you started without me."

Actually she was glad she'd been late. Kept her away from that initial awkward meeting between these two. Bent knew little about Eric, but he must suspect there was more to the story. Eric, on the other hand, knew all about Bent. Vera had spilled her guts about her first love to the man who could have been her second love if she'd opened herself that far. Instead, he'd been more of a best friend—as well as a respected colleague.

"We've only chatted briefly," Eric said. "Sheriff Benton wanted to wait for you."

Vera looked to Bent. "Shall we get started, then?"

Bent began with "Nolan Baker, a local reporter, disappeared about seventy-two hours ago. We first believed he'd been taken by a repeat perpetrator we've referred to as the Time Thief, but that turned out not to be the case."

Vera hoped Bent wouldn't go into the story about Elizabeth. The woman was the epitome of a small-town rich woman of privilege who wanted all the attention on her family. So not worth the discussion.

Bent looked to Vera then, as if he'd read her mind.

"We first became aware," she began, "there might be someone affiliated with the Messenger involved in Baker's disappearance when he left a message for me."

Bent leaned forward and spread the crime scene photos from her house across his desk. It wasn't until that moment that Vera realized her nightshirt and panties lay on the floor between the shower and the toilet in the corner of one photo. The creep of red up her neck was like a flame licking a path. If she were lucky, no one would notice the scrap of black since the tee she slept in was black too. There was no mistaking the face on the shirt, however. Jon Bon Jovi's image, with his eighties hair, had faded but was still there.

"Wow." Eric looked to Vera. "I'm sure that was one hell of a surprise."

"To say the least." Though, at the moment, she wasn't sure they were talking about the same thing. She eased deeper into the chair, told herself to relax. Didn't help that both men were watching her. "In keeping with the Messenger MO, no evidence whatsoever was left behind. No one saw or heard anything. Frankly, there are no close neighbors in either situation to have seen or heard anything."

"He did step outside the usual MO," Bent said, "when he left the message on the mirror in Baker's apartment. He picked up the key from the victim's father, Carl Baker. We have a sketch artist with him right now, though we're not particularly hopeful about the results."

Eric's smooth forehead lined just a little. "So he didn't get a good look at him when he provided the key?"

"He didn't," Bent explained. "The perp wore a baseball-type cap. Dark sweater—black, he thought—and maybe jeans. And sunglasses, so Carl remembered basically nothing about his face or even his age. I have my doubts whether anything he recalls at this point will be accurate."

"Mr. Baker wasn't suspicious that the man didn't wear a uniform?" Eric's eyebrows pulled together in surprise.

"Baker was worried sick about his son," Vera explained. "His entire focus was to do whatever necessary to help get him back safely. Anything else was irrelevant."

Eric nodded his understanding. "Of course."

"What have you found on your end?" Vera felt confident there wasn't that much to share, but she could hope.

"Not a lot, unfortunately," he admitted. "I checked various databases, called my contacts and found no known activity matching that of the Messenger." To Bent he added, "Obviously there are plenty of serial killers who send their victims messages, but not like this one. He always—without exception—announced his intentions. Never deviated. Never left a job unfinished." He turned to Vera then. "Until Gloria Anderson."

Bent looked to Vera. "You didn't go into a whole lot of detail about how you came to be involved with the investigation."

"I was interviewing an elderly woman who'd claimed that she saw a man and woman struggling by an unfamiliar vehicle in the street in front of her house," Vera explained. There were things she still didn't want to tell Bent, but with Eric here she might have no other choice. "The woman couldn't say what the couple looked like, other than that they were White. She didn't recognize the make of the vehicle. It was too dark, and she'd been frightened. A patrol unit had come to her home and found nothing amiss, but the lady demanded to speak with a detective, and I landed the call. As I was leaving the interview, I heard a sound . . . like a crash at the house next door. It was an old neighborhood with those small post–World War Two houses right on top of each other."

"Like in Huntsville's medical district," Bent suggested.

"Yeah." Vera nodded. "So I listened for a moment, then I started for my car again, and"—she shrugged—"I just got this feeling that I should knock on the door. I can't explain it. Maybe it was something the woman said that stuck in my head. I have no idea."

"It's called *cop's intuition*," Eric reminded her, "and yours was very highly developed early in your career."

"Anyway," she continued, "I knocked on the door. No answer. Knocked again and again. Every time I knocked and there was nothing but silence, my skin tingled, heart rate climbed. I couldn't stop. Then I heard another sound. Not a crash, not a scream, but something muffled. I walked slowly around the house, knocking on walls and windows until I heard it again, louder this time—a muffled cry."

"That," Eric said, "is when she kicked in the back door." He grinned at her. "She always leaves that part out. But she burst into that house and found Anderson, naked and bleeding. She saved the woman's life."

"But then the Messenger was pretty pissed," Vera admitted. "He started sending me messages."

"Ironically," Eric put in, "Vera fit the profile of his preferred victim. Smart, blond, attractive. The game was on. He intended to have her." His gaze locked with Vera's. "That's how she and I met. I was on the task force."

"So," Bent suggested, "you used her as bait to reel in the Messenger."

Eric's jaw tightened.

Vera sent Bent a look.

"She volunteered," Eric countered. "If you know Vera, you know once those messages started coming, she wasn't backing down."

"In the end, we trapped him and he confessed," she said, moving on.

Even now, all these years later, she wondered if they really had trapped him or if he'd set the trap. The fact was, in those final days of the investigation, the whole task force had been so focused on her and the messages she was receiving that Gloria Anderson was taken a second time right under their noses. No one had seen that one coming. It was bad enough the woman had gone through that hell once, but to live it twice was the worst kind of nightmare. Particularly considering the second time around was for one sick, sadistic purpose—to send Vera a message. Her insides twisted at the memory.

And that final message was delivered right to Vera's doorstep. Carved into the flesh on the back of Gloria, his final victim: *I'm going to enjoy killing you.* The upside was that, like Nolan Baker, Gloria was alive. As Vera looked back, it was obvious that it was the Messenger who had set the trap. Maybe, after all these years, he'd finally decided to make good on that promise.

She shook off the thought. Not going there until she had no other choice.

"Which brings us to where we are now," Bent said. "Palmer Solomon is in prison—has been for more than twelve years. There's been no other activity matching his MO until now."

"Which can only mean," Eric admitted, "that we have a copycat who has access to information that was never released to the public." He turned his hands up. "Since there was no trial, there were things that simply never came up publicly."

"Or," Vera argued, "he has a surrogate doing this for him. We need to know if he got close to anyone who was recently released. The other option is the one no one wants to consider—that there was someone else involved before he was caught and that protégé has decided on a comeback now."

Eric acknowledged her points with a nod. "Which is why I'm here. The more eyes we have on this case, the better. We do not want a repeat of what happened before."

Vera cringed inside. Like the part she had not told Bent. That she hadn't told Eve or Luna. It just wasn't the kind of thing you shared.

"So you'll follow up on any close associates he may have had in prison?" she asked, skirting the subject he'd brought up.

"Absolutely," Eric confirmed, looking a little confused. "We're already looking for ways he may have reached out to someone beyond those prison walls, which, as you are aware, is the most logical scenario."

For those involved with the original case, it's the cleanest for sure, she opted not to say. Not to mention it happened all the time.

"I'm sure you're ready to settle in," Bent said to Eric. "We can reconvene in the morning at eight and go from there."

"Excellent." Eric stood, reached a hand across Bent's desk. "I look forward to working with you, Sheriff Benton."

Bent gave his hand a shake. "We'll take all the backup we can get."

Vera pushed herself to her feet, picked up her bag, and hung it over her shoulder.

"Vera, are you free for dinner this evening?" Eric asked.

She produced a smile. "I am. I was about to ask you the same thing." It would be rude not to. Plus, there were things they needed to talk about. "Are you staying at the Hampton Inn?"

"I am, yes."

"The cantina next door at seven sound okay?"

"Sounds great." He gestured to the door. "I'll walk you to your car."

"Can you stay a minute, Vee?" Bent asked.

"Sure." She smiled at Eric. "See you at seven."

When he was gone, she settled her full attention on the man watching her so intently. "Eric really is one of the best analysts at Memphis PD. He will be an asset."

"I'm sure." Bent studied her another moment. "Did you two have a thing?"

She stiffened, though she had fully expected the question. "Define *thing*."

"Is he the one you said you almost married?"

Shit. She had mentioned the one serious relationship during the two decades they were apart. She just hadn't said with whom. "Yes, but that was a long time ago. We're just friends now. We have been for a long time."

Bent nodded slowly. "Got it."

"See you in the morning."

Vera walked out of his office, surprised he didn't insist on accompanying her or demand to know her schedule for the next couple of hours. Maybe he was as unsettled as she was. There was something—she couldn't pinpoint the feeling that welled inside her as she walked away from him. Something she didn't want to touch . . . something with the potential for pain . . . for disrupting her life further. Something old that had never let go.

By the time she reached her SUV, she felt ready to run.

Her cell vibrated, and she was grateful for the distraction.

Eve.

"Hey," she said as she climbed into the driver's seat.

"We need to talk."

Vera stifled a groan. Whenever her sister called needing to talk, it was never a good thing. "The usual place?"

"I'm headed there now," Eve confirmed.

"On my way." Vera ended the call.

She hoped this was not the "what else" she'd wondered might be coming.

24

Rose Hill Cemetery
Washington Street, Fayetteville, 5:20 p.m.

Dusk had crept over the landscape by the time Vera parked on the side of the street that ran along the rear of the cemetery. Eve was already there. Her vintage Toyota was parked a little farther up. Parking was never easy, particularly if a service or an event was happening at the cemetery.

Vera walked through the gate and surveyed the rows of headstones that covered the hillside. It was a beautiful old cemetery—as cemeteries went—with ancient trees all encircled with an old-world stone fence. Their mother had loved this cemetery. She'd come every year to the historic walks and, of course, to every burial of a friend or neighbor. Sometimes Vera wondered if Eve had gotten her fascination with the dead from their mother, but she'd never known their mother to be quite as obsessed as Eve. Their parents had been more about paying respects, as was the way of things in their day. You might not have seen a recently deceased person for decades, but you didn't dare miss the funeral or, at the very least, not drop by the viewing. It just was not done.

Eve waited on the bench they'd had placed at the foot of the family plot. She looked up as Vera approached. "I'm really pissed at Bent," she announced.

Vera had spent half her life pissed at Bent. What else was new? "I can't imagine why." She sat down beside Eve. "He didn't arrest you or Suri. You should be thrilled."

Eve glanced around, her fingers gripping the edge of the bench. She was visibly agitated. More so than Vera would have expected, given Suri had confessed to killing the man Eve had whacked over the head with that cast-iron skillet. The idea that this level of stress could send her sister hurtling off the wagon wasn't lost on Vera. Eve had been sober for a long time now. The mere thought of her losing all that hard work gnawed at Vera.

"What if this goes the wrong way?" Eve glared at her. "I know what Bent said about the DA. I get it that Suri is more sympathetic since she's the victim. But . . . I'm worried."

"Bent is right," Vera assured her, reaching for the nearest hand and prying it from the bench. She squeezed her sister's fingers in her own. "This really is the best route. We probably should have done it months ago. Both of you have carried this burden for far too long."

But Vera was well aware of human nature. It was difficult to trust anyone completely with a secret like the one Eve and Suri had carried. Self-preservation was a strong instinct.

Eve stared at Vera's profile until she met her gaze. "What's the deal with this Messenger case?"

"What have you heard?" Vera was surprised she had heard anything other than what she'd told her sisters. Bent hadn't given a statement to the press just yet, but he wouldn't be able to put that off much longer. No matter how confident they were that the Messenger or his cohort was here for her, the public needed to be aware of the potential danger.

"Nothing really. When I was talking to Bent earlier, he said I should help him keep an eye on you. He said this serial killer might try to hurt you." Eve glanced around the cemetery. "I can't believe he doesn't have anyone following you around."

Vera scanned both streets that stretched along the perimeter of the cemetery. "I'm not so sure he doesn't. He hasn't mentioned it, and I find that in itself strange." She should call him and simply ask. Then again, if she were wrong, he'd be prompted to assign someone. It was a double-edged sword.

"Maybe he thinks you can take care of yourself."

"Ha. Wouldn't that be nice." Plus, if that were the case, he wouldn't have been telling Eve to keep an eye on her.

Eve laughed abruptly.

Vera frowned. "What on earth do you find funny in any of this?"

"I"—she slapped her palm against her chest—"have always been the one in trouble. Alcohol. Drugs. Sneaking out of the house and going to crazy parties. Skipping school." She drew in a big breath, let it go. "I mean, really, I've done so much crazy stuff, and not once—in my whole life—have I ever had a killer after me. You"—she pointed a finger at Vera—"on the other hand, are always in some killer's crosshairs."

Vera laughed then, and once she started, she couldn't seem to stop. "Oh my God. You're right. They're attracted to me, it seems."

Eve stared at her for a long time, not laughing anymore. Vera wiped her eyes and pulled herself back together.

"You've always known things," Eve said quietly. "How to fix things and find things, I mean. Maybe you have this instinct about people that not everyone has."

"It's just cop instincts," she argued, reminded of what Eric had said. "Like you with your instincts about the . . . *visitors* you prepare at the funeral home."

Eve shook her head. "No. This is different. You know. Even when you don't know, *you know*. That's why you became a star in Memphis."

Vera made a face. "Like you ever paid attention to what I did in Memphis."

"I did," Eve countered. "Bent did. We discussed your work plenty of times before you came back."

Eve had never told her that. "You did?"

"We talked about your cases. Bent said it was really something how you could analyze the situation and find the trouble. That team you helped create—"

"The one that failed," Vera reminded her.

"It failed because someone else made a mistake. You didn't make the mistake."

"But I should have seen the mistake before it turned into a tragedy." But she hadn't. She had allowed trust to get in the way of discernment. Vera didn't really want to talk about this, but if it helped her sister to get right with the decision she and Suri had made today, then she would do it.

"See," Eve said, "that's what I mean. You have this uncanny knack for seeing things that are about to happen based on what's occurring at the moment." She shrugged. "I can't explain it, but Bent says it's a gift."

Or a curse. "We both have our talents," Vera reminded her. "You should never forget what you do. It's so important to the people who are left behind. What you and Suri both do."

Eve exhaled a big breath, stared at the ground. "I had a bad dream last night, Vee."

"You did?" When they were kids, Eve used to tell her all about her bad dreams. Especially after their mama died. Vera was the person Eve clung to. She couldn't remember the last time her sister had talked about a bad dream.

She looked to Vera then, her face clouded with worry. "It was you, Vee. You were on my table, and I couldn't wake you up."

That instinct they were just talking about swelled inside Vera. She ignored it and forced a big smile for her sister. "It was just a dream. Besides, when I die, you'd better not put me on that damned table. Cremate me."

She stared at the headstones in front of them—their dad's, with their mom on one side and the witch of a stepmother on the other. But when Luna had wanted to bury Sheree's remains here, what could they say? Vera and Eve's father was Luna's father too. Besides, how could they argue about anything after what they'd done?

"And don't even think about trying to poke me into a hole with this group," Vera tacked on.

Eve worked up a smile. "I would never do that. I'll put you in an urn on my mantel so I can talk to you about everything until Suri or somebody puts me in one right there beside you."

Vera hugged her. "Don't get too excited, I plan on being around for a long time."

Assuming whoever was playing the Messenger game didn't get the jump on her.

25

Las Trojas Cantina
Redstone Drive, Fayetteville, 6:55 p.m.

Vera parked in the lot and waited. She could see Eric just inside the door, waiting for her. But there was something she needed to confirm before she went inside, and to do that she had to wait.

About ten seconds after she'd parked, another car slid into a slot a few spaces away. Then she waited some more. A full half minute later, and no one had emerged from the vehicle. She smiled. She had been right. Satisfied, she climbed out of her SUV and secured it. Rather than walk toward the entrance of the restaurant, she moved in the direction of the other vehicle. Black—of course—two door and quite sporty. The windows were tinted, but she was far too confident in her conclusion to be put off by the lack of visibility.

Vera walked right up to the driver's window and rapped on the glass.

It powered down, and a man of twenty-five or so, maybe thirty, stared up at her without saying a word. The look on his face told her all she needed to know. He'd been caught, and his boss was not going to be happy about it.

"Deputy . . . ?" She sent him a questioning look.

He exhaled, stared forward. "Kershaw."

"Deputy Kershaw," she said, "I'll be in the restaurant for a couple of hours, give or take, and then I'll be heading home. Did the sheriff assign you to keep an eye on my house tonight as well?"

"Until further notice, ma'am."

"I guess I'll see you later, then." With that, she headed toward the entrance of the restaurant.

The hostess smiled. "Welcome. How many in your party?"

"She's with me," Eric announced, appearing at Vera's side. He ushered her toward the dining room. "I have a table already, and our waitress is on standby."

Eric was always fully prepared for every occasion. Had never allowed a "play it by ear" moment in his life. He'd likely already tipped the waitress well to ensure she appeared the moment Vera arrived.

The table was in the corner farthest from the small crowd already seated in the dining room. Vera would wager no one would be seated close to them. *Never leave anything to chance* was her old friend's motto.

When they'd settled, the waitress took their drink orders. Vera decided she was due a margarita. Maybe two, depending on how long the evening lasted and just how much Eric was willing to share. He ordered a margarita as well.

Once they were alone, he leaned forward. "I just had a call from Agent Alcott. He tried to visit Solomon again this afternoon," he said in a hushed tone.

Vera wasn't surprised. The FBI would want to put to rest any notion of this situation being *the* Messenger or someone who had worked with him. The possibility might make them look bad and would certainly raise questions and have reporters nosing around. The copycat scenario was much more palatable from their perspective.

"Have you heard how the meeting went?"

"Solomon refused to see him. Insisted he had nothing to say to the agent."

Not a complete surprise. "He never liked Alcott."

Eric nodded. "But he did have a message he wanted to pass along."

The waitress arrived with two rather large glasses rimmed with salt and festooned with lemon slices. So maybe one would be her limit. Vera sipped the tangy drink. "Hmm. Nice." She licked the salt from her lips. "What was the message?"

Eric ignored his own drink. "He said he had something to tell you, but he would only pass it along in person."

Wasn't she the lucky one? "Really?" She indulged in another, deeper swallow. "He wants to see me. Interesting." Not really. The Messenger had had some bizarre fascination with her from the beginning. The idea that it still lingered made her more than a little uncomfortable. "If it helps with our case, I'm happy to oblige."

The prospect had made sense back then. She fit the profile of his preferred victim. But, if she was completely honest with herself, it had felt like more. Eve had touched on it when they talked at the cemetery, but Vera would never admit as much out loud. On some level she understood there was a connection between her and Solomon . . . a knowing. Vera had only felt that deeper connection to a perp a couple of times. Explaining it to anyone would be like attempting to describe the shape and texture of air. It was impossible to put into words. She downed more of her margarita.

Eric's expression had gone somber. "I don't like this, Vera. I'm concerned that he's up to something. Unlike Alcott, I'm not convinced that what's happening here is the work of a copycat. But if it's him, I don't think it has to do with his past activity either. I think this is purely about you and his sudden need for revenge."

"Could be, I suppose. I can pay him a visit first thing tomorrow. No problem. But why now? That's the real question, don't you think?" Vera felt a little buzz of something like anticipation and maybe just a little fear, which likely prevented his words from evoking a deeper reaction. "Better than twelve years is a long time to wait."

The fact that Eric was even suggesting this case was actually related in any way to the Messenger screamed loudly that he knew something she did not. The man was trained to always CYA when it came to the MPD.

"He's dying."

The impact of those two words jarred her. And there it was, the "something" he knew that she didn't. Wow. Vera cleared her head, then her throat just to buy time.

"I . . . don't know anything about his current circumstances. Frankly I haven't even thought of him in all these years," she responded. That last part might not be entirely true. Every so often she googled him. Made sure he was still where he was supposed to be. And once in a great while, the things he'd done found a way into her dreams.

"He found out just before Christmas," Eric explained. "Pancreatic cancer. It's quite advanced. They've given him only a few months at most. Alcott claims he was unaware of this development. I have my doubts on that one."

The Bureau never liked sharing until necessary. As for Palmer Solomon, he had just turned sixty when Vera first met him. That would make him seventy-two now. His wife had died the year before his arrest. He had no siblings or extended family other than his children. A son, Christopher, and a daughter, Pamela, who had a son of her own, Patrick. Christopher had valiantly done all possible to keep his father out of prison. In addition to retaining the very best criminal attorney in Memphis, he had called in a high-powered psychiatrist to try and prove his father was insane and should be in a hospital, not a prison. Then Solomon had turned it all off. He had confessed in calm, vivid detail. The daughter was appalled and took her son and went into seclusion. According to the prison visitor logs, Christopher had been the only one to visit Solomon in prison.

The news unsettled Vera, perhaps far more than it should have. "I can see how this might prompt a renewed interest in revenge," she agreed.

The timing, which had been the sticking point in her opinion, now made sense. And if revenge was the Messenger's intent, he would want the connection to be obvious—his MO would need to be clear. Furthermore, he would want it to happen fast, before he was dead.

"You can see now," Eric said, his worried eyes searching hers, "how I would be concerned for your safety."

"You shared this with Bent already?"

"I told him when I first arrived. I wanted to tell you privately."

He'd pulled one of her maneuvers. "You made sure Bent was aware before I could suggest limits or additions to what you intended to share."

"I felt he needed to be fully aware," Eric confessed.

The waitress returned, and Eric ordered for the both of them. God knew they'd eaten together enough times at their favorite Mexican restaurant in Memphis for him to be well versed in her preferred choices. She let him. Her mind was elsewhere, and she needed a moment to tamp down the rising frustration.

When the waitress had moved on, Vera said what was on her mind. "Like I said, I'll go see Solomon tomorrow. Maybe I can end this thing." It was always possible that all he wanted was her attention anyway. He had tried repeatedly those first couple of years of his prison sentence to open a line of communication with her. She had ignored him.

"The chief and Alcott have requested a conference call for eight tomorrow morning," he said, rather than commenting on her decision.

She wanted to tell him that whatever her former boss and Agent Alcott had to say was irrelevant in her opinion, but this was Eric. He deserved better than her frustration with the higher-ups.

"What they say or think won't matter," she warned. "Not really. You know this." The truth was, she should have been warned. There was always the chance that a heinous killer's impending demise could prompt desperate actions.

"Lincoln County and Fayetteville may not have the bodies or the skill level for this kind of manhunt, if it comes to it," Eric argued. "*You know how this can go.*"

The point was a valid one. The Messenger had known how to hide. If someone went missing—someone besides her—finding that someone in time to save his or her life would be impossible. They hadn't been able to do it in Memphis with a hell-of-a-lot larger division and the help of the FBI—not to mention years of data on the bastard.

Clearly whoever was playing the part of puppet had already proven capable of the same. They hadn't found Baker until the perp was ready for him to be found.

Fury twisted in her belly. Son of a bitch. Solomon was already several steps ahead. He'd had weeks—months to plan.

Forcing her head back into the conversation, she asked, "Are they planning to send someone else to help out?" They certainly hadn't given that impression in today's call. The whole thing could turn into a major clusterfuck.

"Obviously that's the sheriff's call."

Part of her felt certain Bent would want to keep this in his department, but then, he might feel that in this situation, having outside help would be the best way to protect the residents of his county.

Deep down she had hoped—really hoped—this was not the Messenger orchestrating this show. That maybe it really was just some copycat. A part of her had known better . . . but that knowledge had not kept her from ignoring the possibility, allowing her to sleep better at night. Denial was a powerful emotion.

"So," Eric said, "that is *the* Bent. The one who stole your heart when you were only seventeen."

Why in the world was he bringing up her old love life? Then she followed his gaze, which was no longer on her.

Bent sat at the bar, his back to them. As she watched, the bartender placed a bottle of beer on the counter next to his hat. Bent's gaze remained on the mirror behind the bar . . . the one that likely allowed him to see them quite clearly.

Irritation was her first reaction. More of the frustration she'd been dealing with since they'd sat down came next. But then all of that went away as something like satisfaction filled her. Was Bent jealous? No, that was impossible. Men like Bent never felt that green-eyed monster. Never had to.

Don't be juvenile, Vee.

Vera forced her attention back to Eric. "That's him."

Eric's gaze rested on hers once more. "He didn't escape unscathed. I could see it in his eyes when he looked at you and every time I said your name before you arrived at the meeting. You left your mark."

Vera laughed. Then she finished off her margarita. Maybe she would have that second one after all. "Eric." She rested her attention on the man she had adored . . . the man she had wanted so desperately to fall in love with but somehow it just wouldn't happen. "Your imagination is running away with you. There are some fairy tales that just don't have happily ever afters, and my history with Bent is one of them."

Eric pointed to Vera's drink and nodded to the waitress.

God, the man read her like a damned book.

"But you admit that it was a fairy tale–like affair."

She shook her head, pushed her empty glass aside. "I suppose to a seventeen-year-old it was, yes."

"Have you told him everything?"

Vera wished that second drink would hurry up and get here. She made a noncommittal face. "There are some things you don't talk about with just anyone." This was why she wished he had consulted her before telling Bent new information about Solomon.

"Except someone who lived them with you," he countered.

That was the thing. She and Eric had lived through something . . . an event that changed both their lives. Not to say that their relationship was based solely on that singular, shocking time, but it was the little things leftover afterward—the almost-intangible ghostly tethers—that had tied them together for months, maybe years.

"I haven't told him. No."

The sad smile that appeared on Eric's lips made her chest ache. "We got through it. That's what matters."

Vera's throat felt dry. "I should have killed him when I had the opportunity." She had never said those words out loud, no matter that she had thought them hundreds of times. The bastard was nothing but a drain on the taxpayers of Tennessee, just sitting in prison all these years. Now he was even more so, considering his medical treatments were likely exorbitant.

He deserved none of it.

The waitress arrived with her margarita, and Vera's relief was palpable.

"No." Eric shook his head. "You did the right thing. He was disabled. You called for backup. That was the right choice."

Palmer Solomon had lured Vera into a trap using Gloria Anderson. Eric had been assigned to keep an eye on Vera, which landed him in the same hellacious situation. It was a mistake she would not make again. Oh no. After that she had made it her life's goal to immerse herself in all the training available. She never passed up an opportunity to learn how to better her self-defense skills.

But back then she had been eager. Eager and ambitious. Totally focused on solving the biggest case of the time. She'd ended up captured by a serial killer. Landing Eric in that trap too. Nearly three days of sheer hell . . . but it was Eric who bore the scars of her mistake.

The Messenger had intended to leave a message for law enforcement—carved in the skin of one of their own. Vera pleaded for the bastard to use her instead. She fully realized it was her fault Eric was there. Her pleas only made the Messenger more determined . . . fueled his disgusting desires. On the last day, he decided to make Vera finish the carving. The second biggest mistake of his twisted life. She used his trademark filleting knife to slice a hole right through his gut.

But she hadn't killed him. Her aim narrowly missed any vital organs, damn it.

He survived . . . they both did.

And then, in the end, he officially confessed to everything.

Vera and Eric were heroes. They'd become friends and, in time, more—to some degree because of what they had shared.

"I'm sorry." The words were out of her mouth before she realized she intended to say them.

He frowned. "Sorry for what?"

Eric Jones was one of the kindest, smartest, damned coolest men she had ever known.

"For not being a better friend . . . a better part of *us*."

He laughed, sipped his margarita. "You didn't love me the way I loved you. It wasn't your fault; it just was."

"Thank you for understanding and for still being my friend."

"Always, Vera. I will always be your friend."

Their food was served, and they ate. By the time dinner was over, Eric had told her about a new friend. A lovely woman—he had dozens of photos on his phone—who made him happy. Vera was thrilled for him.

Eric suddenly frowned. "We should have called Bent over. Now he's gone."

Vera glanced in that direction. He was right. Bent was no longer at the bar. She looked around. Not in the dining room.

"I'll let him know we got busy catching up and lost track of time." She smiled at her friend. "He'll understand."

"He'll do a hell of a lot more than that if he's smart." He reached across the table and squeezed her hand. "You are an amazing woman, Vera. He would be very lucky to have you."

Vera laughed. "On that note, I think we should call it a night."

They reminisced a bit more while he settled their tab, and then he walked her to her SUV. They hugged, and for a split second Vera wished again that things had been different.

But there were no true do-overs. There was only moving on.

In her rearview mirror she watched him watching her as she drove away, her detail right behind her. Eric had insisted he wanted to walk back to his hotel. To get a little air, he'd said. Vera powered her window down. She needed a little air herself.

26

Boyett Farm
Good Hollow Road, Fayetteville, 9:30 p.m.

Fayetteville was a small town. Only a few minutes were required to reach the road that led to her farm. But she was exhausted by the time she'd unlocked the door and taken care of the alarm. It had been a long, emotional day. And she could not wait to crawl into bed and put it behind her. At least as much of it as her traitorous mind would allow.

Thinking about Bent at that damned bar, when he knew she and Eric were going to that restaurant, was slipping deeper and deeper under her skin. The reality that Solomon refused to speak with anyone but her . . . the fact that he was dying . . . burned on the fringes of her thoughts.

She didn't have a freaking clue why the news that he was dying would disturb her, but it did.

"You are so screwed up," she muttered to herself as she climbed the stairs.

Despite the desire to go to bed without doing her nightly routine, she forced herself to go through the steps. Forty was almost here, and she needed to do all within her power to avoid more wrinkles and age spots. She tucked her hair up with a claw clip, scrubbed her face with the gritty stuff all the best influencers recommended, and then rinsed repeatedly. She followed with a moisturizer that had cost far too much.

"You're worth it," she said to her reflection, then rolled her eyes. "Yeah right."

Her blouse and slacks went in the hamper. The bra too. Rather than a sweatshirt or sweater and jeans, she had actually made an effort to dress up tonight. Since moving back home, she hadn't done a lot of that. She was back to being just a plain old country girl. All she needed was a cow to milk and chickens to feed, and life would be perfect. She tugged on her nightshirt and hugged her arms around Bon Jovi's face.

She dropped her cell onto the charging pad on the bedside table, then collapsed onto her bed and dragged herself onto the pillows. She moaned. God, it felt good to lie down. She pulled the clip from her hair and tossed it in the direction of the bedside table.

Her cell vibrated.

"No," she grumbled into her pillow.

Reaching out without even looking, she grabbed her cell and pulled it to her. She forced her eyes open and stared at the screen.

Bent.

She tapped the screen to accept the call. "What?" she grumbled.

"I'm at your door."

Adrenaline swam through her veins, as if she were seventeen again and he was waiting for her to sneak out to him. "Why? Did something happen?" She sat straight up, pushed the hair out of her face.

"We need to talk."

"Fine. I'm coming to the door, but you can't come inside because I'm already in bed."

"Fine," he said back.

Phone in hand, she climbed out of the bed and stormed from the room. Some part of her considered that she probably should have checked the house before she came up to bed. Yes, the windows were all screwed shut and the monitors on the doors would have set off the alarm if someone had come inside before she got home. Still, she should have looked. Damn it. The Messenger had started something. It was no longer a theory; it was real. Diligence was necessary.

She checked the peephole, even though Bent had said he was at her door. There he was, hat making it hard to see his eyes. His long, shaggy hair hanging around his too-handsome face.

After deactivating the alarm, she unlocked and opened the door. Shit. She had on the damned nightshirt. She kept her lower body behind the door and leaned around to look at him. "What do we need to talk about?"

"I need to come inside, Vee."

Well hell.

The hall was nearly dark, since she hadn't turned on any lights. But the night-light that had been plugged into an outlet next to the staircase for as long as she could remember allowed her to see well enough. She opened the door wider, then closed it behind him. With her back to the door, she faced him. Yeah, she was half naked, but it was dark enough to prevent a close inspection. She wasn't sure when she'd last shaved her legs. She was too old for this.

Bent braced his hands on his hips, stared at the floor, then at the wall. Maybe he was embarrassed by her manner of dress. Big deal. It wasn't the first time he'd seen her in this old tee. Not to mention he'd seen her naked dozens of times . . . more than two decades ago, of course. Anyway, she'd told him she was in bed.

"Jones told me how this Messenger guy refused to speak with anyone but you."

"I didn't know until tonight." She suddenly felt bad again. "We were going to come over to the bar and talk to you or invite you over to our table, but we started talking and then you were gone."

"I had to . . . go." The subtlest shift of one shoulder was apparently his way of dismissing the subject.

"Can you please take off your hat and look at me when you're talking?" She hated when he wanted to have a conversation and he used that damned hat as a shield so he wouldn't have to look her in the eye. He'd been doing a lot of that lately. She remembered the move well from back when she was seventeen. Fury roared through her. She was not seventeen now.

He pulled off the hat, ran his fingers through his hair, and her body trembled.

She swore silently at herself. What the hell was wrong with her?

"He—Jones—said," Bent told her, "we needed to talk about what happened before with the Messenger."

Damn Eric. He shouldn't have put the idea in Bent's head. "It doesn't matter. That was a long time ago. The man who did those things is old and dying now."

Bent's gaze zeroed in on hers. It was impossible not to feel the heat even in the near darkness, even across the four or five feet of floor space that separated them. "But the man he sent here to write that message on your mirror—on Baker's back—isn't."

Vera lifted her chin and gave him the answer. Why not? If this thing dragged on, it would come out anyway. Reporters loved recaps. "He wanted to scare me, so he tried to make me feel as if he intended to do things to me. Like he did to his other victims. But he didn't. Instead, he did them to Eric."

"So, he didn't . . . *hurt* you."

"No." She moistened her lips, her heart suddenly beating too fast. "He didn't hurt anything but my feelings." That was putting it mildly.

The Messenger was a torture-murderer. There was no end to his imagination when it came to inflicting pain and fear.

Bent nodded. "I read the things he did to the others, and . . . I was worried."

She took a step closer to him. Suddenly wished she had told him this before. They were supposed to be friends and colleagues now. His gaze locked on hers, and no matter that it rattled her somehow, she dared to take another step. "What he did to his victims was unthinkable, and I'm glad he's dying. But he didn't do anything to me except make me regret that I didn't kill him when I had the chance. Eric is the one who ended up with all the scars."

"He couldn't stop looking at you," Bent said, his voice too low . . . too soft . . . too wanting. "Your friend from Memphis."

Vera wasn't sure how to react to the statement.

"I kept thinking about him touching you . . . you," he said, his voice barely more than a whisper, "touching him."

Vera tried to find the right words to say, but her head was spinning. Her body quivering. This thing that had been simmering between them for seven months now was swallowing her up.

Bent claimed that last step between them. He tossed his hat to the floor and put his hands on her arms, his fingers curving around her. The feel of his palms against her skin made it impossible to breathe. Her phone slid from her hand, clattered onto the floor.

"All I could think," he murmured, "was that it should have been me."

His head came down, and his lips brushed against hers. Then his mouth claimed hers.

There was no more talking . . . only touching.

27

Khatri Residence
Morton Drive, Fayetteville, 10:00 p.m.

Eve sat on the side of the bed.

She needed a drink. Dear God, she needed a drink.

She needed a drink more than she had needed one in years. More than she needed to breathe.

The sound of the shower turning on in the bathroom made her blink. Suri was taking a shower. She didn't have to know. No. No way could she cross that line. She couldn't do that to Suri. Suri believed in her. Trusted her. Loved her.

And Suri needed her now more than ever.

"Don't screw up," she muttered. *Don't screw up!*

Her fingers tightened on the sheets on either side of where she sat. But how could she keep fighting when the need got stronger every minute.

She needed a drink!

"Damn it!" She pushed up from the bed. She should call her sponsor.

Vera and Bent were right about getting this Gates business out in the open. It would all work out. Vera wouldn't steer them wrong. Bent either.

"You're good, Eve." She paced the floor. She and Suri would be okay. It was all good.

Still, she couldn't help wishing that cave had never been found by those two kids. That Gates was still hidden away and no one, not Teresa Russ or anyone else, had made the connection between Gates and Suri.

The son of a bitch had gotten what he deserved. All this fuss over him was wrong, just wrong. The stress and worry the investigation into his death had caused Eve and Suri was not fair. They had only been protecting themselves. Well, Eve had been protecting Suri. But anyway, it was self-defense. Suri was the victim.

Eve paced the small room again and again. She and Suri had finally found their place with each other. They no longer felt the need to hide from anyone. But now people would be looking at them with suspicion. Murderers, they would call them. Lesbian murderers. Damn it!

The impulse to rush to the liquor store and buy a fifth was very nearly overwhelming. She couldn't do that . . . couldn't do it.

Couldn't let Suri down.

Keep it together for Suri.

The spray of water in the bathroom suddenly stopped.

Eve took a breath. Suri would be out in a minute, and they could talk. Suri always knew how to talk her down from the mania and get her on an even keel. Deep breath. She could get through this.

A scream jerked Eve from the worrisome musings.

"Eve!"

She rushed out of the bedroom and burst into the steamy bathroom. "What's wrong?"

Suri stood next to the tub, the towel hugged against her like a shield. She pointed to the mirror over the sink.

Eve's gaze followed that route, landing on the steamy glass, where words had been written in the fog.

Eve, you're next.

Ice slid through her body. She had to call Vera.

"Who did this?" Suri cried.

Fury blasted Eve, seared away the icy chill. Just what the hell she needed. Life was complicated enough without this shit. She stepped to the sink and used both hands to swipe the words away. "You son of a bitch!"

"Eve! You shouldn't do that . . . it's evidence," Suri wailed. Tears streamed down her cheeks.

Eve fell back a step. *Shit.* Suri was right. "I'll call Vee." She turned to the woman she loved more than life itself. "Don't worry. Vee will know what to do."

"Let me finish drying and get dressed and I'll be right there."

Eve nodded.

"Don't close the door," Suri urged. "I don't want anything between us right now."

"I won't."

Eve hurried down the short hall to the living room and then to the small kitchen. She'd put her cell phone on the charger. She grabbed it from the counter and touched the screen, but something made her pause before selecting the phone app. She frowned and glanced around the room to figure out whatever the hell it was that wasn't right. The dishes she had washed were drying on the counter. Chairs were all pushed into place at the table. Their boots sat on the floor at the back door.

She looked again. That was it. The door was ajar.

What the hell?

They always locked it immediately when they came in and kept it that way. Frowning, she stepped in that direction.

Something pinched the back of her neck.

When she would have twisted around, a powerful arm locked around her chest, and a hand closed over her mouth.

"Don't move," a voice warned.

Male. Not familiar.

Her heart lunged into panic. The room started to spin, and her cell phone clattered to the floor.

The sound of the hair dryer down the hall followed her into the darkness.

28

Boyett Farm
Good Hollow Road, Fayetteville, 11:00 p.m.

The hum of the hair dryer seemed ridiculously loud.

But Vera was grateful for the noise . . . for the humdrum action of attending to her hair after a long hot shower. She gritted her teeth and swiped at the mirror with her free hand to clear away the last of the fog and the lingering streaks of detergent the bastard had used to leave her a message. Still not satisfied, she unrolled a wad of toilet paper and scrubbed some more. Her life was a mess . . . the past kept coming back to haunt her, and . . .

She'd left Bent in her bed.

Good God. What had she been thinking? Sounds and sensations flooded her. She closed her eyes a moment and blocked the vivid recap. Deep breath. Not an easy feat. She forced her eyes open. The idea of how far across the line she had thrown herself shook her. Hadn't she learned her lesson about personal involvements with colleagues? Sadly, it was done now, and there was no going back.

They had made love.

She and *Bent*.

And it was amazing.

Twenty-two years! Before the crash and burn in Memphis that had sent her running back home, she had not seen him or heard his voice in more than two decades. Well, the truth was, the crash and burn had only preceded her coming home. The remains found in that damned cave were the reason she'd had no choice but to come rushing back here. Otherwise, she might have attempted to ride out the storm in Memphis. But then what? It wasn't like she'd had any place to go in Memphis once the dust settled. Within two weeks of the tragedy that had taken down her team, she'd resigned her post there. In the end, coming back here had been the right decision. It was all like falling backward in time.

And if that wasn't twisted enough, she'd been working with her first love ever since.

Of course it was inevitable that *this* moment would happen.

They were only human, after all. She couldn't pretend she hadn't considered the possibility over and over again. Obviously she should have prepared better.

Vera pushed the thoughts away. This whole business with the Messenger and seeing Eric again had made her vulnerable. Yes, she decided, it was the volatile combination of events from the past coming together in an explosion of unexpected emotions. Otherwise, she would surely have told Bent to go home when he showed up wanting to mark his territory.

Anger sparked inside her. Seven months they had been working together, and not once had he made so much as an overture toward going down that path. Not one single word or touch that suggested he felt anything more for her.

They were friends . . . colleagues. Old acquaintances.

Nothing more. For goodness' sake, he had women like Renae who grew her own hothouse tomatoes and brought him meals. What did he need with Vera Mae Boyett?

She turned off the dryer, unplugged it, and placed it on the counter. Under no circumstances would she ever—*ever*—allow him to see how tonight had affected her. She tugged on a clean sweatshirt that had been hanging on the back of the bathroom door. Sans a bra, since she'd have to go back into her room if she wanted a bra. Not happening.

Pretending to be unaffected would not be easy. Obviously he'd been in the room when she was losing her mind with multiple orgasms. Damn it. But he didn't have to know how touching him, smelling his skin—her respiration quickened even now—had made her feel. How his hands moving over her body and . . .

Okay. Enough of that. She dragged on a pair of jeans she'd pulled from the hamper. He likely recognized desperation when he saw it. But just because he had pushed all the right buttons and driven her over the edge physically didn't mean he had to know how he had moved her emotionally. He couldn't possibly understand how being with him had felt more right than sex with any other man. How she had missed him so desperately and had spent her whole life comparing every other lover to him.

Damn it all to hell.

She smoothed her sweatshirt and squared her shoulders. She would never share those thoughts with him. He already had her at a distinct disadvantage. The face that stared back at her from the mirror warned there was just one big problem with her plan.

How did she keep him believing she was unaffected and at the same time make sure this happened again?

She groaned. If she was completely honest with herself, she could not recall when she had felt so alive . . . so satisfied.

"Pathetic, Vee," she grumbled.

Since she couldn't stay holed up in this bathroom forever, she slung her towel over the shower-curtain rod. Made sure the Bon Jovi tee and her underwear were in the hamper. Then she drew in a big breath and exited the room that felt more like a sauna. She'd stayed in here entirely too long.

A quick peek in her bedroom revealed no sign of Bent. He must have gone downstairs. The rumpled sheets made her cringe. The urge to rip the sheets from the mattress and rush them to the washing machine was a vibrating need.

No way. She'd just washed the scent of him off her skin. She wasn't touching those damned sheets.

Where was her phone? She'd taken it downstairs when he called to say he was at her door.

The distinct memory of hearing it clatter to the floor told her where she'd left it.

Braced to deal with the reality of the past hour, she descended the stairs. Her phone was no longer on the floor. It was on the hall side table. He must have picked it up when he came downstairs. His hat sat next to her phone. He'd picked that up too.

She pocketed her phone. Where the hell was he?

Moving as silently as possible, she wandered through the downstairs until she reached the kitchen. He stood at the back door, staring out into the darkness.

His shirttails hanging untucked was the only readily visible indication of what they'd done. Dear God, she'd been such an idiot.

As if he'd sensed her presence, he turned around.

His hair was a little tousled, and a day's beard growth shadowed his jaw. His shirt front was held together by only two or three buttons. For an instant he looked almost vulnerable. Like the twenty-one-year-old guy who had stolen her heart all those years ago, who'd rarely allowed anyone to see this side of him.

"I was just thinking." His voice was low, deep . . . sexy as hell.

Holy hell, she was in trouble here.

She folded her arms over her chest. "That you succeeded in marking your territory," she snarked.

Holding her gaze, he started toward her. "Is that how you see it? If so, I'm surprised you didn't send me packing before we climbed the stairs."

He always had an answer for everything. Damn him. "I considered it, but . . ." She shrugged. "We all have needs."

He reached up with those hands that had made her feel things she could never adequately articulate and fastened another button of his shirt. "Glad I could help out." Then he fastened another.

Before she could dig up a proper response, her cell vibrated in her pocket. She snatched it out, her gaze still boring into his. "What?" she said to the caller without even looking at the screen.

"Vee, it's Suri."

The high-pitched, hysterical sound of her voice warned something was not right. "What's wrong, Suri?"

"Eve is gone. The back door is standing open, and I can't find her anywhere."

A burst of uncertainty sent Vera's heart into a gallop. Where the hell would her sister go? She wouldn't likely be called to the funeral home in the middle of the night. Wouldn't leave without telling Suri. Surely today hadn't caused her to need a drink. Then again, the business in Bent's office had been pretty stressful for Eve and for Suri.

"Suri." Vera steadied herself. "Has she been drinking?"

"No!" A keening sound rose from Suri's throat. "Vee, there was a message on the bathroom mirror."

Terror blasted through her veins. "Tell me exactly what it said."

"Eve, you're next."

Oh God. It was the Messenger.

"Suri, lock yourself in your bedroom. Slide something in front of the door. We're on our way."

29

Khatri Residence
Morton Drive, Fayetteville, 11:55 p.m.

Bent walked through the house in search of Vee.

He had deputies crawling all over the property and the surrounding area. There weren't any streetlights along this stretch of county road, and the neighbors were few and far between. The chances of finding anyone who had seen a vehicle or a person in the vicinity of the house at this time of night was next to nil. Since they hadn't found a vehicle that didn't belong in the area, either, there was no reason to believe Eve was out there fleeing on foot with some scumbag right on her heels. Whoever had come here had gotten what he came for, and now they were both gone.

But Bent had to be sure . . . that her body wasn't out there somewhere. The thought twisted inside him.

He'd called Conover to the scene, but it would likely be a waste of time. They'd already learned that, like the Messenger, this perp didn't leave evidence. Still, there was always a first time. Better to be safe than sorry. If there was anything here that would help them figure out what happened to Eve, he intended to find it.

Vera had called Luna, and Bent had sent another deputy to her house. He wasn't risking that this scumbag wasn't finished.

He located Vee in the small bathroom. She leaned against the wall opposite the sink, arms folded over her chest and gaze fixed on the mirror. Suri had explained that Eve had gotten angry and swiped the message from the glass. Not that it would matter at this point. They all knew who had left it.

"We'll find her," he promised.

"No question," she responded without looking at him. "I'm not worried about finding her, Bent. I'm worried about what condition she'll be in when we do."

The lack of emotion in her voice told him she was in that place—the one an investigator had to reach in order to keep going when the worst of the worst happened to someone they cared about.

"Baker was alive," he reminded her.

Her eyes widened with realization. "She could be at the house or barn right now." Her lips trembled. "Or at that fucking cave."

Bent had already considered that possibility. "I have deputies searching those areas right now."

She closed her eyes and blew out a breath. "Thank you."

"I also called Jones." He hadn't wanted to for reasons that were purely selfish and out of place. But he'd done it anyway. This was about the job . . . this was about Eve. "He's on his way."

"I appreciate it." She shook her head. "I was going to call him, but I came in here, and I just couldn't do anything but stand here staring." Her lips tightened. "I have regretted so many times that I didn't kill that son of a bitch. Eric said I did the right thing. Now I realize the real right thing would have been to follow my instincts."

Bent moved closer, his gut tangling into knots. "I will find her, Vee."

She managed a small smile. "I know you'll try your best, Bent. We both will." Her lips trembled again, and a tear slipped down her cheek. She scrubbed it away. "I'll tell you a little secret."

He held her gaze, wanted with his entire being to reach out and touch her but didn't dare. He couldn't risk she would see it as him taking advantage of the situation.

"Tell me," he urged when she remained silent.

She swiped at her eyes again. "I cannot do this life . . . without her."

"I know." The two had clung to each other after their mother had passed. They'd kept their secrets and protected each other all these years. Truth was, he couldn't imagine one without the other either. "Right now, Eve needs us to put aside our personal feelings and to focus on finding her. We have to think like cops, Vee—not family, not friends. Just cops."

"You're right." She pushed away from the wall. "I'd like to talk to Suri again." Her breath caught. "Did you send someone to Luna's house? She could be in danger as well. God damn it, where is my brain?"

"I did, and I've explained everything to Jerome. He's taking time off from work to be with her until this is finished."

"Jesus." Vee shook herself. "I can't believe I didn't think of that already."

She was only human, but Vee had never liked admitting as much.

"Come on. Let's talk to Suri again. See if she's remembered anything more."

As they reached the small living room, Eric Jones walked through the front door. He went straight to Vee and gave her a hug—something Bent had worried he shouldn't do. He'd spent the past seven months trying to figure out where he stood with Vee. He wasn't sure he would ever really know. But he had no one to blame for the distance between them except himself. He was the one who had walked away in the first place.

Walked. Yeah right. He'd run. He told himself it was to protect her from making a mistake. But maybe he'd been protecting himself from something that scared the hell out of him.

"I'm so sorry," Eric was saying to her, his voice low. "We're going to do everything possible to get her back unharmed."

Vee nodded. "I know."

"We were about to talk to Suri again," Bent said, rather than what he wanted to say, which was something along the lines of *Go home, we don't need you.*

He was having more trouble keeping the personal junk away than he'd anticipated. And here all this time he'd thought he was immune. Vee was the only person who'd ever made him feel like he might be vulnerable to his emotions.

Jones, Vee at his side, followed Bent to the larger of the two bedrooms in the house. The bedrooms were on one end of the house, while the living room, kitchen, and bathroom were on the other. It was a small home, with a couple of acres of woods around it. Suri's grandmother had left it to her since both her parents were deceased and her brother had already moved to Huntsville to start his business. Bent had suggested Suri call her brother and let him know what was going on. But he doubted Suri would be willing to go and stay with him until this was done. She would want to be here just in case. Bent would assign a deputy to her as well.

It was a damned good thing he'd gotten his personnel quota up to where it needed to be. He had a good, solid team now.

Vee sat on the bed next to Suri and put an arm around her shoulders. "This is Lieutenant Eric Jones. He's an analyst I worked with in Memphis. He's familiar with the perp we believe is behind what's happening, and he's going to help us."

Suri glanced at Jones. "She'll be pissed."

Jones frowned. "What do you mean?"

"Anything or anyone that threatens the people she cares about makes her angry. She'll give him a hard time." Suri's tears started again in earnest. "That's the part that worries me the most. She won't be easy to handle. He'll wish he hadn't taken her."

A shaky smile tugged at Vee's lips. "She will. She'll give him hell."

Bent suppressed a chuckle. They were right about that. Eve was a fighter. She wouldn't take this lying down unless she was unconscious. Otherwise she would be fighting tooth and toenail. Not to mention raising hell.

"Walk us through what happened once more," Bent suggested.

"We both had stressful days." She glanced at Bent.

The confessions about Gates. He asked, "Did the two of you go back to work after leaving my office?"

Suri nodded. "We were both behind for the rest of the day. We didn't get home until around nine. We ate. I took a shower, and when I got out . . . the message was on the mirror." She closed her eyes and shuddered. "*Eve, you're next.* I screamed for her. She came and saw it. It made her angry, and she scrubbed it away. I told her she shouldn't have done it, but it was too late."

"She didn't harm anything," Jones explained. "It's unlikely that the person who put the message there left any prints or other usable evidence."

A slow nod, and then Suri continued, "We both understood we needed to call Vee." She glanced at the woman next to her. "She said she would, so I got dressed and dried my hair. When I finished, I went looking for her since she never came back and told me if she got in touch with you. That's when I found the back door standing open and Eve's cell phone on the floor." She moistened her trembling lips. "There was a chair overturned like she had reached for it . . . there was blood on the floor too."

Bent gritted his teeth. It wasn't a lot of blood, but enough to suspect Eve hit the floor face first. Her nose or lips may have been injured and bled from the impact. No way to be certain.

"I called Vee," Suri went on. "Locked myself in here like she said and waited."

Vee gave her shoulders a squeeze. "I'm so sorry about this, Suri."

Bent looked to Jones and then jerked his head toward the door. The other man followed him out of the room. When they reached the living room, Bent turned to him. "At this point, I think we can accurately assume he's been here for at least four or five days." He kept his voice quiet to prevent Suri overhearing. "Whoever this guy is, he's been watching and getting the lay of the land."

"Which means he has a landing place," Jones said, concurring with the scenario. "I wouldn't doubt he's been here even longer." He exhaled a heavy breath. "My advice would be to do a press conference. It's time to warn the public. Have people call in any strangers they've seen. Any suspicious behavior. Basically, anything or anyone that doesn't belong."

"That's what I was thinking," Bent agreed. "We can't really provide a description other than the image the sketch artist came up with, based on Carl Baker's account of the man he encountered who claimed to be from my department."

Frankly the image could be anyone. No definitive hair or eye color. Medium height and weight. Baseball cap. No logo Carl could remember. Jacket and jeans. It was basically worthless.

Jones grimaced. "That sketch is so generic I'm not sure I would even use it. We don't want people ruling out anyone because some tiny characteristic didn't fit the sketch."

"I agree." Bent mentally ticked off the folks he would need to call. "I'll set it up."

By dawn he wanted to have a community-wide search in place, just as they had done for Baker. He couldn't even fathom how terrified Eve would be right now. It was true that she would be fiercely ticked off, but beneath all that bravado, she would be scared, and he hated the idea of her going through that. Eve had suffered plenty in her life, and she didn't need this kind of crap. She was like a little sister to Bent.

Wherever she was, he intended to find her and bring her home. And if this bastard had harmed her, he would see to it that he didn't need a trial.

30

Saturday, March 8
Lincoln County Sheriff's Department
Thornton Taylor Parkway, Fayetteville, 8:20 a.m.

Vera couldn't really concentrate on the ongoing conference with Memphis PD. She, Eric, and Bent were in his office, crowded around the conference table. Voices floated from the phone's speaker, but Vera couldn't focus.

They had found no sign of Eve.

The pain of that reality stabbed deep into Vera's belly. Her sister was missing.

Someone sent by Dr. Palmer Solomon had taken her. Fury writhed inside her like a snake shedding its skin, desperate to break free.

Bent had done everything right. He had started a search party and had the teams in the field by dawn. He had done one quick press conference urging folks to look for anything out of place . . . anyone they didn't recognize. If it wasn't there before or had changed in some way, they were to call the sheriff's office. A special hotline had been set up to handle the calls. Volunteers were manning the lines.

He'd contacted the sheriffs of the surrounding counties and had a BOLO out for Eve. Since they had no idea what make or model vehicle the perp was using, there was no way to include anything other than Eve's description.

A more in-depth press conference was scheduled for nine. Bent would give what little information they had to the public. Because all indications pointed to Solomon, the story would no doubt go statewide at least. Eric had set up a call to Talbert and Alcott to bring them up to speed.

Vera and the way her career ended in Memphis would come up in the media, but she didn't care. Let them rehash the dirty details. All that mattered right now was getting her sister back safely and stopping the piece of shit the Messenger had sent.

He's dying. Eric's words reverberated inside her. Running out of time above ground. Funny how facing death often made people attempt to settle unfinished business. She would think, for the sake of his son and daughter as well as his grandson, Solomon would just go out peacefully. Was stirring up his old reputation going to help his grown children who had to go on in this life? Maybe one or the other intended to publish a book, and Daddy was providing a little media boost as well as a killer ending.

Around three this morning, with Eric's help, Vera had done a deep dive into Solomon's offspring. Pamela Solomon Hamilton divorced her one and only husband after only a few months of marriage just last year. She had one adult son named Patrick. Pamela lived in London. She'd kept an almost invisible profile since the arrest of her father. No social media accounts or interaction at all. Her son had been only seventeen at the time of the arrest. Based on her age when the boy was born and the fact that his last name was Solomon as well, he had been a surprise, and she hadn't married or acknowledged his father. Whatever the case, the kid had gone on to do well. He had finished medical school at Vanderbilt University and was currently in his final year of a residency at the Vanderbilt University Medical Center. His academic profile was outstanding. Although he had social media accounts on the most popular platforms, he did little interacting. A social media prowler, she imagined. One who only liked to scroll.

Christopher Solomon had pretty much carried on with his life after the sentencing of his father. He had never married. He was forty-six. Had no children. A mediocre career in real estate. His business had floundered for a while after his father's arrest, but he appeared to be back on his feet now. No social media profiles. His private life was vague at best. She supposed being the son of a notorious serial killer wasn't the best way to win friends and develop influence.

Nothing remarkable about the history of Solomon's offspring before or since his arrest had jumped out at her.

Eric had called both Christopher and Pamela and left voicemails. Both deserved a warning about what was coming. Daddy was up to no good again.

Vera had no sympathy for either of them. Christopher had spoken to her outside the courtroom after his father was sentenced. Blaming her for what happened. Pamela hadn't bothered with an appearance, but her son was there.

You did this to him, Christopher had insisted, his nephew at his side.

She supposed loyalty for one's father and grandfather was appropriate. No matter that Dr. Palmer Solomon had murdered ten women. Then again, Eve had certainly protected their father all those years. And Vera had protected Eve.

But it wasn't the same. Their father hadn't been a murderer. Eve wasn't a murderer. Not even remotely in the way Solomon was.

Vera closed her eyes. *Please, please let her be okay.*

"Any additional thoughts, Vera?"

She blinked. The voice that had asked the question belonged to her former boss, William Talbert.

Scrambling to reorient herself, she looked to Bent and then Eric. Both were watching her, their faces showing worry and a hint of sympathy—neither of which she appreciated. What she needed was to be out there looking for the son of a bitch who had taken her sister.

"Vera has made it clear," Bent said, when she failed to find a response in a timely manner, "how she feels about the subject. Whoever this is, Solomon is involved."

She gave him a subtle nod. "We're all aware," she began, "there was no evidence to support the theory that Solomon had a partner back when we finally caught him. Given what's happened, we have to take a harder look at that possibility, as well as the possibility that this is a new protégé—a surrogate. Either way, the perp we're dealing with is following the technique far too precisely for this to be coincidence or even a mere copycat."

"There's no guarantee," Will spoke up, "that someone involved with the investigation didn't leak the details you're seeing. We all recognize such things happen even in the best departments."

This was true. Before she could argue the point, Eric jumped in. "If that was the case, why was it never in the news? I'm sure there were plenty of reporters itching to get the hidden details for a big story. Based on that, we must assume those details were never leaked and that neither Gloria Anderson nor Solomon ever provided those details to anyone until now—otherwise we would surely have heard about them before."

"I suppose you're right," Will admitted. "I can't deny that I'm still hoping this is unrelated and we haven't allowed Solomon to reach beyond the bars. Or, worse, left a killer's apprentice in the wild."

"Exactly," Vera muttered. But then that wouldn't explain the bastard's obsession with her unless he was being guided by Solomon himself. "Eric mentioned that he's had no visitors besides his son."

"That's correct," Will confirmed. "No visitors. All correspondence is reviewed, so we can say with certainty there has been no discussion or preparation related to anything like this via the official mail."

"Nothing at all from his daughter?" Vera would have thought the woman would at least write to him after she learned of his diagnosis. Then again, how did you forgive someone or even look past a decade-long trail of murders?

"Nothing," Will confirmed.

"For the sake of full disclosure," Special Agent Alcott said, "I have personally reviewed everything we dug up last time about Solomon. I interviewed his son, Christopher, yesterday afternoon by phone in hopes of gaining any of his insights. He has not seen or spoken to his father since Christmas, when he was told about the cancer diagnosis. He insists his father told him not to return and would refuse to see him if he did. To that end, he claims he's had no further contact of any sort. I also called his sister, but Pamela isn't taking my calls."

Vera had only spoken to the son on one occasion beyond that day at the sentencing, and he had been the one doing all the talking. He had seemed shocked by the investigation and in deep denial about his father's guilt. He'd given every indication that he was wholly unaware of his father's secret criminal activities. The daughter had stated the same in a private interview with the feds. Her son had been a part of that interview, and he had claimed to know nothing either.

Nearly thirteen years later there really was only one reasonable explanation for what was happening. Palmer Solomon—the Messenger—had himself a puppet, whether from before or new to the game . . . someone who was willing to do his bidding.

Alcott went on, "I'm sending two agents who worked the original case to support your efforts."

And just like before, they would find nothing. This Vera kept to herself. Her fear and anger were making for a bad combination. Had her wanting to lash out.

"We're grateful for the support," Bent told him.

"Jones," Will said, "stay as long as you need to. Give Sheriff Benton whatever help he requires."

"Will do, sir."

"Vera," Alcott said, speaking again, "I'm guessing that you've decided against visiting Solomon in light of what's happened with your sister."

Bent looked from her to Eric. Vera realized then that she'd failed to share this information with Bent. They'd been a little busy, and then Suri had called about Eve.

"Agent Alcott tried to visit Solomon again last evening," Eric explained. "He will only speak to Vera and claims to have a message for her."

"I'm considering it," Vera answered, ignoring the look Bent pointed in her direction. "I wasn't aware of Solomon's request until last night, and then my sister was taken, so I've had no time to evaluate the merit in either option." She hadn't been able to think of anything else except Eve.

But she hadn't forgotten the invitation.

The call dragged on for a few more minutes before Bent put everyone out of their respective misery and ended it.

"If," Eric said as he pushed to his feet, "you have no different directions for me, I'd like to check in with the search commanders." He turned his hands up. "I don't need to be here for the press conference. That's your platform, not mine. I'm here to help you, not take the podium."

Vera recognized what she had to do. But no one in the room was going to like it.

"I'll hook you up with my second-in-command. He'll see that you get wherever and whatever you need." Bent looked to her. "Vee, I don't want you out of my sight." He hitched his head toward Eric. "Or Eric's. I don't care what this bastard Solomon wants. You need to be where one of us can see you at all times."

She appreciated the gesture. Really she did, but his edict was personal. It was about her safety—not about the best way to handle Solomon's request. "Well." She grabbed her phone and stood. "In that case, one of you better be ready to move, because I have things to do."

Vera knew better than to tell either of the two what she had in mind now that the fog of fear and worry about her sister was thinning enough for her to think clearly. She headed out of the office, and as it turned out, it wasn't necessary to tell them anyway. They both followed her toward the front exit of the building.

"Vee," Bent warned.

She imagined he had figured out what she intended to do. So she ignored him.

"Vera," Eric echoed, "slow down a—"

She pushed out the door and walked into the sunlight. It was a chilly morning, but the sun was giving its all. No less than a couple dozen reporters stood by for the scheduled press conference that was mere minutes away.

Vera walked directly into the crowd that instantly surged forward. Right up front was Patricia Patton. Vera barely restrained the need to roll her eyes.

"I have a preconference sound bite for you," she announced. She didn't have to look back to know both Bent and Eric had stalled and were now watching her and hoping she wouldn't say anything one or both would regret.

"You may have heard," Vera said, "that my sister Eve has been abducted." Hurt swelled so fast inside her that she couldn't speak for a moment. "We all know this is no longer about the Time Thief. You'll hear more about the person we feel is responsible in a few minutes. But right now, I want to send a message to that person."

Eyes and cameras zeroed in on her face. Recording devices extended toward her. Vera ignored all of it and focused on what she had to say. The message was simple and direct.

"I know why you're here," she said. Then she smiled. "It's not my sister you want . . . it's me. So let's make this easy. You let her go, and I'll take her place. You know where to find me."

She turned away, ignoring the barrage of questions thrown at her like bullets in a shoot-out. Bent and Eric followed her back through the front entrance, away from the crowd she'd riled up.

"Do you really think that was smart or beneficial?" Eric asked. He looked disappointed in her.

Bent, on the other hand, looked fighting mad. "She knows it wasn't smart. She's trying to force a reaction." He glared at her.

Ah, Bent knew her well. Didn't matter. She no longer cared what anyone thought. This was about finding Eve before that piece of shit did something Vera couldn't fix.

She looked from one man to the other. "I'm ready to go to Nashville to see Solomon."

"No way," Bent said flat out. "I'm putting you in protective custody."

"Like hell you are," Vera fired back. "You're not thinking like a sheriff, Bent." She didn't have to say the rest. He knew exactly what she meant.

"Just hold on a minute." Eric held up both hands. "She's right. He's refusing to talk to anyone except Vera. It's possible if she gives him the attention he wants, he'll back his guy down. We have nothing to lose but a few hours' time by giving it a try."

Bent was not the easiest guy to make angry. He generally took everything in stride. She supposed he'd learned that kind of patience and restraint after all those years of having his father beat the hell out of him. His mother had died when he was just a little kid and wasn't there to protect him. Then there was his time in the military. But despite all that, she, apparently, had the power to rile him up . . . to scramble his focus, because he was thoroughly pissed right now.

"If she goes," Bent said to Eric, "you go with her. I'll take care of things here." Then he pointed that weighty glare at Vera once more. "I do not want her going anywhere—particularly that prison—alone."

Vera didn't argue. She could live with his terms. "I want to go now," she said to Eric. "Right now."

He nodded. "Okay."

"Bring your car around back," Bent suggested. "You can get away while I start the press conference. We don't need anyone following you. There's a side entrance to the parking lot at the end of the corridor past my office."

Eric headed in that direction.

Bent's blue eyes, still fiery with anger, settled on her. "You do what you think you need to do, Vee, but don't do anything else as careless as what you just did."

"We can wait for his next move," she argued, exhaustion pulling at her now, "or we can make the next move. It's that simple, Bent."

She wasn't going to apologize for taking the necessary steps to prompt a reaction. Of all the people who had worked the Messenger investigation, she knew Solomon on a sort of intimate level the best.

He or his surrogate wanted a reaction from *her*, so she'd given it to him.

Now it was his turn.

All she had to do was give him the right opportunity. But first she had to see the bastard who'd started this thing.

It was always better to take some measure of what you were up against.

31

Riverbend Maximum Security Institution
Cockrill Bend Boulevard, Nashville, 10:30 a.m.

Eric made the turn onto Cockrill Bend Boulevard.

Before they could begin this journey, Vera had insisted on stopping by her house and changing. She couldn't have cared less about what the reporters thought of her sweatshirt and jeans, but this was different. She needed Solomon to see the professional person he'd been drawn to all those years ago. With that in mind, she'd chosen a black suit. The skirt was tight, and the heels she wore were high. She'd even gone the extra mile with the makeup. Today she needed a full arsenal. Solomon might be an old man with terminal cancer, but he wasn't dead.

And Eve was counting on her.

The drive from Fayetteville had been filled with equal stretches of silence and spurts of small talk. They hadn't discussed the case or Solomon. Eric had asked about Eve, and Vera had told him about some of their adventures as children. She had laughed and barely held back the tears, but all in all, those moments had kept her from obsessing on the worst-case scenario.

She would get her sister back alive. Any other option was unacceptable.

"Bent is exactly what I expected," Eric said as he parked in the visitor's lot.

Vera turned to him. "That tells me I spent far too much time talking about him when you and I first started a personal relationship."

He leaned against the headrest and pointed his face toward hers. "Sometimes, but only because I asked. I knew the impact he'd had on you, and somehow I couldn't stop digging. Glutton for punishment, I suppose."

"The whole situation was entirely your fault," she warned. "I had sworn off relationships until you came along, so you opened that old can of worms."

He smiled then. "I guess I did." He searched her eyes for a moment. "Do you ever miss *us*?" He frowned. "I mean, I'm completely in love with Anna. I've asked her to marry me."

Vera smiled, despite the shitstorm of emotions sucking her into it. "Congratulations. That's great. Really great." Her smile faded a little. "I do miss us . . . sometimes." Why lie? "I miss the way we laughed together and how I knew without a doubt that I could always depend on you and that you would always be there."

"Something Bent hadn't done," he suggested.

She nodded.

"But he's older now," Eric said. "He knows how to do it right this time."

Vera laughed softly. "Who can say? Maybe it was me. Maybe I'm the problem."

"Don't lie to yourself, Vera," he rebutted softly. "I saw how he looks at you, and I didn't miss the way you look at him."

"On that note," she said, reaching for her door handle, "I think we should move on."

He gave a single, firm nod. "Good idea."

Warden Wyman Halston was waiting for them after they'd made their way through the security protocols.

Once the pleasantries were behind them, Halston moved on to the reason they were here. "Solomon refuses to see anyone but you, and as you're aware, we can only record personal visits under certain circumstances, and this is not one of them. Therefore, we will be relying completely on you to handle whatever comes up in conversation. Make no promises that you are not authorized to make."

"Understood." This wasn't her first rodeo.

"You will have a private interview room, but there will be guards right outside. Solomon will be secured, and there is a panic button if the need arises."

She nodded and repeated, "Understood."

"I'll be right outside the door," Eric assured her, "with the guards."

"Very well," Halston concluded. "Don't make me regret the extra effort."

From the warden's office, two guards escorted Vera and Eric to the interview room. The wide gray corridors in a prison were always the same. Too brightly lit and full of echoes and whispers of anger and hate and agony. And the smell. Sweat, fear, with a hint of urine. Never a pleasant place.

The row of interview rooms for private meetings was short and no less gray. Their progression stopped at the door marked with a number two. There was a very small window in the door for peering inside, but she opted not to look. She did not want the man waiting there to catch her taking a peek at him. She wouldn't give him the satisfaction.

"The panic button is under your side of the table on the right, ma'am," the taller of the two guards explained. "He's in full shackles, which are secured to the floor. He won't be able to reach all the way across the table, but he can raise his hands and reach a few inches. You should not lean across the table or approach him in any manner."

"Got it." Vera's heart pounded. Her entire body had gone numb and on high alert with the flood of adrenaline roaring through her.

Eric reached out and squeezed her upper arm. "Don't let him get to you."

She gave her friend a nod, then turned to the guard who'd spoken. "I'm ready."

He unlocked the door and opened it. Vera walked in, her heels clicking on the polished tile. The room was more beige than gray. An equally beige table sat in the center, a generic chair on either side.

Dr. Palmer Solomon sat on the side farthest from the door. He smiled at her as the door closed with a solid thud, then the lock slid into place.

"Hello, Vera."

She gave him time to look her up and down before she crossed to the table and pulled out her chair. "Hello, Dr. Solomon." She sat down and stared at him. "I wish I could say it was a pleasure to see you again, but it's not, so I won't pretend."

"The pleasure is all mine then." He inhaled a deep breath, as if attempting to draw in her scent.

She'd spritzed on just a little of the perfume she'd always worn whenever she bothered. Soft, subtle, just a hint of citrus. "Let's get straight to it. After all this time, why now?"

It was a simple question. He'd had a dozen years to reach out for revenge. Why wait so long? Had the news that he was dying prompted the need? Or was it because he knew she was closer, geographically speaking? She felt sure he'd kept up with her. Relished the tragedy that ended her career in Memphis, no doubt. Anger bled into the adrenaline pulsing inside her. *Bastard.*

"I'm sure you're aware," he said, "that I have only a very short time to live."

He really didn't look like a dying man—just thinner, wearier maybe. As much as it chafed her to say, he remained quite handsome—as killers went. His hair was that white color so envied by those who didn't have it as they reached later life. Gray eyes still clear and attentive. Fewer wrinkles than your average seventy-two-year-old. Obviously, until his illness stopped him, he had stayed physically fit. But those details were fading. The cancer was stealing all the strength and vitality from his body, and there was not a damned thing he could do.

The thought made her inordinately happy.

"Yes," she said, "I heard. If you expect sympathy, you're looking in the wrong place." The images of all those women he had killed flashed one after the other before her eyes.

"I saw you on the news this morning. They allow me to have a television. Did you know that? It's one of the benefits of cooperating with the FBI from time to time." He chuckled as if the idea were quite funny. "Advice from a serial killer is a very marketable commodity."

"Then you know why I'm here." She repositioned in her chair so she could cross one leg over the other.

He watched the move with interest. "I knew you would come." His gaze shifted to hers. "As soon as I heard what was happening, I was worried about you."

Vera laughed out loud. "Of course you were."

He leaned forward. Chains rattled. "I'm quite serious, Vera. I am very worried about your safety, as well as your sister's."

A new burn of fury blazed inside her. "If you hurt my sister . . ." She dared him by leaning forward the tiniest bit, as if to meet him in the middle, and lowering her voice to a whisper. "I will find a way to make your last days a living hell."

That he watched the movement of her lips so intensely was unnerving and yet satisfying. He was still intrigued by her, which meant, she hoped, that he would play along. Perhaps make a mistake.

"I would never hurt your sister," he said, drawing back, his respiration a little faster than before.

She drew back as well. "I don't have time for games, Palmer." He liked when she called him Palmer. In fact, while he held her captive, he'd insisted she use his given name. "Tell me who's doing this, or just call them off. I can live with either choice."

"He has been watching you, Vera. For months. He knows where you live. Where your sisters live. What you do and who you do it with."

Outrage mounting, she gritted her teeth for a moment to prevent the wrong words from erupting. "Tell me," she said as calmly as the emotional whirlwind inside her would allow, "who did you send to do this?"

He leaned forward again. "He knows all your secrets. He's studied you so closely. Even I was impressed. He knows how to hurt you, and he won't stop until he has done the most damage possible."

She barely restrained herself from lunging across the table and shaking the truth out of him. If she had a gun, she would shove it hard into that soft place beneath his chin and blow his fucking head off.

"Who is it?" she repeated.

"I told them," he said, as if she hadn't demanded a name. "I told them you were in danger as soon as I learned of the plot, but apparently no one listened. Otherwise, you could have been watching all this time and stopped him."

His words penetrated the haze of anger. "You told who what?"

"Why, Agent Alcott, of course. Shortly after my diagnosis, I told him I feared you were in danger."

What the . . . ? Vera pushed away the uncertainty that attempted to intrude. This could be a trick. His way of throwing her off balance.

"When was this?" She uncrossed her legs and sat up straighter.

"February third. They told me in December there was nothing to be done for my condition. By February I realized what was happening, and I told Alcott he should warn you."

Vera clasped her hands together in her lap to prevent herself from reaching over and ripping his throat out. "I'll take that up with Alcott. *This* is between you and me. Tell me who it is."

He shook his head, as if what he had to say next made him sad. "You should have followed your instincts, Vera. You knew there was someone else. You felt it in your bones, but you were afraid to bring it up. You were so new at the business of being a detective." He looked away, as if needing a moment to collect himself. "I was wrong to do what I did. But I thought it was the right thing at the time." He searched her eyes once more. "Can you understand that?"

She understood nothing except that this man was a monster. Still, she played along. She couldn't take any risks when Eve's life hung in the balance. He was suggesting that she recognized he might have had someone working with him back then. And she had. But there had been no evidence, and she hadn't pushed the issue. She'd let it go. They had their killer. End of story.

"You're only human," she offered. She wanted—needed—to understand what he was talking about. Every nerve ending in her body tingled. He was about to tell her something important—maybe something that would save her sister.

He nodded. "I knew you would appreciate my dilemma. You've done things you needed to do as well. You've covered for the people you love—no matter the bad deeds they've done."

The realization of what he was saying bored into her brain, shook her as if an earthquake had begun deep inside her. "No." She drew away. This could not be right. "I was there. *You* kidnapped me, and *you* kidnapped Eric Jones. I saw what you did . . . you confessed. Why would you change your story now?"

He stared at her, saying nothing, a look of . . . not triumph . . . a look of defeat in his eyes. No. No. This couldn't be.

"I wanted to protect my family," he said quietly. "I had no choice, really. It was my fault after all. Genetics." He shrugged. "One was bound to inherit those more unpleasant genes."

"No." She could not get right with the words he was saying. "You had every detail down to a science . . . every single detail. Gloria identified you."

"Well, I was there, after all . . . guiding my prodigy." He closed his eyes a moment, his face in a tight grimace.

Pain, she surmised. With cancer came pain. She felt no sympathy . . . she felt only horror and dismay at what he was insinuating to her. The need to rush out of the room was a barely suppressed throbbing impulse inside.

Prodigy? What the hell? Was he suggesting his son, Christopher, had been a fledgling serial killer?

When his eyes opened once more, he went on. "You came so close. I realized then that I had been deluding myself. Evading exposure for an entire life's work is rare. It requires a certain level of skill. I recognized this one, sadly, was not like me. I had to make a way out—you understand. We do what we must for those we love. So, I promised to reveal myself if—"

"Jesus Christ," she snapped, cutting him off. "You are a fucking psychiatrist. You are well aware that he cannot just cut it off. Any more than you could." This meant only one thing—the Messenger had worked with a partner. How the hell had that partner been finding a way to assuage his needs all this time?

"I had to offer the opportunity," he argued. "It was the least I could do."

Dear God, how many more had been tortured and murdered without their killer being caught?

"Is it Christopher?" Serial killers were far more likely to be male than female. The reality of what he was saying made the bottom drop from her stomach. And the bastard had Eve.

"Anger is the guide now," he said softly, as if Vera had said nothing. "I'm dying, and my family is feeling true, bone-deep loss for the first time in their lives. I suppose I protected them far too well. At any rate, the goal is revenge." His gaze fixed on Vera. "The concept that we would never have been caught if not for you is in play. You were the first to make me see the possibility. I may have said as much."

"How many others?" The urge to vomit had her throat tightening.

"You mean before the FBI became aware of my work?" Pride twinkled in his eyes. "One each year since I was twenty. My methods evolved, of course. As did those of the FBI, which eventually brought my work to their attention."

Vera had known he hadn't suddenly started at age fifty. Son of a bitch. But right now, his history wasn't relevant. "How many others has your prodigy killed without you?"

He made a face. "I don't believe there have been others," he insisted. "He loves his work. He saves lives now. He doesn't take them."

He.

"Oh my God." Her jaw fell slack. She snapped it shut and summoned a steady tone. He wasn't talking about Christopher or Pamela . . . he was talking about Patrick, his grandson—the doctor. "Wait." She held up both hands. "Your grandson was only seventeen when you were arrested."

Solomon laughed a sad sound. "His first adventure with me was when he was nine. His mother failed to look after him properly. His father was never in the picture. I was all he had, really. This was something special we shared. By the time he was a teenager, he was taking the lead." A smile tipped up his lips. "He was a very good student."

Vera's insides expanded with the need to expel the horror he'd just dumped on her. She had to get out of here . . . had to stop the bastard. If he was this profoundly affected by his grandfather's looming death, he would be reckless . . . and even more dangerous.

"In retrospect, while it's true that his mother neglected him, it was me who ruined him," Solomon went on. "I eventually understood that I had to try and save him. It was my obligation to him and to my daughter."

"You wanted him to stop." It wasn't a question. She got it now. Her heart thundered . . . throat felt dry . . . palms were sweating. "You set up that whole finale with Gloria Anderson so you could give your grandson a second chance. You arranged it so I would find her. You did all of it—abducted me and Eric—to expose yourself . . . to steer us away from him."

"No." The chains rattled again with the movement of his hands as he waved off her suggestion. "You found Gloria all on your own." He lifted his shoulders, let them fall in a shrug. "Perhaps only because of his mistakes. You see, he left me out of the planning on that one. But that is irrelevant. Then you started digging, and as you grew closer, I knew you were going to find us because you were—are—better than all the rest." He stared directly at her then. "It was then that I recognized his vulnerability. I had to do something."

So many emotions that she could not begin to name even a portion of them were roiling inside her. "Where is he? Where did he take my sister?"

"I only know that he is in your hometown. He is angry that I'm dying. Angry that it was he—and you—who caused me to spend my final years here. He will not listen to reason."

So he had spoken to him. No matter that she wanted to go ballistic on the man, she held back . . . focused on speaking calmly. "Where is he exactly?"

"I swear to you," he pressed. "I do not know."

"If," she warned, "you fail to tell me the whole truth and my sister pays the price"—she leaned closer—"I will gut him like a fucking pig and watch him die in pain. You have my word on that, Doc. It won't be like last time."

"If I knew, I would tell you. Once I realized what he was planning and confronted him on his last visit to me, he disappeared."

Her gaze narrowed. "I was told you had no visitors except your son, Christopher."

"There are things that even the warden doesn't know." He smiled that charming expression he was known for. "Trust me when I say I have seen and spoken to him on numerous occasions. Perhaps the visitor logs list him as someone else—as Christopher, I would guess." His brow furrowed then. "Be advised, I've contacted all my sources, and no one can find him."

"Your sources?" What the hell?

Another of those faint smiles slid across his lips. "You know how it is in prison: if you can pay the price, you can learn anything—get anything—from the outside."

Oh yes, she was well aware. Disgusted, she stood. "Give me a moment."

She walked to the door and banged on it. It opened instantly, and the guard waited for her to step out. Eric looked her up and down, as if ensuring she was unharmed.

"I need a Sharpie."

"A what?" The guard stared at her as if she'd lost her mind.

"A permanent marker," she clarified. Who didn't know what a Sharpie was?

"Ma'am—"

"Here." Eric thrust a pen at her. "It's the only thing I have on me."

It was an ink pen, but she supposed that would work.

"Ma'am," the guard repeated, "you cannot give him that pen or anything else."

"Don't worry." She backed deeper into the room and away from the door. "It's not for him. It's for me."

"Just close the door," Eric said when the guard would have argued.

He muttered something about telling the warden and slammed the door.

Vera crossed back to the table and leaned over. "Hold out your hands."

Solomon extended his hands, palms up, as far as his restraints would allow. Chains rattled. "Don't move," she ordered. On the underside of his left forearm, she wrote her number. Then she leaned away from him. "That's my cell number. If you find out anything at all, you let me know."

He stared at the number, then looked up at her. "You have my word."

His word wasn't worth shit, but she'd already given him her word about what she would do if he didn't give her a heads-up. And she suspected he understood this was a promise.

When she would have turned away, his voice stopped her. "He taunted me about being inside your home."

The fury she'd kept under control for the most part threatened to boil over again. "How nice of him to give his old grandpa a few jollies."

"I warned him that I was going to tell you, but he only laughed. He said he'd left you a gift—a secret message that only you would understand—somewhere in your house, but it would likely be too late when you found it."

Vera pointed a finger at him. "You better not be lying to me."

"As I said, you have—"

"Yeah, yeah. Your word."

She walked away from him. As she reached the door, he said, "It was good to see you again, Vera."

Fucking piece of shit.

She banged on the door and got the hell out of there. She didn't speak to anyone, just walked away. It took every fiber of self-control she possessed not to run.

Eric hurried to catch up with her. "The warden will be waiting to hear how the meeting went."

"No time," she said. "We have to get back to Fayetteville." Eve needed her. This was Vera's fault, damn it. She had to fix it.

"He told you who's working for him?"

"I'll tell you everything on the way."

Vera didn't say another word until they were in Eric's car, headed south. The walls in places like that prison had ears.

"We screwed up," she said. The weight of what she now knew had parked like a dump truck on her chest. Fear snaked around her throat... squeezed to the point she could barely breathe. And Eve had gotten the short end of the stick.

"I'm afraid to ask what that means."

"Palmer Solomon set us up to protect his grandson."

"That's impossible." Eric glanced from the road to her and back, his head moving side to side in denial. "The grandson wasn't much more than a kid."

"Patrick was a serial killer in training who came into his own at a young age. Solomon was so proud, until he recognized the kid couldn't protect himself. It was too late then; I'd already discovered his latest victim." She scrubbed at her eyes. God, she needed sleep, but that was not possible.

"Gloria." Eric's fingers tightened on the steering wheel. "Son of a bitch."

"Yeah." She rubbed at her forehead and the ache pounding there. "Because I got too close, dear old Palmer decided Patrick wouldn't ever be able to avoid being caught the way he had, so he made a deal. The grandson would stop killing, and Palmer would take one for the team."

Eric cut a horrified look at her. "Just the sort of grandfather every teenage boy needs."

"But now the grandson is angry that his beloved mentor is dying." She shrugged. "Maybe he had a breakdown after all the pressure of med school and his residency. Add to that his grandfather's imminent death. Who knows? Whatever tipped Patrick over the edge, he's out for revenge." She closed her eyes for a moment to pull herself together. "Alcott should check on the mother—Pamela. Solomon mentioned that she hadn't taken care of the kid. I don't think he would have mentioned that fact if it wasn't relevant."

"Got it." Eric glanced at her. "Anything else I should know?"

"He's been watching me for weeks at least." The words ripped at her soul. "He's been in my house. He knows everything I do. Everything my sisters do."

"And he has Eve."

Vera stared at the highway ahead of them. "Yeah."

32

Boyett Farm
Good Hollow Road, Fayetteville, 2:45 p.m.

Vera watched Eric drive away.

It hadn't been easy to coax him into leaving, but she'd managed. As soon as they'd arrived, despite the fact that a deputy was watching her house, Eric had insisted on coming inside and searching the place for any hidden intruders. Didn't matter that her security system had still been armed and every window in the house was screwed shut.

The only reason Bent hadn't been waiting for her return was because she'd called him on the drive back and filled him in on the meeting and because he had another press conference scheduled at three. He'd wanted her to come to him, but she'd complained that she was far too exhausted. He probably saw right through that story like peering through a screen door. But he'd let it go. He had his hands full—even more so now.

Bent had downloaded a recent photo of Patrick Solomon—who looked eerily like his grandfather had when he was young—and was issuing a BOLO. He would release the photo in his press conference.

On the drive home, Eric had set up a three-way call on his cell phone with Will and Alcott to inform them about Solomon's latest confession. Alcott was sending an agent familiar with the case to Nashville to be near Palmer Solomon in the event some sort of intervention was needed. He was also contacting someone in London to make an official notification to Patrick's mother, Pamela, since she refused his calls. She, as well as Christopher, would be under close surveillance. During the same call, Vera had confronted Alcott about Solomon's claim that he had warned the agent about potential danger to Vera. Alcott had insisted that, at the time, he'd felt certain Solomon was only jockeying for a meeting with Vera one last time before he died.

Vera wasn't entirely sure she believed Alcott, but it was irrelevant now. There was no time for raising hell. She had a mission that couldn't wait. Solomon had said his grandson had left a gift—a secret message—somewhere in the house for her. She intended to find it ASAP. If there was any possibility that it could help lead her to Eve, she had to find it. Then she was going to find him.

She went to her bedroom first. It was the most likely place, if he'd left something especially for her. Disgust tasted bitter in her mouth. Sometimes she wondered how she had survived this long with so many monsters in her orbit.

She started in her closet. Didn't take long. She had donated most of her business wardrobe when she sorted through her stuff from Memphis. Nothing unexpected in the closet. Since there was no carpet, just the old hardwood floor and a few throw rugs, she lifted each one and checked beneath them. Under the bed was next. Between the mattress and box springs, and then she tore the bedding off the mattress, removed sheets and pillowcases. The effort proved futile, as far as her search was concerned. But the scent of the man who'd shared this bed with her less than twenty-four hours ago lingered on the sheets . . . the unmistakable smell of their lovemaking had her trembling.

Probably hadn't been the best move she'd made since returning to Fayetteville. Likely wouldn't be the worst.

Moving on, she searched all pieces of furniture, shelves, and any little niche that might hold an item.

There was nothing new in her room. She exhaled a big, weary breath.

Why should he make it easy?

From there, she picked methodically through the other upstairs rooms. One by one, including the bathroom.

Back downstairs, she shoved her sheets into the washing machine and then executed the same search, moving from one room to the next. Her mother's library proved the most difficult. There were literally hundreds of books and dozens of photo albums. Hoping for the easier avenue, she started with the albums.

By the time she was halfway through the pile, she'd sunk to the floor and had photo albums spread all around her. Each album was big and thick and loaded with pages and pages of family pictures. Memories sifted through her, making her heart swell.

It was the eighth one she selected that opened to a nine-by-eleven envelope made of stock brown kraft-style paper with a metal clasp. Her name was scrawled across the front. Anticipation buzzed along her nerve endings. The weight of the envelope warned there was something more inside than a single note.

She unfastened the clasp and removed the contents. On top was the expected note. Beneath it were eight-by-ten photos. The images captured there had her eyes widening in surprise and her breath stalling in her lungs.

Her mother . . . naked save for a sheet draped over her from her chest down, lying on a mortuary table. *The missing funeral home photos.* Vera's shoulders slumped as her entire being seemed to melt into an invisible puddle of muck. These had been missing last summer when she had tried to find them.

Seven months ago, the former county medical examiner had suggested Vera's mother was murdered by a family member. The very idea was ludicrous. Their mother was in the final days of a horrible battle with cancer. She'd either fallen asleep or gone unconscious while taking a bath and slipped under the water. It happened far too often to those already feeble from illness and then pumped full of pain drugs.

Except—Vera's fingers felt stiff and icy as she shuffled through the photos—there were bruises just like the ME had said. The placement of the bruises suggested she'd been held down prior to death. The marks were on her shoulders and just above her breasts . . . there was even one near her throat. How . . . ?

Not possible. There had to be another explanation. The photos had been doctored. Something.

Except the images were right in front of her eyes. The photos slightly yellowed by time. Maybe the bruises were made the day before she died, but how and why and by whom?

This was insane . . . completely crazy.

How the hell did Solomon's grandson, a.k.a. the other half of the Messenger, know about these missing photos? Solomon had to have told him all sorts of things about Vera. Things not known until seven months ago.

Fingers trembling, she picked up the note the piece of shit had left.

> Dear Vera,
> Found these hidden in your sister's house. I guess she kept them so she could look back and relish her first kill. Did you know?
> Cheers,
> Your First Mistake

Rage ripped through her. Yes, apparently the Messenger case was her first big mistake. His pointing this out was only to remind her that the crash and burn of the team she'd helped build was not her first career failure . . . it was her second.

But why send her these photos in the middle of his big return to his first career—killing? How was it relevant to what he had planned for her and Eve? Was it just a distraction? A prompt for her to think any less of her sister?

Or a clue?

Vera reshuffled the photos and stuffed them back into the envelope. The bastard's note went next. It was all she could do not to tear it into a thousand pieces. Then she hid the *gift* back in the album and hurriedly returned all twelve to their proper shelves.

She drew in a deep, calming breath, smoothed the too-tight skirt, only then remembering she was still wearing it. First, she had to get out of these clothes. The heels had landed somewhere. She found them by the front door. Grabbed the pair of pain-inducing footwear and hurried up the stairs. It was still a little cool outside, so she dressed with that in mind. Jeans, thick socks, and a tee, along with a sweatshirt. She snagged a baseball cap and tugged it into place. Downstairs she found her sneakers and pulled them on.

She had searched the house. There was nothing else related to the Messenger to find. He'd come into her house at least once, maybe twice before she'd screwed the windows shut. Palmer Solomon had said his grandson had been watching her for months. Since Christmas possibly. So he could have come in numerous times she didn't know about. But why wait so long to make a move?

The whole thing made no sense. Did it really take him that long to prepare? Maybe so. He'd spent weeks, sometimes months watching his other victims. The amount of time spent might be a part of his process. All serial killers had processes—MOs. A way of doing things from which they rarely deviated.

Then again, maybe he'd just been rusty.

In any event, he would have carefully chosen where to keep Eve—which was Vera's biggest problem at the moment. Baker had been nothing more than a teaser, requiring far less preparation. Most likely he'd been merely an opportunity that arose from the fake Time Thief business. Eve was the one he would use to hurt Vera. Worry and hatred welled inside her. For Vera he would have planned extensively.

This farm was where she and Eve had grown up. Where they'd played as children. Lived and lost and survived. This was where their mother had died and then, not even two years later, their stepmother had taken her last breath, here in this very house.

Bent had people searching Fayetteville and the surrounding area. There were official searches with county and city law enforcement personnel as well as civilians in the community simply checking their own property and that of their immediate neighbors'. During this morning's press conference, Bent had urged folks to check in on their neighbors, particularly the elderly or otherwise vulnerable. To report any suspicious activity in or near abandoned homes or buildings.

The whole county was on alert.

But the evil could be right here on her farm. No matter that Bent had searched the farm. Not once but twice. After the message was left in her house and then again after Eve was taken. But no one was looking here now. Which was likely exactly what the bastard had wanted. Executing his plan here would be in keeping with his previous MO of leaving his victims in a location relevant to their lives. He'd left Nolan at Vera's barn because this farm was relevant to Vera, and Nolan's abduction had been about her, not the young reporter.

Anticipation funneling through her, Vera grabbed a coat and a flashlight and headed for the door. She'd just gotten down the front steps when the deputy currently assigned to surveillance duty approached.

"Is everything all right, ma'am?"

"I need to have a look around the property."

Deputy Mitchell, according to his name tag, glanced about the yard. "I'm not sure that's a good idea, ma'am. Why don't I call the sheriff and run it past him? It would be better if you stayed inside."

"Call him," she agreed. "But I'm having a look around."

She started around back, taking her time to really look at the house... the landscape... everything. It hadn't rained lately, and the snow had all melted quickly, the moisture immediately absorbed into the dry ground. There was no chance of tracks. A quick peek in the potting shed and well house revealed nothing out of place—just like the last time she'd looked.

Had that been yesterday or the day before? Time had blurred into one long stream of consciousness.

The barn was her next destination. Mitchell was right behind her as he ended his call to Bent.

By the time she reached the barn on foot, Bent had pulled up in his truck. He'd taken the narrow dirt road just past the house that led directly to the barn.

That was fast, she decided, even for him. He must have already been en route.

Deputy Mitchell headed back to the house.

Vera entered the barn without a backward glance. She was on a mission. Bent could either join her or wait for her to finish. Her sister was in trouble, and she would do whatever necessary to help her.

"This was the first place I had my deputies look when Eve went missing and we didn't find her in the vicinity of Suri's house."

Vera glanced at him through the building gloom. It would be dark soon. "I know. But I need to do this."

"All right." He climbed the ladder and checked the loft while she poked around the lower level.

It only took a few minutes to confirm there was nothing to find. Nothing out of place. Defeat tugged at her, but she refused to give up.

Her grip tightened on the flashlight. "Did they look in the cave?" The thought of going in that damned hole in the ground had her stomach cramping.

"They did. But we can look again if you feel the need."

Need. That was the reason they'd ended up in bed together last night. Flashes from those moments whispered through her head, sent heat searing through her. The idea that Eve had been taken around that same time ripped her heart to shreds.

"I do," she said, "feel the need." She moistened her lips. She needed this relationship—the friend and professional one—between them to work out, and now she feared she had screwed that up by surrendering to that more intimate need.

Worse, she may have lost her sister. Agony ached through her bones. No way. Nope. She would not allow that to happen.

He nodded. "I'll get my flashlight from the truck."

She followed him outside the barn and waited while he went to his truck. From there they walked through the woods, picking their way through the underbrush. Didn't matter that it would be dark soon; muscle memory would have guided her along the overgrown path even if Bent hadn't been leading the way.

"Have you checked out the old hospital?" she asked. Baker had been abducted from there by this piece of shit. But if the grandson was anything like the grandfather, he was like lightning and never struck in the same place twice.

"We did. As well as the shack on McDeal Road and at the funeral home." He glanced over his shoulder at her. "Any place else you've thought of that I might have missed?"

"The high school Eve and I attended." There were two high schools in Fayetteville now, but there had been only one back then.

"Done already."

She tried to think of any place this resurrected Messenger could hole up in that meant something to her or to Eve. "At the park, under the bridge?"

"Yep. Checked the cemetery too."

Vera racked her brain for other options. "What about that bar where she used to hang out before she got clean? The one just off Lincoln Avenue that's closed now. All boarded up."

"Checked there too. And the church where she goes to AA meetings."

So far it sounded as if he'd thought of everything. But Patrick Solomon had to be someplace. God, she hated this shit . . . hated that she had brought this to her family.

No losing it yet, Vee.

They reached the clearing where the mouth of that cave rose out of the ground like an enormous eyebrow.

"You want me to go first?" he asked.

"I do." Otherwise he'd be staring at her ass until she crawled through on her hands and knees. God, she was so tired.

He removed his hat and placed it on a nearby boulder, then dropped to his knees. He lit the flashlight and tossed it through the opening before crawling inside.

Vera went next. Once she was deep enough inside, he offered his hand, giving her an assist to her feet. She swiped her knees, then turned on her own flashlight.

More of those echoes from the past whispered through her. Before, when they were just little kids, she and Eve had come here to play. They hadn't known all the secrets this cave held at the time—at least Vera hadn't. Years later this was the place they had used to stash their stepmother's body. The sound of infant Luna wailing reverberated in her ears. She shivered at the memories. She really had hoped to never come in here again.

They studied the ground and the walls to ensure there was nothing new. Beyond the graffiti, of course. Teenagers had sneaked onto the property and left ugly words and drawings. Vera ignored them. Her family members were now the most infamous residents of Lincoln County. She'd been inundated with requests for tours of the cave and surrounding woods back during Halloween.

She'd considered having the mouth of the cave walled up with brick or concrete. Maybe she would when this new level of insanity was over.

After twenty minutes of careful examination, it was clear there was nothing new inside this big hole in the ground. Bent had checked the second, deeper chamber. Vera had declined that adventure.

When they were outside once more, he picked up his hat and asked, "Have you eaten today?"

The way he looked at her—as if he might hug her—had her bracing to run. If he touched her . . . she might just fall apart. She could not do that under any circumstances. Not until she found Eve . . . not until she took care of that bastard.

Instead, she lifted her chin and looked at him as if he'd lost his mind. How could she think about food right now? "Eric forced me to eat a burger on the way back from Nashville."

"He seems like a nice guy," Bent said as he made his way back toward the barn.

Having moved past the denser area, they were able to walk side by side. Vera glanced at him. "He is a very nice guy."

"You still have feelings for him?"

Now there was the question he'd really wanted to ask. At a time like this? Jesus. She swallowed back the whale of emotions. "As a dear friend, yes. He's in a serious relationship now. Her name is Anna."

Bent glanced at her. "Good for him."

"Yeah, good for him and Anna." Eric would be a wonderful husband, and father, if the latter was the route they chose to take.

When she and Bent reached her house, he followed her inside. It would be full-on dark soon. The idea that they still had no idea where Eve was churned in her belly, twisted in her chest. *Please, please let her be okay.*

Poor Eve would likely be pissed as hell at the bastard who'd taken her. And worried sick about Suri.

"Suri is staying with Mr. Hurst," Bent explained, as if she'd said the thought aloud. "He and his wife insisted when they heard what had happened."

Vera was surprised. The Hurst family had always seemed a bit standoffish. In light of Suri's confession, Vera was actually stunned he hadn't fired her. Hurst was the biggest funeral home service in the county. Like most businesses, reputation was immensely important.

"Good." She scrubbed at her forehead, realizing she was still wearing the damned makeup. "I should call Luna. Make sure she's okay."

Bent hitched his head toward her living room. "I have some calls to make. After that, you mind if I catch a quick nap on your couch?"

She was confident that, like her, he hadn't slept much if at all since the night before last. After downing that hamburger, she'd actually dozed once or twice on the way back from Nashville.

Funny how the exhaustion and the rumpled clothes looked so good on him. Oh well. No one knew better than her that Bent would look good wearing mud.

"Sure." She caught herself before she suggested he take her room. Particularly since she had stripped the linens off the bed. He would immediately think of last night. "I'll be in the kitchen."

She hurried away. First, she moved her sheets to the dryer, then she grabbed a wad of paper towels and washed her face. She needed a shower after spending time with Solomon in that prison.

But she refused to get naked again with Bent in the house.

Instead, she made that call to Luna to check on her, and then she rounded up a pen and pad. She sat down with a cup of coffee to start analyzing what she knew about Solomon's grandson and the moves the two had made during the ten murders of which the authorities were aware. If she could create an accurate profile . . . she might just be able to figure out where he had taken Eve.

Hang in there, sis! I'm coming for you.

33

Eve used her bound hands to swipe at her face. She had tried really hard not to cry, but as the hours had passed, it had become more and more difficult. Daylight had come and gone, and judging by how tired and hungry she was, an entire day had passed.

Suri and Vera would be so worried. Luna too.

A burst of anger chased away the tears. She glared at the man who sat on a stool watching her. She wanted to kill this son of a bitch more than she wanted to take another breath.

Blasts of fury erupted in her chest like a series of explosions in a fireworks display. Her feet and legs hurt from being bound together too tightly at the ankles. Her hands were going numb. He'd taken the gag out when he'd wanted to ask questions, and he hadn't put it back. She'd told herself to keep her mouth shut so he wouldn't be prompted to stuff it in again, but she wasn't sure how much longer she could keep quiet.

"You know your sister was a big hero when she took down my grandfather and saw that he went to prison." His mouth twisted in hatred. "Everyone thought she had rescued them from 'the' monster." He emphasized the word by making air quotes.

"And you were a coward," Eve said. "Otherwise you wouldn't have left your own grandfather to rot in prison alone for the crimes you helped him commit." He seemed kind of young to have been killing for so long, but what did she know. He had that creepy blond hair—almost white—and pale-gray eyes.

As if she'd said as much out loud, he shot to his feet and charged toward her.

Heart racing, she held perfectly still. It wasn't like she had much of an option. She was on the floor, leaning against a wall. There was nowhere to go unless she attempted to roll to her right or left. As numb as her legs felt, she wasn't sure she could do that quickly enough. Instead, she braced herself and rode it out.

"You," he growled, so close spittle flew in her face, "have no fucking idea why I did what I did. We were partners, and all he wanted was to save me . . . now he is dying."

"Seems pretty clear you just sat back and let him do it," she said, allowing nothing more than a blink in reaction.

Fury flared his nostrils as air sawed in and out of him.

That nose was so close to hers she considered biting into it . . . snapping it completely off. She imagined his blood spewing all over her face before he grabbed his own and stumbled away, howling in pain. Probably wasn't as easy as it looked in the movies. But oh, she so wanted to hurt him.

Low-life creep. When Eve had first gotten a look at him, she had been kind of surprised. She'd figured the person doing this crap was just some random scumbag working for Solomon. But once she saw the bastard, she recognized this was someone related by blood to Dr. Palmer Solomon. Too young to be his son. Had to be his grandson. Then the shithead had confirmed her conclusion. She wondered if Vee had figured it out.

The ridiculous thing was that with his looks and his money—he wore a Rolex for fuck's sake—he could get plenty of women. Instead, he secretly followed each victim like some pathetic outcast, sneaking around in the shadows. Then he abducted her so he could torture and murder her.

What a fucking waste of a pretty face. Her lips tightened with hatred.

Still, how old was he when he started killing? Two?

"My grandfather said it was his gift to me. He wanted me to be able to live my life. So, to fulfill his wish, I went to college and then medical school. I focused, poured everything into becoming a brilliant doctor—just like him . . . just like he wanted," he snarled, drawing back slightly. "It was the most difficult task I have ever undertaken."

"I get it." Eve nodded slowly, as if some epiphany had dawned. "He thought if he gave you rules and something real to do, you'd stop killing people. Stop being who you are."

His eyebrows pulled down, and his lips rolled back, but rather than spew that fury all over her, he whirled away and started to pace. "It was a test, really," he said more calmly. "To see if I could be good again." He paused and glowered at her. "My grandfather is a very important man. It is up to me to carry on his prestigious legacy."

"*Was*," Eve pointed out.

His expression turned to one of confusion.

"*Was*," she said again. "He *was* a very important man. Now he's just an elderly statistic rotting away in prison."

Patrick laughed long and loud. One of those outbursts that spoke of sheer madness. Oh yeah, this guy was totally over the edge. He started to pace once more.

When he'd said nothing more for several laps of the room, she asked, "So why did you fall off the wagon?" She shrugged. "I've done it a bunch of times myself."

She should have let him sink into that conscious coma again, but somehow she just couldn't resist taunting him. Maybe he'd get so mad he'd have a stroke or a heart attack. It happened all the time, even with people her age, and he wasn't that much younger than her. The image of his face contorting and his hands grabbing at his chest played in her head like a social media reel. She almost smiled.

He sat down on his stool once more and studied her. "Such a clever girl. I know all about you and your big sister. I cannot wait until I have the two of you together. It is going to be so much fun."

Eve was the one laughing this time. "Trust me, I'm the fun one. You do not want to go down this road with Vera. She does not play well with others."

"I found your photos." A grin widened across his face. "Did you enjoy killing your mother?"

Every part of Eve's being went still . . . cold.

He laughed, recognizing he'd struck a deep nerve. "Oh yes. I may have allowed my grandfather to—as you say—rot in prison, but at least I did not kill him with my own two hands." He stared at his hands, laughed as if he'd told a hilarious joke. "Perhaps you and I have more in common than you realize."

"What did you do with the photos?" Eve demanded, a new kind of panic spreading through her.

"Oh." He smiled. "I left them for Vera. A little gift. I am quite certain she has found them by now. I wonder—assuming the two of you survive—if she will ever forgive you for such a heinous act?" He made a tsking sound. "What kind of eleven-year-old child kills her own mother? You could have at least waited until you were old enough to have a real grudge against her."

Eve turned away from his stare. She didn't want to talk about it. Not now . . . not ever.

The desperation and hurt building inside her eased just a little as she considered this new nightmare and the reality of what it meant. In a twisted sort of way, this lowlife had done her a favor. Vera was now aware of Eve's terrible secret. The realization made what she recognized deep down she needed to do far easier. Vera would not understand about the photos. Eve had never wanted her to know, and she could not bear even the idea of facing her now.

Which meant Eve no longer had anything to lose.

She would make sure this piece of shit never got to her sisters, even if it killed her.

If she was dead, Vera couldn't hate her.

34

Sunday, March 9
Boyett Farm
Good Hollow Road, Fayetteville, 6:30 a.m.

Vera pulled a hoodie over her tee. She was ready to go. The question was, Where?

She'd spent hours last night trying to figure out the moves Patrick Solomon would make. Bent had said he'd wanted to take a nap, but she'd heard him on the phone at least a dozen times last night, checking in with his deputies and, at least twice, with Eric. He hadn't taken a damned nap. He'd only wanted an excuse to hang around in her house.

Finally, when he was on the phone yet again, she'd come up to her room and closed the door. She'd eventually fallen asleep still puzzling over the possibilities. Waking up this morning on top of the covers, still wearing yesterday's clothes, and without having brushed her teeth had sucked.

She reached for her sneakers. Eve would be wearing the same clothes as the night before last. And she hadn't been able to brush her teeth either. An ache deep in Vera's chest made tears sting her eyes. If her sister was still breathing, she didn't care what clothes she wore or how her breath smelled.

"Just let her be alive," Vera murmured.

Nothing else . . . not even those damned photos . . . mattered right now.

She tugged on her sneakers and tied the laces. She didn't know what time Bent had left last night—if he had—or if he'd come up to her room and found her asleep first. He would have woken her if he'd learned anything new. Same went for this morning. No calls meant nothing new. Disappointment felt like a pile of rocks on her chest.

Then again . . . she stilled. Maybe this was not entirely bad. If past experience with the Messenger MO held true, no news was good news. Once he was finished with a victim, he left her where she was easily found. Eve hadn't been found, so there was still hope.

Her cell vibrated with an incoming text message.

Probably Bent or Eric wanting to know if she was up yet.

Unknown number.

Anticipation roared through her like a freight train rushing out of a tunnel. Had to be Palmer Solomon.

Happy birthday, Vera.

Anger twisted her lips into a sneer. Who cared? Before she could type a response, another message appeared.

He's waiting for you on a hilltop surrounded by woods and pastures and goats. Be there at nine. Alone.

Hope surged through her. But dwindled just as quickly. What the hell? That could be anywhere around Lincoln County! There were all kinds of hills and endless pastures, fields, and woods. Lots of people had goats! Damn it! She squeezed her eyes shut a moment, ordered herself to calm. Proceeding carefully here was extremely important. She couldn't risk making him angry or putting him off in any way. Deep breath. She chose her words carefully as she typed a response.

I'm not sure I can find the location in time. Any other details?

Vera held her breath and waited.

Wind chimes. The sound is driving him mad.

Wind chimes? Her mind rushed in a dozen directions. Where the hell could that be?

She sent a reply. Let me know if you hear anything more from him . . . I need more.

The ellipsis that told her he was typing appeared. Then, his message: Be careful, Vera. If you choose not to go alone there will be consequences.

Her lips tightened to hold back a string of curses. And there it was. The warning that she should go alone—assuming she figured out the location in time. It would be nice to believe dear old dying Dr. Solomon was not playing games this time, but he was. She got that. He might not want his grandson to continue killing, but he didn't want him jailed or killed either. And it was obvious he was enjoying this game with Vera.

"Bastard." She called Eric—only because his resources would be quicker.

"Vera, you okay this morning? We've been going all night and—"

"Is Bent with you?" She didn't need to hear him say they still had nothing despite hours of effort.

"No. I haven't seen him this morning. I'm at the command center. We're set up in the department's conference room."

"I need you to call Alcott's guy in Nashville. Tell him Palmer Solomon has contacted me via a cell phone this morning. If there's any chance his grandson has been in touch with him using that same phone . . ."

"Then we might be able to pinpoint his location," Eric finished for her. "What did Solomon tell you?"

"There's no time," she urged. "Make the call. We'll go over the rest when I get to the command center."

"I'll call him now."

"Eric, if Solomon learns the agent is coming, he'll send his grandson a warning, and then it's game over." The mere thought of what that would trigger crushed against her rib cage.

"Got it."

"Thanks. I'll be there soon."

"Hey," he said, waylaying her, "happy birthday."

"Yeah." She ended the call. This was the most god-awful birthday of her life.

Okay, focus, Vee.

If the worst happened and she didn't survive this, she hated the possibility of her last words to Eric being a lie, but it was the only way to ensure he didn't grow suspicious too soon.

As much as she wanted to figure this out on her own, she wasn't a fool. Whatever she did, there was a chance she might not make it—that Eve might not make it—but she intended to ensure they both had the best opportunity possible. For that, she needed Bent.

She walked out of her room, at the same time putting a call through to him.

Halfway down the stairs she heard his phone ring, and it wasn't just via her phone either.

Bent was here.

She followed the sound to the kitchen. He'd just reached for his cell on the island when she appeared at the door. She ended the call.

"Morning." He lifted his mug. "Coffee's ready."

"Morning." She crossed the room, poured herself a mugful, thankful that steam still rose from the dark liquid. She had to stay cool, convince him she was good to go for what had to be done. "How long have you been here?"

He leaned against the counter. "I was on the phone so late, getting final reports from my team, I ended up crashing on your couch. I hope you don't mind."

He was well aware she didn't mind. "We both know you had no intention of leaving." She sipped her coffee.

"What can I say? Protecting the citizens of this county is my job."

"Any news from the team?" She opted not to mention talking to Eric. It wasn't like he'd given her an update. She hadn't given him time.

"Nothing on Eve's location." He set his mug aside. "No reports about suspicious activity or sightings. What we do have is a missing deputy."

Dread welled inside her. "When was the last time he was heard from?"

"Just before dark last night. He was using his private vehicle, and we haven't found it. His fiancée hasn't heard from him. All attempts to reach him have gone unanswered."

"Damn." Vera forced down more of the coffee. She needed the caffeine. When she'd finished it off, she placed her cup in the sink. "That could mean the grandson has access to a radio—assuming he is the reason the deputy is missing and that the deputy was carrying a radio." She turned to look Bent in the eyes. "If that's the case, he will know every move we make unless the team goes to a private channel."

This news complicated things.

"The deputy did have a radio, and I have already directed the team to go to a private channel," Bent confirmed.

Of course he had. He was a good sheriff. Bent was no rookie and definitely no fool.

"By the way," he said, his eyes searching hers for whatever she was leaving out, "happy birthday."

She waved off the birthday crap. Time to come clean. "I heard from Palmer Solomon a few minutes ago."

A frown furrowed Bent's face. "How?"

"When I visited him, I gave him my cell number. He promised to let me know if he heard from his grandson."

Keeping whatever he felt about the news to himself, Bent asked, "What did he have to say?"

Vera was grateful he chose not to rant at her about what she'd done. "Patrick told him—or so the story goes—that he was on a hillside surrounded by pastures and woods. And goats." She huffed a breath. "That could be anywhere in the damned county. But he wants me there—alone—at nine a.m."

"And you're only sharing this with me because you can't figure out the location yourself."

She could deny the charge, but why bother. "Probably."

He stared at the floor a moment, then, "Anything else about the location?"

"Wind chimes. Solomon said the sound was driving him mad, so I'm assuming that means a lot of loud wind chimes. Not just some little rinky-dink cheap ones that tinkle."

Bent nodded, the distant expression on his face telling her that he was mentally playing back memories of the sights and sounds around the county.

She had done the same. But she'd only been back home for seven months. There was a lot she hadn't seen yet. Twenty-one years was a long time to be gone. She'd forgotten far more than she remembered . . . except Bent. Her face flushed. Not the time. Damn it.

"The Carter goat farm," he said, still obviously in deep consideration.

"I don't know the name." Hope stirred because he recognized the location.

"Over on Coldwater Creek Road," he said as he pulled out his cell phone. "Old man Carter—Deke Carter. His farm is high on a hill off Coldwater Creek. He and his wife started raising goats years ago when cattle got to be too much for them."

Vera put her hand on his when he would have made a call. "How old are we talking?"

"I'd say mid- to late eighties. Mrs. Carter passed last year, so it's just him. I got the call when his wife died. When I arrived, the ambulance was already there. And I remember there were wind chimes on the wraparound porch, all around the house. Carter said his wife had loved them."

Adrenaline charged through Vera. "Then that's the place." At least as long as the bastard in that prison hadn't lied to her.

"We need to get a team moving," Bent said.

She held on to his hand—again delaying any call. "If he figures out I'm bringing the cavalry, he'll kill Eve."

Bent's head was already moving side to side before she finished talking. "You are not going in alone."

"No." She released his hand, held up both hers in a *wait* gesture. "We assemble a group of trusted deputies and have them cover any potential avenues of escape around the farm."

"The property is thickly wooded along one side of the hill it sits on." His forehead furrowed deeply. "The other side is open pastureland sloping downward. I can have the team surround the base of the hill. Staying clear of the open areas."

"With that missing deputy," she said, realizing the potential misstep, "I'm thinking now that if we go radio silent, he'll know something is up. He has to believe your search is ongoing and we have no new tips."

"I'm aware of how this is done, Vee," he said, his expression hard. "I have certain members staying on the open channel and tossing out questions and comments from time to time. My only question is how do *you* factor into the plan?"

Well, he'd certainly told her. Furthermore, he wouldn't like this part, but that was too bad. "I'll go in. Just drive my SUV up to the house as he's requested. You can be close behind in the tree line. It's the only way we can hope for Eve's survival. The man has nothing to lose, Bent. What's one more dead body?"

"Two," he fired back at her, "if he gets you in there."

She took a breath, forced back her emotions. "Like you, I know how to do this, Bent. I'm good at it. Let me go in and make him think he's getting what he came for." She gave a knowing gesture. "If anyone is going to die today, it'll be him."

Five, then ten seconds ticked off. "I'm not saying it's a good plan," he finally admitted. "But it could work."

Relief flooded her. "Thank you."

He didn't look fully convinced, but he hadn't said no.

"I'll have deputies covering the most likely egress routes," he told her. "But I'm going all the way up the wooded side. Once I'm in place, you can drive up alone."

Vera wasn't so sure having him that close was a good idea, but it could work if they were careful. "Can you be certain Mr. Carter doesn't have any sort of alarm or those field cams for watching his animals?"

A lot of folks around the area had them. It was the best way to catch poachers and to determine what sort of predators were snatching from a herd. The cameras could be bought just about anywhere.

"No," he admitted, worry creasing his brow again. "But I don't recall seeing a keypad for an alarm system near the front door. I didn't see a computer or laptop. Nothing like that. The man didn't even have a cell phone. He still used a landline."

That news gave her hope. If he didn't use a cell phone or any other electronic device like an iPad or laptop, he likely didn't have field cameras. "What about dogs? Do you remember seeing any dogs?"

A nod this time. "He has dogs. Great Pyrenees. Two that I recall, but they'll be in the pastures on the other side of the hill with the goats."

Damn. Risky at the very least. "If a deputy gets too close, the dogs will be his alarm."

His expression turned to stone. "If—and I do mean *if*—we're going to do this your way, you will let me handle the logistics outside the house."

"Fine. Let's get it done." Every minute wasted was another that Eve's life was in danger. Vera didn't want to consider when she'd last had a drink of water or eaten . . . *please, please let her be okay.*

The preparations were fast . . . faster than Vera could have hoped for. The owner of the last farm on the left of Molino where it ended at Coldwater Creek was more than happy to allow his place to be used as a staging area for the operation.

Vera called Luna and warned her not to leave the house or to talk to anyone she didn't know until this was done. Two deputies were assigned to keep her safe, and her husband was there, so Vera felt reasonably confident the bastard wouldn't try to get to Luna. No matter, Luna cried. She was worried about Eve and Vera. Vera assured her as best she could. She promised to do all in her power to get Eve and herself through this safely.

Vera went upstairs while Bent finished arranging the team. There were small preparations she needed to make as well.

In the bathroom she gathered a couple of potentially useful items. Her mother's metal fingernail file. Six inches long and pointy on the end. Could make a decent close-contact weapon. She slid it into the sock on her right foot—on the inside next to her ankle.

Then she dug around until she found her father's old straight razor. He'd stopped using it ages ago because the rivets that held the blade to the handle had broken and come loose, leaving the razor in two pieces. The razor had been passed down from his father, and he'd used it for as long as Vera could remember. He'd always kept it nice and sharp. Her mama had hated it. She was glad when it finally gave out and he had to stop using it.

Vera tucked the blade portion into her left sock, again on the inside next to her ankle. If her feet were bound together, the weapons were less likely to be noticed by the person doing the binding. Then she returned to her bedroom and retrieved the small handgun she kept in its original wood case. She'd used her department-issued firearm for so long back in Memphis that she'd all but forgotten about her personal weapon. When her household goods had arrived here after the sale of her Memphis condo, she had discovered lots of things—including the handgun—she hadn't thought of in years. She had cleaned it and tucked it, case and all, into her bedside table.

She hadn't really expected to ever use it.

Until now.

35

Carter Farm
Coldwater Creek Road, Taft, Tennessee, 8:50 a.m.

Vera parked on the road, a quarter of a mile or so from the turn for the driveway that would lead up to the Carter home. The location was shielded by the woods on the left, preventing any possibility of being seen from the house.

Bent turned to her, studied her for a long moment. The hat, that face . . . almost made her wish . . .

"I will be careful," she said before he could, and in an effort to prevent her mind from going down that other path. "You need to remember that I was a well-trained homicide detective before I became a criminal analyst with the Memphis Police Department. I know how to handle myself in situations like this."

"All the training in the world doesn't make you bulletproof, Vee."

She nodded in acquiescence. "I'm aware."

"Wait two minutes once I get out, then go." He looked away a moment before saying, "Just don't get yourself killed."

Before she could think how to respond, he grabbed her by the head and pulled her to him. He kissed her hard and fast. He released her just as suddenly and climbed out of her SUV.

She watched in her rearview mirror as he moved around the back of her vehicle and then disappeared into the woods. Her attention shifted to the digital clock on the dash and waited. One minute. Felt like a lifetime. She held her breath, waiting for that digital clock to click over once more. Two.

Staring straight ahead, she tightened her fingers on the steering wheel. "Showtime."

She removed her foot from the brake and rolled forward. When she reached the driveway, she started to turn into it, but the vibration of her cell phone stopped her. She hit the brake and stared at the device on the console. It vibrated again.

She picked it up and studied the screen.

Unknown Caller.

She tapped the screen to accept the call. "Keep driving," a voice said.

Male. Not one she knew. The grandson . . . *Patrick?* Maybe. Fear and anticipation exploded in her chest.

"I'm here," she blurted. Caught herself and forced a sense of calm. "Alone, like you said."

Laughter echoed over the line. "Good girl. Now, drive straight ahead. Quickly, before your friends catch up to you. You will know what to do then."

"Where am I going?" she demanded, but the call dropped.

"Fuck." She tossed her phone onto the seat and rammed her foot against the accelerator. The SUV lurched forward. If she hesitated too long, Bent would rush back to her vehicle to find out what was going on.

She hadn't gotten fifty yards before her phone started to vibrate again. She glanced at the screen. *Bent.*

She drove faster. *Quickly, before your friends catch up to you.* The bastard's warning echoed in her brain.

A curve had her slowing slightly, and then she gunned the accelerator again.

She blinked . . . what the hell? A white van sat sideways in the road . . . blocking her path. Someone stood next to it. There was no way to go around . . . the ditch on either side was too deep. She couldn't risk trying to go around.

She slowed. Banged a fist against the steering wheel. As she drew closer, she recognized the wording on the side. A television station's call letters. Then the person standing outside it . . . *Patricia Patton.*

"Son of a bitch!" Vera slammed on the brakes, squealing to a stop. She rammed into Park and wrenched the door open. "Get out of my way!"

"You have to come with me."

"What?" Had the woman lost her damned mind?

Patton's throat worked with the effort to swallow. "He said you have to come with me. Now. Hurry."

Vera reached back inside her SUV, grabbed the handgun, and tucked it into her waistband beneath the hoodie. "What the hell are you talking about?"

She started toward the woman, who stood mute and staring at her like a frightened animal paralyzed in a hunter's crosshairs.

"What are you talking about?" Vera demanded again as she grew closer. Then she noticed the spots of dirt and maybe blood on Patton's high-dollar white sweater and slacks.

The reporter's lips trembled, and tears flowed down her blush-enhanced cheeks. "He has my friend . . . if we don't hurry, he'll kill him and your sister."

Vera charged the rest of the way up to her. "If you're lying to me—"

"Please." Patton shook her head. "We have to hurry."

"I'm driving." Vera climbed into the driver's seat of the van, adjusted the position of her weapon and then the seat while Patton hurried around to the other side. "Where are we going?"

"Keep going straight on this road."

Vera cut the steering wheel sharply to the right, hit the accelerator, sending the vehicle rocketing forward in the direction Patton had said. She thought of Bent and how he and his deputies would be frantically searching . . . damn it all to hell.

"Where's your cell phone?" Patton asked, her face cluttered with fear. "I'm supposed to toss it out the window."

Vera's fingers tightened on the steering wheel. "I left it in my vehicle." *Shit.*

"If you're lying," Patton cautioned.

"Give me the damned directions," Vera growled, like a woman possessed by the devil himself.

"Just keep going. It's a couple of miles."

Vera pressed the accelerator harder. A minute ticked off, then another. Her heart pounded harder with each second. Where the hell were they going?

Patton leaned forward to stare out the windshield. "It's not far now."

"Am I taking a left or a right?" Vera asked, glancing at the reporter, who was not acting like herself at all.

"Left. See the satellite dish and that little red barn. It's the next left. A gravel road."

Vera braked hard and slid into the turn. Patton grabbed for something to hang on to.

This was wrong. Vera's cop instincts were screaming at her. "How did he know when I got to the Carter farm?" she demanded as she wrested back control of the vehicle and sent it bumping along the narrow gravel road.

The bastard had set up some way to watch for her approach. There was no other explanation. If this woman admitted to having been his lookout, Vera might just stop this van and kick her ass.

"He set up those little battery-operated cameras. The whole parade of law enforcement vehicles appeared on the app on his phone. But he was never at that location anyway."

Had Vera been thinking straight, she would have realized he would do something exactly like that. The guy was nearly ten years younger than her. He would be versed on all the latest gadgets. "What next?" Several mobile homes in various stages of disrepair sat on either side of the narrow road. All looked abandoned. Probably uninhabitable. Vines, trees, and bushes, as well as undergrowth, had all but swallowed them.

"Go left at that last one. There's a shed. Pull the van into the shed."

Vera made the left. She stared a moment at the shed, assessing if the van would fit. Only one way to find out. She rolled forward, eased into the derelict structure that looked as if it might fall any minute. She shut off the engine and turned to the woman who had been the bane of her existence far too often.

"Get out," Patton said, her voice wobbling. "We close the shed doors and go inside."

"How did you get involved in this?" The idea that Patton was somehow just trying to get the story, frankly, scared the hell out of Vera.

"He called me. Claimed to be a guy who had some information about you and what happened with the Messenger last time."

Vera rolled her eyes. "And you fell for it."

"I always follow every lead." She reached for her door, climbed out.

Vera did the same. "So you met with him," she prompted. "What happened?" She really did not have time for this. Damn it.

The shed doors creaked as Patton closed them. She turned to Vera then, her movements disjointed. "The man, Patrick Solomon—I didn't recognize him immediately—got into the back of the van. Then he introduced himself, and I knew something was off. Mike prepared to start filming and . . ." Her face crumpled. "He stabbed him. Then he told me to drive." Her voice caught. "Then, a little while ago, he sent me to pick you up. He said if I didn't bring you back . . ."

Vera wanted to shake the woman. "Well, you always did jockey for a front-row seat." The woman had damned well gotten herself one this time. As soon as she had said the words, Vera felt a little bad. Patton's friend was injured. Damn it. How many more had to die or be hurt because this sick bastard wanted to get even with her?

"I'm sorry," Patton sobbed. "I was only doing my job." She gestured to the dilapidated mobile home next to the shed. "We have to go in there . . . he's waiting for us."

"Is my sister in there?" Vera held her breath, pulse racing, heart pounding.

"She's there. My friend too." Patton searched Vera's eyes. "We're all going to die, aren't we?"

"Not if I can help it." She started toward the dilapidated mobile home, surveying the landscape as she went. The whole area appeared abandoned. Slowly being devoured by nature.

Vines had grown up the side of their destination. The windows she could see were broken. Probably vandals. "Is anyone else in the house?"

"I don't think so. There's no electricity. No water."

"You didn't see anyone else with him?"

"No. Just me, Mike, and Eve." A sob ripped from her throat.

"Did you see any other weapons besides the knife?" Knives were the weapons the Messenger used on his victims. Apparently he'd used one on her friend.

"No."

"Okay. Just stay calm and ride this out. Let me do the interacting with him. I will get us out of this. You just have to trust me."

She nodded.

Vera hoped to hell the ambitious reporter would do as she was told. The Patricia Patton she knew always broke the rules.

They had that in common.

But now wasn't a good time for the woman to go rogue.

As soon as they approached the narrow steps, the front door opened.

Patrick Solomon stood in the doorway. The jeans, sweatshirt, and hiking boots were completely out of character for the young medical resident whose photo she had found on the Instagram page of one of his friends.

He had the same pale-blond hair as his grandfather and mother. He appeared fit. Also like his grandfather. Obviously he was intelligent. But it was his gray eyes—cold, fathomless—that warned just how bad the situation was. This man—this monster—appeared to have just one goal: act out his revenge before he was captured or killed.

Vera's gut told her that this was also in part about him having held in those desperate urges all this time, and he just couldn't do it anymore.

This was the eruption . . . the meltdown. He'd blamed it on his grandfather's situation, but it had likely been coming all along.

"If you are carrying any sort of weapon, toss it on the ground," he ordered.

Vera held up her hands. "I'm unarmed."

"She's lying," Patton said, her voice too high pitched. "She has a handgun. I saw it."

Vera sent her a scalding look. What the hell was wrong with her?

"Toss it on the ground, Vera," he ordered, "or I will stick your sister."

Vera removed the handgun from her waistband and tossed it to the ground beyond the porch. She sent Patton another withering look she hoped conveyed her thoughts. *Stupid bitch.* Did she really think following an order like that one was going to save them? It was one thing to make a bad move but a whole other level of stupidity to give away a secret unnecessarily. How would he have known Patton had seen the weapon if he found it?

He wouldn't have, damn it.

"Come inside," he ordered.

Vera climbed the three rickety steps and walked in first. Patton stayed close behind her.

"Nice of you to join us, Vera." The door slammed to a close. "Though I do not appreciate your foolishness."

She turned around slowly, her gaze seeking and finding her sister. She was alive. Thank God.

"I wouldn't have missed it for the world." She shrugged. "Your grandfather didn't mention that I couldn't come prepared—if that's what you mean."

"Mike." Patton rushed to the man on the floor. Judging by the blood on the front of his clothes and the fact that he only vaguely reacted to her presence, he was barely hanging on.

Shit. Shit. Shit. This was bad.

Eve sat in the opposite corner from the others, hands and feet bound. She nodded, only the slightest dip of her chin, but said nothing. Vera did the same. Eve showed no visible injuries. No blood on her clothes. So far so good on that count. The room was empty, save a couple of chairs and an old cabinet-style television. A bag and about an inch of dust sat on top of it.

"My grandfather insisted you were too clever for your own good. It seems he was correct."

Vera turned back to the man leaning against the closed door, a long-bladed knife in his hand. A sheath hung at his side. Probably attached to his belt the way a hunter would wear one. Only this man didn't hunt animals . . . he hunted humans—women who fit a certain profile. The occasional male who got in his way or suited his purpose.

Pushing aside all the thoughts and realizations that would change nothing, she asked, "How do you want to do this? It's only a matter of time before the sheriff and his people find us."

"I'm aware." He held Vera's gaze. "Patricia, secure her," he barked.

Patton scrambled to her feet. Grabbed something from the bag on top of the television and rushed to Vera.

"Put your hands together," she said, her face still clouded with that fear.

Vera held her hands together in front.

"Behind her," Patrick ordered. "I cannot trust this one."

Vera rolled her eyes and shifted her arms around so that her hands were behind her back. Patton tightened the zip tie into place.

"On the floor," Patrick ordered. "Next to your sister if you like."

Vera walked to the corner where Eve leaned against the wall and sat down. Patton quickly secured her ankles with another zip tie. She didn't meet Vera's gaze. Unquestionably she understood how utterly stupid what she'd done was. Then she hurried back to stand before the asshole orchestrating this shitshow and to await his next order.

"I have waited a long time for this," Patrick said, drawing Vera's attention to him once more. "You took my grandfather away from me. I needed him . . . needed his guidance." He looked away a moment, as if overwhelmed by emotion.

Vera wanted to puke. How dare he pretend to be emotional.

"Now," he glared at her once more, "he is dying."

There were many things Vera would like to say to that, but she resisted. No need to egg on his wrath.

"By the way," he said with a sickening smile, "happy birthday."

Vera gritted her teeth to hold back a *Fuck off.*

"Let us all sing happy birthday to Vera," he directed. "Happy birthday," he began, waving his arms in encouragement to the others.

Patton joined in. Eve turned to Vera as she did the same. The guy bleeding out didn't appear to have the energy. Vera wasn't sure whose voice sounded the most pathetic, Patton's or Eve's. Her sister blinked back tears as their gazes met.

Vera wished she could hug her.

When the singing concluded, Patrick clapped loudly. "Bravo."

"Look," Vera said, "why don't you release the three of them, then you and I can go somewhere private and get this party started. Someplace we won't be found."

He smirked. "You would do that, would you?" he said to Vera.

"No question." She leaned forward. "Call it my birthday present. The truth is, it's me you want. You don't need all this baggage slowing us down."

"You are exactly right," he said.

In a swift, unexpected move, he stabbed Patton. Deep. Then he shoved her to the floor near her friend, who appeared to have gone unconscious. Shock claimed the reporter's face as blood bloomed across the front of her white sweater.

Vera bit her lips together for a moment to ride out the scream burgeoning in her throat. Her chest tightened to the point of stopping her heart. She had to do something. Now!

But there was nothing she could do . . . except . . .

"Look," she urged. "We should go. Finding us will be way too easy if we linger here too long." If they left now, maybe Bent or some of his deputies would find Patton and her friend before it was too late. Dear God . . . they were dying right in front of her.

Ignoring her completely, Patrick reached out and sliced his blade first across the cameraman's throat, then Patton's. Blood spewed from the ugly gaps created. Then, as if he'd only been butchering hogs, he swiped his blade clean on Patton's white trousers.

Next to Vera, Eve started to sob. *Deep breath.* Vera had to regain control . . . couldn't let this piece of shit get to her with his theatrics. She could grieve the dead later. Right now she had to stay focused on stopping him . . . somehow.

"Really," she said more firmly, barely able to press out the word, "we should go."

"I want you"—he turned back to Vera—"to know how this level of loss feels."

The idea that he meant killing Eve speared through Vera. Fear erupted inside her, rained down like volcanic ash. "We don't have time for you to play, Patrick. If you're going to do this, we need to move."

"In good time." He smiled, the expression evil. He walked out and slammed the door, as if he had all the time in the world.

"You shouldn't have come," Eve whispered, her teary gaze connecting with Vera's.

"How could I save you," Vera whispered back, trying to sound strong and confident, "if I didn't show up?"

Eve laid her head on Vera's shoulder. "Bent will be pissed."

"Yeah." Vera allowed her cheek to rest against her sister's hair. The only thing that mattered to her right now was saving her sister's life.

"I'm scared, Vee," Eve whispered, as if she feared the bastard outside would hear her.

"Don't worry," she whispered back. "I'm going to kill this piece of shit."

36

Carter Farm
Coldwater Creek Road, Taft, Tennessee, 9:35 a.m.

Bent struggled to catch his breath. He'd run all the way up and then all the way back down that damned hill. Deputy Fowler had rushed to get his vehicle so they could follow Vera. They were now barreling in the direction she'd gone. The county cruiser just wouldn't go fast enough for Bent.

Three other deputies had checked the house and barn. No sign of anyone or any indication that someone had been there besides the owner.

Old man Carter had been home all day the day before and all night last night. He'd been surprised by the deputies and had no idea what they were talking about.

There were far too many side turns and not nearly enough time to assemble roadblocks on the other end of this road or any of the many others.

What the hell had Vera been thinking? Instead of turning into the driveway, she had driven away. The only reasonable explanation was that she'd gotten a call informing her of a change of plans.

Or she'd set this whole thing up as a distraction.

He swore under his breath. Didn't want to believe she would go that far. But then this was Vee. She would do whatever she thought was necessary to save her sister.

A silver vehicle appeared in the distance. He leaned forward, his pulse surging faster.

"That's her SUV," he said to Fowler.

The driver's side door stood open. A blade of fear sliced into his gut. Fowler slowed just a little. "You want me to call it in, Sheriff?"

"Let's check it out first."

They parked, exited Fowler's cruiser, and walked toward the SUV, weapons leveled and readied.

The engine was running, but the vehicle was empty.

Her cell phone lay on the passenger seat.

Fob was still in the cup holder.

Damn it, Vee.

He surveyed the area . . . open fields. No houses within sight. Empty highway. No one to have noticed anything. Desperation climbed up his spine, camped at the base of his skull, and throbbed. Had the bastard been waiting here for her?

His cell vibrated. *Jones.* "Have you heard anything from Vera?" Bent asked rather than bother with a greeting.

"I haven't. I just got off the phone with the agent in Nashville. Solomon flushed the phone down the toilet," he said. "We can't confirm anything he told Vera."

She had insisted on leaving Jones out of this covert op. Now Bent knew why. He had no freaking idea what Jones was talking about. "This is news to me, Jones. What the hell are you talking about?"

"What's going on, Bent?" The other man's tone warned he understood there was trouble. "When I spoke with Vera, she said she'd been contacted by Solomon, but she didn't give me any of the details. She hasn't answered my calls since."

"We followed the instructions Solomon sent her via text message," Bent explained, defeat kicking him hard. "The location he directed us to was a ruse. Now Vera's MIA."

All this was assuming what she had told him was the whole truth. Every part of him ached at the realization of what he had allowed to happen. His gut twisted into a tight knot.

"What's your location? I'm coming there."

Bent cleared his head. He had to think. "You at the command center?"

"I am."

"Tell Deputy Olson to bring you to my location. I'll text him the address."

"Bent, was she armed?"

"She had a handgun."

Jones exhaled a worried breath. "Okay. Thanks. See you soon."

Bent shot off a text message to Olson with the Coldwater Creek location. Then he turned to Fowler. "I'll use this vehicle. You go back to the team we left at the Carter farm and orchestrate a grid search along this road. I want you to check every house, every barn, under every damned rock. If you see or hear anything even remotely suspicious, I want to know about it."

"Yes sir." Fowler hesitated. "I just heard . . . they found Deputy Riggs. He's dead."

God damn it! Bent had expected that would be the case, but he still hated hearing it. "Thanks, Fowler. Make sure the news doesn't get out until I have a chance to notify his family."

Fowler nodded, then hustled to his vehicle and executed a three-point turn and headed back to the Carter farm.

It wouldn't take Olson long to get here with Jones. But it was far too long to suit Bent. His mind was already playing over and over a collage of possible things that bastard could do to Vera . . . could do to Eve.

He picked up her phone and reviewed the messages she had received. He'd been right. She'd left him at the Carter farm because she had no choice. She had received a call from an unknown number. He gritted his teeth and tossed the phone back into the seat to prevent himself from calling that number. He couldn't take the risk. Then he checked her text messages and confirmed the instructions she had received from Solomon. She'd told him the truth.

Bent felt sick. Wanted to bust something with his bare hands.

County cruisers barreled past him, first one and then another, turning down the side roads up ahead.

The one thing that gave him comfort was the reality that Vera would not go down easy.

He smiled.

But if he got there first . . . Vee wouldn't have to bother.

37

The vehicle bumped, bumped over uneven ground.

As best Vera could estimate, they had been driving around for better than half an hour. Where the hell was he going? Away from Fayetteville? To some secret location he had set up over the past couple of months?

The sound of tree limbs or bushes scratching at the sides of the van had her instincts going on alert. Had he left the road? Taken a narrow, rarely used dirt road, maybe? There were certainly plenty of wooded areas in any direction going out of Fayetteville. She thought of the shack off McDeal Road, where they'd found evidence planted to keep the Time Thief case going. No trees or bushes close enough on that road to scratch a vehicle. Not unless the driver purposely drove more in the ditch than on the road to mislead her.

Possible. He would know Vera was paying attention.

Solomon had dragged first Eve and then her to the back of the news van and hefted them inside. A canvas tarp had been thrown over them. Since Patton had secured her, luckily the nail file and the blade end of the straight razor tucked into Vera's socks hadn't been noticed. That was the only bit of good luck so far.

As completely as she had despised the reporter in Patricia Patton, she felt sick that she and her colleague had been murdered. No one should die that way. Damn it. Patton and her friend had families. Now they were dead because the bastard had wanted to get Vera. It made her want to tear him apart. God, she hoped she got the chance.

She forced away the thoughts and focused on the moment. Nothing she could do about it right now. Whatever he had planned next, she and Eve needed to be ready.

She nudged Eve with her forehead. Vera whispered, "Daddy's straight razor is in my sock on the inside of my left ankle." Her sister nodded. Vera felt the move more than saw it. Almost no light filtered through the tarp. "Can you try to get it out and cut me loose if I pull my feet up to your hands?" Another nod.

With Vera's hands secured behind her back, it would be very difficult, probably impossible to reach down and retrieve a damned thing, much less use it. She pulled her knees to her chest and scooted backward, being careful not to make any sound while placing her feet even with Eve's hands. The move dragged the tarp from her face. She tilted her head back and looked toward the driver's seat to ensure he hadn't been alerted. He appeared focused on navigating the vehicle. Good.

She shifted her attention to the windshield as her sister's cold fingers dipped into her sock. Trees just beginning to put on leaves were visible beyond the glass. Their limbs scrubbed at the sides of the van. Had he taken a trail through the woods? More of that swaying and bumping around seemed to suggest they were not on paved or graded ground. She tried to assess where they might be. He'd driven too long to still be in Fayetteville.

Unless he'd spent time just driving around to confuse her.

The tight band around her ankles suddenly released. Eve tapped on her knee. Vera scooched her upper body closer to her sister. "What now?" Eve asked.

Vera checked the driver again. Still focused straight ahead. "My hands," she whispered.

She rolled onto her stomach and then onto her side to put her hands against her sister's. Eve felt for the zip tie. For a few seconds she just held onto it. Vera suspected she was afraid of cutting her. Better to be bleeding and unrestrained. She nudged at her sister's hand with her own. Eve inhaled a deep breath, then began.

Vera felt the cold steel against her skin as Eve sawed back and forth against the plastic restraint.

A slice through skin and the sting that followed had Vera swallowing a grunt. Eve's hand stilled.

Her attention on the driver, Vera nudged her sister's foot with her own and then held herself as still as possible while Eve started again. Another slice. Vera bit the inside of her jaw as the fresh sting radiated up her arm. Tears burned her eyes. Eve kept sawing. Vera gritted her teeth as warm blood slipped down her thumbs.

Then her hands were free.

Vera took a breath, then rolled onto her other side, facing Eve, and reached for the razor. Vera held it firmly and waited as her sister pushed her bound hands toward her.

The van braked to a hard stop.

The blade sliced across Eve's arm.

Vera's eyes went wide.

Eve kept her own closed in pain. Her lips tightly pressed together.

Heart thumping, Vera tried to see how bad the cut was . . . exactly where it was. Above the wrist on the front of the forearm. Not too deep.

Thank God.

The driver's side door opened. No time. Vera tucked the blade back into her sock.

Heart pounding, she pulled the tarp back over their heads, then positioned herself as if she were still bound, feet together, hands behind her back. She needed him to believe she was still secured. And she needed him close . . . close enough to injure.

Leaves and sticks crunched beneath his steps as he moved toward the back of the van. Vera's gaze collided with Eve's as those rear cargo doors wrenched open. Vera hoped her sister knew how very much she loved her. She suddenly wished she had said as much while she had the chance.

"I'm sorry I didn't tell you about Mama," Eve whispered abruptly.

Before Vera could tell her that right now nothing but survival mattered, Eve was jerked from the van by her feet. Her shoulders and head hit the ground. She cried out.

Vera bolted upright. Scrambled into a crouch.

Patrick dropped Eve's legs and charged toward Vera.

She lunged at him.

They hit the ground together. She grabbed at his throat.

Something rammed into her shoulder.

Sting.

Needle.

She tried to squeeze his throat, but her arms felt limp, wouldn't work.

She crumpled atop him, her respiration slowing . . . her body helpless.

He rolled her off.

His face floated above her . . . the image wavy, as if she were looking through water.

"I knew you'd try something like that. Nighty night, Vera Mae."

She sank beneath the blackness.

38

Lincoln County Sheriff's Department
Thornton Taylor Parkway, Fayetteville, 12:00 p.m.

Three hours.

Vee had been out of communication for three hours.

Bent stared at the maps spread across the conference table. All area grids were being searched. County and city law enforcement personnel as well as civilian volunteers were covering ground as quickly as possible. Bent had issued new BOLOs for Vee, Eve, and Patrick Solomon, as well as the news van from Memphis. Everyone who had watched the news or listened to the radio had been alerted and asked to call in any sightings or suspicious activity. But it didn't feel like enough.

Worry gnawed at him. He had called in a favor in hopes of getting air support. If they could get a couple of copters in the air, it would help, but that took time.

They might not have time.

Fury burned hot in his gut, and he barely held it inside.

He fisted his hands, braced them against the table to prevent roaring with a mixture of rage and anguish. Worse, the bodies of Patricia Patton and her cameraman, Michael Brown, had been found. Solomon, Vera, and Eve were long gone. The abandoned mobile home where they had been held hadn't been lived in for a decade or more. There were no utilities at all on that narrow side road. Bent and his deputies had driven right past those damned rusty structures the first time because they were looking for a vehicle.

The only blood discovered inside was the pools that had leaked from the two victims left behind. As gutted as he felt for the reporter and her cameraman, Bent hoped that no other blood meant Vera and Eve were uninjured.

The handgun Vee had taken from her house was found on the ground outside, so she was no longer armed.

Where the hell are you?

Bent straightened, set his hands on his hips, and kicked aside the emotions that would do nothing but splinter his attention. He needed his full attention focused on finding them.

All they had to do was locate the van, and maybe, just maybe, they would find Vera and Eve.

Unless the bastard changed vehicles.

Jones appeared on the other side of the table. "I've got a call in to the news station," he told Bent. "I'm hoping they have trackers on all their vehicles. It's Sunday, so not everyone is at the station. As soon as they have an answer from someone in management, they'll call me back."

"Thanks. That was a good call." When Jones had first arrived, Bent had wanted nothing more than to send him straight back to Memphis . . . but now he was glad to have the help.

Jones scrubbed a hand over his face. Like Bent, he hadn't slept much in the past two days. The weight of uncertainty and a load of fear were bearing down heavy.

"They've interrogated Dr. Solomon repeatedly," Jones said, "and he's still giving us nothing new. Part of me wants to say he probably doesn't know more. But this just doesn't feel right." He looked from the maps on the table to Bent. "The whole situation is off somehow."

"You believe he's protecting his grandson again?" Bent wished he could have five minutes alone with the bastard. He still might not spill whatever he knew, but he would be sorry he knew it.

"I think we would all be fools not to believe that's the case. Not to mention this situation gives him one final hurrah—even if only vicariously through his grandson." He exhaled a big breath. "But if we put that aside and focus only on the grandson, this is what we know about how he operated as part of the Messenger—or at least how he operated more than a dozen years ago." Jones stared at the maps, went quiet.

Bent waited for him to go on, his nerves firing erratically, urging him to act. It took every ounce of restraint he possessed to stand still.

"He watched each victim for months," Jones said, his voice sounding quiet and distant, as if he were remembering the events far too vividly. "When he made his move, he was quick. In and out. No evidence left behind. No witnesses. Ever. He kept his victims for as little as a couple of days to as many as five or six."

"Any particular reason," Bent asked, "as to why he kept some longer than others?" He had reviewed everything he could get his hands on about the Messenger, but to hear more details from someone who had lived the case would be far more useful.

"The profile created by the FBI," Jones explained, "suggested this is typical for torture-murderers. It's not the murder that drives them, it's the torture. So if the fun with a particular victim grows flat, let's say, then what's the point of continuing?"

Bent shook his head in disgust. "So, if he's no longer getting off on the reactions of the victim, then it's game over."

"Exactly. Torture-murderers are the worst of the worst. Take for instance Patton and her colleague: their murders weren't fun for him. They were a means to an end, so getting rid of them was merely housekeeping. The job quick, precise. No playing around. Like buying gasoline for your car. You do it because you must, not because you enjoy the task." Jones looked away a moment. "Vera and Eve, on the other hand, are his chosen victims. He'll take as much time as he feels he can for as long as it is enjoyable to him."

Bent cleared his throat. Couldn't bear to consider the idea. "If . . . we can't pinpoint his location quickly enough . . ."

"You know Vera," Jones said. "She's smart. She's tough. She understands the Messenger. Understands killers like him better than most analysts. She will buy time. She'll play his game to ensure he gets the biggest thrill possible until she figures out a way to take him."

"Yeah," Bent agreed. "She will." He didn't know that side of Vee so well yet. But he knew the woman all the way to her core. She would do everything in her power to stop this bastard from hurting her sister.

Jones reached into his pocket, drew out his cell phone. He frowned as he accepted the call. "Jones."

Bent braced, hoped to hell this wasn't worse news.

The call ended in just over a minute. Jones tucked the phone back into his pocket, his expression somber. "That was Agent Alcott. His guy in London, who has been watching Pamela's flat, was surprised by the local police arriving at the building, sirens blaring. It seems a downstairs neighbor of Pamela's reported a bad odor and some sort of liquid dripping from her ceiling."

Holy shit. Bent's gaze locked with the other man's. "Solomon's daughter is dead."

"Throat slit," Jones confirmed. "The building's CCTV confirmed Patrick Solomon was the last person to go in and come out of her apartment."

A new kind of panic raced up Bent's spine. The guy killed his own mother. Fuck. "We have to find them."

He and Jones stared at those damned maps again. The voices and activity around them seemed to fade to a hum. Somewhere out there—Bent scanned the lines and symbols on the pages—Vee and Eve were fighting for their lives. Dread swelled wider and deeper inside him. To stand here orchestrating the ongoing activities wasn't enough. He had to get out there. He had to do something.

"Tell me," he said to Jones, "where did he take his victims? Where did he leave them?"

"Back when he was active," Jones began, "he—they—always left the victim at a location that had meaning to her life. Almost as if they wanted those left behind or the police investigating the case to understand that no place was safe from his reach. The profiler on the case insisted it was a continuation of theme—sending messages. They sent messages to each victim warning that she was next or that they were coming. Always, without deviation. The thought was that the drop location was a message as well."

Bent's instincts rose a degree higher. "Give me an example of what you mean."

"For example," Jones said, "Judy Finch, the first victim we know of, was left at an old, abandoned playground. Later, after some digging, we learned that this was the place where her father had a heart attack and died when she was a kid. He was there with her and her brother. She never went back to that park, her mother said. Not ever. Until her body was found there."

"So part of the time he takes watching each victim is to learn all he can about that person," Bent suggested. "Who they are during captivity is not enough. He—they—want to know the victim's history. It makes the interaction more personal, more intimate."

"Right," Eric confirmed. "Shelia Upton—she was victim number six. Her body was found in a long-closed bookstore. That bookstore had been her favorite place when she was growing up. She went there all the time, her parents said, until it closed. She grieved it like a lost friend."

Bent scanned the map again. There were places that had special meaning to the Boyett sisters. "Rose Hill Cemetery," he said. "Their parents are buried there. Vera and Eve used to meet there all the time. Probably still do."

"He might leave them there, but unless there's a place where he can have privacy," Jones explained, "we aren't likely to find them there while he's doing the torture thing."

"The house where they grew up," Bent mentioned. "That's where their mother and their stepmother died . . ." He hesitated. "No . . . the cave." He looked to Jones. "Vee and I checked the cave just yesterday.

I have someone watching her place. You can't get to that cave without going past the house."

"Call your deputy," Jones argued. "He's slick. He could have slipped under even the most skilled deputy's radar. Vera and Eve could be there right now."

Bent attempted to contact the deputy watching the Boyett place.

No answer. Fear spiraled through him.

Jesus Christ. That was it. He looked to Jones. "I think you might be right."

"Let's go."

Bent was already halfway to the door.

39

The sound of sobbing penetrated the haze cradling Vera's brain. She told her eyes to open . . . drew in a breath as if it were the first in hours. Her heart started to beat faster. Damp. The air smelled wet . . . moldy.

Where was she?

Open!

Her eyes refused.

Her mouth felt dry . . . lips. Needed to lick her lips.

More sobbing . . .

Was she crying?

Her eyelids fluttered open.

A spot of light high above her head held her attention. Craggy . . . rocky. What was she looking at?

A cry of anguish pierced the air.

Vera tensed.

Eve.

Vera attempted to move. Her body resisted. Felt too heavy.

Wake up! Move!

She opened her eyes wider and tried to move her head. It felt like a bowling ball. She forced it to turn so she could look around.

Eve. Her attention settled on her sister's profile. Some sort of light sat on the ground, providing just enough illumination for Vera to see her sister's face . . . to see this place . . .

The *cave*. They were in the damned cave on the farm.

Eve lay on the raised ledge where they had placed their stepmother's body what felt like a million years ago. A darker form hovered over Eve.

Patrick. Solomon's grandson.

Adrenaline shot through Vera, and she sat up as if she'd risen from the dead—her movements disjointed. Determination and an unparalleled urgency roared through her.

He was here . . . with them . . . torture . . .

Fuck!

A scream ruptured the dank air. Eve's head whipped from side to side in agony.

Vera went completely still . . . even her heart seemed to stop. But her eyes widened to see more clearly. Her pulse raced . . . heart pounded . . . blood rushing through her veins screamed in her ears.

The Messenger always secured his victim's hands and feet in some manner. And then he made each carefully planned incision in just the right place to exact the most pain.

The remaining layer of fog in Vera's brain cleared. Rage fired through her limbs, giving them the power to move. Her wrists were bound behind her back. She tried to move her feet, but they were fastened together as well. She peered at them. *Rope.* He'd evidently run out of zip ties. She twisted her hands and wrists, allowing the movement to reopen the injuries caused by the straight razor Eve had used to cut her loose in the van. She needed the blood to seep down and help with her escape now. She twisted her feet and ankles, tugged with all she had to loosen the bonds. She would get loose . . .

The bastard should have started with her. Big mistake.

The burn in her hands and her sister's cries only made her work at twisting and tugging harder until first one, then the other hand slipped loose. She lifted her feet and drew them back toward her torso. Fingers fumbling, she didn't relent until the bindings at her ankles went slack. She tugged the rope free, then she rocked onto her feet in a crouched position, using her hands for balance. Eve's tormented moaning covered any noise she made.

She was going to kill this son of a bitch.

Vera pushed upward. Swayed a little. Caught herself.

She glanced around for a weapon. The cold blade burned against the skin of her ankle. She needed something more substantial.

Something . . . like a rock. Her gaze landed on one about the size of a baseball, more oblong than round.

The pounding of her heart thudded in her brain as Vera watched Patrick stoop over her sister. She bent down, closed her fingers on the rock, and picked it up. She weighed it . . . tightened her grip. She was going to bash his head in.

She took a step toward him. *Be quiet. Be quiet.* Then another. Her pulse and heart rate rose with each one.

Just a little closer.

He abruptly wheeled around, the knife in his hand bloody. "Well, well, you're awake." He laughed. "Ready to join the party, birthday girl?"

A new rush of fury crowded in on her. "Can't wait."

He lunged. Vera stepped to the right and twisted around, slamming the rock into his shoulder.

He hit the ground. One grappling hand grabbed at her, took her with him. The fall onto the unforgiving stony surface jarred her to the bone. A gasp escaped her.

He rolled upward. She threw up her left arm just in time to deflect his knife. The blade sliced through flesh. Stinging pain flashed. She growled and smashed the rock into him again, aiming for his head. The contact with his skull vibrated along her arm.

He howled and toppled over.

A smile tugged at her lips even as pain scorched through her.

A new rush of adrenaline had her scrambling up onto her knees and aiming once more. She hit him even harder on the forehead. *Die!*

She had to stop him . . . had to save Eve. Urgency hammered at her. *Hit him again!* She readied to hit him again, her face contorted with the effort.

He plunged the knife at her . . . she blocked it with the rock, sent the knife flying free of his hand and clattering across stone. Surprise flashed on his face.

Now! Kill him! Do it!

Then she was on top of him, ready to slam the rock into his head one last time. He reached for her throat, squeezed with all his might. *Ignore the pain . . . ignore the seizing of your lungs. Do it!*

She raised the rock and slammed it against his head with every ounce of strength she could muster.

His eyes rolled back in his head. Hands went slack, then fell to the ground.

Relief gushed through her, sucking the fight out of her limbs. For a moment Vera only stared at him to ensure he was down for the count. *Move! Move!* Then she scrambled up and rushed to Eve.

"Hey." She surveyed the damage. Dozens of cuts to her bare torso . . . her arms. Her top was gone, but she still wore her sweatpants. No blood on her pants, so no damage there, it seemed.

She was alive. Oh thank God! Thank God.

This time the relief was so profound, Vera's knees nearly buckled.

Eve moaned. Her eyes fixed on Vera. "Did . . ." She moistened her lips. "Did you kill him?"

Vera glanced back at the bastard on the ground. "Not sure, but he isn't moving." She reached for the blade at her ankle and severed the zip ties binding Eve, then she helped her to sit up. "I just need to get you out of here, then I'll take care of him. Can you walk?"

Eve stood, her legs shaky. "Think so."

Thank God. Thank God.

It wasn't until they were making their way to the cave opening, more slowly than Vera would have liked, that she realized tears were streaming down her cheeks.

They were almost out of here. Just a few more feet. Slowly, they lowered to their knees.

"You go out first," Vera said, still struggling with the alternating waves of solace and fear. "I'll be right behind you."

Her movements sluggish, disjointed, Eve crawled out.

Vera felt giddy that her sister was free . . . away from the danger. Now she could escape.

The sting of a blade sliding into her side sent Vera diving away from the threat. She twisted around.

Blood slipping down his face, Patrick drew back his knife and dove for her again.

She dodged the move with a blast of adrenaline. Grabbing for him, she wrapped her fingers in his hair and slammed his head into the rock wall. The knife sliced across her free arm. Pain radiated along the limb. She cried out, but still she rammed his head into the wall again and again until he collapsed on the cold, uneven ground.

Air sawing in and out of her lungs, she watched a moment to ensure he stayed still.

"Piece of shit." She glanced at the knife lying on the ground and then the blood pouring from her side and her arms. Gritting her teeth, she lifted her sweatshirt. He'd cut her, but not too deep, she didn't think.

Big breath. She reached for the bastard, then—dragging him by the arm—she crawled out of the hellhole that had haunted her life for more than twenty fucking years. He snagged on rocks, and she jerked harder. She didn't give a damn if she pulled his arm out of its damned socket. A new massive boost of adrenaline gave her the strength to keep going. The need to end this once and for all kept her pulling, dragging, stumbling.

"What're you doing?" Eve called, pain in her voice.

"Not taking a chance on him escaping," Vera said. She wrenched him the last few feet out of the damned hole, then she collapsed onto the ground.

"Oh my God, you're bleeding. It's bad, Vee."

Eve was suddenly next to her. Dozens of little cuts on her chest and stomach oozing blood. Despite the fire and ache swelling in her body,

Vera worked up a smile. "I'm okay," she lied. She wasn't okay. She could feel the blood leaking from her torso wound faster than she would like. "We have to get to the van."

They didn't have a cell phone unless there was one in the van. They needed out of here, and she needed medical attention.

"Help me up." She held up her free hand to her sister.

Eve struggled to assist in pulling her up. The accompanying discomfort took Vera's breath. Had her gritting her teeth.

"You are not okay," Eve wailed.

Vera rode out a particularly nasty surge of pain. Grabbed the bastard's arm again. "Just get me to that van."

They took a step, then another, the weight of Patrick's body dragging at her arm.

"Just let him go," Eve cried, tears streaming down her face. "We can't keep going with you dragging him."

"The only way I'm leaving him behind is if he's dead."

Eve's face went hard. "Then let me kill him."

Vera stalled. Almost laughed out loud. "Don't think I'm not tempted."

"Vee!"

Bent's voice.

Her body sagged with relief. "Over here!"

Eve hugged her tight and started to sob once more. Vera hugged her back. Grimaced at the pain pulsating through her torso.

They were going to be okay. Bent was here. *Thank God!*

She stared down at the bastard on the ground. He was still breathing. Too bad, really. Then again, sudden death was too good for him. Let him suffer over time the way he'd made his victims suffer. She wanted to kick him, but she couldn't find the strength to move her leg. She was fading fast. Everything hurt. Her brain was getting foggy again.

But they were alive. She kissed Eve's forehead. "Love you," she murmured.

Bent was suddenly there, pulling her into his arms.

Eric was right behind him. He took care of Eve.

Vera tried to smile, but her lips wouldn't cooperate.

A half dozen deputies emerged from the woods and surrounded the piece of shit on the ground.

Vera laid her head against Bent's chest and closed her eyes.

She was done.

40

Lincoln Medical Center
Medical Center Boulevard, Fayetteville, 4:00 p.m.

Vera's eyes opened. Eve was staring down at her. Vera managed a smile, though she felt seriously loopy.

"You scared the hell out of me," Eve said.

Vera laughed a rusty sound. Her side hurt, and she winced. She lifted the blanket and stared down at the hospital gown. "Any serious damage?" She looked to her sister.

"Just a lot of blood and stitches."

Vera studied the bandages on her arms. She remembered some of the stitching. Mostly she remembered Bent being there and how worried he'd looked.

She glanced around the room. She was still in the ER. Good. She did not want to be admitted. She wanted to go home. The sooner the better. "Where's Bent?"

"He had to go see the Riggs family and tell them about their son—the deputy that bastard killed. He almost killed another one, too—the one watching the house—but he survived. Thank God." Eve drew in a big breath. "Now he and Eric are holding a press conference in front of the hospital. They had no choice. Reporters had taken over the lobby. It was crazy. They were shouting your name."

"Seriously? Were they planning to hang me?" Oh God, every part of her hurt.

"No," Eve scolded. "They all know you're a hero."

Vera thought of Patricia Patton and her cameraman. And Deputy Riggs. Damn. She was not a hero. People had died. "What about Patrick?"

"He's locked down in a room." Eve eased onto the edge of the exam table. "Apparently you gave him a pretty bad concussion, so he's under observation."

"I should have killed the son of a bitch." She remembered thinking that exact same thing last time . . . except it had been about his grandfather. Such a twisted family. Then again, hers wasn't exactly ideal. The thought made her head hurt. God, she was sore.

"I'm sorry I didn't tell you about the photos."

Vera looked up at her sister. She was no longer the thirtysomething grumpy mortician. Instead, here was the little girl who'd stood at the door soaking wet and not knowing what to do about their dead stepmother on the bathroom floor. Vera thought of all the little cuts that bastard had inflicted on her torso.

"Forget about that," Vera argued. "Are you okay?" She tried to sit up and grimaced at the pain.

Eve helped her rise the rest of the way up. "I'm okay. Nothing too deep. It took a while for the grogginess of the drug he used to wear off."

Vera moved a little to find a better position on this damned hard-ass examination table. Treatment rooms weren't designed for comfort. She finally decided to lean back against the wall. No matter what she did, the pain was still there. Oh well, at least they were alive.

"Yeah. It takes a minute." She studied her sister a moment. "I love you, Eve. Nothing else matters, okay?" She frowned. "Has anyone called Luna?"

It suddenly felt like forever since Vera had seen her baby sister.

"Bent called her. He told her not to come to the hospital because of all the reporters." Eve tidied Vera's hair. "Look, I can't just forget about it. Mainly because when all this has calmed down, you won't be able to stop thinking about it. You think you will, but you won't. So just hear me out, okay?"

Vera nodded, not sure she wanted to know the details. Sometimes it felt like she knew too many bad things already. Her mind desperately needed a major helping of good, or at least a break from all the bad.

"Mama said she couldn't bear the pain anymore. She'd had that last chemo treatment, and we all—including her—knew she didn't have much time. She wanted me to help her. She said she wanted to take a bath and she wanted to go to sleep. She took extra pain pills. The plan was I would leave her in the tub, and she would go to sleep and slide under the water. Then it would all be over. She said it would be better for everyone. That she wouldn't be in pain anymore and we could be happy again. She promised." Eve closed her eyes against the shine of tears.

Vera struggled to restrain her own. "I'm sorry she put that burden on you. You were way too young to deal with something like that. It should have been me."

"I guess she thought I would be okay because of how I understand dead people."

Vera supposed that made a sort of sense. But still, their mother should have considered what she was asking an eleven-year-old child to do. Possibly that last chemo treatment had messed with her ability to reason. Or maybe the long-term use of powerful pain meds.

"When she woke up, spitting and sputtering water," Eve went on, "she just kept trying to do it, but she couldn't stay under the water. She asked me to help her." Her voice had softened to a near whisper now. "But I couldn't do it." She picked at her fingernails. "I just couldn't. So Suri did it for me."

Vera held her breath for a moment. She wasn't sure she trusted herself to breathe, much less to speak.

"Mama begged us, Vee. I guess she was desperate. She knew she would go any day, and she was just tired of the pain."

Vera nodded. "Of course she was." She reached out, ignored the fiery twinge the movement generated, and hugged her sister. "You and Suri did what she wanted you to do. I'm just sorry you had to carry that burden all this time."

How perfectly horrible for her sister. Vera only wished she had known and could have helped. All these years Eve had lived with that nightmare. Anguish squeezed her heart. Made her wish she knew the right words to say to make it better. But she wasn't sure that was possible.

Eve drew back, searched Vera's eyes. "After it was over, I was so torn up. It was like, I had murdered my own mama. I couldn't stop thinking about it and I couldn't tell you. I was afraid you wouldn't understand." She shook her head. "All I could think was that Mama had lied because it didn't feel better."

"I understand." Vera ached for her. "It was a terrible thing you had to do, but it was her wish, and that's all that matters." She pulled her sister close again and hugged her hard, no matter how much it hurt. "I would have done the same thing. I promise." Tears sprang to her eyes, and she struggled to hold them back. Eve didn't need tears; she needed her big sister to be strong for her.

They held each other for a long time. Vera just wanted the past to stop haunting them. It was time they were able to move on without looking back. Maybe now they could.

A rap sounded on the door just before it opened. Bent poked his head in. "You ready to go home?"

Vera had never been more ready in her life. She gave Eve one last squeeze. "Yes. Please."

Bent walked in, Eric right behind him.

"Hey," she said. "Looks like we got him." But, dear God, the cost. Patricia Patton . . . Mike Brown . . . Deputy Riggs. Damn it. Her heart ached for their families.

Eric gave her a gentle hug. "*You* got him, Vera. Patrick Solomon is going away for the rest of his life."

"Good." She wished she could see the look on Palmer's face when he heard the news.

"We think," Bent said, "we have a deeper understanding of why Solomon was eager to work with you to stop his grandson."

Vera scoffed. "I'm not sure I would give him any credit at all. That goat farm he told me about turned out to be a ruse."

"True," Bent admitted. He looked to Jones. "Why don't you explain the rest?"

Jones gave Bent a nod. "Patrick killed his mother several weeks ago. We think just before he came here to start watching you. The consensus is that he had some sort of breakdown, and maybe Solomon was actually trying to stop Patrick, given he had murdered his daughter."

She studied Eric a moment. Sounded reasonable anyway. "I suppose time will tell." She made a sad face. "I guess this means you'll be heading back."

"I am. I have work to do, and Anna is anxious to have me back home."

Vera hugged him. "I expect to be invited to the wedding."

"Count on it." He shook Bent's hand. "Good working with you, Bent."

"Thank you for the assist, Eric."

Vera liked that her two favorite men seemed to have made friends.

When Eric was gone, Bent turned to her. "You wearing that home?"

Vera laughed. "No way. If you'll get out of here, I'll . . ." She frowned. Where were her clothes?

Bent snapped his fingers. "Damn. I think they cut your clothes off when you first arrived."

Vera groaned.

Another light knock on the door, and it opened. "Got those scrubs for you, Sheriff." A nurse walked in holding a bag and smiling for Bent as if he were her idol.

"Thanks, Shelly." He accepted the bag. "Much appreciated."

She glanced at Vera and Eve, but her gaze lingered on Bent. "Let me know if you need anything else." Then she was gone.

Vera resisted the urge to shake her head. The man could charm anyone. She held out her hand for the bag.

He handed it to her and stepped out of the room.

Eve helped her dress in the scrubs. It was a slow, uncomfortable process. Luckily she still had her sneakers.

"We match," Vera said, only then realizing that Eve was wearing the same green scrubs. Well, of course she was. Her clothes had been missing or all bloody as well.

"Just like twins," Eve teased.

Vera smiled at her. "We will always be more than sisters, Eve. Best friends. That's what we are. Forever."

"Damn straight." Eve hugged her once more, making Vera wince.

Before walking out, Vera had a quick glance in the mirror. The reflection there was horrifying. She washed the remaining blood and dirt from her face while Eve finger combed her hair. Then they joined Bent in the corridor.

"Is it okay if Suri and I stay at the farm tonight?" Eve asked as they started along the wide corridor, with its white tile floors and shiny white walls.

"Absolutely," Vera confirmed. "It's your farm too."

"Just a heads-up," Eve added, "Luna's doing a big surprise birthday party for you. She's been working on it ever since she got word we were coming home."

"Got my invitation an hour ago," Bent tossed in.

Vera groaned. Forty sucked already.

"We're going out the staff entrance," Bent said, directing their forward journey.

Vera suddenly had a thought. She knew exactly how she wanted to spend the rest of her birthday. "You should stay tonight too." Vera looked to Bent. "The Boyett sisters always seem to be in need of a hero." She moistened her lips. "Some more than others."

He chuckled. "I think the only hero in all this is you."

Vera just laughed at the idea. She put her arm around her sister's shoulders. "Just say yes," she encouraged. "It is my birthday after all." She might as well embrace the crazy.

"It will be my honor," he assured her. Then he suddenly stopped and reached into a pocket. He withdrew a cell phone and handed it to her. "You left your phone in your SUV."

"Oh." She made a face. "Thanks."

She had several missed calls, but the latest notification was a text message.

Unknown number.

> Thank you for not killing my grandson. Stopping him was essential. He could not control his urges and he stole away my beautiful Pamela. Bravo to you, Vera. Now you can sleep at night . . . at least until the next monster finds you.

Palmer Solomon. Bastard.

Vera wasn't ruining this moment by mentioning the text. In fact, she decided it was time for a new number.

She slid her free arm around Bent's waist and rested her head against his shoulder. No question there would likely be a next time. Helping find the bad guys was her job.

And she might not be a hero, but she was damned good at her job.

ACKNOWLEDGMENTS

What fun I'm having with the Vera Boyett series! Using my new hometown of Fayetteville, Tennessee, as the setting is just the best.

As always, with fiction it's often necessary to edit things, even real-life settings—for instance, the old hospital, which I may have embellished here and there for the sake of the story. The truth is, I never want any real-life person or place to be negatively impacted by one of my stories, since I do write about murder and people who do bad things. With that in mind, I've created a fictional farm and house on a real-life road for Vera's family. Though some town shops and city or county offices in my story are similar to real-life ones, all are fictional, as are all characters in the book.

I am so grateful to be able to share this story with you, thanks to my amazing publisher, Thomas & Mercer, and my incredible editor Megha Parekh! And a special thanks to editor Charlotte Herscher for helping me find the extra spark this story needed. Authors write, but it is the editors and publishers who provide the finishing touches and put the stories in the hands of readers.

I hope you enjoy this story, and if you live in Fayetteville or nearby, know that I adore living here! This is a special place with the greatest neighbors!

Thank you, readers, for allowing me the privilege of entertaining you! A special thanks to the Molino FCE Book Club, Shannon Bartlett Cornwell, Faye Coble, Belinda Davis, Lillie Galvin, McKenzie Lemley, Debbie Motlow, Bonnie Pond, Debra Quarles, and Gayle Sandlin. You guys rock! Also, thanks to the Book Inn! Independent bookstores are amazing!

ABOUT THE AUTHOR

Photo © 2019 Jenni M Photography LLC

Debra Webb is a *USA Today* bestselling author of more than 175 novels. She is the recipient of the prestigious *Romantic Times* Career Achievement Award for Romantic Suspense, as well as numerous Reviewers' Choice Awards. In 2012, Debra was honored as the first recipient of the esteemed L.A. Banks Warrior Woman Award for her courage, strength, and grace in the face of adversity. She was also awarded the distinguished Centennial Award for having published her hundredth novel. Debra has more than ten million books sold in many languages and countries. The author's love of storytelling goes back to her childhood, when her mother bought her an old typewriter at a tag sale. Born in Alabama, Debra grew up on a farm and spent every available hour exploring the world around her and creating stories. To learn more about Debra and her work, visit her website at https://debrawebb.com.